Imaginary Friends

Alison Lurie divides her time between London, Key West, and Ithaca, New York, where she is Frederic J. Whiton Professor of American Literature at Cornell University. Her books have an enthusiastic following in Britain, from *Love and Friendship* through *Foreign Affairs* (Pulitzer Prize 1985), *The Truth About Lorin Jones* (Prix Femina Etranger 1989) and, most recently, her collection of short stories, *Women and Ghosts* (1994). She is also the author of *The Language of Clothes* and a collection of essays on children's literature, *Don't Tell the Grownups*.

ALISON LURIE

Imaginary
Friends

Minerva

A Minerva Paperback
IMAGINARY FRIENDS

First published in Great Britain 1967
by William Heinemann Ltd
This Minerva edition published 1995
by Mandarin Paperbacks
an imprint of Reed Consumer Books Ltd
Michelin House, 81 Fulham Road, London SW3 6RB
and Auckland, Melbourne, Singapore and Toronto

Copyright © Alison Bishop 1967

A CIP catalogue record for this title
is available from the British Library
ISBN 0 7493 9786 1

Printed and bound in Great Britain
by Cox & Wyman Ltd, Reading, Berkshire

For David Jackson and James Merrill

Seek, and ye shall find

1

I've spent a lot of time over the past months thinking about what happened to Tom McMann and me last winter in Sophis: asking myself exactly what it was the Truth Seekers did to us there, and how. Could any group of rural religious cranks really have driven a well-known sociologist out of his mind, and his assistant almost out of the profession? Or were they just, so to speak, the innocent flock of birds into which we flew our plane? And was the crash real or imaginary? There is a very good possibility, you see, that it was partly stage-managed. And is McMann really mad now, or not? What does 'being mad' mean, anyhow?

The problem presents itself constantly, since this office is directly across the corridor from the one McMann used to occupy. A lot of his stuff is still in there; that long, smudged shape you can see through the frosted glass, hanging on the back of the door, is his raincoat.

When I first got to the university, a year ago last fall, I used to look at that door and think that behind it sat Thomas B. McMann, the author of *We and They: Role Conflict in River City* – one of the first books of its kind in the field, and one of the best; a classic of descriptive sociology. Yes, he was right across the hall; and I was one of his colleagues.

If he doesn't come back this summer, I suppose the janitors will clear everything out of that office before the new small-group man arrives in September. Meanwhile, there is an impressive library in there: books, journals, reports. Bob Onland, my office mate, says I ought to offer to keep part of it – the back files of the AJS and ASR, for instance, which McMann had been saving for at least twenty-five years – since he was in graduate school at Chicago. But do I really want to stock up my shelves, and by implication my mind, with all those years of footnotes and data? What good did they do him?

Apart from his professional reputation, McMann was known around the university for his good nature. He was the straight man of a rather eccentric and withdrawn department, the walking proof that social scientists can be social beings: big, slow, good-looking for a man of his age (early fifties), with a taste for Scotch and sports events, a rough but not sharp edge to his speech. He was the natural choice for any liaison operation with non-professionals: heads of other departments, administration, groups of students or alumni; he lectured on Parents' Day to large, enthusiastic crowds. He was good at explaining things in print, too (*Harper's*, the *New York Times* magazine section, the student paper), under titles like 'The Social Scientist Today: Seer or Statistician?' He is missed around here: all sorts of people, from janitors to deans, keep asking me for news of him.

The official story, outside the department, is that McMann is on leave of absence for reasons of health. But naturally there are all kinds of rumours going around; some quite fantastic, others pretty near the truth. 'Listen, what happened to Professor McMann?' I overheard one student asking another in the campus store the other day. 'I was planning to take his course.' 'Well, you know what I heard,' the other said. 'He took off in a flying saucer ... Yeah, he's at the laughing academy.'

Though he got on with everyone else so well, when I arrived at the university McMann would hardly give me the time of day. When someone you admire like that obviously has no use for you, it's discouraging. If you are a naïve, brand-new Ph.D., as I was then, you think to yourself, This great man sees right into my soul, and there he sees an insignificant worm. At first I hoped that if I kept on being agreeable, McMann's dislike of me would go away before anyone else noticed it. It didn't though. If anything, it increased.

2

Finally, after a couple of months, I got up nerve to ask Bob Onland if he knew what the hell McMann had against me. Oh sure, Bob said; didn't I know that? Well, don't worry, it was nothing personal; it was just that from McMann's point of view I was a snotty young Columbia intellectual who had been hired behind his back last fall while he was away, instead of some guy he wanted from Chicago. The fact that, like McMann, I was the empirical type of social scientist, didn't make any difference. The way it looked to him, Ginsman and Mayonne and the rest of the tenure staff had brought me here to annoy him.

After this I stopped edging up to McMann at every opportunity (in the lunch line at the faculty club, for instance) and asking him if when he did the survey of such-and-such in 'River City' he had ever thought of doing thus-and-so. I had thought I was showing flattering interest in his work; but it must have seemed to him as if I were officiously pointing out holes in it.

McMann's rudeness moderated into a cold politeness now, no more. But I was determined to get to know him, to demonstrate my respect. I started going to him when I had a problem: asking as respectfully as I could what to read on a certain topic, or how to handle a difficult student. For months McMann remained chilly, though he gave me some excellent advice. He was still suspicious, obviously; he suggested several times, in a sort of angry joking tone, that I was probably going to report what he had said to Mayonne or Ginsman, who would then recommend some other book or procedure.

The first crack in the ice came one day when I happened to make a joke about the Parsonians. I said something about Boxes and Arrows, which was how we used to refer to their work when I was an undergraduate, and he really lit up. I was a joke in his favour now, an ally in the other camp. Barry Ginsman, with all his high-level abstractions and talk about dissociated interaction norms, had gone and hired himself a kid from Columbia who was laughing at him behind his back.

3

When he found out I wasn't too sold on Steve Mayonne's rarified brand of statistics either – The Numbers Racket, we used to call it – he really started to like me.

We had a term for the kind of sociology McMann was trained in too – all those volumes of case histories and somewhat simple-minded social diagnosis that were still on reading lists when I was in college — Nuts and Sluts. *River City* was a Nuts and Sluts book in its way; but then so were *Street Corner Society* and *The Lonely Crowd*.

I seldom saw McMann outside the office, and not too often there. If he was in town he would be at a committee meeting, or a football game, or giving a speech, or showing some visiting celebrity around. He was always going off on the plane to places like Washington and Texas to be on a panel or give a talk. He had no family to tie him down: he had been divorced years ago. His wife was remarried, and lived in California. McMann described her to me later, one of the few times he ever mentioned his marriage, as 'a crazy, mercenary bitch' – both a Nut and a Slut.

I had no family either, but I was home most of the time. The only people I knew that first term were young couples like the Onlands with two or three small babies apiece. The students were out of bounds, and the girls in the office either stupid or married. There was a girl in New York I went down to see every month or so; which was all I could afford but wasn't so good for our interaction rate. Sometimes I went out to a concert or the movies, but mostly I sat in my apartment and corrected papers, or felt sorry for myself.

After a while, McMann began to talk a little about his own work as well as advising me on mine. One of his current concerns was with the effects of internal opposition on small groups. He was interested in what kinds of antagonism or disagreement would break a group up, or weaken it, and what kinds would strengthen it, and under what conditions.

Recently, through a newspaper item, he had heard of a

4

spiritualist cult group in Sophis, a town about a hundred miles from the university. These people, who called themselves the Truth Seekers – or Seekers, for short – believed they were in contact with other planets. They had proof, they said, that beings of a higher order of Christian development, in another solar system, were watching over our affairs, and observing us from flying saucers; preparing to visit our earth. McMann had been looking for something like this for years, he told me. He wanted to get up a team to go and study the Seekers in action. The social isolation they must be facing would give him an ideal, almost laboratory situation. In most small groups (a graduate seminar, a Scout troop, even a Communist cell) there is some positive reinforcement from outside. In the case of the Seekers, all support would have to come from within, so that any expression by a group member of doubt or disagreement would be thrown into high relief.

McMann's basic hypothesis was that a certain minimum amount of opposition would actually be good for such a group. For one thing, up to a point the energy which the members would have to expend answering the doubts, or combating the opposition, would unite them and involve them as individuals more deeply. Even a disproof from the natural order (as, for example, the non-appearance of men from outer space) would not necessarily be fatal. His theory was that a disconfirmation of this sort would not really weaken a well-established group, as long as the members faced it together. They would simply rationalize what had happened, and alter their convictions just as much as was necessary to preserve the belief system and the group – both of which probably existed for non-ideological reasons anyway, and filled important social needs.

When McMann finally asked if I would be interested in working on this project with him for a few weeks, I didn't even wait to think it over. I could see the title of the article already, floating mirage-like in the air about three feet in front of me: 'We and It, or Role Conflict in a Belief Group' by MCMANN and ZIMMERN. I rushed back to my office, and blurted out my good fortune to Bob Onland.

Bob took it very flatly. He moved some graph sheets around on his desk, and arranged his six sharpened pencils in a line; and then he said that though it was none of his business, maybe he ought to put me straight. If I really wanted to make it in the department, as well as in the field, I had better not get too chummy with McMann. Sure, he was a nice guy; he had a big public reputation; but professionally, in Bob's opinion, he was on his way down. As he put it, that type, 'the old-fashioned non-specialized, so-called humanistic social scientist, is becoming extinct'. I could howl about what a shame that was, if I wanted to waste my energy on nostalgia. But what I ought to understand was that McMann, even if he was a great man, was a survival from the past. All he was good for now was speaking at conferences and writing popular pieces for the magazines. Since *River City,* over fifteen years ago, what had he accomplished?

I didn't pay too much attention to this. Bob is the kind of statistician who hasn't been in the field personally since he graduated from NYU; the kind McMann once described as 'a walking IBM machine'. All he does is take other people's raw data and feed it into the Computing Centre, and he isn't really interested in anything less than a hundred cases.

Besides, the remark about *River City* was unfair, I said. It was common knowledge that McMann had been working for the past eight years on a longitudinal study of a town called Hesiod about thirty miles from the university, along with two other sociologists. A preliminary descriptive survey of the place, written by his collaborators, Sniggs and Murt, had come out several years ago, and I was looking forward to McMann's final report.

'Listen, you don't know what you're talking about,' Bob told me. 'That study is never going to be published. . . . Why? . . . Because he can't get the data to complete it. Those people out in Hesiod wouldn't let a sociologist within ten

6

miles of the place now. . . . Well, I don't know the whole story. It was all before my time. But originally, as I heard it, Hesiod was going to be the big project for this whole department. They worked on the preliminary report for about two years, and then there was some methodological conflict, or personality clash, and Sniggs and Murt quit the project. They left the university too. Anyhow, as soon as they got out of here they went ahead and published their findings separately. Well, somehow the book got back to Hesiod, and everybody in town read it. Sniggs and Murt hadn't bothered to disguise their data much, so there it all was. How much each of the principal citizens took in per year, how the wife of the bank president was a junkman's daughter, and the Presbyterian minister had been born an Irish Catholic; how there were two bookies in Hesiod and one full-time professional whore; how one out of seven girls had to leave high school because she got knocked up; and a whole lot more. This information was no surprise to them, they already knew it; but now it was out in public, in a *book*, where outsiders could see it. The next time McMann and his students hit town, they practically ran them out of Hesiod on a rail.

'Sure, all right, all right,' Bob continued. 'Maybe he did get a raw deal. Some people think so. But another version is that he got Sniggs and Murt fired from the department, and was planning to publish their data under his name, only they beat him to it. . . . I didn't say I believed that. But you know, it might have been the best thing that could've happened for McMann's reputation. It gave him the perfect excuse for not putting out another book. . . . No, it never occurred to me to investigate it. I don't *want* to find out who was right. It was a long time ago, and I've got enough troubles of my own. . . .

'Anyhow, if I were you,' he concluded, 'I'd just forget the whole thing. Tell McMann you're sorry, but it turns out you haven't got time to work for him. If he insists, you can go talk to Steve Mayonne about it.'

If there had been a chance before that I would decline to

7

join the Sophis Project, there was none now. I was determined not to have Bob Onland think I had taken his craven advice.

There were some things about the project that bothered me a little, though. I wasn't a small-group man, and the thought of spending days or weeks out in the sticks somewhere with a bunch of religious fanatics made me uneasy. But I liked the outer-space aspect of it: the idea that science now dominated the culture to the point where people were sitting round a table conjuring up ectoplasmic rayguns and little green men instead of ladies in white veils.

What would the members of such a group actually be like? Social misfits, obviously; dreamers. People who weren't satisfied with life in a declining rural area, but for some reason hadn't had the energy, or enterprise, to get out. You read a lot about alienation and loss of identity in the city; what about the small town? Who were these people, for instance, in terms of age, sex, income, race, religious background, politics?

I might get a couple of good articles out of Sophis myself, I thought. That would be one up on my friends in New York who were so sorry for Roger Zimmern when he had to leave civilization. I started seeing more titles: 'Anomie in a Small-Town Setting.' 'Science as a Belief System – a Rural Case Study.' When I left for vacation, it was definitely arranged that I would work with McMann on the Sophis Project, starting in the fall.

McMann had everything set up when I got back to the university in September. He had a small grant from NIMH for a pilot study, and had hired a secretary. The Seekers were still in operation; he had been following the local paper, and though there hadn't been any more news stories, they had run two announcements of their meetings among the church notices. This was good: it meant the Seekers were looking for new members, and we should have no trouble making contact. As McMann put it, all systems were Go.

8

The news item picked up by the AP last spring had said that messages from the other planets were being received by Verena Roberts of 119 West Hawthorne Street. This was the same address given for the meetings of the Truth Seekers Discussion Group. We had checked the Sophis area phone book, but there was no one named Roberts on West Hawthorne Street. If Verena Roberts really lived there, she must be a boarder, or a dependent relative: a nutty mother-in-law, or peculiar maiden aunt. The simplest approach would be to go to West Hawthorne Street and ask for her.

It was McMann's idea that I should drive to Sophis some week-end, look the place over, and make the initial contact. If things seemed promising, he and a couple of graduate students who were planning to work on the study would move in later. If I ran into trouble, or made a fool of myself, they could alter their approach accordingly. In other words, I was somewhat expendable.

So, one Friday afternoon after the term had begun, I found myself packing my briefcase and getting into the car. It's about three hours' drive to Sophis in good weather, and the weather was fine that day. Crisp and clear; the trees along the highway just beginning to turn. Hills, barns, clouds, cows; all the pastoral props.

Sophis was a let-down. The country around it is flat and monotonous, and the town has no kind of charm. I approached it through flat, ugly outskirts: gas stations, fruit stands, trailer camp, roadhouse, used-car lots, lumber company, grain and feed store, more gas stations. Then the centre of town, which was indicated by J. C. Penney's and the First National Bank. If you lived here, I thought as I drove down the main street between their two traffic lights, you'd need to be in communication with distant planets: the more distant the better.

Past the second traffic light was Sophis Junior College (faculty 103, student body 1100). Two converted Victorian mansions and a windowless stack of yellow brick were visible from the street; also a nondescript shingled College Inn. I

9

by-passed this; we didn't want to run into any possible colleagues.

On the far side of town, out where the gas stations began again, I found a weather-streaked green stucco building called Ovid's Motel – not a bad name, considering the source of most of its local trade. It was Ovid himself who showed me to a room: a sullen, dried-up man, very uncommunicative. We wanted privacy; we would have it there.

I paid Ovid, shut the door, and sat down on the faded chenille spread of a Hollywood bed like any of a hundred thousand beds in cheap motel rooms all over America. The walls were damp-mottled, the furniture varnish and red leatherette. Over the bed was a framed cardboard print of two sentimental circus clowns in paint-by-the-numbers style. In the microcosm of that room, it represented Art. Literature was represented by an old copy of the *Post*; and a four-page coloured pamphlet titled 'Picturesque Central New York State' would have to stand for all of history, geography and natural science if the Martians put up at Ovid's Motel when they landed here.

I wasn't feeling very confident. I had never interviewed in a small town before, let alone in a group of religious fanatics; and I had never gone into any group playing so obviously false a role.

I had assumed at first that we would present ourselves to the Seekers in our real identities. Certainly not, McMann said. Admitting we were university professors was absolutely out. If I had any idea of the resentment and suspicion of academic intellectuals there was in that sort of milieu, I wouldn't even suggest it. We would say we were visiting the town on business, and were interested in spiritualism.

I didn't think I could pass as a spiritualist businessman; I didn't even want to try, I said. Besides, it seemed to me that in any study you should proceed as straightforwardly as possible. That way you avoided the nervous strain of playing a part, and the trouble that was bound to arise when your subjects found out who you really were. As the Seekers

10

would have put it (they were always quoting these old saws, as seriously as we cite references), honesty was the best policy.

I was being very naïve, McMann told me, the old chill coming over his voice, and speaking from what was obviously a limited research experience. In a town where you were known, or on your own campus, it was foolish to try and disguise the fact that one was a social scientist. Outside the university, the situation was different. If you wanted unbiased data on a sensitive topic, in fact if you wanted any data at all, you had to filter your presentation. You could tell a group of college kids you were making a study of their religious beliefs, and get up to 90 per cent co-operation; with any other sample over half the people you approached would slam the door in your face. And these Seekers weren't an average sample. They were probably already more or less on the defensive, suspicious of criticism and ridicule. As he put it: 'If they know we don't even *begin* to believe in their system, they'll be so threatened that we won't find out a God-damned thing.'

McMann did finally agree that I wouldn't have to try and pass as a businessman; I could say instead that I was doing public opinion survey work. That would give me a chance to sample local opinion formally if I wanted to, and it was a little nearer the facts. He invented an organization I might be working for, and an elaborate rationale of his connection with it, in case anyone should ask.

This side-step towards the truth, from a considerable distance away, had relieved my mind. It hadn't occurred to me yet that the whole thing was a particularly ironic version of the means-justify-ends argument: with the excuse that we were seeking Truth, we were proposing to lie ourselves blind to the Truth Seekers.

All the same, as I sat on the bed in Ovid's Motel, I felt uncomfortable. Through the half-shut slats of the blind I could see narrow horizontal sections of two parked cars, a billboard, and some yellowing leaves – essentially the same

11

view available at that moment to ten thousand travellers in motel rooms in strange towns.

The leaves outside the window trembled as the wind shook them, and then subsided; trembled and subsided. The longer I sat, the more possible hitches in our plan I could think of. I might as well get going.

2

West Hawthorne Street, as McMann had predicted, was marginal lower-middle. Frame houses forty to fifty years old, built close together, each with its front porch, strip of driveway, backyard, and one-car garage. Number 119 was typical: white paint, grey shingled roof, grass cut close, sagging chrysanthemums tied to stakes below the porch. Some dishtowels hung on a revolving clothes-drier by the back door. The driveway was empty: maybe they weren't home.

I went up on to the porch and rang the bell. There was a worn rubber mat in front of the door, with WELCOME cut into it, only minimally legible now. Net curtains at the windows, shades drawn exactly half-way. The whole place made me uneasy; it was so ordinary, so average, like that mid-point on a distribution which has no positive correlative.

'Yes?' The woman who had opened the door was as typical as the rest. White Protestant American middle-class middle-aged housewife, in a housedress and flowered apron. This one was about forty, smallish and dumpy, with faded red hair and freckled white skin. She looked suspicious at seeing a strange young man on her porch. Though I wasn't carrying a briefcase, no doubt I planned to sell her something she didn't need or want. Her Yes was 75 per cent No.

'I wonder if you could help me.' The defences I had learned from months of interviewing began working automatically: boyish smile, educated accent, mildly incompetent manner. 'I'm looking for Miss Verena Roberts.'

'She's resting.' This was said flatly. The aperture in the house remained about a foot wide; it did not open. On the other hand, it did not close. Mentally I added ten or twenty years to Verena Roberts's probable age. She must be sixty at least, or she wouldn't be resting at four in the afternoon.

'Oh?' A pause, while I tried to look innocent, disappointed, etc. Apparently with success.

'Could I help you? What was it about?'

'Well, you see. My name is Roger Zimmern.' I gave my real name, which sounded out loudly wrong for West Hawthorne Street. Roger was too upper-class, and Zimmern too Jewish. 'You see, I heard about the Truth Seekers, and I wanted, uh, to speak to someone. . . .'

'Oh, yes?' Her face changed: a dimly favourable though still uneasy expression appeared. 'You know about our work?'

She held the door open farther. There was space now, and half an invitation, to step into the hall. Like any salesman, I took it.

'Yes, you see, I'm in town on a survey job, and someone told me about the Truth Seekers. And since I've always been interested in that kind of thing; well, I just had an impulse to come here.'

This got me through the hall and into the parlour. I was invited to sit on a maple platform rocker and told that Verena would be up soon, and if I didn't mind waiting I could see her. Verena had to rest to conserve her vital spiritual energy. She usually went to her room every afternoon to meditate, and most days she was down by four, but today one of the neighbours, who was not sympathetic, had insisted on running his power-mower. Could she offer me some ginger ale?

I said she could, of course, though I dislike it. Once someone's fed you, you're in, as every stray dog and cat knows.

She got me the ginger ale, in a glass with a pink knit holder, and we sat in that room for the better part of an hour talking about spiritualism. I knew very little about the subject then, but fortunately my hostess, who now introduced herself as Mrs Elsie Novar, was more interested in instructing than in examining me.

She seemed quite ready to talk. The Seekers were not affiliated with the National Spiritualist Association, she explained, though some of them had been members of the

14

Spiritualist church up in Atwell. They had been gathering together for about eight months now informally, and had also held a couple of public lectures which were very well attended – nearly forty people at the last one. They believed in meditation and spiritual healing, but unlike the Association they did not encourage attempts to communicate with those who had passed over from the material. It was an error trying to call our friends there back towards earthly things, interrupting their soul development. It was wrong, besides, to limit our own search that way, to form any picture of what was on the other side of the veil, in the true universe. Because now we only see through dark glass, as the Book says. We have to learn to get into a state of mental readiness, and free our minds of all heavy images and worldly things, so our higher consciousnesses can rise up like a radio wave and tune in to the vibrations, and hear the secrets of the universe. Knowledge is Power, and once we get in touch there's no telling what we can do that we never dreamed of, here on this earth.

Mrs Novar's voice was quite matter-of-fact as she explained these things. It was the voice of a schoolteacher explaining long division for the twentieth time: frank, patient, flat, a little condescending. She looked like a schoolteacher too, with her bright eyes, pink cheeks, and badly pinned-up hair. Under the housedress was a small frame with middle-aged padding; she was an ectomorph with endomorphic overlay, or, as we used to say in Sheldon's course, mostly bird with a bit of muffin and no horse.

It was only gradually that I realized she was evading all my questions about the things that interested us most, or answering with vague generalities. No, no one had been critical at the lectures or made any trouble, not at all that she could remember. Yes, she was certain that there were consciousnesses on other distant worlds. We mustn't think of these worlds as distant, though; the universe was curved, you know the scientists have proved that now. Besides, we have to realize that all spiritual beings inhabit another dimension

15

from the ones we can see with our material eyes. Contact with these beings? Oh yes, it was possible, she believed, through a suitable relationship to Mind. Well, they might be holding another lecture downtown next month that I could attend if I was still here; she wasn't sure of the date yet. But she could give me the names of some books now that would be very helpful to me. She began to dictate a reading list, with comments about levels of Being, and the truths of other great world religions.

I interrupted her between references. I said I had heard that the Seekers were actually getting messages right now from beings on other worlds, other planets, who had visited or were going to visit Earth. This stopped her; she looked at me hard sideways and asked in a sharper voice where I had heard that. I told her I didn't remember exactly; I thought somebody had said it was in the paper.

'Uh-huh. I thought so,' Mrs Novar said. 'Small low minds. Small materialist minds, I know the sort, that can only see things in crude physical terms. It's the same terrible Error so many of our scientists and leaders are making right now, trying to explore the universe with material vehicles. Rockets,' she sneered. 'Going round and round the earth like fools in those machines, same as a rubber ball on a string. They'll never get anywhere that ways. They've got no spiritual knowledge. The universe isn't heavy and dense like they think, just made of molecules and substances. Why, the real best scientists know that already! It's on a much higher order, all kinds of electrical waves it's composed of. And it's all in motion, constant motion. Isn't that so?'

In my warm, unfinished glass of ginger ale bubbles still formed and rose slowly, like suns and planets in a miniature golden galaxy. 'That's what they say,' I assented.

Mrs Novar smiled. Then she cocked her head, listening to some sound I had not caught. Rising, she said she would go see if Verena was ready to come down.

Once she was out of the room, I opened my notebook and began to record observations. But after a line or two I

16

stopped. I was convinced we were on a false trail. The Seekers were only one more of the thousands of well-meaning religious uplift groups you can find everywhere in the backwaters of America. They would never run into more opposition than a noisy power-mower next door. And they might as well be studying flower arrangement or Great Books for all the use they would be to McMann.

'Eh – Mr Zimmern?' Mrs Novar called. I shut my notebook, and went out to the hall, prepared to help a feeble or arthritic old lady downstairs. Instead I saw, standing above me on the half-landing and looking over the bannister, a tall young girl. She was about eighteen or nineteen at the most; pale, with a bush of crinkly dark hair pushed back from her face and falling to her shoulders over a long robe or housecoat of an intense chemical yellow colour. It was like one of those pre-Raphaelite paintings: Burne-Jones, or Rossetti's *Blessed Damozel*. As she came down the stairs towards me, I could see she had all the classic features: the full throat and breasts, the broad forehead, heavy straight brows, and baroque pouting mouth, naturally red – as well as the dreamy, half-awkward way of holding herself.

'This is Roger Zimmern. My niece, Verena Roberts.'

'Roger Zim-mern.' Verena said it slowly, as if memorizing. 'I'm glad to see you.' She looked at me searchingly with immense, thick-lashed dark eyes. 'You've heard of our work, and come to us from a long way off,' she announced, and held out her hand. It was strong for a girl's, and warmer than mine.

'Yes, well, I was in town already.' I felt the effort of contradicting her romantic version (which was also literally correct), but thought I had better tell the truth – or rather the lie we had temporarily designated as truth. So I went on through the account of my survey job and my interest in spiritualism I had already given Mrs Novar. Verena gazed at me so intently while I spoke that I began to interrupt myself with nervous reservations ('of course I don't really know, I just felt, but I wasn't sure', and so on). In a way it was the

17

same discomfort I feel when I walk into a classroom full of pretty undergraduates, each with an invisible DO NOT TOUCH sign round her neck. They come into your office too, wearing these signs back and front like sandwich-boards, lean over the desk, and look deep into your eyes, waiting for you to give judgement: C-plus or B-minus? while you think, If I had to meet this girl, why did it have to be here? But in this case, it was Verena who was judging me.

When I stopped speaking, she gave me another, or the same, burning stare, and said, 'You must be looking for something, or you wouldn't be here. You have some special purpose. Isn't that so?'

It was a cliché of her faith, but I didn't know it then, and thought she had found me out. Some extraordinary intuition had told her that a person like Roger Zimmern wouldn't have come to West Hawthorne Street without an ulterior motive.

I looked down, possibly even reddened, mumbled, 'Well, yes; not exactly.'

'I hope we can help you.'

'Anyhow, we'll try,' Mrs Novar put in. 'That's all any of us can do.' Two more clichés; but I recognized these.

'Thank you.' I was safe, for the moment.

Verena stared into my eyes again. 'He has a true leading,' she announced. I had no idea what this meant, but realized it was favourable.

'Thank you.'

'Maybe there'll be something for him at the meeting to-morrow,' Mrs Novar said. It was the first time she had men-tioned any meeting; she must have been holding off until Verena had looked me over. 'Can you come here tomorrow night at seven-thirty?'

I assured her I could.

'I'd like to try and get a Message for him now.' Verena's tone was half declarative, half defensive.

'Now?' Her aunt frowned and countered with objections.

18

The conditions were wrong now, there was too much radial and solar interference, and without the others present they wouldn't have the right prayers and responses; besides, Verena might tire out her powers. It was clear that asking for a 'Message' in the middle of the afternoon was highly irregular; also that Verena, though she might suspect I was a fraud, was better disposed towards me than her aunt.

'Let him come to the meeting tomorrow,' Mrs Novar concluded. I seconded her, insisting that I would be happy to wait. I was supposed to observe the Truth Seekers from the sidelines; not to be the centre of attention at an impromptu seance.

Verena paid no attention to either of us. With the sweet stubbornness, the deafness to others' contrary opinions that was to prove characteristic of her, she simply kept repeating that she would like to try now.

She led the way into the parlour and seated herself in a tall armchair covered in tapestry print, waiting. Mesmerized, or resigned, Mrs Novar and I arranged ourselves on the sofa facing her. I sat stiffly, as if in a doctor's office.

Verena had shut her eyes; now she frowned and opened them again. 'I feel he's troubled in some way,' she announced. 'Did you see his aura, Aunt Elsie?'

Mrs Novar turned her head and squinted at me.

'Not very clear,' she said. 'I thought it might be kind of greenish when he first came in, but I don't make it out hardly at all now.'

'Um-hm.' Verena didn't sound surprised.

'I don't get any other vibration,' Mrs Novar added. 'He's a complete blank.' She and Verena exchanged glances – two doctors of the soul consulting. I looked at the rug. I was supposed to have come here to observe them, and now they were observing me. Well, at least McMann wasn't there to see this failure of field technique.

'There's some confusion in his mind,' Verena said, staring at me. 'I can sense it.' I bent my head, waiting. I suppose everyone, no matter how rational, is vestigially superstitious. When you break open a fortune cookie, or read the character analysis of a weighing machine, you suspend your disbelief for a moment and smile if the news is favourable. 'Well, we'll see what I can receive for him.'

'Do you want some music?' Mrs Novar asked.

'Yes. It might help.'

Verena closed her eyes again. Her aunt went to the upright piano in the corner and began to play, holding down both the soft and the sustaining pedals, a medley of simple chords and hymns. Her rigid back and the deliberate movements of her round freckled arms expressed resigned disapproval.

I looked at Verena. The softly shut eyelids gave her face (again inclined towards the ceiling) an even more classic perfection. Her right hand lay in her lap, palm up; the left was extended awkwardly on the table beside her. It was grasping a pencil.

Two or three minutes of blurred religious chords, followed. Then I noticed Verena's left hand twitch. More chords. It twitched again, more vigorously – an abrupt, inhuman movement, like the kick of a laboratory frog touched with an electric current. Verena herself sat back in the chair quite motionless, eyes shut, relaxed, breathing a little loudly. The jerking hand seemed unconnected with her, something that had come out of the empty sleeve of her robe of its own violition.

A series of muted triads. Aunt Elsie was playing 'Abide with Me'. The hand twitched again, and began to crawl sideways across a pad of yellow paper, dragging the pencil with it – a white frog with a stick in its mouth. It wriggled to the edge of the pad, stopped; and took a spasmodic jump back. It repeated the trip and the jump, repeated it again, crawling faster each time. I leaned forward, but I was too far across the room to see what had been written. Four lines, five lines. The hand was slowing down, quivering less violently. On the seventh crossing it stuttered, jerked ahead once or twice and came to a stop. Another chord, and the pencil fell from

20

its jaws. It slumped sideways, and lay dead on the table-top, next to a china lamp painted with flowers.

For a while Mrs Novar played on. I am one of the least religious people I know, but those soft chords struck me as inappropriate background music for whatever had got into Verena's hand. She finished the hymn with a sweet Amen, then turned round. Verena sighed, shuddered slightly, and opened her eyes.

'Did you get anything?' Mrs Novar asked.

Verena sat forward to see. 'Yes, there's a Message,' she announced in a faint voice, surprised and pleased. 'It's sort of hard to read.'

'Let's have a look.' Aunt and niece bent over the table together. I waited a moment, then got up and joined them. I don't know what I expected to find written on that sheet of yellow paper: an abracadabra in medieval Latin; a complete list of my vital statistics, including birth and death dates; or a denunciation of my purpose, motives, and character.

'Can you make anything out?' Verena handed the pad to me. I saw seven lines of interlocking loops, like a nineteenth-century exercise in penmanship; that was all.

'We've been told over and over the conditions for reception aren't favourable this time of the day cycle,' Mrs Novar said, apologizing to me and rebuking her niece simultaneously. 'You see, you only tired yourself for nothing.'

In fact, Verena looked a little pale and wrung: a sibyl after a session with some small but evil spirit. Her eyes seemed larger; bits of damp hair stuck to her forehead. But she ignored the rebuke; frowning at the scrawled message, she suggested that it might be U-U-U or V-V-V. Her aunt refused to speculate.

'It's getting on for five-thirty,' she remarked, craning to see the clock.

I took the hint and got up to go; none too soon, her expression seemed to say. Psychically, I was a failure: I hadn't read any of the right books, I had no aura, and the spirits wouldn't even speak to me.

21

I thanked Verena and her aunt for their time and efforts, and said I was looking forward to seeing them again at the meeting next evening. Mrs Novar made no reply, though she did not actually withdraw the invitation. But Verena repeated it eagerly, clasping my hand again. This time hers was cold and even a little clammy.

'You will come, won't you,' she stated rather than asked, leaning close and giving me her pale, intense stare. 'It's very important for you, for your whole future.'

'Hmf.' Mrs Novar took a step back, frowning as if she had come upon a couple embracing in public – and not without reason, for there was something of that in the way Verena looked at me.

'I'll be here,' I promised.

'That's right. And take this Message with you. Study it when you get home. You might find some meaning there for you after all.'

As I drove away from West Hawthorne Street, the Message lay on the seat beside me like an uninvited companion, a malign hitch-hiker. Meaningless, threatening nonsense – I felt like tossing it out of the window.

But of course, nonsense or not, it was part of our data – the first item for The Sophis file. And why are you assuming that McMann will want to study the Seekers? I asked myself. All you know for sure is that you want to study Verena Roberts.

Still, whether we went ahead with the project or not, McMann would want to see that piece of paper. So I took it back to Ovid's Motel, where I shut it into a clean filing folder, and put a heavy book on top, so it couldn't get out.

I'm sure most experiences with automatic writing are less unnerving than mine; for one thing, no possible statement is as uncanny as one you can't read at all. The term 'Automatic writing' itself didn't occur to me until I had left the Novars' house. When it did, I felt better, though it was still the same series of events.

Illogical, of course. But I think people can be divided into

22

those like me who are more secure with a nice long word between them and phenomena, and those who are less so – who aren't reassured, but frightened, when the doctor tells them the technical name of that funny feeling in their stomach. Maybe that's how you tell the intellectuals from the sheep – or from the goats. In these terms, though, both Verena and Elsie Novar would have to be classified as intellectuals. Their religion followed the traditional pattern: In the Beginning Was the Word.

I spent most of the next day in the public library, doing research on Sophis. Geographically, economically, and historically it was an undistinguished region; but it had been a locus of psychic activity. Wilson Edmund, the famous clairvoyant, was born near there, and in the 1850s there was a poltergeist outbreak on a nearby farm. But this wasn't exceptional in the nineteenth century. Upper New York then, like Southern California today, was the centre of all kinds of strange happenings and religious fringe groups. It was in this part of the country that Joseph Smith met the Angel Moroni and received from him a new authentic book of the Bible written on golden plates; the Cardiff Giant, a fake petrified man ten feet tall, was dug up not far from Sophis; and the Oneida Community, where free love was a moral duty, flourished not far off. Verena Roberts was right in the local tradition, only about a hundred years too late.

After lunch I drove around town a little, with the idea of doing some background opinion-sampling on the same socio-economic level as West Hawthorne Street. I had some questionnaires in my briefcase, but I never took them out. For one thing, I wasn't sure McMann would want to go ahead with the Sophis study.

But aside from this, I had already picked up some of his scepticism about survey data. As he put it, accuracy is partly a matter of milieu. 'If a group of academics tells you they're in favour of some social goal, let's say non-discriminatory housing, you can assume they think this is so, and maybe even that they might act in support of their views. When you go after most other groups with a questionnaire, what you get half the time is a significant sample, laboriously coded and programmed and analysed, of the answers your subjects felt it was appropriate to give to a polite young man from the city. Damn it, if you want to know what people feel, and what they're willing to do about it, you've got to go and spend some time with them.'

At the meeting that evening, my first reaction was surprise at how many Truth Seekers there were. Only seven besides Verena and Mrs Novar, but in the little parlour they seemed like a crowd. Here is the list I made afterwards:

> Peggy Vonn – Sophis College coed, plump blonde, Lower Middle
> Sissy Freeplatzer – older sister of above, LM, quiet, late 20s
> Bill Freeplatzer – Sissy's husband, LM clerical, nervous, about 30
> Miss Vanting – 60s, thin, M or possibly UM
> Mrs Munger (Milly) – 50s, fat, M or LM
> Rufus Bell – SC freshman, radio eng., acne, LM or UL
> Mr Novar (Ed)

It seemed remarkable that in a place the size of Sophis you could find nine people who believed in spirit voices. Well, eight people: it was never really clear whether Mr Novar believed or not. He attended most of the meetings, but he never opened his mouth except to sing a hymn or recite in unison. He treated everyone who came to the house, or lived in it, with dim reserve. He was a large, pale man, whose face was a clumsy, inert version of Verena's: large dark eyes, sensitive nose, heavy brows, full mouth and chin. Though he worked for the telephone company, I have never met anyone less interested in communication, whether with this or another world. When he was at home, he spent most of his time in his workshop in the basement.

Verena wasn't present when I arrived. I was introduced round by Mrs Novar, in the character her niece had invented for me: the stranger from distant parts, drawn to West Hawthorne Street by a 'leading' – in other words, someone sent by the spirits to join the group. My appearance was a demonstration of the power of the forces they were in touch with, a minor miracle, Mrs Novar pointed out – though she seemed to give me an occasional look of Not Proven.

We sat down in a circle around the parlour – a rather formal, crowded party, ill-assorted as to age and class. The meeting opened with a couple of hymns. I had never sung a hymn in my life; in fact, I'd never been to a Christian service except for weddings and an academic funeral or two. Since there were only typed word-sheets, no song-books, I faked it by opening and shutting my mouth in a fishlike way, humming in a monotone under my breath. As time went on, I got to know all their favourites: 'Lead, Kindly Light', 'Angels Guard You', 'Nearer My God to Thee', and the rest. But I never really sang them. Something – racial memory traces maybe – baulked at the idea of my shouting out loud to music statements like 'Bless me now, my Saviour, I come to Thee', I kept to the fish technique; if anyone seemed to notice, I gave the excuse that I couldn't carry a tune.

After the second hymn, Verena came in. She had on her golden robe again, now tied round the waist with a heavy gilt cord like a ballroom curtain. But instead of seeming theatrical, she made the other women present look pathetic, with their pink-powdered faces and skimpy cotton clothes. No question about it, she really was beautiful. Only, I had to remind myself again, she was probably crazy.

Verena sat down, and announced that Milly Munger would give the Invocation tonight. 'We will all bow our heads,' she added. I stopped looking at her, and looked at the carpet.

Mrs Munger had a pleasant uneducated voice, reminiscent of bake sales and roadside vegetable stands. She asked the Lord to send down his light, to look upon this gathering with grace, to lift up our hearts and minds and increase our understanding so that we could make contact with the spiritual world which was all around us. There was a lot more, and she repeated herself, but this was the general idea.

26

We sang another hymn, and then Verena opened a loose-leaf notebook to review the minutes of the last meeting.

By this time, I had more or less decided that the Seekers weren't what McMann was looking for. Their 'delusions' were nothing but a slightly modernized version of the ordinary Protestant delusionary system. Far from being isolated, they shared their faith with millions of other Americans. I was fascinated by Verena and her automatic writing, but this was a phenomenon for psychology, not sociology. But now, as she read from her notebook, I began to realize that I was really on to something. Mrs Novar's vague volubility the previous afternoon, and her uninteresting answers to my questions, had been a deliberate act.

The truth was that the Seekers *were* in communication with beings from another world, who were watching over the members of the group individually and guiding their spiritual development towards higher planes. These beings lived on the planet Varna, which revolved around a sun many light years away according to our scientists' calculations, but only a vibration or two off for them. The Varnians were not physical entities like us; they were 'clothed not in flesh'. Aeons ago they, too, had been tied to the material body, but over the centuries, through study and practice, they had progressed to another level of density; they were not mortal now, but more or less permanent, like electricity or self-propagating radio waves.

The Varnians had become aware, through cosmic vibrations and the reports of scouts who had observed this solar system from 'dish-shaped vehicles', that there was a race of beings on Earth (or as they called it, Sol-III) who were developed enough spiritually to receive enlightenment. They had been trying to make contact with us for years (possibly for centuries, time wasn't the same on Varna), but very few minds on Sol-III were able to put themselves into the right conditions for receptivity, and there was a terrible amount of material static. Lately, in fact, things on this planet had got into such a bad condition, and there were so many dark

27

vibrations, that sometimes it had seemed to them as if Sol-III was going to blow its fuse before they could establish contact. That danger was over now, though. The Varnians had multiplied their efforts, and finally got through to Sophis, New York, U.S.A. They were in communication with the Truth Seekers, and through them they aimed eventually at the enlightenment of the whole planet. Some day in the future imperfect – it might be next week, or next decade – the Varnians themselves were going to visit Earth.

What the Seekers were doing now was attending a class – I hadn't been so far off yesterday when I thought of adult education. This was a weekly seminar in, let's say, science and the philosophy of religion. The teacher was invisible to me, but some members of the course were far enough advanced by now to see him in the form of a pale golden fog hovering over Verena's hand when it wrote. If all the conditions were right, page after page of lessons would be received, on a variety of topics.

A being named Ro was in charge of the course, but he had some help from guest lecturers. Last week, according to the minutes Verena read, a Varnian named Vo had spoken on physics. The balance of neutrons and protons in our atmosphere, Vo said, had always been precarious, and it had been further upset by the testing of atomic weapons and by waves of hate-thoughts between men and nations. At present, to the spiritual perception, Sol-III was becoming more and more thickly covered by a kind of smog of psychological and nuclear darkness. That was why it was so terribly important for the Seekers to keep their channels of communication open, not only at the weekly meetings but at all times. During every waking hour they must try to concentrate as much as possible on higher things, to lift up their minds away from material clinging, and avoid broadcasting hate-thoughts and worry-thoughts. Vo had wanted to remind them especially of the daily half-hour they were to set aside for meditation. This time was sacred. If they could really rid their thoughts of the trivial and material, then

28

they would feel waves of tremendous light and power flowing into them, their nuclear balance would be improved, and a little hole in the smog would be cleared around their dwellings.

Verena closed her notebook. She knew they had been endeavouring to follow Vo's lesson this past week, she said. One proof they were working together the right way, and starting to send out a strong positive spiritual vibration, was that a new friend and seeker had been led to them here, into their light. She knew that all of them, especially those that had the most experience, would do everything they could to welcome Roger among us and help him to understand our lessons, wasn't that right?

Of course it was. Everybody grinned at me; I grinned back, hoping I was doing all right. I was really untrained for this sort of intensive small-group work, out of place in it; I remember thinking the phrase.

'I know you're troubled in your mind, Roger.' Verena addressed me, her voice ringing with encouraging emotion. 'You feel like you're a stranger here, out of your right place; you have doubts of what could be your right place in the world. Isn't that so?'

'Yes, it's so,' I said, struck by what seemed telepathy, though maybe it was only intuition, if not mere technique. Is there anybody who doesn't feel out of his right place?

'I meditated on your trouble last night, Roger. And what I want to say to you now is, it came to me that that's right for you. It's your true leading, to be a stranger on the earth, always travelling about and seeking the light of truth, asking questions and waking people's spiritual curiosity that is sleeping. That's your true purpose, not to settle down somewhere in ordinary human contentment.'

'Thank you.'

'You've been led here to us now by your spiritual guides, because you're ready for new understandings. But you know, Roger, if you're going to move ahead, you can't just do it in one evening. The lessons our guides have been sending to us

29

are full of very difficult, high-level information that's never been revealed before. You've done a lot of studying, and you know, a little learning is a dangerous thing. You've got to join together with us seriously, work hard on the lessons and come to every meeting. If you don't intend to do that, it'd be better for you to get up now and walk right out the front door.' She pointed with a white hand. 'That's what I'm guided to tell you.'

There was a heavy silence; I did not move. What would McMann have said in my place?

'You're going to stay with us then, Roger, and help us in our search for Truth, is that right?'

'Well; I'll try.' My voice sounded a little flat.

'It seems hard at first, I know that,' Verena said gently, 'when there's so much to learn. You have to get inner strength. That's what we all need, but we've got to realize that it can't come from our own material wills and desires.' She was addressing the whole group now. 'We've got to give up our hiding and seeking among material things and shadows, and follow the teachings of God and the lessons of our guides and friends above. . . . Now we'll have our discussion period.'

Folding her hands in her lap, and sitting back a little in the chair, Verena called for questions and reports on the past week's experiences. Most of the members had got into pretty good contact with Varna during their meditation periods, but Milly Munger complained that she was having some trouble. She set aside time every day after supper, but there were so many mental interruptions. Yesterday, for instance, she began wondering if mould was starting on her grape preserves down in the cellar, if she had put on enough paraffin, and she just couldn't get that thought out of her head.

Verena answered her very tactfully. Milly mustn't be discouraged or feel at fault. She had seen for herself that some of the group meetings, even, were more successful than others. It depended on so many things: the bodily state of the Seekers, the atmospheric conditions here and on Varna, and so on. She must just keep trying. As for the jam, it was in perfect condition.

Almost everyone had some question to ask about messages they had received during the week. I should explain that Verena wasn't the Seekers' only channel of communication with Varna, though she was the main one. But 'we all have psychic powers, if we only know how to develop them', and several of the others had psychic specialties. Elsie Novar could see people's auras. Catherine Vanting sometimes heard voices; when her attention was distracted elsewhere they would whisper in her ear phrases like 'There, there', or 'Time a dozen', which she would write down and bring in for interpretation.

Peggy Vonn, the apple-cheeked blonde, had 'feelings' about people. Often, when the attention of the Varnians was on a certain member of the group, she would announce that they were surrounded by a joyful vibration, or a very intense vibration. Her sister, Mrs Freeplatzer, was an automatic painter. Under the influence of music (mainly Tchaikovsky) she produced faint, rather pretty spirit-drawings which looked like abstract expressionist paintings seen through white smoke. She didn't understand them herself, but Verena and Ro supplied detailed explanations.

When Bill Freeplatzer looked at you hard, if you had a pain anywhere, or were going to get one soon, he could feel it in the same part of his own body – through sympathetic magnetic waves, he said. This had gone over better at the Spiritualist church than it did with the Seekers. One of the lessons frequently received from Varna was that there is no material pain for advanced consciousnesses; at any rate, it is something on which we mustn't dwell if we want to make progress.

The Seekers' theology was a mixture of Calvinism, Christian Science, spiritualism, and straight science-fiction. They believed that the Bible was divinely inspired; every word of it was true, in a symbolic sense. God the Father and God

31

the Son were prayed and sung to at every meeting, but the important member of the Trinity for them was the third one. The Holy Spirit, or the Spirit of Light and Power, or simply Spiritual Light, was everywhere, around us and inside of us and permeating all material things: this table, that chair, your hat, and my overcoat; so that sometimes it seemed as if the Novars' parlour was full of invisible doves.

The Seekers subscribed to some, but not all, of the principles of the National Spiritualist Association, as set forth in its handbook. They believed 'that the phenomena of Nature, both physical and spiritual, are the expression of Infinite Intelligence'; they affirmed 'that the existence and personal identity of the individual continue after the change called death', and 'that the doorway to reformation is never closed against any human soul here or hereafter'. Hell didn't exist; there were just different planes of development in the spiritual world. It might take you anywhere from one to ten thousand years to graduate from one plane to the next, depending on your degree of enlightenment and the efforts of your spirit guides. They believed that every soul has a 'band' of spirit guides; but whereas in Spiritualist doctrine these are all earthly beings who have 'gone before', often one's own ancestors, the Seekers had learned that entities from other worlds (who were much further advanced than most human souls) played the principal roles in this band.

Truth Seeking was a kind of do-it-yourself religion: each member of the group added something to it, or stressed the aspects that suited them most. Milly Munger and Catherine Vanting were always talking about the development of other souls who had passed over, mainly their relatives. Peggy Vonn kept trying to fit the standard Christian cast into the scheme – the Virgin Mary, she felt, was an important astral influence. Rufus Bell, the other Sophis college student, was more interested in super-mental powers and space-warp. He had read nearly everything printed in favour of flying saucers, and both he and Bill frequently pointed out that the information Varna was sending us was really *scientific*. Verena, or rather Ro, accepted everyone's contributions to the system impartially; so that usually as soon as one Seeker found a Truth, the whole group began to believe in it. The result was a communal hodge-podge of logical impossibilities.

Sociologically, or even semantically, speaking, mass delusions are not the same as individual delusions. If a large number of people imagine they are getting messages from outer space, we say they are mistaken; if only one person thinks so, we call him insane. Madness can even be defined as a conception of reality which is not shared by others in your environment. In the parlour on West Hawthorne Street, that September evening, I began to be aware that I was in the position of the insane man who is craftily concealing his delusion.

From this point of view, my most difficult moment came at the end of the meeting. Verena had received a lesson on the spiritual geography of the fifth plane; after reading it aloud and discussing it, she paused and spoke to Ro directly.

'There is a new friend with us tonight,' she announced, giving first the ceiling, then me her beautiful intense stare. 'I'm sure you know of his presence here, because it is through your guidance that he has come to us.' Everyone was grinning at me benignly.

'He is disturbed in his spirit as he enters this gathering,' Verena went on, in a soft clear voice. 'He comes to us from a dark city, from among ignorant and evil men, and his mind is troubled, and he knows not the Truth. So we request and pray now that you may send down a special Message of light for him, for Roger, so that his purpose shall be made transparent to him and to us.'

I stared at the rug, afraid that I had had it. Verena Roberts knew, somehow, what I was doing in Sophis – maybe not the details of my purpose but the spirit. Or if she didn't know consciously, I thought, Ro did. She wasn't going to denounce me as an infidel and a spy herself; the Varnians were going to do it.

33

Mrs Novar had started the chords again. Raising her voice into a kind of penetrating chant in accompaniment, Verena told everyone to get into position. They should sit back, relax, lay their hands on their knees palms up, and uncross their legs so that the psychic currents could flow freely. As an extra reinforcement, she suggested we close our eyes. I imitated the others, and we all sat like blind beggars in a circle, listening to the muted piano.

'Let us pray silently,' Verena continued in the same singsong. 'Let us concentrate our minds and our hearts on Roger and request a Message for him '

Silence. I opened my eyes slightly. Everyone else's were closed, but all their heads were turned towards me, and I could imagine them staring at me through their eyelids. Miss Vanting, next to me, was breathing hard as she prayed, so that the lace handkerchief pinned to her dress quivered. Mr Novar, in the opposite corner, was frowning and had his mouth open. Probably he had suspected me from the beginning. The Freeplatzers both wore expressions of religious intensity, which I could easily imagine changing to righteous anger. So did Peggy who, sitting across from me on the sofa, had uncrossed her legs so far I could see right up her dress to her white cotton panties.

An impulse to laugh, mostly nerves, came over me. I shut my eyes again quickly. As I heard Verena's hand, on my right, beginning to scratch across the paper, I sent up a half-serious request to the spirits of Max Weber, C. Wright Mills, and Nicolo Machiavelli to get me through whatever lay ahead.

The Message, when it came, was brief:

PEACE AND LOVE TO R TO T TO ROGERSEEKER OF FF LIGHT TRUTH OF   FFEAR NOT ALL WILL BE RREVEALLED
MAKES FAVOUR SEE RIGHT ILLS O MAKE A VEIL HIGH

4

Indian summer had faded to paleface autumn by the time I first drove with Tom McMann to Sophis. It was cool; a heavy grey mist sank slowly through the air, wetting the car windows.

I had been to West Hawthorne Street twice since the first meeting, trying to establish myself as an unimportant but regular member of the group and find out something about its origins and history. It hadn't been hard: the Seekers had kept records of all their meetings, and my wanting to study them proved the seriousness of my interest.

As I had thought, the current elaboration of their belief system was a joint effort. Most of the scientific material had come from Rufus or Bill, and the spiritualist formulae from Elsie. But the original impulse and outline were Verena's. Without her, the Truth Seekers would never have come into being.

It had all started about a year before, when Verena arrived at 119 West Hawthorne Street. She wasn't a sibyl then – only a dreamy, intense teenager just out of high school. Her father was dead; her mother had remarried and had two younger children. The husband was being sent to Venezuela by the company he worked for. You could imagine them thinking, what to do with Verena? Though she probably could have got into a better college or university, they decided to send her to Sophis. She could live with her Uncle Ed and his wife there, and attend Sophis Junior College. This would fill in the time before she found someone to marry, they no doubt thought, and give her some practical skills (shorthand, book-keeping) and a bit of cultural polish – with a fairly cheap brand of wax.

My guess is that from the start Verena wasn't happy in

Sophis. She had been born in the same sort of town, but the last ten years of her life had been spent in more urban and varied surroundings: Rochester, New York; Trenton, New Jersey; even San Antonio. Now she was back in a small town where she knew nobody except her aunt and uncle, and her aunt's friends. Mrs Novar, who had a long record of church-hopping, was currently attending the Spiritualist Association meetings in Atwell, a larger town north of Sophis. She tried to interest Verena in this group, but apparently without much success.

Verena didn't care much for Sophis College either. She found the teachers uninspiring (as I'm sure they were), and had trouble finishing her assignments, especially in General Science and World History. At mid-terms she was already behind in her work; then she came down with the coed's occupational disease, mononucleosis, and by the end of the term she was in danger of failing both courses. Her adviser suggested she drop out of school for the rest of the year on a medical excuse and make up the work.

So there she was, a year ago last February, convalescing in the spare bedroom with a pile of freshman textbooks. She wasn't supposed to leave the house unless the weather was mild and sunny, which in upstate New York in February means never. Her only contact with the world outside Sophis was an occasional letter from South America. Her mother urged Verena to study hard, take care of herself, and try not to be a burden on her aunt and uncle. Verena was expected to write back regularly.

Late one afternoon – it was February 29, Leap Year Day, a fact to which the Seekers were later to attach cosmic significance – she was sitting in her room composing her letter. 'Dear Mom,' it began, in a slow, round script. 'We are still having a bad cold spell. Last night the thermometer on the porch went down to 7 degrees.' She had stopped at this point to gaze out the window at a backyard full of snow, thinking what to say next. When she looked back, she saw to her surprise that several lines had been added.

36

I've seen the letter; it was preserved in the Seekers' records. Cheap pale-blue glazed notepaper; after the first few lines the round script changed completely, into a hurried backhand scrawl. It was mostly unintelligible, dashes and loops run together like the page Verena had first written for me. If you gave it the benefit of the doubt, you could read a few words, in a kind of silent stutter: 'A A aam hhere.' When Verena went down to help with supper, she showed it to her Aunt Elsie as a curiosity.

That was the beginning. Now, seven or eight months later, the words Verena's hand wrote without her conscious control had become a holy revelation in which the Seekers devoutly believed; the occasions on which these words were produced were sacred. The phenomenon was no less (maybe even more) striking because everything in the system was so obviously related to Verena's own subconscious, like the dreams of a child. The parallels Varna–Verena and Ro–Roberts were even remarked upon by the other Seekers, but only as a proof of her divine predestination.

It was easy to see a possible connection between Ro and her dead father, or Varna as a country more interesting and exotic than any in South America (Varna–Venezuela?). McMann pointed out that the academic tone of the Seekers' meetings might be a substitute for the classes to which Verena had failed to return that fall ('Your work is here,' Ro had told her). The content of the meetings, he said, reminded him that the subjects she had been trying to make up were science and world history.

But however you explained them, you couldn't quite explain Verena's abilities away. This nineteen-year-old girl had not only invented a delusionary system, she had got eight or ten other people, some over twice her age, to believe in it. Somehow, she was able to dream for others, or fit them into her own dreams. Through Ro, she brought Miss Vanting messages from relatives who had passed to the realms of brightness, but were still watching over Catherine and observing what fine care she was taking of their furniture and tulip bulbs. She found scientific experts on other worlds to flatter Rufus Bell, and a Varnian art critic named Solo to defend Sissy's paintings that the County Art Association show had refused; they were much too advanced for most of Sol-III, that was the only trouble. Verena, or Ro, discovered and quieted anxieties, sympathized with problems, and suggested solutions. Her influence was by no means limited to meetings. All during the week, and at all hours, the other Seekers visited her or telephoned to get spirit advice and reassurance.

Obviously, I said, Verena had some ability, some kind of force or insight, extra- or super-sensory, call it what you like, that most people lack. She had persuaded Bill Freeplatzer that so many positive vibrations were now surrounding him that he would be able to head the Community Chest drive at City Hall, something he had been afraid to do for eight years; she had reduced the swelling in Mr Novar's knee and cured Elsie's bursitis last spring. I had seen her myself convince Rufus that his brain cells were so full of positive electrical ions that he would easily complete three weeks' neglected English assignments in one and pass the hour exam with a mark of at least 85 (he made 87). And when I lost my car keys she had told me where to find them: they had slipped down behind some piece of furniture, she said – she could see them lying there, next to the wall – and she was right.

None of that had to be ESP, McMann said; it was just simple suggestion or lucky guesswork. Still, it did sound as if the girl had a strong personality, and some natural leadership qualities; he was looking forward to seeing her.

There was a meeting scheduled for that night. McMann wanted me to go over first, to observe the emotional climate of the group, announce that he was coming, and watch how the different members reacted to the news.

I left the restaurant a little before seven, and walked the half-mile or so to West Hawthorne Street. It was cold out, and the mist had thickened to a slow rain.

38

'Oh, Roger,' Mrs Novar said irritably, opening the door. 'Well, come on in.' She was dressed as if to go out, in a coat and boots. 'I don't guess there's going to be any meeting tonight, though.'

'No meeting?'

'No, the furnace is stopped. Can't you feel how cold it is in here?'

'That's too bad.' I came in and shut the door, but not very usefully: it was about the same temperature inside as out. 'Can't you get it fixed?'

'They won't come before tomorrow morning. Just what you'd expect.'

'Euh!' Someone indistinguishable in a coat with a fur collar, scarf, gloves, and a knit hat pulled down to the eyes, came forward from the parlour. 'Good evening, Roger, how are you?'

'Oh, good evening, Miss Vanting.'

'Catherine,' Elsie Novar corrected me impatiently. A recent lesson of Ro's had been that we should all address each other 'simply', that is, by our first names; just as they did on Varna, where all were brothers and sisters in the spirit.'

Catherine took off a wool glove, shook my hand with her dry, cold hand, and put the glove back on. 'This damp chill,' she said. 'It goes right into my bones.'

'Has everyone else left?'

'No, they're down cellar mostly. Ed's trying to get the furnace going.'

'Oh.' I followed Elsie, and Catherine followed me, out through the kitchen and down to the basement. All the rest of the Seekers, in coats or raincoats, were standing around the furnace watching Ed and Bill Freeplatzer work, or giving them advice. The group had grown some since my first visit: Milly Munger had brought her cousin Felicia, and Rufus another college science-fiction fan named Ken, a tall, gawky boy with freckles. They were both there that evening; the cellar was crowded, but its physical and moral temperature was low.

'How're you getting on?' Elsie inquired.

'Not too good,' Bill said. Mr Novar said nothing, but continued to strain at a pipe with a wrench.

'There must be some elemental blockage, that's what I imagine is wrong,' Catherine said. 'You've never had any trouble with it before, have you?'

'Yes, it was like this once last winter. But Ed fixed it then; it didn't take him hardly any time at all.' Elsie gave her husband an annoyed, almost suspicious look.

'The coal-feed regulator's stuck,' Rufus explained, coming over to us. He was wearing a coat fastened with clothes-line and clothes-pins. 'It's one of those automatic gadgets.'

'When did it stop working?'

'Some time this afternoon, I guess. When everybody was out.'

Mr Novar hit the pipe with a hammer: clang, clang.

'What I think is,' Sissy put in, 'I think it's a sign that the galactic conditions aren't favourable tonight. That's how it seems to me.'

'You mean it's a sign from Varna that we shouldn't hold a meeting this week?' Felicia said.

'Well, uh-huh. It could be.'

Clang, clang, clang.

'Or else, what I thought of, maybe it's some negative force working against us,' Milly said.

'That's what I said already,' Catherine Vanting exclaimed. 'I said to Roger upstairs, some antagonist elemental force might be working against us.'

'Well, I don't think it's that.'

'If you ask me,' Ken said, moving over, 'it's probably just some coal jammed up in the chute.'

Ed Novar sighed, and put the hammer down.

'Any luck?' Bill asked. Ed shook his head. 'Looks like the feed just isn't working, hm?'

'That sounds like a hostile force to me.'

'I guess we might as well go on home, Elsie,' Milly said, wrapping a woolly coat tighter round her comfortable bulk. 'Before we all catch our deaths.'

'If there's a hostile force here,' Elsie Novar said firmly, 'it's up to us to gather our spiritual power and overcome it. That's what our teachers and guides would expect us to do.'

'If it's not a sign from them.'

'Ayeh; they could be signalling to us this way, not to hold any meeting tonight.'

'Why don't we ask Verena?'

'We don't have to ask Verena,' Elsie said. 'All we have to do is gather our mental powers and concentrate our minds on the problem.'

'I think we should wait till another time,' Bill announced, wiping soot off his hands.

'I can't stay here much longer,' Catherine complained. 'I'm chilled through already.'

'We could try, at least,' Peggy said.

'Yeah, but if —'

'You don't understand —'

'I think —'

Almost everyone was talking at once now; the general tone was one of irritability and dissension.

'We aren't going to get anywhere just standing around arguing,' Elsie Novar said, raising her voice shrilly. 'Come on, let's concentrate our minds! Quiet, everybody! Quiet, Peggy. Let's have a moment of silent concentration, and maybe we can get some true understanding of what's the will of Varna, should we hold our meeting now or not. Come on, Sissy; let's all recite the Hymn to the Spirit of Light first and then have a few moments of silence.'

'You mean down here in the cellar?'

'Uh-huh. All right, everybody. Oh Spirit of Light . . .'

Only Sissy and Peggy really joined Elsie in the prayer, and they did so half-heartedly. The other Seekers stood about in the cold damp basement more or less silent, or mumbling occasionally.

41

'This is nuts,' Ken muttered to Rufus and me. Rufus gave him a blank look and stepped aside.

I was supposed to imitate the actions of the majority. It was no trouble; for the first time I felt just like them: isolated, disappointed, resentful, and cold.

While the Hymn faltered on, I looked at my watch and realized that McMann was due, and I hadn't announced his arrival. Even if they let him in, there would probably be no meeting for him to attend; and instead of the cheerful, unified group I had promised, he would find a collection of dissatisfied, dissociated individuals.

In fact, Elsie hadn't even finished the Hymn when the doorbell rang.

'. . . Let Power destroy the wrongful works of men. Don't answer it, Ed,' she snapped, as Mr Novar started for the stairs. 'Let Thy Will be done on Earth.'

'I think it's probably a friend of mine from out of town.' I hurried out our prepared story. 'Tom McMann, he's very interested in your work. I forgot to mention, he was in Atwell on business, and I wanted him to meet you, I suggested he should come over here this evening.'

All the Seekers turned and looked at me, not sympathetically. Their generalized resentment had a new object. The doorbell rang again.

'*Well!*' Elsie said. Nobody else made any comment. 'Well, all right. Ask him to wait upstairs, and I'll talk to him in a minute. We'll just have to start over again. Come on, Peggy. Rufus.'

I let McMann in, and explained the situation – he was less annoyed than I expected. In a few minutes Elsie Novar came upstairs. Her face remained set in an impatient frown as I introduced them.

'Mr McMann, I'm pleased to meet you, but —'

'And I'm so happy to be here, and to meet you,' he boomed, and shook her hand warmly.

'Roger should have told me you were coming, I hadn't any idea, most of the time we don't allow —'

'I know; it's very, very kind of you,' McMann said, still shaking her hand.

'And the house is in such a condition tonight, I don't even know if we'll have our regular meeting.' Elsie was visibly beginning to thaw. 'Oh, this is Bill Freeplatzer, and Sissy Freeplatzer.'

'Glad to meet you.'

'Glad to meet *you*,' McMann echoed, non-directively but with emphasis.

'– and Peggy Vonn.'

'Hi.'

'Hi!'

The rest of the Truth Seekers had come up out of the cellar now, and Elsie introduced McMann to them in turn. There was no opposition to his arrival for me to record: he said the right thing to everyone, and even those members of the group who were still not too comfortable with me seemed to take to him. But it was a different Thomas McMann they smiled at from the one I knew. His voice and his gestures were suddenly those of a provincial businessman, and in his gabardine raincoat and a distinctly non-academic tie (perhaps bought for the purpose?) he even looked heavier, made of coarser and simpler materials. It was an impressive performance.

'– Oh, and this here is my husband Ed.'

'Hiya.'

'Hiya.' McMann echoed the flat greeting.

'No use, Else. Just won't budge.'

'You can't start it?'

'Nah. Might as well drive over to North Atwell to that auction. Get warm there, anyhow.'

'Your furnace isn't working?' McMann asked. 'What's the trouble?'

'It's the coal feed,' Bill Freeplatzer said, bringing forth the expertise I had recently seen him acquire. 'See, there's this automatic loading mechanism to feed in the coal, only it's stuck or something.'

'An automatic coal-loading gadget, hm,' McMann repeated.

'Yes, do you know anything about them?'

'It must've been off since lunchtime,' Elsie said. 'Only we were out, we didn't notice it.'

'I used to have a furnace like that. It gave me a lot of trouble, too.' McMann grinned. 'Used to have to go down cellar and give it a kick now and then.'

'You only kicked the furnace, that's all?'

'Well, not much more'n that. Usually it was just some coal jammed in the chute.'

'That's what *I* said,' Ken began.

'I told you so, Ed,' Elsie interrupted. 'I said, I bet it's just a piece of coal stuck in there somewheres.' She turned back to McMann. 'I suppose I shouldn't ask you; but since you're here maybe you could just go downstairs and take a quick look at our furnace, to see if it's like yours, and show Ed what you did?'

'Why, of course. I'd be happy to.'

Elsie led McMann towards the basement, followed by the rest of the Seekers; I brought up the rear. The house was growing steadily colder.

'What I used to do with mine, was just unhitch that dohickey there with a wrench, and hold back this lever over here, and then you can get in and hit the end of the chute here a couple times,' McMann was saying as I came down the stairs.

'Why don't you try that, Ed?' Elsie said. 'Ed?' But Mr Novar was missing. Rufus was sent upstairs after him, but he was either in the bathroom and not answering, or else he had left the house.

'Well, Bill. Why don't you try and fix it?'

Bill Freeplatzer picked up the wrench, and tried to follow McMann's directions.

'Uh-uh, you got to turn it the other way . . . That's right. No, hold back the catch first. That piece there. . . . You're pushing it too far to the left now. Nope! Watch it!'

'Ow.' Bill dropped the wrench on the cement floor and

began sucking his finger. 'Maybe you should do it,' he said.

'Well, I'd be glad to try. Oh, don't worry about that,' McMann added, as Elsie began to object that he would dirty his hands. 'These things are the dickens till you get used to them. Practically took a finger off a couple times with mine.' (Bill smiled at this, his self-esteem a little restored.) 'Thanks.' He took the wrench. 'Now, we'll just – umf – and then we'll turn this gadget here back, and that'll hold it down while we' – McMann used the plural, though nobody but him was doing anything – 'give this a couple good bangs – have you got a hammer handy? Thank you. Okay, here goes.'

Again there was the sharp, ringing sound of iron on tin, followed almost at once by a duller, more varied noise, like a shower of stones on a roof.

'Hey, that sounds like something! Yep.' McMann laid down the hammer. 'Looks like we did it. Your chute was just blocked up, that was all.'

'You fixed it, huh!'

'That's wonderful!'

The Seekers crowded round McMann, thanking him and exclaiming that he had been sent to them by providence, Spiritual Light, or even Ro himself. McMann offered no opinion on this; he kept to non-directive techniques, never disagreeing with anyone, or bringing in a new idea – merely assenting to whatever was said to him, or simply repeating it. But he did it with great skill. Elsie Novar saw his aura very clear, a kind of lovely reddish violet colour; Peggy was aware of a vibration of strength and hope around him.

Only Ken failed to congratulate McMann. 'I could've done that myself, if they'd let me,' he grumbled to Rufus, who replied:

'Oh yeah? Maybe, maybe not.'

The furnace was relit, and we adjourned upstairs. The house was still very cold, but nobody complained; they were eager to begin the meeting.

Mr Novar had disappeared, taking the car with him.

45

Presumably he was at his auction; it even seemed possible that he had deliberately failed to repair the furnace for this reason.

The meeting began well. The hymns came out loud and strong (McMann had a good bass voice and none of my scruples); nobody fidgeted or coughed during meditation, and interaction rates were way up. As Elsie Novar played the hymn that was Verena's signal to come down, I sat forward, watching.

'Welcome, friends and seekers of truth.' Though it was she who had just entered, Verena spoke as a hostess greeting guests. 'Welcome to you all.' She advanced into the room, her golden robe sweeping the carpet behind. 'Welcome to our new friend.' Turning to McMann, she held her arms out, palms up.

'Thank you.' McMann stood up; he stepped forward and nodded, almost bowed; but I saw no sign that he was surprised by the apparition of this beautiful girl in the Novars' shabby little parlour. Instead, it seemed to me that each stared at the other appraisingly from behind their spiritual smiles.

'Our new friend is a lifelong seeker of power and light,' Verena announced to the group. 'For many months, many years, he has been moving towards us. Even before we were first met together on this temporal plane, he was seeking us in his dream life, which is now made manifest. Isn't that so?'

'Yes, that's so.' McMann assented to this truth as blandly as to the platitudes he had agreed with before.

Verena continued to look at him; I expected her to mention the providence which had sent him to mend the furnace (her aunt had been upstairs to tell her about this). Instead, she lowered her voice slightly and remarked, 'I seem to see a shadow over your leg, your left leg. Have you had an injury there?'

'Yeah, my knee. I hurt it in the war.'

'Yes, that's where the shadow is centred.' There were murmurs of appreciation from the Seekers. 'You come to us from a distant place,' she went on: she closed her eyes, then opened them. 'A distant part of our nation. I see a flat, grassy plain, troubled by winds. Is that right?'

'That's right. I was born in Nebraska.'

More whispers of admiration, which Verena ostensibly ignored; but still no sign of real surprise on McMann's face. 'You are welcome among us. Let us be seated, and let us all prepare to receive.'

Ro, like Verena, welcomed McMann into the group without giving him any special credit for his repair job. Instead, he rebuked us for thinking the breakdown of the furnace a sign that we should cancel our meeting. It wasn't the way of Varna, as we should know by now, to act through the material. They were above that – though, of course, if they wished they could stop every furnace on earth.

One day we too would have such powers, Verena said. Through study and active meditation, our wills were already becoming developed far beyond those of other men on Sol-III. With the instinct of a born leader, she stressed the fact that our strength lay in union: *together* we could move mountains of coal.

Down in the basement I had thought McMann too prominent for an observer, but no longer. Non-directively, following Verena's line, he had lowered his voice, retired into the background. I knew by the way he watched everything that went on, sometimes with a brief nod or almost imperceptible smile, that he was satisfied with the Seekers – and felt as pleased as if I had invented them for him myself.

When we got back to Ovid's Motel we were both in a state of euphoria. McMann poured us drinks out of a bottle of bourbon he had brought, with ice from the machine in the motel office, and drank as he strode around the room talking.

He congratulated me on the progress I had made on the Sophis study, and both of us on its physical convenience. 'Hell, you know, look at us: just a couple of hours' drive in the country and here we are! And that poor sap Steve Mayonne has to go all the way to a slum in Puerto Rico to get his material, ruin his whole summer vacation – rats, dysentery, sunstroke.' He laughed. 'You didn't show Steve any of this stuff, by the way, did you?' McMann picked up my loose-leaf notebook. I was now allowed, even encouraged to take notes during the question-and-answer part of the meetings, and to copy the messages received from Varna. This was a great advantage to us; it meant that we could record events as they happened, and keep track of interaction processes in detail. McMann was using a modified version of Bales' schema; we recorded our observations in a sort of shorthand, in case one of the Seekers should ask to use our notes to supplement theirs.

'No.'

'Well, don't.' He opened the notebook. 'Now, let's go over this, and make some plans.'

I had admired McMann for a long time; but it wasn't until that night that I saw him in operation. At the house I had been impressed by the social agility, the genius almost, with which he could go into a strange context and project friendliness and approval, walking upright on waves of shifting social force that quivered like a sea of jelly. Now I was impressed again by his ability to stand back from a mass of data, scrutinize it, order it, and plan for the future; he knew without hesitation what to look for and where to look.

The only thing I didn't understand was McMann's attitude towards Verena. He didn't seem to realize how exceptional she was, how unusual it was to find a girl like that among such a bunch of freaks, I said.

'They're not a bunch of freaks,' he dissented. 'They're just what they look like, respectable small-town people, a lot better adjusted to their lives than most academics. And Peggy and Sissy are good-looking girls.'

'So is Verena.'

'You think she's attractive? To me she looks like something out of Edgar Allan Poe.'

48

I controlled an impulse to protest. It was bad enough to suspect myself of unprofessional feelings about Verena, but I wasn't letting him in on them. 'She's in the tradition,' I said. 'After all, Poe must have got his set from somewhere. I expect prophetesses have always looked like that.'

'You think that girl's really a prophetess?' McMann lay back on the bed and put his feet up, shoes and all.

'Well, she's got something. She knows things about those people they don't tell her. Or else she makes an awful lot of lucky guesses.'

McMann clasped his hands behind his head and narrowed his eyes, looking at me as if I were an experimental subject. 'You're really starting to believe this stuff,' he said, grinning.

'No, but I'm keeping an open mind,' I defended myself. 'I thought it was pretty good the way she knew you came from Nebraska, for instance.'

'She didn't mention Nebraska. I did that. Verena only said I came from the great plains or something. Anybody could have guessed that from hearing me speak.'

'What about her telling you you had a bad knee? And Miss Vanting's headache; Verena picked that up tonight, too.'

'Or else she convinced Miss Vanting she had a headache. That kind of nervous old maid will believe anything you tell her. And Verena knew I had a trick knee from watching me get out of my chair. It's an ability, sure, but it's not ESP. It's just a matter of getting physical clues below the usual threshold of perception. She thinks she does it by magic, maybe, but it's only empathy. When it's not suggestion, or just plain coincidence.'

'And Verena's first message to me? How did she get those three names? You think that was just coincidence.'

'She overheard you, I suppose. Subliminally maybe. Weren't you sitting near her? Probably you spoke under your breath.' McMann began to laugh. 'You think they were trying to get through to you by way of Varna? Come on.

Weber and Wright Mills wouldn't associate with that class of spirit.'

'I guess not.' I grinned. 'Still, it was pretty effective at the time.' I felt relief, doubt, and disappointment at McMann's explanations, like a child who has been told that there are no witches, either black or white.

'You know what I think, Zimmern?' McMann had got up from the bed; he walked across to the window and pulled the cords of the blind. The rain was still falling outside, and the headlights of cars shone through it as they splashed past on the road. 'I think you've been on this project too long without a break. You've got next week-end off, why don't you go to New York? See your girl-friend, or something.'

5

I took my week-end off, but didn't go to the city – there was too much work to catch up on at school. McMann had thought that if I stayed away from Sophis for a while I would get some perspective on it. It worked, but only in reverse. The Seekers didn't seem any less crazy; but now everyone else, especially my students, was starting to resemble them. Essentially, they were all converts to the same religion, or victims of the same illusion: they believed in education, in science, and in the voice of authority.

They had been trying to see me for weeks, they said, those round-faced boys and girls who filed into my office, lowered themselves carefully on to a chair as if in church, and waited for the Word, which they seemed to think I kept in my top drawer. They didn't feel they were getting much out of their courses, what did I think of their leaving college and going to work? Should they change their major to anthropology, or maybe to fine art? They knew this very nice girl, only she wasn't Jewish and she cried a lot, should they marry her? Damn it, don't ask me, I felt like shouting. Who do you think I am, Ro of Varna?

Most of them didn't really come for advice; they had already made up their minds, and only wanted an authority to rubber-stamp their decisions. They wanted an intellectual rationale for what they intended to do, and somebody or something to blame when it went wrong. Sociology can become an alibi even for sociologists. ('Well, studies show 74 per cent of marriages to crying non-Jewish girls end in divorce, so it's not *my* fault.')

All my students reminded me of the Seekers. When a solemn spotty boy who was concerned with mathematical models walked in, I thought of Rufus Bell; a plump girl who

51

had read too much Erich Fromm reminded me of Peggy Vonn. I kept gazing off abstractedly past them, wondering what was happening on West Hawthorne Street, what Verena was saying.

The next week-end I was back in Sophis with McMann. Almost as soon as I walked into the house I could feel that the atmosphere had changed. Everything was more intense: the hymns sounded louder, the Invocation more fervent; the Messages were longer and crazier.

All the questions the Seekers asked that night were answered, all doubts resolved. The superstitious concern of Felicia Kapp about the fact that there were thirteen people present was calmed by a Message from Mo, a Varnian mathematician. Mo explained that whereas for consciousnesses below the second plane the number 13 was unfavourable, in the spiritual world it was a symbol of divine light, of one in three and three in one. Numerology was an enthusiasm of Mrs Kapp's, and she seemed to have temporarily passed it on to the whole group. There was a long lesson about the cosmic significance of various numbers, delivered with many cautions to secrecy. Ro's final Message ended:

TTRESURE ALL THESE THIG UP THINGSS IN YR
HARTS   AND DO NOT TTELL TO THE MMM
MULTITUDES   THETIME IS NOT NOW

As she read this aloud, Verena's sing-song prophetic voice was like that of the girl on the telephone in New York: 'When you hear the signal, the time will be . . .' Not Now.

All of us, but especially the newer members (Felicia, Rufus's friend Ken, McMann, and me) were asked to hold up their right hand and swear not to reveal these cosmic statistics, or any of the other Lessons of Truth, to anyone, anywhere. I didn't like doing that: I felt guilty as I looked at Verena, her eyes raised and the sleeve of her robe fallen back from her round white arm as she lifted it towards the ceiling, intoning, 'Repeat after me: I solemnly promise and affirm, with my whole soul and spirit—'

Would Ro make an exception for the *American Journal of Sociology*? I thought not. My promise was given in the colourless tones of a child crossing his fingers behind his back. Not so McMann's; he spoke it out boldly. But then, I was in Sophis more or less in my own character; he was not. Whatever was said to him there, whatever he replied, affected him personally no more than the curses of the witches affect the actor who plays Macbeth.

When the meeting was over, the Seekers didn't drift off as usual; they stayed on for refreshments and continued the discussion informally in twos and threes. McMann was everywhere: praising Elsie Novar's orange coconut cake, taking down the titles of books on flying saucers from Rufus and Bill, holding Sissy's hand and admiring her psychic insights. I watched him with a respect which was beginning to be overcast by some doubt I couldn't put a name to, and tried to imitate his technique. Whatever was said to me, I repeated it, or exclaimed over it: 'Oh, really?' 'How interesting!' 'Gee, that's too bad.' It worked, all right: they smiled, relaxed, leaned closer, and spoke with a more affectionate, confidential intensity. The disconcerting thing was that none of them seemed to notice that they were no longer talking to another human individual, but to a mechanical echo.

It was after ten this time before the group broke up. I was more or less silent on the way back to the motel, thinking.

'Let's have a drink,' McMann said, after he had shoved the door shut. 'That orange soda of Elsie's tasted like piss.'

He got the glasses from the bathroom, poured whisky into one, and flung himself into a chair, loosening his tie. 'Help yourself.' He passed me the bottle.

'Thanks.' I added ice. 'Want some?'

'Yeah, sure ... That's more like it.' McMann was still using the coarse hearty tones and wide gestures of the provincial businessman he had been playing; they stuck to him like stage make-up incompletely wiped off after the performance. 'Great evening, huh, Roger? Want some soda?'

'No thanks.' I had figured out what was bothering me now. 'I wanted to ask you something, though. About this non-directive technique we're using.'

'Shoot.'

'Well, as I understand it, the reason for our approaching the Seekers this way is to put them at ease with us, and encourage them to bring out more material.'

'Yeah.'

'The trouble is, it seems to me, if you push quantity too hard, it becomes quality. The whole situation changes. I thought I was overdoing it tonight; for instance, agreeing with Catherine Vanting that I could feel the electrical waves penetrating us. I think maybe I should have been more non-committal.'

'Aw, no.' McMann put his feet up on the glass top of the dressing-table. 'You got to give them a decent response; especially with a group like this, where they already have the expectation of being contradicted or silently ridiculed. These people need a strong reinforcement, or they won't trust you. Hey, I wish we had some potato chips, peanuts, something like that.'

I disregarded this wish. 'But look what's happened to the group. You might not notice it so much, you haven't been away, but the whole tone of the meetings is changed since I was here last. It's much stronger now, much more affirmative.'

'You think so?'

'Absolutely. There's more commitment than there was, say, three weeks ago. Don't you agree?'

'I damn well do. And you know something?' McMann slopped more whisky into his glass. 'This is just the start. These people are *really* going to be committed before they get through. This is going to be more than just an ordinary little interaction study. What we have here is an important

54

proposition, and you and I are in it on the ground floor.' He drank. 'Sorry. Go on.'

The idea of working with Thomas B. McMann on an important study pleased me, though it grated to hear him speak as if it were a sales campaign. I ploughed ahead.

'What I wondered was, if we might not be responsible for the change ourselves. We might be creating static – I suppose I should say, electricity.'

'You mean *I'm* creating static.' McMann grinned. 'You think I'm being too positive, huh?'

'Well, yes, occasionally.'

'Yeah, but don't forget the kind of guy I'm working with.' He laughed. 'You got to take into account that you're making electricity yourself all the time, only the negative kind. You cool them off, so I've got to heat them up again. It balances out.' He chuckled, then looked at me. 'Don't worry about it, kid. You can't help it, it's just your spiritual nature.'

'All right; but still —' I stopped, trying to gather enough moral force to make him take me seriously. 'What I meant wasn't that, I meant —'

'Yes?' He grinned encouragingly.

'I think maybe we forgot to consider enough what the effect of our participation would be on the group. If you look at it for a moment: here are nine people, mostly women, insignificant small-town types, insecure, not too well educated, meeting once a week. Then you bring in two urban college-trained males, obviously upper-middle; and whatever the group members say, they repeat it in a loud voice. With a reinforcement like that, what's going to happen? Exactly what has happened.'

McMann smiled, waiting for me to finish.

'You know what Elsie Novar told me tonight, when I was helping her carry the stuff in from the kitchen? She said how wonderful it was that an educated man like you had joined the Seekers, what a big difference it made to them.'

McMann sat forward; he put his glass down on the arm of

55

the chair. 'So what do you suggest we should do?' he asked. 'Pack up and get out?'

There was a pause; I heard a car pass on the road outside. 'No-uh,' I said. 'But I think we should mute our responses more from now on, as much as we can, try to stay in the background.'

McMann nodded slowly, gently. It was only later that I realized he was practising on me the technique I had just recommended, and proving that it worked.

'The way you were doing tonight with Ken,' I continued.

'Ken?'

'Rufus's friend.'

'Mmhm.' He nodded again.

'After all, we can act interested without affirming everything they say so strongly.'

'Mmhm.'

'You think I'm right?'

'You might be right.'

I was so satisfied by this muted non-directive response that I got up and began to make myself another drink, as a reward.

'I was surprised to see Ken again,' I added. 'When I heard he wasn't here last week, I thought he must have given up on the Seekers. He seemed to know just about enough science to realize how impossible their system is.'

'Yeah, and that's what he came back for, to tell them so. Only Elsie Novar didn't give him a chance.' McMann reached for the soda. 'He spent the last couple of weeks in the college library, I bet, finding holes in the Varnian universe. Elsie could sense what was coming, that's why she cut off the question period before he got his turn. She realizes as well as we do where opposition is coming from.'

McMann turned his glass slowly round on the arm of the chair. 'You know, Roger,' he continued, 'I think we've been putting too much emphasis on Verena's role in the group. She's not the only leader; Elsie is just as important, or maybe more. Apart from her dissociated personality, Verena's only

56

an ordinary college drop-out with a certain amount of loose emotional energy. I don't think she could sustain a group like this alone.'

'But the whole thing started with her,' I protested.

'How do we know? It all depends what you mean by "started". It's like the Salem trials. There's often some neurotic adolescents involved in these affairs, but they're just the catalyst. The elements are all there to begin with, set up and ready to go. My guess would be that most of what Ro says now is put into Verena's head by her aunt. She's got a lot of whatever they call it—atomic force, spiritual over-drive—that woman.'

'Nobody likes her, though.'

'You mean you don't like her. That's neither here nor there. You've got to admit she's a very determined woman.'

'Then what does she want to bother with Varna for? Why doesn't she just go down to the Methodist church and be an atomic force there?'

McMann shrugged his heavy shoulders. 'Maybe she likes it better in a small pond. She'd have a lot of competition trying to take over the Methodist women's auxiliary. Or maybe she wants to feel she's controlling her universe through an original intellectual system. You should understand that.' He laughed, and pulled the notebook towards him along the bed. 'Elsie cut off Felicia's questions as well as Ken's,' he remarked. 'There's no danger there, though. Maybe she just got tired of arithmetic.'

'You think Ken is going to provide serious opposition?'

'Yeah, I do.'

'But if he keeps coming to meetings, he must be look-ing for something, as they put it. Maybe he'd really like to believe, and wants Verena to explain things to suit him.'

'Nah. He's just waiting for a chance to tell them all how wrong they are, for their own good, or just for kicks. I think maybe he's hot for Verena, too. Did you notice the way he kept staring at her? It could be interesting.'

'I don't see how he could do much damage. He's not integrated into the group enough yet. Nobody listens to him except Rufus.'

'Wait and see. That kid is going to make trouble. He's the type. And also he's got it in for us personally.'

'Why us?'

McMann shrugged again. 'He's a farm-boy; maybe he doesn't like city types.'

'Well,' I said, 'whatever Ken does, he'll be doing us a favour. It's all material.' I laughed; so did McMann; and the ice cubes in my glass returned a little tinkling laugh of their own.

I had almost forgotten our conversation about Ken by next Saturday's meeting. We had spent most of the afternoon interviewing, or visiting with, Bill and Sissy Freeplatzer, who had also given us supper – the first decent meal, as McMann told them, we had eaten in Sophis. It was almost a social occasion: conversation moved from science and the soul to food, local history, and baseball, in which McMann and Bill had discovered a common obsession.

At West Hawthorne Street everyone was in an expectant mood. It was the fall equinox, a numerologically significant and electronically charged point in the solar cycle. At the last meeting, we had been told to expect an important revelation tonight.

Felicia was there again, and so was Ken. He stood by the fireplace, singing the opening hymn out of tune through his nose. I noticed him again during the Invocation. He seemed nervous; he kept clenching and unclenching his hands, which hung at his sides, the knobby wrists protruding from a jacket he had outgrown. He sat down with the rest, but as soon as the discussion period was announced he leapt to his feet.

'I have a question I want to ask,' he began, before he had even been recognized. In this part of the meeting the Seekers followed parliamentary procedure; Bill and Elsie, especially, were strict about it.

58

'Sit down,' Bill called.

'If you have a question, raise your hand,' Elsie said.

Ken raised his hand; he held it right up over his head. He didn't sit down. 'My question is,' he went on, in a voice trembling with righteous indignation. 'What I want to know is, why are there two professors here taking down everything you say? Him and him.' He pointed. 'They're professors from the university, social scientists, studying your ideas. I found out all about them.'

General consternation. I sat there, holding my pen and the notebook in which I had begun to record the evening's proceedings, confounded.

But McMann behaved magnificently. He showed no surprise or embarrassment; he didn't even sit up to face Ken, just turned his head towards him, smiling, as if he were in class. 'You're quite right, Ken,' he said. 'I am a professor. Where did you find that out?'

Ken was taken aback; he swayed sideways. 'Uh, I well,' he said; and then, regaining the offensive, 'In the library. I looked you up in the Sophis College library. You were in *Who's Who*.'

'Very enterprising,' McMann remarked encouragingly. He glanced round the room as if asking us all to take note of how enterprising Ken had been. Then he stopped smiling. 'And you think there is something wrong with a professor being interested in the lessons of Varna?'

'No,' Ken got out. 'But I wondered. I mean, if you really *believe* all this junk —' He tried smiling round the room himself, but it didn't work; everyone held their expressions of dismay and confusion. He looked at Verena last. White, with round eyes, her face was smooth as that of a stone nymph in a garden, impossible to read. 'I mean —' he said, and stopped completely.

Verena drew in her breath. 'Two scientists, two wise men, have come to us in their search for truth,' she announced, in her clear sleep-walking tones. 'Is that what you have to tell us?'

Ken mumbled something.

'You came here with so many doubts, so much antagonism, that you can't believe anybody else could have faith.' She stated it almost sorrowfully.

'No, sure, I know *you* believe in it,' Ken said. 'It's just, well hell' – several members of the group twitched disapprovingly at the profanity – 'they're *professors*. He's a professor of social science, that means he studies people like you. Mr Zimmern too. He wrote an article on group census. It was called Something and Group Census. No, Consensus. I read it.'

No one paid any attention to these remarks.

'Ken's always been a negative vibrational force,' Elsie Novar said. 'Ever since the first time he came here; isn't that so?' Some of the Seekers nodded; others frowned.

'He's always been troubled,' Milly Munger suggested.

Ken leaned against the mantel for support.

'I can't be a negative vibrational force,' he said, his voice growing louder. 'Listen, I mean darn it, there isn't any such thing as a negative vibrational force in electricity, or in physics either. A force can't be negative.'

'You're clinging to wrong teachings,' Felicia said. 'I think —'

People were beginning to murmur aloud now, and interrupt each other:

'Magnetic poles —'

'Well, Vo's told us —'

'– in the cosmic ether.'

'Most of us are here with open minds,' Bill Freeplatzer exclaimed, raising his voice considerably. 'I know Tom's here with an open mind. And so is Roger. I'm sure of that. But if your mind is closed to the truth, and full of suspicions, if you only want to bring up objections and disregard parliamentary procedure, you don't have any right to come here and disregard parliamentary procedure and break up the meeting.'

'I'm not trying to break up anything! I just want to know what's going on here.' Ken began to shout, then faltered as

60

he looked at McMann. 'I mean, if you really believe all that stuff about negative force and messages from Varna. Actually, it's your privilege. I mean, it's a free country.'

'Yes, this is a free country,' Peggy Vonn said, her tone screwed up towards hysteria. 'We have freedoms, freedom of the press, freedom of speech, freedom of church. You don't push your way into people's houses!'

There were some exclamations of agreement.

'Listen, I came here with Rufus,' Ken objected.

Everybody looked at Rufus, who had said nothing as yet.

'I di-didn't, he didn't t-t-tell me,' Rufus said, stuttering like Ro of Varna. His face was red under the pimples. 'Ken didn't tell me he was going to m-m-make objections. He just said he wanted to come along. I didn't know he was going to be like this.'

'Ken's mind is darkened,' Elsie Novar announced suddenly, in a louder, shriller voice than I had ever heard her use. 'I see a dirty, smoky blur around him.'

'I see it too!' Sissy cried. 'It's all over that part of the room.'

Everyone looked now, and those nearest to Ken moved away from the contamination. Ken lifted his head with a jerk and stared up. The only light in the room came from two table lamps and a bridge lamp by Milly's chair; Ken's side of the ceiling was in shadow.

'It's there!'

'I see it too.'

Now a strange thing happened. Group census, as Ken had called it, took hold, and I too – just for a moment – saw a shadow over Ken's head: a sooty veil of smoke such as is made by burning grease, hanging in the air. The Seekers were all talking at once, loudly.

'He ought to leave.'

'We don't need to have people that break into our meeting and bring dark vibrations.'

'He can't stay here, anyways.'

'Insulting us!'

'All right!' Ken shouted. 'I'm going.' He started across the

61

room, then hesitated a moment in front of Verena. 'I wasn't trying to insult you. I'm sorry; but it's all crazy.' Verena only looked at him. He stumbled on, opened the front door on the November night, and went out, slamming it behind him.

The angry-crowd sound diminished; I could hear individual remarks.

'The dark vibration is gone,' Milly said.

'He took it away with him.'

'It went right across the room and out the door. I saw it.'

Elsie cleared her throat. 'I suggest we begin this meeting again from the beginning,' she said. 'All right? Let's sit back, then, and try to gather our thoughts into harmony. Sissy, would you play?' Sissy moved towards the piano. Elsie raised her hands, palms up, signalling those who were still seated to rise. 'All right, Sissy. "Love Divine, All Love Excelling."'

'It was always a possibility,' McMann said, as we drove away from the Novars' house. 'I had a line of defence worked out just in case, that's all.'

I repeated my congratulations.

'I hope you noticed how I followed your advice, Rog. I kept up the non-directive bit all the way, didn't I?' McMann grinned.

'Mm.' It was technically correct that he had done nothing when Ken accused us but agree and repeat his words. After the meeting, though, I had overheard him telling Elsie and Catherine, as they served cookies and canned Hawaiian Punch, that we mustn't be too hard on Ken. What the kid had said, after all, was no more than some of our colleagues in the university would think if they knew where we were. 'You know, professors' minds aren't always open to new ideas. They're conservative; they like to hang on to the old-established doctrines they learned as students.' 'Their brains are full of old notions,' Catherine Vanting had agreed, playing our part for the moment.

62

But I didn't think of contradicting McMann. With brilliant resourcefulness, he had turned what could have been a catastrophe upside down; and now we were even better established on West Hawthorne Street than we had been before.

6

The next couple of weeks were in some ways the best the Seekers ever had. Morale was high, and there was very little friction. As McMann said, the opposition or disbelief of one individual often unites the rest of a group.

There weren't any visitors at the meetings now. Some of the Seekers wanted to bring friends, but Elsie or Verena put them off. Another public lecture that had been scheduled was cancelled, and a couple of college students (acquaintances of Peggy's) who phoned one evening were met with what amounted to a denial that the group still existed. Ken's outburst had demonstrated that, after all, we couldn't be too careful; most human minds were not ready yet, not spiritually advanced enough, to hear the Truth. The magic circle around the Seekers had grown into a low wall.

This bore out McMann's theory, but it was inconvenient to the study otherwise. McMann had several graduate students he had planned to bring into the group, to observe and ask questions. Some of them were supposed to come more than once, and carry out projects of their own. Now this was impossible.

None of the Seekers seemed to mind the absence of new faces. The group was in a state of happy equilibrium; it was a functioning social institution. These few individuals, who didn't count for much in the local power structure, were now (if only anyone knew) the most important people in town – in the whole world. They were members of a secret fraternal order like the Masons or Elks, but one infinitely more significant; of a church which superseded all other churches.

Not that they broke off relations with other institutions now; even with the local churches. The revelations of Ro of Varna were not, in their minds, opposed to the doctrines of

Protestant Christianity, but supplementary to it, as would be revealed in the fullness of time. Occasionally, after the Saturday night meeting, Milly and her cousin Felicia would go to Sunday morning services at the Methodist church; Peggy Vonn to the Episcopal, and Catherine Vanting to the Presbyterian. Now they sat quietly among the congregation; but one day they would rise up and bring Divine Light to all these divided faiths, drawing them back together into one unified Spiritual Church.

In comparison with most small-town people, the Truth Seekers were notably lacking in local kinship ties. Peggy and Rufus had come to Sophis College from even smaller towns forty or fifty miles off. Peggy was engaged to an Atwell boy, but he was in the army now, in Texas. Milly and Felicia were widows whose children had moved away; the Freeplatzers were childless after seven years of marriage; and Catherine Vanting was an unemployed spinster who had lived alone with her parents until their deaths a few years ago.

The group provided each of them with the undemanding sort of social life typical of their class and locale, centred mainly on the extended family unit. The Seekers were much more like relatives than like friends: they represented a wide age-range (Rufus was eighteen, Miss Vanting nearly seventy) and associated without ever asking themselves whether they 'liked' one another. They were each others' siblings, aunts, cousins, or in-laws. They met often outside of the regular meetings now: Elsie and Verena went out to Milly's place to help her can tomatoes; Sissy and Bill had Rufus to Sunday dinner on week-ends when he didn't go home; Mr Novar moved a gas-range for Catherine Vanting in his station wagon; Felicia taught Peggy to crochet.

When McMann and I were in town we were included as a matter of course in this imaginary kinship system. We went to movies and football games with the Seekers, drove them to the store, watched television with them, or 'just visited', as they put it, which meant sitting around for hours in some-body's parlour or den, making desultory conversation.

65

McMann was a lot better at this than I was. It wasn't just that age and experience had made him more skilful or more patient. This diffuse sociability suited him better; it was closer to the patterns in which he had been brought up. Geographically, Sophis was a lot farther from Nebraska than from Morningside Drive; but it was much nearer sociologically.

It was years since I had been reminded so often, or so uncomfortably, not only of my social but of my racial and 'religious' identity. I was raised by devout agnostics, and never saw the inside of a synagogue until my sophomore year at college, when we had field trips to places of worship in Social Relations 203. Around the university, I hardly ever gave it a thought. But among the Seekers I was starting to feel more and more Jewish. Now that we were practically living with them two or three days a week, we were exposed to all their opinions, including the unconscious anti-semitism that obtains in small-town lower-middle-class communities. It wasn't a matter of active prejudice, but of casual assumption, habit, even metaphor. I couldn't get used to it, though. Every time one of them would talk about 'jewing down' the price of something, or say disparagingly that somebody was 'smart as a Jew' I felt a twitch inside, as if they had pulled on a string tied around my small intestine.

Like many WASPS, McMann had little sense of how prejudice feels when you're on the receiving end. Now and then he would even make some crack about out-groups himself – a good example of Thompson's theorem that members of a majority assume everyone feels and thinks like them. He was scornful when I suggested I should let it be known I was Jewish. 'What for, for Christ's sake? You'll just confuse them, or else alienate them. This isn't a social occasion . . . . What do you mean, "really honest"? If you really wanted to be honest, you'd have to tell them you're an atheist.'

So I went on pretending to be a Gentile, a Christian, and a spiritualist. After Ken's exposure, though, I could at least

66

stop pretending I was doing survey work, and admit to being a college professor.

McMann's reaction was more complicated. He didn't drop the part of small businessman, but added to it. When we were in Sophis, he still dressed and spoke like a small-town insurance agent. But now he began to carry books and papers around; he made notes more openly, almost ostentatiously. He left his galoshes behind at people's houses, and complained humorously of absent-mindedness. At times he murmured aloud to himself as if he were thinking deeply; he would screw up his eyes and look out into intellectual distances, or (sometimes with an ironic glance at me) rest his chin on his fist like the Rodin statue, which he somewhat resembled in physique. He wasn't falling back into reality, but imitating it. And what he was imitating wasn't even a real college professor, but the Seekers' *idea* of a professor.

From their point of view he was much more convincing than I was. They joined in the game and teased him about his galoshes; they began to call him 'professor', or in indirect discourse 'the professor'. It became a source of pride to them that 'Dr Thomas McMann', from 'a world-famous university', was working on a book which one day would make the teachings of Varna known to the whole civilized world.

Anyhow, he was having a good time; and they were having a good time. I was beginning to find week-ends with the Seekers more and more wearing. For one thing, their interaction pattern was so low-key; nobody ever expressed what my family or friends would have considered an idea or even an informed opinion. I was sick of television comedy and football games, hymns and raisin cookies, and limiting my conversation to the echoing of other people's stupid remarks. The long Messages from Varna, which it was my job to copy out after every meeting, seemed weird but boring.

Once you got used to the Seekers' doctrines, their meetings were like any rural Protestant church service: hymns, prayers, responses, announcements, sermon. The Varnian dogmas were no more peculiar, maybe even less peculiar, than others

67

we are more familiar with. Indeed, starting from scratch in a science-dominated culture like ours, I should think it would be easier to believe in flying saucers and positive vibrational force than in a spell which can change crackers into human flesh. Or, if that sounds like prejudice on my part, in a just God.

The only thing in Sophis that still interested me was Verena. I was convinced that she had some sort of ability, some special sensitivity, that most people anywhere lacked. This ability had nothing to do with the superstructure of dogma that had been imposed on it. It existed quite independent of Elsie's spiritualism, Rufus and Bill's science-fiction ideas, and the moralistic Christianity of the rest.

Though uneducated in any serious sense, Verena had a naturally quick intelligence, and once she realized what vulgar and stupid ideas her gifts had got entangled with she would give them up. Without our encouragement, it might have happened already.

I was impatient for the Sophis Project to end, for the group to disband, or go on without her, I didn't care which. I didn't see Verena spending the rest of her life among religious cranks, even of a more sophisticated sort. On the other hand, suppose she were to go back to Sophis College, finish the two-year course, and then get a job in some office here or in Atwell and marry some upwardly mobile local boy. That wouldn't satisfy me either. Like Elsie, I thought that Ken (for instance) wasn't 'good enough' for Verena – though for me the term had different referents.

No, Verena should leave Sophis, and as soon as possible. Half-seriously, I proposed to myself that she might apply to the university. She could get a real college degree here: a creditable A.B. in the social sciences or humanities. And meanwhile, she would be learning to make her powers conscious, and to understand them – with my help.

What interested me, of course, was the sociology of the subject. Assuming that ESP existed, what sorts of people had it? Which variables (age, sex, race, class, education) were determining factors? Did gifts like Verena's operate best alone or in groups, and what sorts of groups? How did they relate to social alienation, both historically and spatially? Why, it was an almost untouched field. I began to plot a series of controlled experiments which Verena could take part in, and maybe later help me to run. And I was seeing titles again: 'Preliminary Notes on the Sociology of Extra-Sensory Perception', and so on.

Meanwhile there was plenty of work to do. McMann and I finished interviewing the group members informally, collecting data on every aspect of their lives: their background, education, daily routines, opinions and associations. There were pages and pages of charts telling who spoke at meetings, when, to whom, and for how long. But we had got little or nothing, since the Ken episode, on internal opposition – which was what we were there to study.

I didn't expect any, either; everything seemed to be running so smoothly. If I'd been in charge of the project, we would have missed the next significant event. The occasion sounded unpromising: Felicia Kapp had invited the Seekers for dessert and coffee on a Sunday night. It wasn't impossible for us to go, but it meant we would have to drive back at midnight, or else get up at six the next morning. I didn't think it was worth it, but McMann insisted.

Felicia's house, though on the wrong side of town, was newer and somewhat more pretentious than those of the other Seekers. Her dessert turned out to be an elaborate sort of jelly roll with sweet whipped cream and candied fruit, served with the most complicated paraphernalia: silver tongs, electric warming trays, hand-decorated napkin holders, lace place-mats embedded in plastic. The house was in the same style; filled with gift-shop clutter. Every chair had a collection of little satin pillows, every table two or three fancy ashtrays; there were two sets of curtains at each window, and extra rugs on top of the carpet.

We were obviously meant to compliment Felicia on all

69

these possessions, the newest of which she pointed out to us ('Have you noticed my new copper planter?'). But whenever somebody asked where she had got that lovely lamp or that cute plaque, she smiled mysteriously, tossed her pepper-and-salt curls, and said, 'Oh, that's a secret,' or 'I can't tell you that now.' McMann went through the routine with every appearance of interest. He was really a pro, I thought as I tried, not too enthusiastically, to imitate him.

After everyone had praised everything in the room and had all the whipped cream he wanted, Felicia set her gilt-edged coffee-cup down and announced that she had invited us here tonight because she had something special to tell us and show us.

'You've all been wondering, and asking me, where I found all the lovely things you've admired so much,' she began breathily. 'Maybe some of you thought I must have come into a little inheritance, or won some money at the races.' She giggled to show that this was a joke. 'Well, it's not that at all. All these beautiful, practical things, and a whole lot more that you haven't seen yet, were so cheap, uh, inexpensive, that if I told you some of the prices you wouldn't hardly believe it. But I'll tell you something even more amazing. A lot of my best things I got Absolutely Free! This pretty lamp, for instance.' Felicia pointed to a shiny brass funeral urn about three feet tall with a pink satin shade.

'I got this elegant, original lamp without paying a single penny! And do you want to know something?' She looked round the room, catching our eyes in succession. '*You* can get a lamp like this Absolutely Free too, or any of dozens of wonderful gifts you want.'

Felicia stopped and took a breath. She had delivered her sales talk (for it was obviously a sales talk, learned more or less by rote) almost perfectly. The response was satisfactory. Several voices, notably Sissy's, were raised to ask how they could get such a lamp. Felicia didn't play coy any more, but brought out a catalogue, and explained to us that through the generosity of something called the Myzner Company, and the wonderful savings possible through their Guaranteed Purchase Plan, all of us could soon be the lucky owners of things we never dreamed we could afford before.

The Myzner Company didn't only carry household goods and stuff women were interested in. There were lots of wonderful gifts for men, too. Felicia batted her eyes at Bill, me, and particularly McMann. Luggage, sports equipment, 'grooming sets' – she leaned over McMann, who was sitting next to her, and fluttered the shiny coloured pages of her catalogue at him. Wasn't this or that smart-looking, elegant, original? McMann replied heartily that it certainly was. Having created a demand, Felicia passed catalogues round to all of us.

'Why, I almost forgot to tell you the best thing about the Myzner Company!' she said. 'And it's just the part you will be most specially interested in. I forgot to tell you about the Lucky Number Prizes!'

Waving her catalogue like a small flag, Felicia explained that when we had picked the gifts we wanted for each month, the next thing we did was to make out our Lucky Number order blanks. Each order blank had a code number at the top, and every Friday at the Myzner Company offices, after all the orders for that week were in, the numbers were added and divided, or multiplied – I forget which – and the sender of the order that matched the result received a Lucky Number Prize. This was *in addition*, Felicia told us excitedly, to the bonus gifts we would earn as a matter of course by accumulating our bonus credits on the Guaranteed Purchase Plan.

The Seekers were going through their catalogues now, pointing out to their neighbours the items they liked. Elsie, on my left, was looking at table-cloths; Bill, on my right, at diving equipment. It was the kind of catalogue trading stamp companies put out, full of shiny coloured photographs of hard and soft goods, heavy on bedding and kitchen equipment. Meanwhile Felicia had got up and was bringing things out of cupboards or in from the kitchen to show us: an

71

electric knife-sharpener for Ed Novar, a pile of linens for Sissy.

The only one who didn't seem interested was Verena. That didn't surprise me; on these purely social occasions, when she chose to attend at all, she often sat graciously silent, or was friendly in a mild, generalized way like some member of a royal family on a public visit. Her catalogue lay open on her lap, but unregarded, though now and then she politely turned over a page.

'But do you really think there's a chance of any of us winning one of those prizes?' Sissy said. 'I mean, they must get just hundreds of orders.'

'Oh, yes! You have a very good chance. All of us have. You see, for one thing there's more than one lucky prize a week. There's two second prizes, and ten third ones. I only joined the plan in September, and I've been a third-prize winner already, just last week. And then we have a special advantage, you and me. All of us. Because, listen everybody. Listen!'

The Seekers stopped talking and turned towards Felicia, who had pulled her vinyl hassock towards the centre of the room. 'You know, we've got extra-sensory development of our mental powers much more than the average person by now. It's really the truth, the way Ro said the other night, we just don't know what we can do along those lines till we try. When I was sending in my order week before last, I thought of that Message. So I just made my mind a blank and fixed all the strength of my desires on it, and suddenly I could hear, just as clear as somebody talking in this room, a voice saying, "Ninety-six". Well, so I went through my order blanks, till I found one that had a nine and a six on it, and a four, because four is my own lucky number, and I sent in my order on that blank. And I was a third-prize winner and got two Irish linen guest-towels, these ones right here, Absolutely Free.'

'Gee.'
'Really?'
'What do you know!'

Felicia looked round in triumph. 'That was a sign, that's what it was, I think. But you know, I bet we can do much better than that. If we all get together next time, and concentrate our mind powers —'

'Yes, that's right!' Peggy exclaimed, getting the idea.

'We could ask for guidance on it, anyhow, and then —'

'Say, that's true.'

'I'd sure like to get one of those lamps, if —'

'Vo could help us, maybe, or Mo —'

'You ought to be ashamed of yourselves.' Verena had hardly raised her voice, but it cut through the babble like a knife. 'Felicia, how could you think of making that kind of use of the lessons of Light? You know how many times Ro's warned us about the heavy vibrations that gather in material possessions. How do you think our teachers and guides are going to feel, if they see our minds darkened with greed for Things, and trying to use the high powers they've given us for personal gain?' Her voice trembled a little. 'We've got a divine responsibility to keep our spirits free of material clingings, that ought to be always reaching and striving upward towards truth and light. Put those dish-towels down, Sissy.'

At this command, Sissy first impulsively clutched the towels to her chest; then, more slowly, she laid them on the coffee-table.

'That's right.' Verena looked round. 'Anyhow, we don't want to have to do with an organization like that, that's trying to get people to sign some agreement where they promise to buy more and more possessions they don't really need in the first place.'

'That's not the way it is,' Felicia interrupted nervously. 'When you join the Guaranteed Purchase Plan, it's only arranging ahead of time to get the things you'd have to go out and buy, anyway, over the next year. It saves you trouble, and you receive all the extra bonus gifts absolutely free, so if you plan it right you save money, and time. Time and money both.'

'Yes, Felicia.' Verena's voice had softened into a resonant persuasiveness. 'But our lesson is to live simply and fix our thoughts on things of the spirit.'

'That's right,' Rufus put in. 'Ro's told us —'

'And besides,' Felicia interrupted, her tone rising shrilly. 'This is such a wonderful chance for us, all us Seekers, because of the special power and knowledge we have!'

'That's true,' Milly said tentatively. 'We have a real advantage there, you know.'

'– Why, if we all work together,' Felicia went on, 'and ask for guidance, one of us might be a *first* prize winner, and then you get —'

'The words of Our Lord were, the Last Shall be First, and the First Shall be Last,' Verena said resonantly and firmly. 'No, Felicia; this is a wrong leading. Anyhow, it'd be unfair to use our spiritual powers, that've been given us for the most highest purpose, so's to cheat other people out of their chance at those prizes, even if we could. No; the best thing for you to do now is send all these catalogues and order forms straight back.'

'But! But I can't, I'm signed up for the plan till —'

'Just write them a polite note, and say you're not interested any more.' Verena turned to address the whole group. 'We'll all pass the books back to Felicia now, and put these kinds of thoughts aside. Rufus.' Verena passed her catalogue to Rufus, who held it dully for a moment, then handed it on, along with his own, to Milly. 'That's right. Milly; you remember your guide's special Message to you last week, about the pie.' Milly closed her catalogue. 'Of course, that Message was for all of us —'

She went on speaking calmly to one Seeker after another as the pile of catalogues circled the room, not giving them a chance to interrupt. Some of them hesitated a little, but nobody protested openly. Without raising her voice once, Verena had changed the whole direction of the group.

McMann gave me a half-grin of satisfaction – I told you

74

we ought to come tonight, it said. I nodded in acknowledgement as I received the pile from Bill and passed it, now almost complete, to Elsie. She handed it on to Felicia at arm's length, like a dead cat.

'I was only trying to help you all out,' Felicia said in the voice of a rebuked child, laying the dead cat in her lap. 'The Company's sent me so many lovely things, I thought I should give you a chance at them too. I didn't mean any harm.'

'Of course you didn't,' Verena said kindly. 'It's just that we have to remember our lessons. The week before last, Ro explained to us then that we've all got to free ourselves of material ties now, as much as possible.'

'That's right,' Elsie announced, looking round the room. 'You've got too many possessions already, Felicia, dragging you down. When you're surrounded with material Things this way, especially all these real brand-new Things that are still emanating so many negative charges, the way we learned, the rays from Varna just can't penetrate to you, through all this low material stuff.'

While Verena spoke to her, Felicia had seemed to turn into a sulky, but basically nice, little girl: her shoulders dropped, her head hung sideways, she clasped her hands in her lap. But at Elsie's voice she sat up straight again, and reassumed forty years of self-conscious respectability.

'There's nothing low about my things!' she said indignantly. '*Some* people might have that kind of cheap stuff, but I've always believed in buying the best. The Myzner Company carries only the most high-quality merchandise, the brands that's sold in the best stores everywhere.'

'It doesn't signify where it comes from,' Elsie said. 'It's obvious it's holding back your spiritual progress; and probably poisoning your brain waves, I wouldn't be surprised, you've got so much. It seems to me you might do a lot better if you were to give away some of these extra possessions.'

Felicia scowled.

'That's a good idea,' Verena said gently. 'Or at least, Felicia, I think you should set them aside for a while.'

75

'Is that so.' Felicia's voice was still a little angry.

'Yes, I think it's so. You'll feel so beautifully free, so light, with your spirit rising straight up towards the stars, once you put some of these things away —'

'Or you could lend them out, maybe,' Elsie suggested. 'Till the worst part of their low negative electricity was dissipated off. Right now, this house is too full of crooked material vibrations for you to make any true progress.'

'Oh, really?' Felicia said. 'And who'm I supposed to lend my things to, you I suppose? Listen, Elsie Novar, I got everything here fair and square, and I'm not going to give it away, neither. I don't know as I believe in all that talk about dangerous vibrations, anyhow.'

'Felicia —' Verena tried to interrupt.

'I don't credit it, I never have, if you want to know,' she went on, breathing hard. 'If you go to church regular and live a Christian life, and follow your lucky numbers, there's no harm that can come to you from your own good furniture and china. That's what I think.'

'Now, Felicia —' Bill Freeplatzer said. 'Let's calm down, now.'

'All that other stuff, it's just a lot of made-up nonsense.'

There was a gasp round the room, as if air had been sucked out of it; then Elsie flung herself into the vacuum.

'That's because your mind is already poisoned, probably, with dark emanations from all this stuff,' she said shrilly. 'The minute I walked into this house tonight, I thought to myself, this place is full of some heavy current, with a kind of bad, greenish brownish aura; but I didn't want to say anything about it.'

'Is that so!' Felicia had completely metamorphosed now into the indignant small-town clubwoman. 'Well, if you feel that way about my home, nobody's making you stay here.' She stood up.

'All right then.' Elsie also rose, clutching her pocketbook as if she were going to throw it. 'Just get me my coat.'

'Elsie —'

'Aunt Elsie, Felicia didn't mean —'

'Hey, wait a minute.'

But Elsie was in the hall already, dragging her coat out of the closet. Several members of the group had risen and followed her.

'Take it easy, Else —'

'I wasn't really suggesting —' Felicia began stiffly. 'I only said —'

'I know when I've been insulted,' Elsie announced proudly. Holding her coat around her, she turned to look at us all, her eyes sparkling with satisfaction. 'Good night, everybody.'

The door and the screen-door shut behind her with a definitive bang, clang.

'I certainly didn't intend anything like *that*,' Felicia started explaining. 'I only meant —' The years of dignity slid off again, and now she was an excited girl, chattering in self-justification.

The scene assumed the usual post-crisis formlessness. Verena spoke to Felicia calmingly, but without much apparent success. Then she and her uncle excused themselves to go after Elsie, explaining that they really couldn't let her walk home all the way across town alone. Nobody sat down again, and they politely declined more cake or coffee. Within ten minutes, all the Seekers had thanked Felicia for a very pleasant evening and found their coats.

McMann and I left, according to our usual procedure, after half the group. When we got outside we found Catherine Vanting and the Freeplatzers standing talking just out of sight of the house; and we were soon joined there by Rufus, Peggy, and finally, Milly.

McMann had theorized at the beginning that if there were any serious opposition to the Seekers' doctrine from one of the members, the group would tend to reject the offending person and reaffirm the doctrine more strongly. He seemed to be right. Inside, they had all listened to Felicia politely enough, and even seemed to accept her explanations. Now, standing under the street light while a cold wind blew round our legs, they remarked that, after all, Felicia had insulted a guest in her own home; and that she really did have more things than any one person, living alone, needed.

There *was* a negative feeling about the house, Sissy said; she had noticed it herself. Milly told us that she had been worried about her cousin Felicia ('of course, she isn't really my cousin, only by marriage') for a long time. All that concentrating on numbers, it never did seem exactly right to her. After all, numbers meant counting, and what else could you count except money and material things? Whereas the Spirit of Our Lord was infinite, or else it was One, which was sort of the same thing.

It was too cold outside to talk very long, but a tone had been set. Catherine Vanting announced as we drove her home that Felicia was probably under a bad astral influence. It wasn't her own fault maybe, but if she were to pay more attention to her spiritual guides, she wouldn't be drawn into trying to peddle material things to her friends, and encouraging them to bet and gamble. Because when you came right down to it, that was what this lucky numbers plan was, wasn't that so? 'That's so,' McMann said obligingly; encouraged, Catherine spent the rest of the ride telling us what she had said to her minister in 1942 when he tried to put in Bingo.

Though McMann had the satisfaction of having insisted on going to Felicia's, I was feeling good too that evening as I wrote up my notes. For the first time, I wasn't only observing the Truth Seekers; I was on their side in a significant, if odd, kind of social protest. Sissy's statement that poisonous material vibrations were leaking out of all the television sets in America, for instance, was about what I believed myself.

Over the next few weeks, as I listened to the Seekers criticizing not only Felicia but each other and even themselves for various 'materialistic leanings', or arguing about whether some object was a luxury or a necessity, I had a

78

sensation of nostalgic *déjà vu*. I was back in my Trotskyist uncle's apartment on 85th Street, looking up over the top of a comic book as he, my aunt, and their friends raised their voices in a tense political and moral discussion.

Was Truth Seeking really a disguised attack on the values (and possibly the institutional substructure) of the affluent society? And if so, what did it mean? People like my aunt and uncle had been mounting this attack for years without making any appreciable dent in the cultural monolith. Maybe a naïve, grass-roots movement, with an inspired young leader like Verena, would be more effective. After all, look what she had done at Felicia's.

Suppose you multiplied the Seekers by a thousand – and why not, I asked myself, if there are ten of them in a town like Sophis? I could imagine the movement sweeping across the country: housewives from coast to coast tearing up trading stamps and returning free trial merchandise to stores. I even saw Verena leading converted mobs out of shopping centres; urging them on as they burned billboards, defaced advertisements, and toppled television aerials – and in these dreams, I was among them.

7

'I got to talk to you,' Elsie Novar exclaimed one Friday afternoon a few weeks later, almost the moment we entered the house. 'Come on in.' She pulled McMann towards the parlour; I followed.

'It's that Ken.' Elsie spoke in a rapid whisper. 'I thought he might be hanging around us, or some other negative influence, but I figured on him first.' She felt for Verena's chair behind her and sat down. 'There had to be *some* reason, the way things've been going since last week-end, when we got all that static and repetition; that same lesson we already had once. You remember how it was.'

She looked at us; I nodded, and so did McMann. It was true that last Saturday's Message from Ro had seemed redundant, but most of his Messages lately were redundant.

'Well, it was even worse Wednesday.' Elsie was kneading the arm of her chair like a plump, nervous mouse. 'We sat till near ten, and hardly a thing came through. You can see it in the book, letters and arrows and dots, nothing you can make sense of. The Message was all broken into pieces, static like. Verena felt real weakened and sick afterwards, she had to stay in bed most of the next day. I knew there was something funny going on. And anyhow, Sissy said when she left to go home she saw a dark vibration, sort of blackish reddish, down along by the front doormat, like it was trying to get in. Well, I knew someone who'd been here at least once had to be sending it, or it couldn't have come that near, not right up on to the porch. Rufus figured it might be Felicia, but I didn't think so. She's an undeveloped soul, but her will is pretty good.'

Elsie stopped and took a gasp of air for the revelation she was about to make. 'Well! You know what Bill Freeplatzer saw downtown *this morning*, in the Rexall drugstore? Ken and Verena, he saw!'

'Ken and Verena were in the drugstore?' McMann repeated not only the sense of Elsie's statement but some of her tone.

'They were together, in a *booth*.'

I could imagine the scene: Bill spying from behind a revolving rack of comic and scenic cards, waterfalls and pratfalls. I saw Ken clearly, crammed into the narrow booth – sitting back against the wall by the juke-box outlet, with his large feet up on the bench in front, wearing a dirty maroon wool jacket lettered SOPHIS. Then I tried to add Verena: in her long golden robe and flowing hair, she seemed as out of place in the picture as a fairy-tale princess. But, of course, she would have been wearing ordinary clothes; the picture faded out.

'Drinking coffee. Verena admitted it to me when she came home. She's seen him twice before this, when she went over to the college store for books. He works there part-time. All this whole week he's been casting a negative aura over her, and poisoning her mind, only she won't admit to it.'

'She won't admit to it,' McMann echoed.

'No; she says him and her didn't even mention the group or the meetings or anything, they only talked about college and stuff. That's his plan, to look like a normal person. All he wants her to do, she says, is go to a lecture with him, tonight. Some *professor*, from out of town, is talking.' Elsie was so engrossed that she forgot her audience – a sneer underlined the word.

'A lecture?'

'Yes, some science thing, about the stars. Some false learning, probably. But even if it's not, Ken knows well enough Verena can't go out tonight. She has to rest at home if she's going to receive tomorrow, or she won't be a good instrument.' Elsie picked at the upholstery of the chair with both hands now, causing dust to rise. Her eyes were round, like the eyes of a rodent in panic, and shreds of faded red hair

81

stood out from the knot at the back of her neck. 'You know that; it's what Ro said himself, didn't he?'

'That's what he said,' McMann agreed.

'I want for you to talk to her.' Elsie turned to him. 'She's up in her room now, resting and praying for guidance, I hope. She'll listen to you, she thinks so high of you.'

'You'd like me to talk with Verena?'

'Oh, thank you.' Elsie visibly relaxed. 'I knew you'd help me. I'll see if she can come down now. She's so unworldly, she doesn't know what's right for her gift. You can tell her she shouldn't go out tonight; tell her she mustn't even think of it. And warn her not to speak with Ken any more. She has to protect herself from that kind of vibration.'

Instead of sitting down while we waited, McMann began to pace the parlour rug, swearing.

'Ah, Goddamn it.'

'What's the matter?'

'What d'you mean, what's the matter?' McMann turned on me, knocking against a floor lamp so hard that it rocked on its base. 'That snotty kid, that Ken, is going to ruin everything for us.'

'But it's just opposition. What we need.' Since Felicia's party, nothing had happened to test the Seekers' commitment to their belief system. Felicia had been invited to come to the next meeting and repudiate her errors, but had declined. To make sure that they did not fall under the same 'earthward-tending' influences, all the Seekers except Milly had stopped seeing her, more or less.

'The hell it is. This is the wrong kind. I don't want any external interference now.'

'You really think it's that dangerous? Verena's so strong in her faith, I don't think anything Ken could say to her, or anything she might hear in a lecture, could influence her. I don't think it's that important.'

'Then why was she concealing it?'

'She was only keeping it from Elsie. Probably she knew Elsie'd get upset.'

'And what about the trouble with the Message?'

'There've been illegible messages before.'

'Maybe.' McMann subsided heavily on to a hassock and took his 'Thinker' pose.

'Listen, I have an idea,' I said.

'Yeah?'

'We can't stop Verena from going to the lecture if that's what she wants; but we can go too. It's probably open to the public. Why don't we go? Maybe we could get Elsie to come along.' McMann half smiled. 'I bet, whatever the speaker says, they'll deny it, or else fit it into their system somehow.'

'Maybe. I'd prefer not to risk it.'

'But it's not up to us.' Scientifically speaking, we had no business trying to keep anyone away from either drugstores or lectures on astronomy. 'I mean —'

'Shh.'

'Tom . . . Roger.' I had half expected to see Verena sulky or defiant, but she made a sublimely poised prophetess entrance, sweeping across the parlour towards us, her arms extended. She had on a dark yellow dress, the same colour as her long robe; her thick crimped hair was held back from the high forehead with a gold velvet ribbon. Her eyes shone.

'Light be about you.' She greeted us formally, in one of the phrases Ro had suggested.

'Light be about you,' I repeated. Superfluous; it obviously already was.

'Roger.' She turned to me, holding out her hand. 'I feel that your bodily trouble has been lifted. On the first and second day after we last saw you you were still in distress, but towards the end of the third day the negative waves were dissolved, isn't that so?'

Last Sunday I had begun a bad cold. Verena had commanded me to go to bed as soon as I got home and stay there for twenty-four hours, playing piano music constantly on the phonograph to absorb the damp atmospheric vibrations. Suggestion, of course; sympathetic magic (I used Chopin's Études mostly); but it had worked. 'That's so,' I said.

83

'You are perfectly well now.'

'Yes, I am, actually.'

'I know it.' Verena smiled and let my hand go.

'We'll have a positively charged, restful kind of evening tonight,' Elsie promised. 'Just congenial minds: Milly and Catherine are coming over, and I've made some chicken stew. Then we can all retire to our meditations early.'

'I'll be with you in spirit,' Verena said. 'I'm going to a lecture tonight.'

'You're going to a lecture?' I was angling non-directively for an invitation, but Elsie chose to take it otherwise.

'Roger sees that it's not wise for you, going out a night like this.' An exaggeration: it was cold and crisp, good weather for mid-November. Verena did not respond. 'Some other time maybe, but this is Friday. You have to rest your mental processes tonight and receive your inspiration.'

Verena drew herself up impatiently. 'Inspiration comes from many places,' she announced. 'Truth is blown on many different winds, and carried into many hearts.' She shook her hair back, a darkly burning bush, full of sparks.

'It's not carried into that Ken's heart. He's a negative force.' Verena frowned, but did not answer. Her full sculptured mouth shut obstinately. 'We know that,' Elsie went on. 'He's working against us.'

'No one is working against us,' Verena contradicted her. 'Those are hate-thoughts.'

'I'm not saying he's doing it of his own will.' Elsie's eyes were glittering; she kept gathering up the hem of her pink-flowered apron nervously with one hand. 'He's an undeveloped spirit, that's all, and elemental forces of anger and confusion have got into him, taking possession of his mind. I don't hold it against him personally.'

In the Seekers' theology, as expounded by Ro of Varna, there was no conscious evil, no Satan. All men were naturally good, at least in potential. The pain and horror of life on earth came about either through human error or through the imbecile flailing about of 'elementals' — violent, low-IQ

84

entities or forces, somewhat like loose electrical fields, or monstrous poltergeists, which wandered through the universe breaking and smashing whatever they touched, causing wars, earthquakes, fire and flood, cancer and Communism. Varna, needless to say, was seldom troubled by them.

'It's not so,' Verena said. 'Why, he was top of his class in physics and math last spring.'

'His consciousness is tangled in lower things.'

'It's not so!' Her denial resounded through the parlour.

'It is so.' Elsie's voice had gradually shrunk to a mutter, but now it picked up a little whiny volume. 'You're such a child, Verena, you don't see it, but everybody else can. Tom and Roger, they re-alize. I told them about him asking you to go out tonight, taking you from your true work. They both agreed with me, it's a wrong leading.' She stood back, giving us the floor now, looking from my face to McMann's eagerly and wringing her apron with both hands. 'Isn't that true?'

I swallowed: non-directive technique, as far as I knew, had no rules for this situation.

'Your aunt feels it's a mistake for you to go out.' McMann followed the letter of his law, but not its spirit. I waited for Verena to protest, since he would also logically have to repeat whatever she said. But for the first time that afternoon her straight look flickered, as if there were a fault in the current.

'You think it's possible Ken is under a dark influence, too,' she said, slightly scornfully.

'I think it's *possible*.' He spoke heavily; the provincial businessman giving the word on a dubious venture.

'But I know his will is good. He says a lot of our science is moving towards spiritual ends now, trying to understand the work of the whole universe through higher mathematics, reaching out to all kinds of new ideas, just like Ro told us, and sending their signals into space. That's what the lecturer is talking about tonight. They've found out space is really curved, and they know now that all matter is made up of

85

electrical forces, the same way we learned. Some day they'll be able to make anything in the world, Ken said, just out of the electrical waves of the universe; even coffee and doughnuts. He's interested in all that; he's studied it a lot.'

Elsie's face sagged, conceded, 'Mmhm.'

'Ken is interested in making coffee and doughnuts out of the electricity of the universe.' McMann's tone was bland, noncommittal; but Verena got the point.

'It was just an example.'

It had taken Elsie a little longer, but now she joined in. 'Doughnuts! It's like I said, his soul is tied to the material. It's a painful thing, to think what great scientific powers are going to be placed in the hands of undeveloped spirits like Ken, in this world. Up on Varna, only their purest souls are admitted to the real high knowledge.'

'Ken's spirit may not be developed,' Verena contradicted, 'but it's one of good will.'

'Good will! It's beyond belief how you can say that, when you saw how he behaved the last time he was here. Calling names, and all kind of rudeness, throwing suspicion and scorn on our belief, didn't we all see that?' This time she looked from McMann to me.

'No, I mean yes, but —' I tried to frame a neutral response.

'We saw how he behaved,' McMann said distinctly.

'You see, everyone knows it. He's been casting a negative vibrational force over you, Verena, or you wouldn't talk that way. His emanations are confusing your mind.'

Verena took half a step back; she touched her forehead tremulously. Neither McMann nor I said anything, but in spite of this we appeared to be in agreement with Elsie. If Verena will only defend herself, I thought, I'll reinforce her. But instead she turned to McMann, looking up to him – for the first time that phrase came to mind; though since he was a head taller she must often have done so.

'Do you feel there's a shadow on me too?' Verena's cloud of hair stood out in all directions. Her face was very pale, and an actual bar of shadow, thrown by one of the branches of the

86

ceiling light fixture, lay over it diagonally. If he says he sees that shadow, I'll quit the project, I told myself.

'I don't know.' McMann spoke deliberately, his voice full of warm concern. 'What do you think?' It was our standard response to any direct question.

'I *have* felt strange lately.' Verena ignored us now, speaking only to him. 'This morning, when I was walking up to town, I felt this strange trembling. It went all through me, just for a minute, like something was shaking me.'

'That was probably, you were walking into Ken's electrical field, his atomic field,' Elsie said. 'That's what it probably was.'

'And just this afternoon,' Verena went on, paying no attention to her aunt. 'I was lying on the bed, thinking over what Ken had been saying, and I started hearing this noise, kind of a low vibrational hum, that went on and on. It seemed to come from everywhere around me at once. And I had this funny hot sensation inside my body.'

'You had a hot sensation.' Though McMann looked at Verena and spoke solemnly, he was really addressing me, and in effect roaring with laughter.

'Yes. It was like when I was sick last year, and ran a fever. Only this was more concentrated. Mostly in my side, sort of.'

'In your side?'

'Yes, right here.' Verena put a white hand below her other arm, crushing the cloth to her full breasts.

'Hmmm.' Elsie let out her breath like a train starting. 'You got this just today,' she said, 'it must have come from Ken. Did he touch you? Anywheres?' The whistle of the train, shrill. Elsie leaned forward; a cord in her neck stood out, pulled tight.

'He just put his arm round me, when we were walking.' Verena looked at none of us now. 'A couple – two times, maybe. His hand – well, his fingers . . .' She gestured half-heartedly.

'I knew it! You know what that was, he was transferring those elemental vibrations to your body, right then.

87

Confusing the patterns of your brain and setting up negative waves. It stands to reason you couldn't receive nothing Wednesday.... Like I told you, you remember,' she said to McMann. 'We didn't get anything then, just a mess of letters and static.'

'You told me.'

'I didn't know.' Verena raised her head now and spoke out. 'I wanted to help him. I feel it was given to me to help him. He has problems, serious decisions about his career.'

'Ken has problems about his career?' I jumped in, echoing her remarks rather randomly.

'Yes, he feels like he isn't getting a real education here at Sophis. He thinks the professors in his courses don't know their material very well. He's impatient, wondering if he should try to transfer somewhere else. He needs a leading.'

'He's blocking your receptive faculties, Verena. You have to think of others besides Ken. You're our main channel of communication, you know that. You want to cut the Seekers off from the true light, just so's you can guide one undeveloped spirit into some college?'

'But for a few days —' Verena began.

'How do you know it's for a few days? When your mind patterns are disturbed that way, how do you know when you'll be able to get back into communication? You think you're helping Ken, but already you're infected by him with elemental confusion. You could be giving him a negative leading right now instead of a true one. Maybe it's right he should leave Sophis. Anyhow, you got to avoid him completely, if your mind waves are going to be cleared. Ro is waiting to get through to you, trying to send his Messages to the earth before it's too late for us. You got a duty, Verena, to the whole *universe*.' Elsie had glanced towards the ceiling as she mentioned Ro; now she turned to McMann and me, including us in the universe. 'Isn't that so?' she demanded.

'That's so,' McMann replied strongly. 'We need you here.' I frowned; this was stretching the rules. He saw it, but bull-dozed on: 'Don't we, Roger?'

Stubbornly, or maybe confusedly, I said nothing.

'Now, Roger,' Elsie insisted. 'You can't deny that. Verena's helped you much as she has anybody.'

I could not deny it, or so I thought then: social politeness as well as social psychology forbade it. Maybe I would have, if I could have thought of a way to take Verena's side non-directively. The trouble was, I was really on Elsie's side; for my own half-conscious, wholly unprofessional reasons, I too wanted to keep Verena away from Ken.

'Mrm,' I said.

'We all need you. You know that, Verena.' McMann stared at her persuasively.

'I know that.' She gave a sigh, and pushed back her cloud of hair – a sibyl recalled to the tripod after a long day off. She looked at none of us, but up into the air.

There was a slight pause, almost of embarrassment.

'We ought to ask for guidance,' Elsie suggested. It was the Seekers' recourse in every uncertainty; effective, since it turned a random, awkward social silence into a deliberate religious hush. 'Let's meditate now, then, and ask our spirit teachers for advice.'

We had been standing under the centre light; now Elsie stepped back and turned it off. Only one lamp by the sofa remained, and such of the grey November daylight as could make its way past clouds, trees, glass, and net curtains. Up out there somewhere was the sun, but it seemed a long way off.

Elsie sat down on the sofa. She crossed her ankles precisely, left over right, and laid her hands, palms up, on her lap, in the prescribed position for individual meditation. Now the spiritual electricity, when it came, could flow in freely through her hands, and would be retained within a closed circuit, unable to leak out through her feet. The rest of us assumed the same position. We shut our eyes.

'Oh heavenly light of the spirit, oh light of God, oh light of Varna,' her thin, intense voice implored. 'Pour down upon us now, and send us your healing forces. Send them to all of

89

us here, and especially to our sister Verena; for she has fallen under a dark influence, and been touched by unclean hands. For she is no longer a proper vessel for communication; she is a filthy unclean vessel.' Elsie cleared her throat, as if of some impediment.

Against the gold of her skirt, Verena's fingers twitched. For a second all her grand, calm, smooth features were squeezed up together, as if something had been thrown in her face; the curved eyelids narrowed into a squint of pain, but did not open.

'Let us pray.' Elsie's expression was rapt, her mouth slightly open. McMann, on the sofa beside her, seemed unmoved, even a little amused. I willed him to look at me, to say something; but this message didn't get through.

'Small evil minds, negative forces . . .' Elsie was still going on.

For the first time in my life, I found myself actually praying, more or less. God damn it (I addressed Ro of Varna), this is going too far. Do something, if you exist. (He did exist, of course: according to psychological theory, he was a fragmented portion of Verena's mind. Why didn't he protect her, then?) Go on, Ro. Give us a sign. (Praying to somebody else's unconscious! I had fallen into a trap thousands of years old, if that was any consolation; because where else have gods ever come from?)

'Cleanse her of all filth and sin . . .'

Wake up, Verena. Don't let them get away with this. (Now I was speaking, or praying, to her directly. Did I really believe in telepathy, then? Why didn't I do something myself? But what could I have done?)

'Light and power are streaming down!' Elsie squeaked suddenly, bouncing about on the sofa. 'I feel them, I feel them flowing into me!' I shut my eyes, in case she should open hers. 'I feel vibrations of golden light here, everywhere. They are flowing into us, all of us!' Elsie gave a strangled cry. 'Can't you feel them?'

'Yes, I can,' McMann's voice agreed.

90

'We are being cleaned, cleaned and purified. Isn't that so?'
'That's so,' he replied enthusiastically.
'That's so.' Verena's voice, but faint and forced.
'Pouring down, pouring down on us!' Elsie sounded shrilly triumphant now.

I opened my eyes again; but closed, in fact clenched, my hands against the current from the Varna Light and Power Company. McMann and Verena still had their eyes shut, and Verena looked stunned.

'Pouring down, down!' Elsie was almost shrieking. The flowered apron hung loose between her spread knees; her shoulders were twisted round, and her head tilted up and back as if she were wildly star-gazing. The whites of her eyes showed below the grey irises – a middle-aged provincial Saint Teresa in ecstasy.

'Oh we thank you, we thank you! We kneel down and thank you.' Elsie slid off the sofa on to the parlour rug. 'Verena, Tom, Roger!' She held out her pink, sharp-fingered mouse hands.

McMann was the first to join her. He left the sofa heavily, and grasped one of Elsie's hands. Verena followed blind, her eyes still shut, and took the other hand – or rather let Elsie take hers. I moved very slowly, but I have to admit I moved. McMann's hand felt normal; Verena's limp and so cold I expected her to faint at any moment.

'We unite our hands and our spirits, that your cleansing and scouring powder may flow through us.' Elsie went on gabbling something of this sort. 'Oh thank you, thank you!'

'Thank you; we thank you,' McMann echoed matter-of-factly.

I remained silent.

'We thank you.' Verena's voice was thin and strained. But her hand grew firmer, though no warmer; it grasped mine now with desperate force, as if she were drowning. I squeezed back – friendly but ineffectual.

'We are cleaned now, and made pure and whole again.'

91

Elsie sounded less hysterical, more simply self-conscious. She looked at us instead of the ceiling.

'I am cleaned and made pure,' Verena said in that same thin mechanical voice, her nails digging into me painfully.

'And we thank you, our teachers and guides. Amen.'

'Amen.' McMann, Elsie, and I dropped hands.

'Amen,' Verena uttered. Her grip loosened and I recovered my hand, cold and aching. She swayed, caught herself, dropped into a limp sitting position, and finally opened her eyes. Pushing back her hair, she looked about, as if she were puzzled to see us all kneeling round her on the floor, in the dusk. We rose awkwardly, while she went on staring at us, and finally spoke.

'I'm tired, Aunt Elsie.' Her voice had changed again; it was that of a petulant child. She held out her hand. 'Help me up. I have to rest now.'

8

No use going over the rest of that day in detail. Verena did not come down again, and there was no sound from upstairs all evening. As Mr Novar, Milly, and Catherine arrived, Elsie gave each of them an overwrought version of what had happened, vague in detail and full of references to 'infectious negative auras', 'thought-power', and 'cleansing force'. McMann and I were called upon again to reinforce her ('We felt the healing light pouring down on us, isn't that so?') and he complied heartily; I was mostly silent.

There were also stage-whispered asides and dark hints: for example, to Milly as we helped clear off the chicken stew and bring in pineapple upside-down cake ('He *touched* her, you know'); but Elsie wouldn't answer any direct question. ('We won't talk about *that*. Our lesson has been to put all unfit thoughts and pictures out of our minds and concentrate on bright images of progress.') The total effect was to make Verena's meeting with Ken seem extremely lurid. Milly and Catherine couldn't have looked more shocked if she'd actually been assaulted.

I was pretty shocked myself to see what pleasure Elsie took in contemplating her niece's fall from grace, and describing her confession and humiliation. Before this I had always thought of them as in partnership: Verena the calm young sibyl ensconced in her Sears Roebuck temple, and Elsie scurrying round the sanctuary like a plump, devout little church mouse. Now she had turned into a monster in mouse's shape. Her pale eyes, edged with red, seemed to expand as she spoke, and the squeak of her voice grew louder, as if amplified.

How could this have happened? How could we have let it happen, or maybe even made it happen? I was so worked up

I didn't wait until we got back to Ovid's Motel to raise these questions; I hardly waited until we had got down the front walk.

'That was a pretty bad scene, this afternoon,' I said as I got into the car.

'It surprised you, huh?' McMann slid in heavily behind the wheel, and slammed his door.

'Yes. Didn't it you?'

'Nah. In an unstable group like this, where there's no tradition, no formal organization to speak of, you've got to expect these sudden shifts in the power structure.'

'Maybe. But it looked to me like this wasn't so much a group matter as a personal one. Elsie was trying to destroy Verena out of personal spite and envy, that's all. It almost makes you want to leave the profession, when you have to stand around and watch one person treat another that way.' I applied only the thinnest layer of irony to soften this remark.

'Come on.' McMann started the Pontiac and shifted smoothly into reverse. 'You're being melodramatic. Elsie doesn't want to "destroy" Verena; there's no percentage in that for her. She just wants her to stay home and keep the group going.'

'That's not what it looked like to me.'

'Wait and see. I'll bet Verena'll be back in business to-morrow, handing out advice and receiving lessons and the whole works. They'll fit this Ken episode into the doctrine just like they did the last one.'

'I know that's your theory.' I didn't say this ironically. I was frowning as we drove through the dark streets, wondering if McMann were right. After all, he had twenty years' experience in the profession against my twenty months'.

As if he read my thoughts, McMann remarked, 'I suppose anybody is apt to have this kind of reaction when they first start out in the field. I remember something like it myself. What it boils down to is, whether you take your job seriously or not. Isn't that so?'

94

'Mm.'

'The basic question is, can you remain scientifically objective on a study, or are you going to let yourself get emotionally involved and fuck up your observations.'

McMann had not put this as a real question, so I didn't have to answer. Silent, I felt myself shrinking. Suppose it had been one of the other Seekers who had been made to confess their error and infection with bad vibrations this afternoon, I thought. Sissy or Bill Freeplatzer, say. Would I have been emotionally involved? Probably I wouldn't have given a damn, any more than I did when Ken and Felicia were told off, and they both had nearly the whole group against them. But then, on the other hand —

'There's another thing,' I said. 'The way we were backing Elsie up this afternoon against Verena.'

'How do you mean?'

'Well, taking a stand like that on one side, when there were only two group members present. Doesn't it bias the data? Without our reinforcement, I don't think Elsie could've convinced Verena she'd done anything wrong.'

'Here we go again.' McMann signed noisily. 'You're so scrupulous, Zimmern, you should have gone into statistics. And anyhow, you're wrong. If we hadn't been available this afternoon, Elsie would just have waited until Milly and Catherine got there. Or possibly she would have called in some of the others. The effect would have been the same in the end, because all of them are solid against Ken.'

'You think they would have backed Elsie up.'

'Christ, I'm positive of it. . . . Whereas if we'd supported Verena, encouraged her to go with Ken, we would have been deliberately acting against the consensus of the group. You can see that.'

'Mm,' I agreed.

'Besides, Verena didn't give us anything to support, like Elsie did. All she ever did was ask if we thought she was under a bad influence. . . . Well, here we are. Only nine-fifteen.

95

Let's get it all into the record, and then maybe we can go out for a beer, okay?'

'Okay.'

In the motel, McMann plugged in his tape-recorder and began telling it what had happened that day. I sat across the room and opened my notebook. For the first time, I wished we had had the machine with us on West Hawthorne Street, so there would be some record independent of his version and mine.

McMann would have liked to use a tape-recorder, at least at meetings. He had tried it twice already. The first time he left it in the briefcase out in the hall, and though the volume was turned up as high as it could go, he didn't get much. Next he tried a much smaller machine, only about four inches long, which he wore underneath his jacket in a shoulder-holster. The trouble with this one was that it had a very short range: if a speaker were more than a couple of feet away, it wouldn't pick up his remarks; and when the person carrying it moved, the rustling of his clothes made static. McMann moved all the time, and the only thing that came through clearly was his own remarks.

After we were known to be professors, he tried the straight-forward approach. He suggested to the Seekers that we should record the meetings for them, and then give everyone a copy of the proceedings after his secretary had typed them up. Elsie liked the idea, so Verena asked Ro about it at the next opportunity. His answer was No. Ro said that the flow of electrons into the machine, which had a negative vibrational charge, would empty the atomic field around it and weaken reception; that is, the tape-recorder would eat up the messages from Varna before they got to us.

A few days later I listened to the tape McMann had made that evening. By that time I was pretty well convinced that he was right; that my perceptions had been distorted by emotional bias, so that the record of that afternoon in my memory was actually incorrect. All the same, there was something unpleasant about his flat, objective version. It reminded me of those pictures that appeared in the *New York Times* not so long ago, candid snapshots of prisoners being tortured in Vietnam. You couldn't help asking, 'Why didn't the photographer do something? He was right there, wasn't he?'

We weren't supposed to go to the Novars' again until next evening. But I drove over after breakfast, on the pretext of borrowing the notes of Wednesday's meeting, to see how things were.

I found Verena cleaning the parlour, in a flowered Mother Hubbard apron. I had never seen her doing any housework before; maybe it was a sort of penance. But then, I had never been to West Hawthorne Street so early without an invitation. Verena's bush of hair was tied back with a piece of black string, and except for her extraordinary eyes she looked less like a sibyl than I had ever seen her. But she was calm, and seemed quite in control of the situation, just as McMann had predicted.

She greeted me pleasantly and asked how I was, as if we had last met a week ago instead of yesterday. After wiping her hands on her apron, she went to fetch the notes of the last meeting. She didn't think they would be much use to us or anybody though, she said. You see, she had already been in a negative field at that time, and these writings, even if we could make any sense out of them, couldn't be considered a true lesson. And now, if I would excuse her . . . Verena turned on the vacuum-cleaner again.

I wondered how she would manage the meeting that night; but everything went off as usual. Verena sang the hymns (she had a nice clear voice), greeted the Seekers individually, and gave them personal guidance. Maybe it was only to me that she seemed blurred, a little mechanical.

When the lights were turned down for meditation, there was a long wait before her hand began to move across the pad as the Message from Varna came through. I wouldn't have been surprised if it had been another page of loops and

97

scrawls; I feared a repetition of Elsie's attack, and hoped for an attack on Elsie. But when Verena finally read it aloud, it was just the ordinary exhortation to faithful study and warning against doubt, with a few new remarks on auras. There was no change in her prophetic manner either, only a subtle diminution. Part of the intensity, the high electrical charge, seemed (at least to me) to have gone out of her overnight, and part of the colour; she was like a painting in reproduction.

Afterwards, while we were having refreshments, she appeared to be chatting quite normally. Only it wasn't right somehow: it was as if she were imitating herself, or reading from a script she had memorized earlier.

Elsie, on the other hand, was nervously lively and full of ideas, dashing in and out of the kitchen, opening soda bottles and dropping ice into glasses as if a high wind were blowing behind her. 'A wonderful meeting tonight!' she said, her little eyes sparkling, as she poured me a Coke. 'Wasn't it a wonderful, wonderful meeting, Roger?'

'Mmh.'

'I felt the current of mind power right in the room, so strong. You know what that means; great lessons are coming to us soon.'

'Mmh?'

'Oh, I know we've had many, many valuable teachings already. But there's much more that we don't know yet. When the connection was first made, we weren't prepared here. We weren't ready for the highest knowledge. We've had to study and discipline our minds, uuh' – Elsie strained to open another bottle – 'and progress by slow steps, like little children, going from grade to grade.' Pop! 'Pass me another couple of glasses, Roger. We've had to cast off false ideas and negative associations, and cleanse our souls. Even those of us who thought we were educated already and knew all there was to know, had to throw away their old notions and learn the true understanding. Isn't that so?'

I had to agree again, but it was a strain. Non-directive

assent, which once had seemed such an easy, energy-saving way of relating to the group, was now difficult and painful.

'Yes, there's wonderful things on their way to us,' Elsie said, taking another tray of ice from the freezer. She set it on the sink and pulled the handle hard, so that blocks of cold, sharp frozen water jumped out in all directions. 'A change is coming. You just wait and see.'

It was so: during the next couple of weeks there was a change in the Truth Seekers. Nobody but Elsie Novar could have called it wonderful, though. What happened was that, surely and not so slowly, Elsie, and Elsie's views and opinions, began to dominate. As McMann put it, there was a shift in group structure. We had a diadic system now, with a formal leader (Verena) and an informal one (Elsie). Elsie took up her niece's practice of giving advice to the other group members during the week, and holding individual conferences with them. She talked much more at meetings; she started giving short sermons on various topics before Verena came downstairs. During the question period she spoke almost as much as Verena, and initiated the largest percentage of action-producing suggestions, or APS.

McMann had more or less abandoned Bales's system by this time, and was using one of his own. He had started keeping sociograms on which he and I recorded, not only who addressed whom, and who initiated each topic, but where people sat in Elsie's parlour, what postures they assumed, how often they smiled, frowned, got up, and so on. It was a job to keep track of it all, and I still didn't understand what use he was planning to make of the data, but I did my best.

Previously, the emotional climate had always been one of optimism and uplift. The universe was full of benevolent power; Spiritual Light and Cosmic Love were flowing more and more towards Sophis, New York. Ro's messages and Verena's advice were filled with joyful reassurance: Catherine

Vanting's neuralgia would get better soon, Rufus would pass his exams, and Bill's boss would recommend him for a raise. Now a more Manichean tone, a kind of metaphysical shadow, began to spread over West Hawthorne Street. There were terrible weaknesses within our spirits, we had to realize, and menacing forces without. We heard much more about the elementals now. They were no longer just a kind of spiritual bad weather, gusts of invisible cold, dark wind blowing about the world; they were sentient forces, full of contagious, stupid malevolence.

It wasn't just Elsie who took this line: it infected the whole group. Verena had changed too, though not as much as the rest. Now and then she would give the old sort of comfort and encouragement. But more often, when she addressed the meeting, she seemed to speak with Elsie's voice, and even to use some of Elsie's small, abrupt gestures, as if her aunt were pulling her strings. She would look up at the ceiling and announce that she felt the presence of chaotic vibrations and static; there was wrong thinking among us, and the mind of someone present was cluttered with material images, dragging us down. Then one of the group, usually Rufus, Milly, or Peggy, would admit shamefacedly that they had allowed thoughts of a toothache, or what to have for dinner tomorrow, to enter their minds. Self-accusation of this sort (even when not specifically called for), and the confession of spiritual faults, became very common.

Saturday evening at the Novars' had nothing about it now of an informal Great Books discussion. When it wasn't a sort of Oxford Group meeting, it was definitely a course for credit, with no auditors allowed. The whole thing got to be like a relentless parody of higher education. There was the same intense seriousness about a body of accumulating data which was, to say the least, unverifiable; the same assumption that here was a small group of enlightened, thinking persons who understood the universe correctly. As for the messages from Varna, aren't most articles in professional journals a form of automatic writing? It is another self who speaks there, solemn and oracular, in a cryptic jargon the real man would never use.

The Seekers had lectures, they had readings in approved texts, they had assignments (twenty minutes of meditation on set topics before breakfast every day, short essays on matters of special interest). They were expected to take notes at meetings, and copy out the messages received. Between times, they had to study the 'lessons' and memorize the prayers, lists, and definitions dictated by Ro and his friends, preparing themselves to be questioned on them at any time: in effect, called on to recite in class.

The worst part of all this was that McMann and I were subject to the same academic requirements. But while he fulfilled them with a carefully calculated average efficiency, I was an involuntary D student. I have never had a good memory for small, stupid details, names, and numbers. When I passed my Ph.D. orals I said to myself with relief that never, never again would I have to prepare for or take another examination. Still, for some time after that, I dreamt (though with declining frequency and force) that I was being examined in public, usually on some preposterous subject.

Now it was as if those bad dreams had begun again, in three dimensions. I was the object of general pity and scorn when I stated, for example, that a yellow-green aura and the release of positively charged delta rays was characteristic of the first stage of the third level of enlightenment, instead of the second stage of the fourth level. McMann grinned as I stumbled through the Invocation to the Spirit of Middle Light, and Verena looked hurt.

The same thing that I had seen happen in my courses when the recognized class dunce stood up to recite, was now happening to me. Nothing fails like failure. And (like success) it tends to spread from one area to another. About this time, the Novars' washing-machine started leaking. Instead of calling Sears, Mr Novar took it apart one Saturday afternoon and laid it out on the cellar floor. Then he and McMann put it back together. I couldn't help them.

My prestige in the group, as measured on McMann's scale, declined correspondingly. Fewer remarks were addressed to me now, and almost no questions-seeking-advice. The group members who were most maternally oriented, Milly and Sissy, offered to coach me in my lessons. Technically I should have accepted, but I couldn't stand to. I was exhorted to meditate more often and study harder – even harder than the others. (Two hours a day devoted to study and meditation on the lessons of Varna was not too much, Elsie told us emphatically. If it interfered with our worldly occupations and amusements, well, we would just have to give some of them up.)

You might think the Seekers would have rebelled against this new rigid, depressing régime. They didn't. Apparently, although people like to hear that they and the universe are good and getting better all the time, they like even more to be told that they are wicked sinners in a dark pit, and can only be saved through great effort, the repetition of magic formulae, and the aid of invisible beings.

McMann pointed out cynically that the group was doing more for its members now: reinforcing not only their wishes but their guilts and fears. It also satisfied their affective needs more fully. There was lots of talk now about how the Truth Seekers were united to one another by pure Cosmic Love, and they were encouraged to demonstrate the fact. There had always been a good deal of intense hand-clasping on meeting and parting; now there was even more, and they had introduced the custom of exchanging a 'kiss of light' (on the forehead, between the eyebrows). According to Ro of Varna this kiss had strong protective qualities, when it was given with a pure spirit.

The increase in physical expression was accompanied, just as in other religions, by a verbal rejection of the physical. It went way beyond the disapproval of commercial materialism I had found so congenial. Now the whole material world, and

102

especially the human body, was revealed as low, coarse, heavy, and filthy; best treated with strict austerity. The spirit must not be allowed to dwell on the cares or pleasures of the physical body, to wallow in thoughts of head colds or hot baths.

Some of the Seekers made more of this lesson than others – but not those you might have expected. Milly and Catherine, the oldest group members, both confided in us that they thought Elsie was going too far when she stopped serving refreshments after meetings – what was the harm, after all, in a piece of angel-food cake; or devil's-food, for that matter? – while the youngest Seekers, Rufus, Peggy, and Verena, seemed most eager to mortify their flesh.

Rufus had given up drinking with the fellows at college, even beer, he announced proudly. Peggy told us of the wonderful electric-clean feeling she got the afternoon she went into the dorm bathroom and washed off all her make-up with strong soap and water. She had stopped setting her hair too, and now it hung like coarse, ragged straw around her shiny face; the natural look didn't become her as it did Verena. But Rufus and Peggy had the consolation of all puritans: they could be as intensely, continually, and publicly concerned with sensual indulgence as the most confirmed hedonist, and feel righteous at the same time. They were obviously enjoying themselves.

It was Verena who bothered me. What she was giving up wasn't just lipstick or beer: she seemed to have stopped eating. At meals she just pushed the food gently back and forth on her plate, or ignored it completely. Several times, against our rules, I found myself encouraging her to eat something, in a disguised way – passing her the bread very often, or asking if I could get her a glass of milk from the kitchen when I got one. 'No thank you, Roger,' she would reply in an unnaturally sweet, vibrating voice, opening her great dark eyes even wider. 'I don't feel the need of anything more now. I have so much spiritual food.'

.   .   .   .   .

By Thanksgiving week-end I was really worried about her. McMann and I had four days off, and he wanted to spend them all with the Seekers. I could go down to New York for the first couple of days if I liked, he said, but he was going straight to Sophis. There was a special meeting Thursday evening, at which we had been promised a 'Message of blinding light', and he wanted to be there.

I had tickets for a new play in New York and a girl I was planning to take to it. I knew my parents would be (politely) indignant if I called and told them not to expect me for Thanksgiving, and I didn't blame them. It was easier for McMann: both his parents were dead, and for such a gregarious man he had few close ties.

All the same, I finally decided to go to Sophis too. Partly I wanted to look out for Verena, and partly I just didn't want to miss anything important.

The Seekers were delighted to have us with them for the holidays. It proved, if any of them still doubted it, that Varna was the most important thing in our lives. We were invited to Thanksgiving dinner on West Hawthorne Street, and Catherine Vanting asked us to stay with her. Before this, we had always declined to be anyone's house-guests, because we valued our privacy, but this time McMann accepted. Maybe he thought anything would be better than four days in Ovid's Motel.

The new anti-materialist régime had no effect on Thanksgiving dinner. Elsie served a fifteen-pound turkey with the classic side-dishes, and we all ritually over-ate. Except Verena. She let them pile the food on her plate, and even dug a little reservoir for the gravy in her mashed potatoes, like a child. But she didn't swallow anything, as far as I could see, except a couple of sticks of celery. She was starting to lose weight, too. She wasn't thin yet by any means, but the sleeves of her dress hung looser on her round white arms, and her chin had lost some of its Victorian fullness. It wasn't unbecoming, but was it healthy? Through the centrepiece of chrysanthemums, I urged her to have some hot rolls; she did not even seem to hear. Tomato aspic salad; pumpkin and mince pie; ice cream; and finally coffee and after-dinner mints. Verena gazed at the ceiling with a blank, fixed look, and neither spoke nor ate.

After the feast, she excused herself and went upstairs to rest and meditate for the meeting that evening. Catherine and Elsie started on the dishes; Mr Novar went back to his workshop in the basement, and we left.

Catherine Vanting's place, where we were staying, was near the centre of town, a block off Main Street. It was a big, old, shapeless stucco house, painted cocoa-grey with beige trim, and kept up as a kind of museum of Catherine's parents, who had died six or seven years ago. It was full of cold, cluttered sun-porches, steep polished stairs, shelves of bric-à-brac, and worn hooked rugs. We had the guest room: twin brass beds, tall chests of golden oak, and a north light.

'Oof.' McMann sat on the edge of his bed and pulled off his shoes, bending over with difficulty. 'Christ, did we stuff ourselves this afternoon! These damned atavistic behaviour patterns – you'd think we were all Indians preparing for a winter of famine. I should have left that mince pie alone.' He groaned and loosened his belt.

'Verena didn't eat anything. I mean literally, anything. I was watching her.' McMann's expression showed no concern. 'I think she's deliberately starving herself, out of some crazy religious conviction.'

'Verena's not starving. She's putting on an act, and you're obviously her best audience.'

'I don't think so. But even if that's true, she's getting thinner and thinner. It kind of worries me.'

'She could stand to lose some weight.' McMann burped, and lay back on the spread, which was patterned with lumps of fluff.

'Not all that much.'

'You like them big in the can, huh?'

McMann was still using the voice and diction of the coarse,

105

provincial man he had been playing all day. Or did he always speak that way off campus? Maybe, I thought, it was the other McMann who was an act.

'And she's so quiet now,' I went on. 'She hardly spoke at all today.'

While I watched, McMann changed roles, drawing his thick brows together and propping his head on his hands.

'Listen, Verena may look pathetic to you,' he said in his seminar manner, bluff but highly educated. 'But she can take care of herself. You've got to remember, that girl has already changed a number of people's lives rather profoundly. Elsie, Milly, Rufus, the whole lot of them. Don't let her fool you. Ahhh.' He shut his eyes.

I was standing by the window, looking through yellowed net at a view of sky, branches, and the grey backs of houses. There were two more lives Verena had changed, I thought, that McMann had overlooked: his and mine. It was the end of November now, and since school started I had been spending all my free time in Sophis. My real life – family, friends, students – had faded into a sort of dim middle distance, like the view outside this window. But that was nothing compared to what Truth Seeking had done to Verena; or what Elsie had done to her.

'Yes, but that was earlier,' I said. 'She hasn't had much influence lately.'

McMann sighed and opened his eyes.

'Well, of course she was humiliated over the Ken incident,' he said. 'Sexual guilt. But that's all been channelled. It's been incorporated into the value system. A damn-near perfect example of the cathartic process.' He grinned.

McMann's professional satisfaction made me more worried, not less. I thought of Verena, shut in her room with the gods she had created and the material body they disapproved of, weak from lack of food. Maybe she was having a nervous collapse right now. I imagined her in a catatonic stupor: seated on her bed, leaning against the flowered wallpaper, with her hair tangled over her staring eyes, her clothes disarranged. Eventually her aunt and uncle would find her there, and telephone for the doctor, the police, the ambulance. Verena would be taken away to Atwell State Hospital, an ominously isolated group of brick buildings on a hill some fifteen miles beyond Sophis, and I would never see her again.

'I think there's more going on than that,' I said. 'Something's really the matter with her. I think we should consider it.'

McMann yawned. 'Let's consider it some other time,' he said. 'I'm going to rest and meditate now in preparation for the meeting.' He burped again, and shut his eyes.

Everything warned me to let it alone, but I couldn't. 'What it looks like to me,' I insisted, 'is the disintegration of a personality, going on right while we watch. And I don't like it.'

'Aw, hell.' McMann shifted on the high brass bed, which squawked under his weight. 'Verena's all right; she's still functioning.'

In any quarrel, people tend to fall back into the forms of verbal aggression they first learned. I reverted now too, and matched the prissy intellectual superiority of the Ethical Culture boy against the crudities of the tough small-town kid.

'You really don't see anything? It seems to me anyone who took the trouble to look would recognize what's happening. It's not only her not eating, of course. She's becoming completely cut off from normal life. She never goes outside any more, anywhere. She hardly speaks to anybody except about Varna. Most of the time she's shut up alone in her room, meditating. It looks to me like a classic case of' – I paused a moment, gathering nerve – 'incipient schizophrenia. That limp handshake she gives you now; it's like, what do they call it, waxy flexibility. The blank way she looks at everybody, as if she saw right through you and out the other side. And that kind of flat voice, especially when she gives advice, and goes along with whatever Elsie suggests, without any argument.

Maybe "functioning" is the right word. She's *functioning*, like a machine.'

McMann rolled over on to his side and looked at me coldly.

'Suppose I were to accept this amateur diagnosis,' he said. 'What would you like me to do about it?'

I gave the logical answer, though it surprised even me as I heard it. 'I think Verena should see a psychiatrist. There must be someone at the college here. I'm not suggesting she should go into therapy necessarily,' I added. 'The way things are now she probably wouldn't anyhow; Ro would object. But at least we would have a professional opinion.'

McMann sat up and faced me. The heavy folds of flesh from which his eyebrows grew drew together in a hard stare.

'And what about the study? You realize what will happen if we take our principal subject out of the group milieu and drag her to a head-shrinker? From that minute on all our data is invalidated.'

Angry, McMann was even more formidable. I had to make myself take a breath before I replied stiffly, in the apologetic plural, 'We might decide that some things, like the sanity of an individual, are more important than any project.'

'Oh, might we.' McMann leaned forward; for a moment I had the idea that he was going to hit me. Instead, he smiled slightly to himself.

'You know, Roger,' he said, 'there's something a little in-authentic here. I'd be more impressed if I thought all this concern was really for the girl. But it looks to me as if you're mostly interested in reassuring yourself. You're afraid Verena is cracking up, all right, but you're not proposing to get her into treatment; you just want to pass the buck, hand the responsibility over to somebody else.'

'That's not true. If she needs treatment now, I think she should have it.'

'And suppose she doesn't want to go?'

'You could persuade her.'

'And Elsie?'

'You could convince Elsie if you wanted to. In her terms: tell her the mental strain of communication with Varna is getting so great Verena needs to see a mind doctor.'

'At twenty-five bucks an hour?' McMann snorted with laughter as he forced me out on the limb of the stand I had taken. 'Who's going to finance that?'

'There are clinics,' I said, clinging on stubbornly. 'Or if she couldn't get into a clinic, I think we might contribute. We've got some responsibility here.'

'For Christ's sake. You're proposing *we* should subsidize a course of psychotherapy for Verena Roberts, on our salaries?'

'If it's necessary, yes,' I said from among the small branches at the end of the limb.

'Well, help yourself.' A crude grin passed across McMann's face, followed by a slow frown.

'You know, I'm beginning to see something,' he said. 'I think your position in the pecking order here is getting you down. All this guff you've been giving me all along, about moderating our impact on the group, not creating static. It was nothing but envy, the whole time. Who's creating static now? You have no training in psychiatry, but you think you know what's best for Verena, you want to step in and direct her life. Yep, Roger's tired of being bossed around by everybody. He wants to play God; he wants to be Ro of Varna himself.'

'I d-don't,' I stuttered under the attack.

'I never would have expected it of you, Roger,' McMann continued, laying about with his sledge-hammer of irony. 'I've always pictured you as such a quiet, retiring type.' Now he began to grin again. 'Then there's another point. Why are you so concerned about *Verena's* mental health?' I started to speak, but he rode over it, raising his voice. 'Hell, all the Seekers are more or less nuts, or they wouldn't be in the group. Sissy has hallucinations; Milly Munger hears voices; and our hostess here is convinced her dead parents are still hanging around the house. That's why we had to bunk together; she didn't want to put either of us in the best bedroom because Mother's and Daddy's spirits might not like having their things disturbed. But I don't notice you getting all worked up about Catherine Vanting's sanity ... There must be something special about Verena. You may not know it, but you're hot for that fat girl, Roger. That's what it is.'

'You're all wrong,' I lied firmly. 'It's not that at all.'

'Yeah? Think it over.' I said nothing. 'And while you're thinking, I'm going to have a nap. Throw me that afghan, will you?'

'Huh?'

'That brown knit blanket, hanging over the rocker. Thanks. Just like the one my granny had. . . . Ahhh.' He yawned. 'Better get yourself some rest too. I've got a feeling we're in for a long meeting tonight.'

9

McMann slept on the brass bed; I went out for a walk. It was cold and cloudy. The air hung damp between the wooden houses, and everything looked flat, toneless – the way it does when you shut one eye. Shut the other half-way, so that shapes and colours are blurred, and you'll have an idea of last Thanksgiving afternoon in Sophis, New York.

I walked around a couple of blocks first, composing the clever, effective defences I might have made to McMann's accusations, and making some accusations of my own. My boss gave the public impression of being a nice guy, a friendly, warm-hearted fellow, I explained to an imaginary jury of our peers; more so than I did. But his real concern for human values was less than it seemed. He had worked himself into the confidence and affection of the Seekers, but he had no interest in them as individuals. What he cared about was keeping his investigations going, and to this end he would employ any means, any offensive (in both senses) strategy. If he thought he could block a threat to the study by accusing me of being personally interested in one member of the group, he would, I complained in a high-minded tone, without any reference to the truth, even the plausibility of —

That last was no good. The twelve imaginary social scientists smiled and shook their heads.

But suppose I *was* interested in Verena, what was wrong with that? the lawyer for my defence piped up. Wasn't it better to be interested in people than disinterested? At least I cared what happened to her after the project was over: I wanted her to leave Sophis and come to the university, where she could get a decent education, take part in interesting experiments, and meet intelligent people.

But what was the purpose of this superior education?

Wasn't it mainly to keep her in town and give her something to do when she wasn't busy in the laboratory, putting out the data that would make Roger Zimmern's name famous in his field? And who were these intelligent people I imagined her associating with after her work was over? Principally they were this same Zimmern.

I had been congratulating myself on being the good guy, the humane scientist, but in fact I was as bad as McMann. Or worse; he only wanted to make use of Verena for the duration of the project. I was as bad as Elsie and the other Seekers, who planned to exploit her powers for an indefinite period. The only difference was that they hid their schemes under the flag of religion, instead of science. It was as if Verena were the golden goose of the fairy-tale, and we the ugly brothers and sister squabbling over her, snatching at her and pulling at her feathers, dragging her bewildered this way and that.

I had been walking in a circle, and was back at Catherine Vanting's house, now half obscured by fog. Instead of going in, I went down the path at the side to the backyard, under a row of spindly bare lilac bushes. Meanwhile, having convicted me on one of McMann's charges, the jury began to take up the rest.

I had accused McMann of being willing to do anything to keep the Sophis Project going. Maybe, they suggested, I was equally eager to stop it. It wasn't easy to admit that what I really had in mind was quitting a job I had taken on and letting McMann down. All right. Suppose it wasn't Verena but Roger that I wanted to help escape from Sophis.

It wasn't so hard to suppose. When McMann first suggested this study, he had spoken as if it would last only a short time. Six weeks, a couple of months at the most, and I could get back to my own work. It was Thanksgiving now, and here we still were among the outer space cranks.

I thought of Sniggs and Murt. I had marked them down in my mind as black hats – but now that I had seen McMann in action, turning a 'little interaction study' into an ever more

112

complex and long-range project, I could imagine what they might have been up against in 'Woodsville'. I could picture their desperation as a few weeks of research stretched into months and years, their professional need to publish something, anything – it was still a low thing to do, of course, but not so completely inexplicable.

I could imagine some of McMann's motives for extending that project too. He was established professionally; there was no pressure on him for results. Besides, maybe he didn't want to leave 'Woodsville'; probably he was enjoying himself there. I had seen the same thing happen in Sophis. McMann was a small-town, lower-middle-class boy; he was really more at ease out in the field than back at the university among academic types.

But the Seekers had begun to make me feel uncomfortable weeks ago. In my new position as group ignoramus I found them and their meetings unbearable; for good sociological reasons.

Roger Z— (I could see the write-up) had been considered intelligent by everyone for over twenty-five years. He was a Ph.D., a university professor, the author of two published articles. His current position in Sophis was a clear case of role reversal; naturally he felt disorientated. It wasn't only Verena who was being driven crazy by the Truth Seekers. Someone else stared at people glassily, spoke by rote, and went into a stupor at meetings; felt his personality splitting apart like kindling – into Clever Zimmern and Stupid Roger.

Maybe I was exaggerating Verena's condition, then, or at least her need for immediate professional help. I didn't have all that much confidence in psychiatry, anyhow. There were good psychiatrists and bad ones, and the local shrink might just make Verena worse.

Catherine Vanting had a long, narrow backyard between high board fences. The faded grass was trimmed short, and edged with flower-beds where nothing grew but sticks and string. In the centre of the foggy lawn was a sundial on a

113

cement pedestal, not working. I had come to this small town to look for anomie and alienation, for people unable to get out of a situation they hated except in imagination and through impractical schemes; and what do you know, here they were.

It was Stupid Roger who was causing all the trouble, I decided. Assistant Professor Zimmern, my real self, looked at things intelligently and objectively. He realized that he had an obligation to finish the Sophis Project without making any more trouble for McMann. We had a lot of data now, and it couldn't take much longer.

Zimmern's interest in Verena was professional, detached, and altruistic. He recognized that she was physically attractive, of course; but someone like him, who had always managed to control his feelings so well in all his associations with sane, sophisticated, educated girls, would never become emotionally involved with a small-town teenager who got messages from flying saucers. It was Stupid Roger who had done that, just like any cult member. Rufus was obviously in love with Verena, and so was his friend Ken, and Bill Freeplatzer was certainly stuck on her in a way, so why not Roger? It was the natural response in his situation.

Once the study was over, this obsession (because it was getting to be an obsession) would vanish; Stupid Roger himself would vanish. Everything would look different. As for those plans for research on the sociology of ESP, I had better hold off on them until my mind had cleared. The special abilities Verena had, if she had them, were beyond the norm, off the graph as it were. If I tried to find them in an ordinary population, I might just make a fool of myself, chasing the invisible moth of ESP through a thicker and thicker forest of statistics.

Meanwhile, until the study was finished, I would just have to keep Stupid Roger under control, and not do anything out of the way, I resolved. All my actions would be as pale and restricted as Miss Vanting's backyard, which was turning even paler now as the light failed and the air thickened with

114

damp. I would be the detached, intelligent scientific observer again; nothing more. I would make no demands on anyone, initiate no action, whatever happened.

It was beginning to rain. I started back to the house, now even greyer and less visible than before.

The special meeting Thanksgiving night was a kind of test case for the Seekers. To attend it, each of them had to leave their family hearth, or even their dinner, on the principal holiday of Family Americanism. A mortification of both body and spirit, when Rufus Bell gobbled down half his squash pie and rushed out of his mother's house to catch the bus to Sophis; or when Peggy Vonn left her fiancé and his parents in Atwell without having a second cup of coffee or offering to help with the dishes as usual. It was just as hard for the Freeplatzers and Milly, who had relatives visiting and had to walk out on their own guests.

All of them left surprise and dissatisfaction behind them, angry words (Peggy had a bad fight with her young man on the way to the bus station), and hurt feelings. They arrived at West Hawthorne Street already martyrs in their faith, sorry for themselves and a little cross.

Elsie was ready for them. Rising to open the meeting, she announced that this was a very important occasion. 'For many weeks, many revolutions of Sol, Ro and the other friends and guides on Varna have been revealing the truths of light to us. They've been watching and testing us, to see if we were serious in our intention and truly deserving of their higher knowledge. Isn't that so?' She paused.

'That's so,' Peggy agreed, but dully.

'All day the vibrations have been strong about this house,' Elsie continued. 'The scientists of Varna have been concentrating their rays, their emanations on to here. Positive force has been piling up. There's a power over this whole place now, enclosing it in.' She paused again and looked round, encouraging the other Seekers to feel this power.

Nobody spoke. Elsie's public manner was not inspiring:

she either lectured the group like an irritated schoolteacher, or confided in it in a whiny small-town gossip's voice.

'Today we all celebrated Thanksgiving,' she went on. 'We thanked the Lord for making us rich in food and material gifts. But our friends up on Varna have a higher gift for us. What they're trying to send us is a spiritual message of light and power that will take us up out of our material selves and make us truly thankful. Some of us are kind of sluggish in our bodies and minds now from overfeeding, heavy from taking in all that earth matter.' She looked round disapprovingly. 'Well, we've all just got to struggle extra hard against this heaviness; we've got to raise our minds way up now' – Elsie lifted her hands – 'and open our hearts to receive.'

Still no one responded. 'We'll just sing a few hymns,' Elsie concluded, 'and then Verena will come down to us and we'll hope for a good message.'

She went to the piano. Slowly, the Seekers got to their feet. McMann and the others raised their voices in 'We Gather Together' and 'Lead, Kindly Light', while I lowered mine as usual into an anonymous hum. As the last 'Amen' died away with a creak of the pedals, Verena came in.

'Light be about you!' she greeted the Seekers.

'In the Eternal Mind,' they replied in semi-unison – the new formula response.

'Be seated, brothers and sisters in the spirit.' Verena crossed the room and stood in front of her chair, gazing at us hypnotically.

'The currents of universal power are strong, I feel them so strong tonight,' she intoned in a penetrating sing-song. 'Right now, right at this moment, we're held in the centre of a beam of spiritual light that's streaming towards us, straight across the universe to us from Varna!' Elsie had just told us the same thing, essentially, but Verena's style of delivery, her appearance and manner, turned the meeting from a sluggish sixth-grade class into a religious event. Though there was a tense edge in her voice, she was in good form, better than she had been for weeks. The Seekers felt it: they looked up, more alert, and sat forward.

'Across the galaxies, across the dark spaces of the universe, our many, many teachers and guides on Varna are sending out the bright waves of their mental power towards us, to each one of us. The atomic positive vibrations are gathered here in this room, so that we feel our minds expanding, getting clearer and stronger than they have ever been before, isn't that so? The cells in our brains are being energized. I can sense your mind cells expanding, Bill, when I look at you now, and yours too, Sissy, all of yours —'

'You know, I was wondering about that,' Bill Freeplatzer said. 'I've been having this kind of tingling in my head, ever since I came into the room almost.'

'I'm getting it too,' Catherine chirped. 'Oh, yes. It's growing stronger and stronger.'

'Yeah, mine too —'

'My brain's so clear,' Rufus interrupted, 'I feel like I could do a whole page of calculus in a couple of minutes. I guess my IQ must've gone up about seventy-five per cent.'

'What I feel, well, it's sort of like pins and needles across the back of my neck —'

'Yeah, that's kind of what I have —'

Verena sat smiling gently, letting the delusion take hold. When they had finished their testimony, she continued in a vibrating tone, 'We're being prepared, that's what it is, you know. Yes, we're being helped to receive the Message of great light that's coming to us now, and our minds are being made stronger and clearer so that we can take it in and understand it. But we've got to help too. We've got to strive together to clear our thoughts of all material ideas and needs, and raise our consciousnesses up to their highest level, so that we can receive this wonderful news. So I want to ask you all as you sit in meditation and readiness to stretch your minds towards Varna, raise your spirits up from earth now, way up! ready to meet the golden words of light that are coming.'

She sat down. Elsie turned off the switch by the door, and

the room was dark except for one lamp, under which Verena's hand lay still on the yellow paper. We waited in silence.

Quite soon, a scratch on the pad announced that Ro was with us in the room. The white hand wrote rapidly several times across the top of the page, and then stopped. Verena was slumped back in the chair, her head fallen sideways against the wing. There was a long pause. The Seekers looked at each other awkwardly.

'Verena.' Elsie spoke to her softly. 'Verena, there's a Message.'

No response. Elsie got up, but as she started across the room the hand jerked on the table again, lunged about blindly in the air, and then found the pad. It crossed and re-crossed the paper, stabbing at it with the pencil as if it were chopping it full of little holes. Verena still lay in a heap in the chair, her eyes shut, her mouth half open.

The end of the page was reached, and the hand tore it off violently, flinging it up towards the ceiling. From there it descended slowly, gliding down to the carpet on invisible currents of air.

The pencil slowed now and wrote more slowly, scratching rather than stabbing. Finally it stopped, and dropped its weapon. Verena opened her eyes. She rubbed them as if they hurt, breathed loudly, and sat forward. Rufus retrieved the paper from the rug and passed it reverently to her by one corner.

We waited in silence while she studied the Message. As her eyes crossed the page they seemed to grow larger, darker. I felt the expectancy in the room; but I reminded myself not to expect too much. Important news had been promised before, and it had turned out to be that a high Varnian bureaucrat had agreed to speak to the Seekers, or that they had all been promoted from the Mura to the Nura radial plane; things like that.

Verena laid the sheets of scribbled paper on her lap, and raised her face towards the parlour ceiling. 'Oh teachers of

118

Varna!' she cried. 'I thank you! I thank you for this great Message of light and promise that you have given us this day.' Next she lowered her head and sat in silence, prolonging the suspense. Finally she looked up.

'Friends and Seekers of Truth!' Her voice sounded hollow and musical, as if she were singing down a corridor. 'Hear the words of light and power that have come to us!

> 'GREETINGS AND THANKSGREETINGSS IN THE ETERNAL MIND REREJOICE FOR WE WHO ARE NOWN TO YOU IN MIND WILL BE KNOWN AND SEEN IN BODILY PREPARE AND PREPARE FOR SOL APPROACHESS TO THE ZZURA FIELD EMANATIONS ARE GATHERED TO THE WHOLE LUNE THE TTENTHE DAY IN THE WHOLE LUNAR VIBRRATION ANDD DDARKENESS OPPOSITING   PREPARE ALL AND FOLLOW LIGHT INSTRUCTIONS OF RREADINESSS'

I looked round the room. Puzzled confusion on every face except Verena's, Elsie's, and McMann's; there I saw joy and triumph.

'They are coming!' Verena sang. 'Our guides on Varna are coming to us at last, in the body, on the tenth day after this day. Isn't that wonderful!'

'Oh, we're blessed!' Elsie squealed.

'Our guides from Varna are coming to us,' McMann repeated in strong affirmative tones – technically, too soon.

'Coming to this earth?' Sissy asked, rather nervously.

'Yes, to this earth,' Verena affirmed.

'Next *week*?' Milly said. 'Is that really so?'

'Yes, it's so,' Elsie insisted. 'Ro has just told us.'

'Say, that's grand!' Bill exclaimed.

'Why – it's wonderful.' Catherine looked towards the ceiling.

The tide had turned – consensus began to take over.

'Ooh, gee.'

'That's really great!'

'I always knew they would visit us some day.'

119

Verena smiled as faith swept round the room – the fixed, ethereal sweet smile of bad religious art everywhere.

'It's a wonderful day for us, isn't it?' Catherine said to me.

'Uh, wonderful.' I agreed lukewarmly.

'I will read this first great Message of light again,' Verena announced; 'and then I'm going to read the instructions our teacher and guide has sent us tonight, telling us how we are to prepare for this wonderful Coming. Listen fully; hearken to these words with your whole mind and spirit. Yes, let's all of us concentrate with every atom of our spiritual energy while I read, so that these great words can fill us all with their healing vibrations.'

In the same echoing voice, Verena read out the Message again. This time the Seekers all had more or less foolish expressions of intense concentration; frowns with jaws set hard; eyes closed tight; gaping mouths. McMann was frowning too, but when I looked over at him he wiped the mask off for a second and grinned.

Of course he was pleased. The announcement that beings from Varna were going to appear on some definite, immediate date, was a wonderful break for the study. It would be a much more severe test of faith and commitment to the group than anything that had happened before. Even a sceptic like me is willing to consider the possibility that there may be intelligent beings on other planets. It's a lot harder to believe that some of them are going to visit Sophis, New York, next week. The extent to which each of the Seekers accepted the prediction, and acted on his belief, would be fascinating to observe. And when the announced date arrived and the Varnians didn't show up, we would have a perfect example of the sudden and complete withdrawal of justification for a group's existence.

Verena told the Seekers to get out their notebooks so they could write down the wonderful Message. She read it over to them once again, very slowly and with emphasis. What I say three times is true, as Lewis Carroll remarked. The harder something is to believe, the more often it has to be repeated.

120

When we had finished writing, she went over the text a fourth time, discussing and explaining it word by word. Ten days from today, the moon would be whole, or full, and our solar system would have entered the Zura atomic field – a combination of events highly favourable for inter-galactic travel. Verena spoke calmly and clearly now, in a normal tone of voice, emphasizing the important points.

The Seekers were scribbling happily and industriously in their notebooks, and so was I. I, too, had got my wish: the Sophis study was coming to an end. In a few weeks, at the most, all this would be over, and I would be free of Stupid Roger and his obsession.

'Is everybody finished?' Verena asked. 'Good. Now let's all turn to a new page. I'm going to read our first instructions. We'll be receiving many more instructions soon, because we have a great deal—oh, a very great deal to do to prepare ourselves for the Coming. We've got to strive the best we can to reach a state of spiritual readiness, so that our guides will be able to come through to us in the body, across the great darkened spaces of the universe and right down through all the heavy vibrations and layers of matter that surround this earth. We're going to be so very busy now, all of us.' Verena looked round at the group with a hectically bright smile, which several of them returned.

'Now let's take this down,' she continued. 'SILENT SILENCE.' Pencils scratched. 'Our first instruction is to be silent about what's coming. We know that most people here on earth aren't ready for the highest truths yet, they aren't mentally awakened and strong enough in their minds, like we are. Well, if that's so, then we know they're certainly not going to be ready to experience the wonderful miracle of our guides from Varna appearing right here in their true body of light. So our first lesson is to treasure our wonderful news up in our hearts and not reveal it to anyone outside, no matter how much we might be impelled to do that. We might meet friends, we might be talking with somebody, and we'd like so much to tell them about the great event that's approaching;

121

but we've just got to hold ourselves back and refrain from it. Silent Silence. We've got to remember all the time that up on Varna our guides are watching each one of us to see if we are carrying out their instructions faithfully, so that they can come on down to us. Because when they do come, there can't be any strangers here, anyone that hasn't really worked and studied the truths of light.'

'Yes, but if nobody else sees our guides, then —' Rufus began.

'It's not just for our sakes, Rufus,' Elsie broke in. 'It's for their own sakes too, isn't that so? Because we do know that most of the individuals here on this earth, they couldn't stand to be exposed all of a sudden to the mental power and light of Varna. If they were to meet our guides all unprepared the way they are now, all that bright mental power would flash through their undeveloped minds like blazing sheet lightning, and blind them with positive vibrations, so they wouldn't see nothing anyhow. We've got to remember that, and that's another important reason we've got to keep silent. Isn't that so?'

'That's right.' Verena nodded.

'That's definitely correct, it's logical,' Bill Freeplatzer said, breaking into the formal diction he was apt to use at meetings. 'We've already been given some lessons that're too strong for the weak overclouded minds of most persons around here. If persons like that, with their untrained mentalities, were to experience seeing our guides in the body, sending out their vibrations of atomic light and power at close range, their brain cells might even be injured.'

'It's the truth.' Sissy backed up her husband as usual. 'There've been times, when a picture was being transmitted into me, I've felt a kind of electric burning feeling going through my whole head, so bright. If I wasn't prepared and made used to it gradually, I couldn't have stood it more'n a second.'

'It's for their own good, Rufus, to keep them safe, that we mustn't tell our friends,' Peggy exclaimed, bouncing forward on the sofa. 'That's what we oughta say to them, when they ask what our wonderful news is about. I'm sorry, we should say, I can't tell you, for your own best good.'

'We have to do more than that,' Verena said. 'Our instruction of silence means not even to reveal that this wonderful news has come to us. We mustn't say anything about it at all.'

'Oh.' Peggy sat back, pulling her skirt down over pink knees. She looked disappointed.

'And if any of us comes to feel an urging to share our great secret with friends, or speak of it to anyone, we must say to ourselves, Stop, and remember that The Time Is Not Now. The time will come later. We know that when we're fully enlightened, many of us will be sent out as teachers of spiritual light all over the world, so that this planet may be freed from its darkness and confusion.'

'That's right,' several of the group murmured.

'Now let's go on. Here is our first instruction. PURIFY COSMIC BODIES REREJECT AND AVOID DEAD FOOD MATTER. Have you got that? I'll read it again more slowly, so you can take it down.' Verena did so. 'You know we've heard something about this before. We've had leadings that one thing that's holding down our progress here, making us heavy spiritually, is that our earthly bodies are full of so much disintegrating dead food matter; and every day, every breakfast, lunch, and supper, we're adding to that heavy weight.

'Now we can't go without material nourishment completely yet, like our guides on Varna and other fully developed beings do. We're not progressed to anywhere near that level. But we do have to realize that some of the foods we've been taking into our bodies are atomically heavier than others; they drag us down much more. There's other things that aren't so harmful, because they contain natural life vibrations which are still emanating after they're consumed into our bodies. Now I want to go into this in more detail.'

While the Seekers scribbled in their notebooks, Verena outlined the rules which were to control our menu during the next ten days. In general, the less we ate the better.

123

Light-coloured foods were preferable to dark ones, and a low specific gravity was good.

All dairy products (milk, butter, cheese) had strong life vibrations, we learned. Fruits and nuts, especially when uncooked, were also excellent. Vegetables that could be eaten raw, like carrots and lettuce, still contained some vital neutrons. Cooked vegetables, and bread, cake and cookies, were less desirable. Eggs were questionable; while steak, chicken, ham, and fish were full of heavy, decaying electricity: not only were they dead, they were murdered, food matter. In effect, what Verena now offered the Seekers was the diet of a tame rabbit.

'Are there any questions?' she asked. Voices and hands were raised all round the room. What about coffee and tea? What about baked beans, ice cream, pizza, and 7-up? My pen jumped nervously back and forth from the right-hand page of the notebook, on which I was recording the instructions from Varna, to the left, where I was making notes for the study in a kind of shorthand. McMann and I took turns at this; it was supposed to be his turn that evening, but he was recording posture changes again, so I had his heavy, black loose-leaf book.

Coffee, occasionally; tea, no; white bread rather than brown. They were all taking it down carefully. The complicated food phobias which Verena had been developing over the past few weeks were becoming the norm for the group.

Wheaties and other cold cereals, yes; hot cereal or oatmeal, no. I finished the page and turned to the back of McMann's notebook for another, unsnapping the stiff metal rings. Pasted on the inside back cover was a dated outline of the Truth Seekers' meetings we had attended, from my first trip to Sophis ('Sept. 24: welcome to RZ. Present: VR, EN', etc.) to this evening ('Nov. 25: 1st announcement of Coming').

I took out the paper automatically, snapped the rings together, turned forward, unsnapped them again, and paused, holding the sheet suspended. Then I turned back the

124

pages again. All this had taken a couple of seconds at the most, while I went on attending to the meeting. Now there occurred one of those vacuums in time when the hands of the internal clock stick. 'Nov. 25: 1st announcement of Coming.' I couldn't say whether I looked at those words half a second or five minutes. They were a perfectly innocuous and accurate description of this meeting; the only trouble was that they shouldn't have been written yet. Unless McMann was gifted with precognition. He had somehow known in advance what Ro of Varna was going to tell us that Thanksgiving night.

10

Later that evening, when we were back in Miss Vanting's spare room, I asked him about it. First I tried to get at the problem sideways, saying I was surprised the Coming should be predicted now; hoping that he would volunteer some simple explanation.

'What I don't understand,' I added as if joking, 'is why they should pick a date in December practically winter. This is a damned unlikely time of year for anyone to visit Sophis.'

'Unlikely?' McMann grinned. 'Hell, it's traditional.'

'Traditional? What tradition is that?'

McMann stared at me, then laughed out. 'What tradition? Christ, talk of sub-group isolation!'

'Oh, you mean Christmas.' I made an effort not to be offended; I smiled. 'I guess I didn't think they'd ever come. I thought the Seekers would probably continue in a permanent state of Seeking.'

'Naturally.' He was laughing still, or again. 'That's what you would think. You people have been waiting around for your messiah a couple of thousand years.'

I gave up any attempt to be subtle then, and mentioned the notebook directly. I didn't make any accusations, just asked how he had known that the Coming was going to be announced that evening. McMann blinked once, and replied that it was only a guess: he had had a hunch the dynamics of the group were working in that direction. So much emphasis had been put on the Thanksgiving meeting, it seemed likely tonight would be it. He hadn't said anything to me because he wasn't sure he was right.

It sounded plausible, but I wasn't convinced. I still suspected that somehow McMann had suggested to Elsie and Verena that it was time for the Varnians to arrive. Or maybe they had decided it themselves, and then told him; but in that case, why conceal it?

The best way to find out what had happened was to go and ask Verena or her aunt. They would never suspect me of anything but stupid curiosity. I hadn't forgotten that only that afternoon I had resolved to stay neutral; but I told myself this sort of inquiry didn't count. I wasn't initiating an action, I was just seeking the truth, and I was stupidly sure that I could keep the two separate, even if nobody else in Sophis could.

It would be easy to see Elsie and Verena alone: all I had to say was that I had a problem and wanted a private conference. The Seekers did it all the time. Rufus and Catherine still always consulted Verena; lately the Freeplatzers usually went to Elsie. McMann had tried them both with one set of questions, to get comparative data. It was really about time I did the same. Which only shows what elegant excuses your mind can make up for doing what you want to do.

I drove over to West Hawthorne Street Friday morning, and found Elsie alone, cleaning out her kitchen and throwing away the foods Ro had proscribed. She wasn't surprised to hear that I had some problems about the Coming. Bill had been over earlier for the same reason, before he went to work, and Milly was coming that afternoon, while Catherine was upstairs with Verena right then. Was it about sugar or salt? They were both all right, Verena had asked Ro about it this morning.

'No, it wasn't about that,' I said. 'What I was wondering was, Tom told me you and he had got some news of the Coming even before last night.' I uttered this lie with a flat, innocent air. 'Is that really true?'

Elsie was lining up cans of soup on the table, separating beef from pea. She met my question blandly.

'We've all had signs, Roger,' she said. 'Many of us, anyways. We've known for a long while some wonderful blessing was on its way to us.'

'Oh?'

127

'Mmhm.' Elsie emptied half a pumpkin pie out of its dish into the garbage can. 'When I woke up yesterday morning, there was a tingling through my whole body. It was like there was some great electric current travelling straight to me from a long ways away. I was sensing it the whole day, off and on.'

'And so you mentioned it to Tom, and you both had the feeling we were going to hear about the Coming?' I tried to keep suspicion, and even interest, out of my tone, but may not have succeeded.

'Oh, no. I couldn't do that,' Elsie exclaimed. Two slices of Catherine's old-fashioned brandied mince pie followed the pumpkin into the garbage pail. 'Our guides wouldn't approve it. It wasn't a real definite sensation, anyhow.'

I wondered if she were lying.

'I see.'

Elsie opened the refrigerator again and took out the Thanksgiving turkey on its platter, wrapped in aluminium foil.

'You know our guides are broadcasting their shining power in this direction constant now. Not just off and on like before.' She peeled the foil off the turkey; there was a lot left. 'It's streaming down on to us every minute, protecting this whole place, you realize that.'

'Mmhm, that's swell,' I said enthusiastically at random. It was only about eleven, but I was still hungry after Catherine's spiritually nourishing breakfast of Rice Krispies and coffee. Was Elsie really going to throw out that whole roast turkey? Not at once, anyhow. She let it sit on the table while she got rid of a cup of congealed gravy, three hot dogs, and a cold baked potato.

'Oh yes, you're safe now, Roger; as long as you're in this house. You don't need to be afraid of elementals or anything.' She gazed at me with the round, reddened eyes of a demented mouse.

'Fine. I won't worry, then.'

'Of course, they could still get at you when you're outside.

128

You know they're everywhere around, this time of the lunar cycle. We got to be careful every minute now, not to let our brain dwell on low ideas or suspicious negative thoughts, because that's when they have their chance.' She gave me what might have been a pointed look. Then she stamped on the pedal of the garbage pail again, picked up the platter, and shoved the rest of the turkey, about five pounds of murdered bird-food matter, down into it. 'You don't want that to happen, do you?'

'Uh, no.'

'Because those elementals, they're so awful hard to dislodge. They just get a death-hold on to your spirit, and stick to it like Elmer's Glue, driving it to negative acts. Like the elemental that's got Ken in its hold still keeps driving him back towards this house, to do harm and spread negative electricity.'

'Has Ken been here again?' Instant jealousy, like instant coffee, boiled up. Irritated with myself, I turned it down as well as I could and added in a different tone, 'I didn't know that.'

'Well, no. Not in the body. He's been telephoning, that's all, trying to get at Verena and poison her mind some more. But I guess there's too much spirit power over this place right now for him to approach.' She smiled. 'You ever get a call from him, while you're staying at Catherine's, don't take the message. Just say she's not there, and hang up.'

'But he's not going to call Catherine's house if he wants Verena.'

'You don't know. He already tried the Freeplatzers' a couple of times. Those elementals are full of moronic will and negative magnetic persistence. They just keep on beating at wherever they're impelled to go.' Elsie shook her head. 'But I know you want to ask me about the lesson. So let's put Ken and all troubled thoughts out of our minds, from now on. All right?'

She wiped her hands, sat down on the kitchen stool, and looked at me.

'I don't have any other special questions really,' I said. 'But I sort of thought I would like a consultation with Verena.'

'Well, she's upstairs with Catherine now. You'll have to wait. I tell you what, why don't you climb up and reach me down what's in that cupboard over the sink, so I can get all the destructive matter sorted out.'

'Roger.' Verena held out one hand and pulled me into her room, shutting the door behind us with the other. She looked young, pale, very pretty, and rather tired. This morning she was wearing moccasins and a short, faded red robe which fell loose to the knee; her hair hung forward over one shoulder in a thick braid. She resembled the ideal Campfire Girl on the cover of my sister's handbook: about fifteen, in semi-Indian costume. 'Light be about you,' she said.

'Thank you.'

'In the —' She prompted me gently.

'Sorry. In the Eternal Mind.'

'That's right.' Verena smiled sweetly and seriously. 'We can't forget our lessons, not now. Sit down, Roger: here.' She pointed to her desk chair, painted white with a faded blue cushion tied to the seat.

I crossed the floor rather consciously. It was the first time I had been in this small, neat but shabby young-girl's room, with its worn dotted swiss curtains and braided rug.

'Now.' Verena pulled a stool forward from her dressing-table and perched on it like a little girl, with her knees up and her hands clasped round them.

'I knew you wanted to see me,' she said in a childishly earnest voice. 'I felt it early this morning. It's about the Coming, isn't it?'

'Well, yes. In a sort of way.'

'I sense that.'

'You see, I don't understand why it should happen *now*,' I began, taking an equally naïve tone. 'I mean, gee —'

'Shh. I know. You're asking yourself, why should our

130

teachers and guides come to us now; why at this special time? What have we done to deserve that?' I nodded. 'Can it be true, you're asking, that they're going to manifest now just because some of us want it so much? That's your question, isn't it?'

'Yes, that's right.' I was so impressed by her guess that I dropped into my own voice.

'But you see, Roger, our guides have been ready to come to us for a long time. They've only been waiting until we were advanced enough in knowledge, and our longing and desire for this blessing was great enough.'

'Tom's desire was especially great,' I said.

'Oh, yes.' Verena smiled. I frowned, wondering how to phrase my next question. The trouble was, even if McMann had put the idea of the Coming into Verena's head, she probably didn't know it.

'I know why you're troubled,' Verena said. 'You're wondering, am I really ready to meet my guides face to face, in the blinding radiance of their being? Some of us might be prepared for that, you're thinking, but I just don't know if I am. I don't know if it's right that they should come now. Isn't it so?'

'It's so.'

'You mustn't worry about that any more.' Verena put her soft white hand on my sleeve. 'It's true, some of us might be further along in our lessons by now than others, but we've all still got an awful lot to learn. Every one of us has to keep on working and studying and praying to prepare himself. I'll help you, just as much as I can, so that when the blessed time comes you'll be ready for it too.'

'That's awfully kind of you.'

'It's only what our teachers want me to do.' Verena let go of my arm and glanced up towards the ceiling. 'You see, it's so terribly important for the whole world that the light of truth should shine down to us through all our darkness and confusion and material error. Each one of us has to become the best possible instrument and messenger to receive this

131

blessed message of light and carry it abroad. You'll be good at that, Roger.' Verena looked back, fixing me with her great fringed eyes. 'You're a professor; you can speak foreign languages, and you've travelled to places all over the world already. That's why I have to help you.'

'I see.'

'I want to do it for your own sake, too,' she added, lowering the fringes almost shyly. 'You're a serious, thoughtful person, and I've always had a natural leading of sympathy for you, ever since the first day you came here.'

'I feel the same way for you.' It was a standard sociological response, but it wasn't the sociologist who had given it. Irritated at myself, I stood up.

'Well, thank you, very much.'

'You don't want to go yet,' Verena stated calmly. 'We haven't even got a leading into your problem yet. Sit down, Roger, and we'll start working on it together, right now.'

I sat down. (According to our rules, I have to, I told myself.)

Verena drew her straight, silky, dark eyebrows together and stuck out her lower lip, like a child concentrating. 'What I think is, there's something interfering with your mental processes,' she said. 'Something's making it so you can't fix your mind on the lessons and discussion in our meetings, or recite correctly when you're called on. A kind of confusion comes over your mind then, I've seen it. It's not natural to you either, because you've got a superior intelligence really.'

'Thank you.'

'It's true. Some people might think it was just slowness, but I know that's not so. I said so.' I wondered to whom she had said it.

'I'll tell you what it is.' Verena leaned towards me, so close that I could see every detail of her face: the white, satiny, convex plane of cheek, the crisp sculptural curve of the full mouth with its indented corners. 'Something's got into your brain cells, and it's blocking them, so you can't think or remember right. Probably you can't receive the vibrations our guides are sending down to us here properly, either. That's why you never get a leading. Because you know, Roger, there are terribly strong positive cosmic waves flowing towards us from Varna all the time, especially now in this period of preparation. They're coming to you just like they are to the rest of us, beating against your head and trying to get into your mind. But they mostly can't get through to you. That's probably what was making your head ache the other day.'

Involuntarily, I put my hand to my forehead.

'You still feel it, don't you?'

'Well, a little.' It was true; and no surprise, considering the situation.

'What we've got to learn now is, what's responsible for this psychic condition, and how you can overcome it best. Isn't that so?'

I agreed that it was so.

'Let's meditate now, and ask for light. I'm going to say the Invocation first, and you join in if you can remember it, and then we'll have a few minutes of silence. You strive to hold your mind as open as you can, and maybe something will get through to you.' Verena looked at me doubtfully. 'And here; take my hand. Maybe that'll help. Oh Spirit of Light . . .'

Verena raised her face to the ceiling and began to recite a prayer that was, after all, not much odder than those my sister used to learn – and in much the same style. She wasn't much older than a Campfire Girl herself, and probably just as innocent. I had to remember that, and pay less attention to how soft and warm her hand was, and how as she breathed harder her full breasts rose and subsided under the loose robe, lifting the thick plait of hair rhythmically. Her eyes were shut, and her other hand lay in her lap, cupped slightly to receive the currents from space. I sat stiff, and tried to concentrate on my professional role.

'Ahh.' Verena let out a final soft breath, and opened her eyes. 'Did you receive anything?'

133

I shook my head.

'I did, Roger. I had a strong, definite sensation; a true leading.' She paused for effect. 'First I didn't sense anything. Just blankness, darkness. They I began to feel a kind of chill. I thought, the room's getting cold, Aunt Elsie must have turned the heat down. Only it got worse; colder and colder. A damp, icy cold – as if we were shut up together inside a refrigerator. My arms went all goose-flesh, and my legs; I could feel the cold running down them in waves, until I was almost frozen all over. Then I realized what it meant, and it started going off fast. It was a sign.'

'A sign?' I prompted.

'Yes, Roger,' she said. 'That cold was coming from you. It was a true manifestation of your affliction, I know it. Some kind of icy coldness has got into you, and your spirit is just gradually freezing up.'

'I don't feel cold.'

Verena put a warm palm to my forehead. 'Maybe not, but you are,' she said. 'I can feel it even out to the skin.' She frowned. 'I don't think it's coming to you from an outside vibrational force. It didn't feel that way to me. It's not an elemental or anything like that, don't worry. It's an internal congestion, from wrong thinking.'

'A congestion?'

'Yes. It's progressive, you understand. You think a cold thought, and it spreads. If something isn't done about it in time, eventually all your higher brain cells are going to turn into – well, sort of like little ice cubes, so they can't receive or transmit.'

'I see.' I did see. Just as Verena's psychic empathy had picked up my worry about the date of the Coming earlier, now she sensed the effort I was making to keep from grabbing her, or even wanting to.

'Don't be disturbed, Roger,' she said. 'Now we know what your trouble is, I can help you to overcome it.'

'Thank you.'

'I couldn't do it by myself,' she explained modestly. 'But

134

there's a wonderful force in the universe, a force of infinite cosmic power, that can melt the ice that's forming in your brain cells and restore your mental processes to normal. Your true inner being is already vibrating towards it and longing to be united with it, anyhow, just like all ours are, but the other parts of your brain are shutting it out; shutting out Cosmic Love.' Verena leaned towards me, very close, her eyes shining, and put both hands on my shoulders. 'You've got to get back into connection with that force.'

'All right, I'll try,' I said.

'I'm going to help you, Roger. Hold my hands, now.'

'I don't want to tire you out,' I protested.

'Heavens, I'm not tired!' Verena almost laughed. 'Come on.' She took my hands as if she planned to keep them for some time. 'That's right. Now I'm going to concentrate and pray with all my soul and spirit for the great force of Cosmic Love to flow into me from the universe and from Varna, and through me into you, so that your spirit may be freed and brought back to its true condition.'

'But —' I started to object, but couldn't think of a convincing non-directive objection. Maybe I didn't want to.

'Shh,' Verena whispered. 'The electrical field is gathering around us already; I can feel it. Don't speak any more, just pray silently.'

She shut her eyes. I was so near now I could see every strand of her long lashes, like fine parallel strokes of Victorian penmanship on the white skin. I looked away, noting neutral sociological details. Item: maple bureau with cut-glass knobs, supporting small mirror of inferior quality, the latter reflecting a non-existent waver in the window-frame opposite. Item: framed colour reproduction, two puppies playing. Item: studio bed with spread pulled tight; narrow, but not too narrow for —

She was right: the whole room seemed to be full of a weak electrical current. I could almost see the plus and minus signs arranged in contracting arcs about us, as in a textbook diagram.

135

Verena opened her eyes. 'I can feel the power flowing, can you?' she whispered excitedly.

'I feel something.'

What Verena had always done with her gift was to guess what people wanted and then give it to them – messages from the dead, a promise that they would pass their exams, the news that they were somebody special and important. Now it was my turn. She had moved nearer, and her knees were pressed against mine.

'Your headache is growing better now, isn't that so?'

'That's so.' But the strain on my self-control was worse. Whether or not it would make static, I had to get out of there. 'You've helped me a lot.' I moved back in the chair, and pulled my hands loose. 'Thank you very much.'

'Oh no, Roger. You can't go now.' Verena grabbed my arm.

'But it's getting late. I know other people want to see you too. I thought, maybe some other day —'

'I'm going to restore your spirit completely this day.'

'That's kind of you, but —'

'Only we've got to get more contact. The vibrations of Cosmic Love are flowing into this room and filling it, but you aren't giving them a chance to penetrate. Let's stand up.' I stood up. 'Take off your jacket.' I obeyed, a little puzzled. 'Now take off your shirt.'

'My shirt? What for?'

'It's necessary, Roger. You've got to expose some flesh surfaces so that the current can enter into you. All that fibrous material is blocking the vibrations.'

'Well, okay.' Against my better judgement, I loosened my tie, undid my shirt at the neck, and pulled it off. I hung it on the back of the chair, and turned round.

'That's right.'

She held out her hands; I took them. Then she stepped forward, so that we were standing arm to arm and chest to chest.

'Verena, listen, this —'

136

'That's better. Hold still, Roger. We're in good contact now. This way, the cosmic vibrations gathered in my body can pass through to you without hardly any blocking. Just stand still now, and concentrate your mind.'

Verena shut her eyes, and leaned lightly against me. I felt a thin cold chill down my chest where it touched the zipper of her robe; on either side of this was a warm area of thin, shiny material through which I seemed to feel every detail of the surface underneath.

'It's working.' Verena's whisper blew warm on my neck. 'Oh, it's working now, Roger.' She leaned heavier on me, resting the side of her face on my shoulder, squeezing my hands, and rubbing her breasts against me with a little moan.

It was too much: I forgot social science and began kissing her hard. I didn't let go of her hands, only pushed them together behind her back and held her to me, so that I could feel the sculptural curves below as well as above her waist.

I remember very clearly that Verena didn't pull back or protest, or even open her eyes. What separated us, a moment later, was a noise from outside the room: steps coming upstairs.

I looked at the door; it wasn't even shut tight, let alone locked. Suppose Elsie, Catherine, or Ed Novar were to walk in now. I let go of Verena; she sighed and sagged forward against me, so that I had to hold her up; I looked at my shirt and jacket on the chair. The steps reached the landing. They approached the door; passed on, and entered the bathroom. Verena gave no sign of having heard them.

'Listen,' I whispered.

Verena opened her eyes, gave the ceiling a glazed, melting look, and shut them again.

'No, Verena, hey.' I tried to hold her away from me; I was beginning to realize what had nearly happened. Except for the accident of somebody needing to use the john, the junior E on the Sophis Project (National Institute of Mental Health Grant No. 789, etc.) would have raped his principal S.

137

'Here, sit down.' I eased, or pushed, Verena into the chair. She blinked as if she were coming out of trance, lifted her head, and focused on me.

'Roger,' she said, like a child identifying objects.

'That's right.'

'How do you feel now?'

'Oh, fine, thanks,' I replied automatically. 'Excuse me.' I reached over her and took my clothes off the back of the chair. 'My headache is much better,' I added, trying to get back into character.

'That's wonderful.' Verena smiled angelically and sat up a little. 'It is grand, isn't it, to realize what great spiritual forces we're surrounded by, all the time. Only we've got to learn to receive them and use them correctly, isn't that so?'

'Oh yeah, that's so.' I swallowed. 'Listen, I'm sorry I got carried away like that. I want to apologize —'

'Apologize?' She opened her eyes even wider.

'I mean, for letting my mind get off Cosmic Love.'

'You didn't do that, Roger. All pure Love is Cosmic, you know that. Our love for each other here and the love our guides feel for us and for one another, it's all from the same source like a wonderful electric fluid running through the whole universe.'

'Uh-huh.'

'It's a blessed thing, too, when we are given the power to help others, and when we can feel the positive spiritual currents of the universe flowing through us to heal our friends on earth.'

'I guess it is.' Breaking our mutual stare, I glanced towards the door.

'We're not through yet, you know. We've got to thank our guides for sending this healing to you.' With a gentle sigh, she sat forward, then dropped to her knees in front of the chair. 'Give me your hand. Come on.'

I got down beside her on the braided rug.

'Oh Spirit of Eternal Light . . .

138

'... Amen.' As she recited, Verena's voice had grown stronger. Now, as we stood up, she pushed her Campfire Girl braid back over her shoulder, and looked at me diagnostically.

'A great part of your brain congestion is melted away now, Roger,' she announced, still holding my hand, 'and your cells are restored to their true intellectual working.'

'That's good. I mean, thank you very much. Well —'

'But there's still some congestion there. Oh, nothing like what it was before, don't worry about that. It's just that the ice isn't completely gone from every part yet.' She moved towards me reassuringly.

'Oh, I see.' The full-length zipper on Verena's robe had a brass ring attached to it at the top. Suppose I took hold, and pulled ... 'Oh, no. I mean, I'm not worried. You've helped me so much, probably whatever's left will go away by itself.' I got my hand back. 'Well, thanks —'

'We can't trust to that, I'm afraid, Roger. It's more likely it'll start spreading again if you let things alone. You've got to work on it till there's no single bit of ice infection left.' Verena thought for a moment. 'I want you to come back here this evening for another consultation. About eight. I'll be meditating then, but I'll tell Aunt Elsie to let you come on up.'

'I couldn't interrupt you then.' I began backing towards the door. 'Not when you're meditating.'

'Yes, you could, Roger.' Verena followed me. 'You're strongly drawn to come here, I can sense it. And I'm guided to help you.'

'Yeah, but I can't come, actually, I —'

'You've got to. With the Coming so close at hand, we can't take any chances. We mustn't have anybody with a negative brain condition here to meet our guides, in all the shining glory of their real presence. It wouldn't be safe for you, either.' She stared at me to let the threat sink in, and then smiled childishly. 'So you be back here at eight; or a little before. All right?'

'All right.'

139

I shut the door of Verena's room behind me, went downstairs, said goodbye to Elsie, and left the house. Then I did the only thing I could think of: I drove back to Catherine's, called McMann (he was at the Freeplatzers'), and told him I had had a phone call from my family and had to go to New York at once; would he give Elsie my apologies? Then I packed my bag, and took a taxi to the bus station.

11

I didn't see McMann again until I got back to Streib Hall the Monday morning after Thanksgiving. At ten o'clock he opened my door without knocking and walked in, looking large, beefy, and annoyed.

'Oh, hi,' I said. 'How did everything go over the weekend?'

'It went all right. You can read the notes. That is, if you're still associated with this project.' McMann did not sit down, so I stood up.

'Of course I'm associated with the project. What do you mean?'

'There's some doubt, when you run out on it like that.' His tone was half-way between a joke and a threat.

'I had to go down to New York ... my mother ...' I brought out my lie again, while McMann gave me a sour smile which suggested he knew it was one. 'I'm sorry I couldn't stay.' Another lie. I had needed those three days in New York to restore me to normality. When I first got to the city, I was only there in body; my disembodied and distracted spirit was still back in Sophis. To give you an idea, I was even arguing with myself that if that was what Verena wanted, well, maybe it would have been the professionally correct, non-directive thing to do ...

Talking about the project to my family and friends helped; gradually I began to see it as they saw it – as I began to present it to them: a short-term sociological study with entertaining comic aspects. When I told one of my friends about the scene with Verena he thought it was a joke and laughed so convincingly that I began to think so too. I hadn't really been in danger of attacking her, I decided; only of being thrown out of the house and probably out of the group if

Elsie had seen us. Of course, I would avoid getting into a situation like that again.

'It wasn't easy trying to keep both books at the meeting Saturday,' McMann went on. 'You'll have a tough job straightening out the notes for Sally. I haven't had any time to look them over.'

I was forgiven, in other words; my punishment would be to transcribe McMann's records as well as my own, and get them in shape for his secretary to type up.

'That's all right,' I said. 'I'll do it tonight.'

'You better start today. There's a lot of stuff.'

'Okay.'

'It's in my bottom file drawer by the window. Here's the key. Don't leave it lying around, and don't show the notes to anybody, remember.'

'Okay, okay.'

Since the beginning of the project, McMann had guarded our data with obstinate secrecy. He kept all the tapes and written material in locked drawers, letting me use it only piecemeal and after an explanation. No doubt his experience with Sniggs and Murt had made him distrustful, but I thought he was over-reacting. It wasn't even logical, because even if I were a Sniggs at heart, I wouldn't want to steal the Sophis data and publish it under my own name. For one thing, it would do me much less professional good that way than under McMann's and mine combined.

It wasn't me he was really suspicious of, but his colleagues Mayonne and Ginsman. I don't know what he feared – that they might appropriate his ideas and methods, or that they might sneer at them – anyhow, he took care it shouldn't happen. His main objection to my keeping any of the data seemed to be that my office mate, Bob Onland, was Ginsman's protégé. He didn't want Bob to get a look at our data, particularly the statistical part of it, as he was convinced would happen if I left it lying around my desk.

'I heard something about your interview with Verena,' McMann went on. He had relaxed now, and was leaning on my desk instead of over it. 'Ice infection in your brain cells, huh? I wondered what your trouble was.' He grinned, and I grinned back in self-defence. 'I hope you got it all down.'

'Yeah, I did.' (Not so.)

'I understand Verena cured you with Cosmic Love. How'd she do that?'

'Oh, you can imagine. She prayed over me a while, and meditated, and held my hand; and then she told me I was better, so I agreed with her.'

'That all? The way you lit out of town afterwards, I thought maybe she'd tried to rape you.' McMann guffawed and sat heavily on my desk, crushing papers. 'But hell, you wouldn't mind that, would you?'

'I can think of worse alternatives,' I said, playing it cool.

'Maybe you'll get a chance at some of them.' He chuckled. 'Elsie told me to tell you, if Verena's treatment didn't work, she'll be happy to try and help you some herself.'

'Oh, yeah?'

'So you better learn the Invocation and the rest of the stuff by heart, or she'll be wanting to, uh, hold your hand next.' McMann grinned at my expression. Apparently he knew or suspected more than he was letting on. 'She wants to hold somebody's hand.'

'You think so?'

'Hell, yes. It's been obvious from the start that Elsie has hot pants. Cosmic Love, huh. I bet she's not getting much of that from her husband, the poor creep. She wants to get laid, and it sounds to me like she's after you. She was really sorry to hear you'd left town.'

'Yeah, I bet.' I only half believed him, or less.

McMann began to laugh to himself. 'You don't have to make that kind of face,' he said. 'She'd probably give you a lot better time in bed than Verena would. Come on, Roger; why don't you give her a try?'

'Why don't you?' I retorted. 'She's nearer your age.'

McMann's laughter burst out; baiting me, he had worked himself round into a good humour. 'Well, it's an idea.'

143

'All right, let's get down to business,' he said finally. 'The Coming is scheduled for next Saturday night, as of now. I want to leave for Sophis Thursday, right after my twelve o'clock. There's a meeting that night, and Elsie's expecting us for supper. And let's take your car this time.'

'I can't go Thursday. I've got two sections of 221 Friday morning.'

'You'll have to cancel them. For God's sake, this is the crisis.'

'Okay, I'll speak to Mayonne. But I don't think he's going to like it.'

McMann frowned, and stared sideways at my bookshelves. 'Maybe you've got a point there,' he said. 'Yeah. I bet he'd refuse. Steve Mayonne would just love to have an excuse to louse up my project.'

'I didn't mean that. It's just, I don't think he'll like the idea of my cutting his section meetings right after vacation. I can ask him, though.'

'Nah, you stay away from Mayonne. I'll handle him.' McMann had picked up a paper clip from my desk, and now he kept twisting it open and shut while he thought. 'No. I'll write him a memo, that's what. I've got an idea. I'll tell him I need you in Sophis, see, and say if it's not convenient he should let me know. I'll date the memo tomorrow, but I'll fix it so he doesn't get it till Thursday. In the afternoon mail.' He laughed. 'How's that?' I said nothing, but must have looked uncertain. 'I'll take the responsibility, for Christ's sake. Blame it on Sally, if he asks.'

'Yeah, but —'

'Listen, Zimmern, are you going to give me more trouble?'

'No, but —'

'All right.' McMann stood up. 'You can pick me up here at one on Thursday, if I don't see you before. And don't forget to go over those notes.'

He marched out of the office, looking shrewd and confident, and I was left staring at the frosted glass in the door, worrying. Months ago I had set up in my mind a kind of Wild West version of McMann's career, and I wanted to go on

144

believing in it. The good old rancher had been tricked by the bad guys, Sniggs and Murt; he might wish revenge on *them*, but he went on being a good guy to everyone else. But unfortunately, as Auden says, those to whom evil is done do evil in return – and not always appropriately as to object.

When Steve Mayonne read that pre-dated memo on Thursday afternoon, and realized he would suddenly have to teach my section meetings, he would be justifiably angry. Right now he probably didn't want to louse up the Sophis Project; but by this week-end maybe he would feel different. He would begin to think McMann was out to get him, and then perhaps he would begin to think how he could get McMann, so that McMann's suspicions would all come true.

Wouldn't it be better if I walked down the hall now and told Mayonne I had to go to Sophis? I stood up; but I didn't leave the office. I imagined Mayonne sitting behind his desk waiting for me to state my business, his thick black brows drawn together over the small wolfish face. 'I'm afraid that's impossible, Zimmern,' he would say. Then I imagined McMann's expression when he heard I had gone to Mayonne against his orders.

No, there was no use doing anything. They had probably been carrying on this quarrel for years, maybe even with a certain enjoyment. The best thing for me to do was remain non-directive, and let events take their course.

We drove to Sophis on Thursday. This time the trip didn't take three hours, but more like five. The sky was already dark when we started, and a few miles out of town it began to snow, for the first time that year. The fields and woods whitened and softened; fans of fine snow like handfuls of granulated sugar blew across the road and into the coarse dead grass on either side.

Dusk was falling as we approached Sophis. Yellow lights shone out mysteriously over the sugar-coated landscape; for the first time, it seemed possible that radiant beings from outer space might appear there.

145

We dropped our things at the motel and went straight to West Hawthorne Street. Verena had already gone upstairs to meditate, but we were greeted with warmth by Elsie. Within the limits of the new rules, she had made an elaborate dinner for us. There were three kinds of salad (moulded lime gelatin with bananas, Waldorf, and greens with thousand-island dressing), two kinds of crackers, milk, orange soda, cookies, and ice cream.

My scientific perspective was holding up extremely well. I was able to observe not only the Seekers but McMann and my Sophis self with interested detachment: McMann supporting all Elsie's statements with a loud non-directive bray; Stupid Roger concealing his dislike of being talked down to and of green jellied salad, by hiding one under a weak smile and the other under a piece of lettuce. This was just a small-group study, after all; and I was only very temporarily part of this group.

Even before supper was over, the other Seekers began to arrive. They pulled chairs up to the table, and Elsie helped them to peach ice cream. By the time we had finished eating everyone was there.

We adjourned to the parlour, and the meeting began. McMann was recording the verbal proceedings this time, with emphasis on questions and expressions of doubt, while I took notes for him on the members' posture, gestures, facial expressions, etc.

First I sketched a seating plan. Everyone had their recognized places by now, just as in any class, though there were minor variations. Bill and Sissy Freeplatzer, and her sister Peggy, usually sat in a row on the sofa facing the window, with Bill or Sissy in the middle. Milly Munger took the maple rocker on their right. To Milly's right was Rufus, on a straight chair, and beyond him was the front hall. Opposite the sofa was Verena's wing chair, placed just to the left of the table under the window, so that she could write with her left hand. In the corner to the right of her chair and slightly in back of it was the piano, with Elsie's piano bench.

McMann usually took the big Morris chair to Elsie's right, in front of the fireplace. On his right, in the corner next to the dining-room, Ed Novar sat in a dining-room chair. Catherine Vanting had the rocker in the opposite corner, on Verena's left, and I sat beyond her, by the hall entrance.

A number of interpretative comments might be made about these choices. McMann had already suggested that the Freeplatzers, Peggy, and Milly, by sitting directly across from Verena, unconsciously constituted themselves her congregation; that Elsie, on her right and a little behind her, was the power behind the throne; and that Catherine, by placing herself on the other side of the table on which the messages were recorded, expressed a desire to be close to Varna rather than close to Verena – as might be expected of someone who in sixty years had formed no close associative ties. One could also conjecture that Mr Novar sat in the corner by the dining-room door in case he felt like edging out unnoticed through the kitchen; while Rufus similarly provided himself with the option of escaping through the front door. Or alternatively, by taking this place, Rufus expressed his sense of being the one who could best mediate the outer world – especially modern science – to the other Seekers.

And what about the two other group members? I thought as I marked the chart. The Truth Seekers frequently behaved as if they thought one or more invisible beings were present at meetings: floating in the centre of the room, or hovering in the warm air over Verena's hand as it wrote. But McMann and Zimmern were under the opposite delusion: in their analysis, they assumed that neither of them was really there. Actually, McMann's preference for the seat at the inner end of the room, between Elsie and Ed Novar, would have suggested several conclusions if he were an ordinary group member. For example, that he considered himself one of the central members of the group, perhaps even part of the family; also, that though he seldom addressed the Seekers, he was in an excellent position to do so.

What might we say about Roger? Well, I had already

147

noticed that in any gathering (party, seminar, faculty meeting) my tendency was to sit on the same side of the room as the host or leader, but not too near to him. I'm not quite sure how to interpret this; but it certainly seems true that in this position I am less likely to be either lectured to or called upon for support. When I first went to the Truth Seekers' meetings I sometimes sat on the sofa; as I became simultaneously more bored and more inept, I ceased to do this. Now, when I found 'my' chair set too near to the others I automatically moved it back towards the wall; whereas Rufus often moved his in towards the centre of the room.

Tonight several chairs had been shoved forward; the tone of the whole group was intimate, enthusiastic. There was a feeling of happy excitement and anticipation; lots of moving about and talking before the Seekers settled down. They acted like – they *were* – a bunch of small-town people planning a reception for some important foreign visitor. Milly and Sissy, for instance, were talking about bringing over some potted plants (the Varnians wouldn't like 'murdered' cut flowers) to decorate the house for the Coming.

As we sang the opening hymn, the Truth Seekers glanced round the room at each other with what they would have called 'smiles and looks of gladness'. It was almost the last moment in which this mood of peaceful harmony was to prevail.

Elsie played the last chords of 'I Need Thee Ev'ry Hour' and stood up. She turned to the group, her hands clenched on the back of Verena's empty chair, and addressed them:

'Friends and Seekers of Truth. We are gathered here in this room together to go on with the great work of preparation for the Coming, which is approaching ever nearer to us. Yes even while we sit right here in our seats our guides and teachers from Varna are moving closer and closer to us across the universe by the power of their magnetic will vibrations. Every minute the beam of spiritual power and Cosmic Love beamed upon this house is getting stronger and stronger.

'And meantime, what are we doing here? Are we working every minute of the day, every second, to clean out of our spirits everything that still holds us down to the earth? Are we meditating and striving to make our whole selves proper vessels for the light of Varna, fit to receive the wonderful gifts of the spirit that our guides are bringing to us?'

Elsie stopped and looked round the room. It was obvious what her answer was going to be. Some of the Seekers dropped their eyes.

'Or are we maybe neglecting our great duty – our duty to ourselves, and our duty to the whole world of darkened minds that's waiting for light? Are we still hanging on to material things and notions, worrying about our schoolwork maybe, or some business consideration, or thinking what some small dark mind will say if we don't keep a certain worldly appointment?' Several members of her audience were looking worried or guilty now. 'Oh, sure, we may *say* to ourselves that we're trying hard, but our teachers from Varna can see right into every heart as they draw near to this planet, into every corner of our souls. They know if we're in a fit spiritual condition for their Coming or not. They know! And they're pretty worried, because the messages they're bringing down to us, they're so powerful, so bright and strong, that if our minds aren't prepared, if we're not truly ready for them, the way our lesson last week told us, we could be in terrible danger when they come.

'You know, it's like when you put a pan into a real hot oven: if it's clean and shining all over it won't be hurt, but if it's got even a bit of food material or grease sticking to it, when you go to take it out it'll be all dirty and scorched, so you might even have to throw it away? Well, when the great light of Varna gets near to this earth, any little bits and left-overs of selfish material thinking and low greedy wants that are still in our minds are liable to catch on fire from their divine nearness; and then you know what's going to happen? The delicate higher cells of our brains are going to be

149

scorched up, and burnt out, till we're reduced to poor mental retarded persons.'

Elsie's abilities as a public speaker had improved. In spite of her thin voice, her rhetoric was effective. The group looked half frightened now; Peggy Vonn was even biting her nails. Elsie paused for a moment to let her words sink in. When she began again, her tone was less shrill.

'We've gone very far already in our progress,' she reassured them. 'All these months we've been working and studying the lessons of higher knowledge, and we've drawn nearer and nearer to the condition of perfect spiritual readiness. But we just can't let up on our effort now, when we're so close. We've got to work even harder in these last days and hours to clean out our minds of the last dirty scraps of greed and selfishness, and lift our spirits up towards the true light.

'Well, forewarned is forearmed. Now let's have a couple more hymns, and then I'm going to ask Verena to come down to us.'

The Seekers sang more raggedly this time, but with more feeling. They didn't smile or glance at each other.

'Light be about you!' Verena entered from the hall as the last Amen faded, and held out her arms. She was wearing a new robe: mauve, with a glossy finish and silver edging. Even over the past week she had grown thinner. There was a theatrical concavity in her cheeks now, and her thick-fringed eyes seemed unnaturally dark and shiny. She smiled slowly round the room at us. It was only for about three seconds that she looked straight at me, but that was enough. Zimmern would have to do more than just observe events with scientific detachment; he would have to watch day and night to keep Stupid Roger out of that room upstairs.

Verena's address to the group was short; it more or less repeated her aunt's without the threats. She fell into trance rapidly, and the hand began to write at once. The Message she received was brief too. It consisted mostly of mild exhortation and reassurance; all except for the final sentence. As she read this slowly aloud, her eyes grew even larger, and she leaned forward, breathing with each phrase.

FFOR YOU SHALL BE CLOTHED NOW IN LIGHT   IN IN ONLY PURE GARMENTSS   AVOID NOW   AND HENCEFORTHWARDS ALL DEAD ORG   ORGANIC MM MATERIALS   GROWTHS OF WORMSSSHEEP   EARTH ROOTED FFIBERS   ALL   DESTROY   NNOW   BURN

With the shine of hysteria in her eyes, but in a fairly controlled voice, Verena explained to us what this wonderful new Message meant. We had accomplished a great deal by omitting from our diet all the dead organic substances which held back spiritual progress by getting into our cells and blocking favourable vibrations. Now we must do the same with our clothing. Henceforthwards we would wear only clothes made of 'mineral and electrical materials' – fabrics like nylon and Dacron which had been created by pure scientists in a clean laboratory, not excreted by worms, torn from the backs of sheep, or beaten out of dead plant fibres. We must cease to cover our feet with the skins of dead cows and pigs, or (even worse) snakes and lizards.

The new rule, she announced intensely, went into effect immediately. Right now, everyone present would remove all dead organic materials which might happen to be in contact with their bodies.

'We must cast them away, we must be free now to rise up from the earth!' In demonstration, Verena stood up, shook off the gold sandals she always wore to meetings, and pushed them aside.

'That's right.' Elsie started on her pumps.

There was a moment's pause. Then Peggy Vonn, with a little murmur, bent down to slip off her loafers. Bill, next to her, raised one of his perforated brogues to untie it. Sissy was next, then Ed Novar. Half the Seekers were taking their shoes off now, so McMann started in, giving me a quick nod to do the same.

'My socks are Dacron,' Rufus said. 'I don't have to take them off, do I?'

'No, Dacron is a synthetic material. The vibrations can pass right through it.'

'Y'know, my feet feel better already,' Bill said. 'More alive, kind of.'

'Nylons are a scientific material too.' Milly looked down at her plump, shiny legs. 'We can keep them.'

'But these are part wool.' Peggy stuck out her red knee-socks. 'I guess I better take them off; they look like they could stop a lot of current.'

'Sure, you got to take those off,' Rufus said.

'My socks are cotton,' someone said; they were beginning to speak all at once. Catherine Vanting (the last to comply) was taking her shoes off; McMann and I removing our organic socks.

'Say, I can feel the current coming through a lot better now,' Rufus exclaimed.

'Me too.' Peggy wiggled her toes, then stopped, holding one bare foot out. 'But what about the rest of our clothing? I mean, this is a wool cardigan.'

'Sheep fibres,' Elsie said. 'You better lay it aside.'

'Okay.' She started pulling at the sleeve.

'Well, then, I better take off my jacket,' Bill said. 'And this angora sweater.'

The Seekers began denouncing and removing their jackets and sweaters, then remarking how much better they felt. McMann, in shirt-sleeves, stretched his arms and loosened his tie; I took off my heavy tweed jacket. Sissy curled her bare legs up under her and leaned against Bill; for a moment, there was a sort of informal, picnic feeling in the room.

'But listen; my skirt's wool too,' Peggy said suddenly, looking down and then up at Verena. 'What am I supposed to do about that? I mean, does it count?'

'Our instructions are, to remove all dead organic cloth-ing,' Verena said.

152

'You mean, right now? In front of everybody?'

'There is no shame in the True Universe, Peggy.'

A slight pause, while the rest of the Seekers glanced at each other. Nobody said anything.

'Well, gee; all right.' Standing up, Peggy slowly unzipped her skirt and let it fall, revealing a white cotton slip. Then Sissy, even more slowly, uncovered a blue one. No one else moved.

'I'm not going to take off any more of my clothes,' Catherine said suddenly. She stood barefoot, tall and thin, in a white blouse and droopy grey skirt, with her bony arms hugged round her. 'I'll get a chill if I do. I catch cold real easy these days.'

The other Seekers looked at her, then at Verena.

'It is kind of draughty tonight,' Milly said.

'That's all right, Catherine,' Verena conceded sweetly. 'You can go along with Aunt Elsie up to her room – she'll find you something else to put on. Won't you?'

'Sure I will,' Elsie agreed. 'I've got a nice warm quilted rayon bathrobe you can have, Catherine. And some extra slippers.'

'I'm a little cold too,' Bill said. 'If Ed's got a sweater or something . . .'

'I guess he might. Anyone who needs clothes, come along with me. Sissy, Peggy? And Ed, maybe you could help the men.'

All the Seekers left their seats now, and began padding barefoot up the stairs to replace their wool and cotton clothes with coverings of pure fibre. Only Verena remained quietly seated. Her new robe was obviously made of artificial fibres. She must have known what was coming, I thought, because her old robe, the one she usually wore to meetings, was cotton velvet. But of course she knew; what was the matter with me? Was I beginning to believe, like the Seekers, that Ro was a separate entity?

It was Verena herself, not Ro, who was putting us through this; who, if she hadn't met with resistance, would have sat

153

and watched while we all stripped naked in the Novars'
parlour. (Or would she have joined in? Only Ro knew.)

It was noisy and confused upstairs, with doors and drawers
banging open and shut, cries and apologies as half-dressed
group members bumped into each other in the narrow hall.
Bill, Rufus, McMann, and I followed Ed Novar to the spare
room, where he began searching in the closet for non-organic
clothes. McMann and I took off our shirts; Bill, explaining
that his was Dacron, loosened his belt and dropped his pants.
Rufus backed into a corner behind the chest of drawers and
began to undress very slowly; not out of modesty, I think, so
much as from shame about his acne, which was even worse
on his body than on his face.

When we had finished, Bill still retained his Dacron shirt
and McMann his synthetic trousers (he demonstrated the
label to us). Almost everything else we had been wearing,
including most of our underwear, had turned out to be wool
or cotton.

Ed Novar now had on the plastic waders he used for duck
hunting and a dirty tan windbreaker. For McMann he had
found a semi-transparent nylon shirt, almost yellow in hue,
which made him look like an auto salesman in the early
1950s; for Bill a pair of pale-green plastic-looking slacks
streaked with paint. They were much too long and rather too
wide, and Bill had to hold them up with his hands, since our
belts were of animal origin. I wore black-and-white-striped
pyjamas, like a comic-strip convict.

Rufus, because it had taken him longest to undress, looked
oddest of all. By the time he had finished, there was nothing
left that Varna would approve of except a pair of maroon
swimming trunks. Faced with a choice between appearing
downstairs practically naked or going home, Rufus glanced
round the room desperately, finally fixing on the end of the
bed.

'What's that?' He pointed to a puffy flowered quilt. 'Isn't
that nylon, or something? Look, here's the label. Thirty per
cent Dacron, seventy per cent reprocessed fibres. I can wear

this all right, for now.' Not giving anyone a chance to object, he wrapped the quilt round his shoulders like an Indian blanket.

'Well, uh —' Ed began.

'Let's go.' Rufus led the way out of the room, his quilt dragging on the floor behind. As we followed, I saw McMann's face tighten up; he was trying not to laugh.

As we descended the stairs, the mirror by the front door reflected us like some group from the Theatre of the Absurd: a tall middle-aged duck hunter, a small convict with horn-rimmed glasses, a plump comedian in baggy paint-spotted pants, and a large used-car salesman, all barefoot; led by a skinny naked lunatic in Dacron socks, swimming trunks, and a flowered quilt.

The female Seekers had managed better. Women's clothing tends more towards the synthetic anyhow, and they had had two wardrobes to choose from. Milly and Catherine wore respectable bathrobes. Sissy had a white nylon dress, rather too small for her, and Peggy a short formal (it looked as if it might be Verena's high-school graduation dress dyed pink), rather too large. Elsie was wearing a semi-transparent blue plastic raincoat through which her slip partly showed.

No one laughed. When we were all assembled, Verena cleared her throat and addressed the unseen world.

'Oh friends and teachers of Varna! We have followed your lessons and done according to your instructions. We are free now of all dead organic materials, and clothed only in garments of light. The beams of power and truth that you are sending down to us now are entering direct into our beings. The space of this room is filled with vibrations of electrical beauty and power, and our spirits move freely within it at last!' Her voice had risen to an intense pitch. 'Isn't that so?' She raised her arms.

'It's so,' Elsie and Bill said, lifting their arms in turn.

'The whole room is filled with a golden electrical vibration now. It's flowing free through all our cells.' She gave me a special smile. 'Isn't that so, Roger?'

'That's so,' I said. Most of the others had their arms up

155

now, so I lifted mine too, feeling a fool. Without my real clothes, my social-scientist's costume, I felt vulnerable, exposed; I knew how ridiculous I must look in the convict-striped pyjamas. When Verena recovers from this delusion, I thought, she'll probably despise everybody who was involved in it. If she recovers.

'I can see it now!' Sissy was crying. 'It's all yellow golden, like mist in the sun!'

'It's warming me, and lifting me up!' Peggy chimed in.

'Yes, I feel it.' McMann's deep voice came in one affirmation too soon.

'I can't see it, but I feel it,' Bill said. 'It's getting stronger and stronger.'

'Let us kneel down, and give thanks for this blessing,' Verena proposed, slipping from her chair to the rug. She bowed her head, then looked up, frowning. 'Wait!' she cried, lifting her hand. 'Don't anyone move! We have been neglectful, and forgotten our instructions of light.'

Rising to her feet, she stood before the rest of the group, who had frozen at her command into various awkward positions. 'Let us hear these words again.' She snatched up the Message.

ALL DEAD ORG ORGANIC MM MATERIALS GROWTHS OF WORMSSSHEEP EARTH ROOTED FFIBERS ALL DESTROY NNOW BURN

Verena indicated the cast-off clothing and shoes. 'We must rid ourselves of these organic fibrous materials,' she said. 'They are unclean; they must be destroyed.' With a sweeping gesture that flung her sleeve back over a white arm, she pointed past Elsie to the fireplace. The narrow grate was empty as usual except for two polished brass andirons. 'Light the fire, Aunt Elsie.'

There was a moment's pause, while the Seekers looked at each other.

'I'll have to find some paper and kindling,' Elsie said, getting to her feet. 'We haven't had a fire in that chimney since last winter, but I guess it'll draw.... Ed, you can bring up some of that old scrap wood you got down in the cellar. Rufus'll help you.' Slowly, as if stunned, Rufus and Ed Novar rose. 'Sissy, let's you and me turn back the rug a bit, so it don't catch.'

Sissy, too, stood up.

'I guess we've got to rid ourselves of organic materials,' Peggy said to Bill, not too firmly, across the space her sister had left. 'Only, gee . . .'

'I don't see why we couldn't just give away what we can't use,' Milly remarked. 'I mean, if we asked our guides first. Otherwise, it's just a waste. . . . Verena?'

Verena did not reply. She stood like a Victorian marble figure, her smooth pale face slightly tilted up, the shiny folds of her robe falling to the floor. Her eyes were shut, the lids sculpturally round and white. Was she in trance again, or just ignoring objections? As usual, it was impossible to tell.

'We could give the clothes to charity,' Catherine suggested. 'Our guides ought to approve that.' She glanced upwards. No one else spoke; the sense of being overheard by invisible presences was too strong.

What was going to happen? I looked at McMann, who shrugged, raising his heavy eyebrows; then at Sissy, who had sat down again instead of helping Elsie.

I had always thought the distinction made by some of my colleagues, between actions which do and those which do not affect future actions, philosophically naïve. But there certainly was a difference, if only one of degree, between anything the Seekers had yet been asked to do and this latest command from Varna. Up to now the search for Truth had consumed mainly time. Reciting the Creed of Spiritual Light, or putting on somebody else's rayon bathrobe, is a limited and reversible act. Burning up your own clothes has practical, economic consequences. I looked at Bill's face, at Milly's, and at Catherine's, all fixed in sour rumination. No, they won't do it, I thought.

The rug was folded back now, and Ed Novar had begun

stacking wood in the fireplace, while Elsie crumpled sheets of newspaper and packed them underneath.

'It's ready, Verena.'

Verena opened her eyes, looked round the room without seeming to see any of us, smiled, and rose. Taking a box of kitchen matches from Elsie, she knelt on the tiles. Her bare white feet stuck out behind.

'Oh fire of earth, burn for us, that we may do the will of our guides of Varna!' she exclaimed, and struck a match. The *Atwell Sun–Advertiser* caught first, then, very quickly, the kindling wood. A sheet of hot yellow flame leapt up the bricks, and a corresponding cloud of dark smoke streamed out into the room. Verena fell back, coughing.

'The draught!' Elsie shouted through the smoke. 'Ed, you got to get the draught open! Push it hard. . . . Ahh. That's better.'

The fire was roaring right up the chimney now, looking much too large. The Seekers coughed and fanned the air. The whole parlour was full of a thick acid-smelling smoke and soot, as if some particularly strong and unpleasant astral force were present.

'Spirit of Light!' Verena turned and held out her hands to the flames. Barefoot, in the glow of burning newspaper and falling ash, surrounded by drifts of smoke, she looked very prophetic. 'I give to you these dead organic materials, that you may consume them.' Some of the group members stood up and edged forward to watch as she took up one of her gilt sandals from the rug, and threw it into the fire; then the other. 'Blessed be the Fire of Truth!'

The soles of Verena's sandals caught first. The gold straps scorched brown slowly, then suddenly burst into lines of bluish flame. She turned and looked at us triumphantly.

'I am purified and made free,' she announced. 'Rufus!' Her great dark eyes fixed upon him; Rufus began to duck his head and fidget. 'Bring your things here.'

Strategically, it was a good choice; yet Rufus hesitated, turning his head from side to side.

158

'Bring them here. Not the shoes, you'll need those to get home. Bring your sweater.'

As if hypnotized, Rufus picked up his Sophis College sweater. He crossed the parlour through the smoke and flickering light, his quilt trailing behind him.

'Oh Spirit of Light,' Verena prompted him. 'Go on.'

'Oh Spirit of Light,' Rufus repeated, 'I, uh, give you these dead materials.'

'That you may consume them.'

'That you may consume them.' He cast his sweater, with its white felt monogram, on the flames.

Everyone seemed to breathe together as it caught. 'Uh!' or 'Oh!' – a communal gasp of surprise, dismay.

'Blessed be the Fire of Truth,' Verena intoned. 'Peggy?'

This time there was less resistance. Peggy, looking childishly pretty in the pink net and taffeta dress, went over to Verena with an air of almost cheerful solemnity.

'Oh, uh, Spirit of Light . . .' She dropped her sweater and red knee-socks one at a time into the flames, looking at Verena after each item for approval.

'Ohh.' The murmur this time was louder but more neutral, as if from spectators at a fire.

'Aunt Elsie —'

Elsie's sweater must have been partly synthetic, for it caught in a flash, sending sparks high up the chimney.

'Blessed be the Fire of Truth! Say it along with me, everybody. Blessed be —'

'Blessed be the Fire of Truth!'

'Now, Uncle Ed —'

Mr Novar's brown coat-sweater and socks, which he had wadded up into a ball, were a disappointment. They burned slowly, creating smoke and a feeling of impatience. Well before they had burnt out, Verena was looking round the room again.

'Milly —'

Milly Munger brought the jacket of her knit suit to the fire with an air of self-sacrifice. As she often said, she was

159

particularly troubled by material clingings. It was hard for her to let go of it; she visibly hesitated for several seconds, took a step back, looked at Verena, and gave in. 'Oh-ooh!' she wailed, though under her breath, as the stuff caught.

'Ahhh!' A sigh almost of satisfaction from the rest of the group, including McMann and me. In some crazy way, I was beginning to enjoy myself.

'Blessed be the Fire of Truth!'

'Good, Milly. You are purified now, and made free. Catherine?'

Miss Vanting stood up, but for a moment she did not move, though we were all willing her to. She was an elderly woman, after all, of a higher class origin than the other Seekers. She had years of membership in a more conventional church behind her, and a strong feeling for her possessions. Her expression was stubborn.

'Your spirit band is about you now, Catherine,' Verena said, in her most vibrating tones. 'Those that have gone before, they are here, watching and guiding you.'

Again Verena's instinct had been infallible. As if, at the thought of her dead kin, she had become a little child again, Catherine Vanting picked up her long grey cardigan and carried it across the room to Verena. Standing beside her, she dropped it into the fire like a dead bird. The flames were hot now, with a foundation of ash and coals, and it caught at once.

'Ahhh!' This time it was a sound of pure pleasure – we might have been watching fireworks. Catherine's sweater glowed and crackled nicely, shooting out little orange and purple flakes of flame, possibly from mothballs.

'Bill —'

'Sissy —'

Verena had the rest of the group on her side now, standing in a rough circle around the fireplace and joining their wills to hers. The Freeplatzers crossed the room, carrying Bill's best sports-jacket and socks, and the elaborately patterned blue-and-white cardigan Sissy had been knitting herself all

160

fall. It was because of this, I realized, that Verena –maybe not consciously but with the instinct of the born leader – had been saving them to the last.

Together, Bill and Sissy threw their things into the fireplace. It was too much: the flames sputtered, then subsided.

It isn't by accident that the more complicated and primitive religions limit visibility in their temples, and emphasize incense and candles. As the light steadied, so did my mind. I looked round the room, mostly clear of smoke now, and thought, This is crazy. Burning up their best clothes, that's crazy. It was as if I had been suddenly transported to the back ward of some state hospital, where a group of patients in grotesque costumes were methodically destroying things. And I was sitting there, recording it all with scientific detachment.

A friend once told me he had shifted his field from experimental to clinical psych because he couldn't stand the look in the eyes of his laboratory animals. I watched the page as my hand and pencil scratched across it almost automatically: pale-blue parallel lines on white, the bars of a cage into which we were putting the Seekers – their names, words, gestures.

'It's gone out,' someone said flatly.

'The fire's out.'

In the grate, Sissy's sweater began to hiss and pop. An acid steam rose from it.

'No, it's catching.'

'Yeah —'

'It's burning now!'

'Ahhh!'

'Blessed be the Fire of Truth!' I didn't shout it with them this time.

'Tom —' Verena called.

I drew in my breath, and held it. Watching the Seekers, I had forgotten again that we were present in the body. Well, McMann would get out of it somehow, I thought. Now, if ever, he would demonstrate the smooth, good-natured social skill for which he was famous.

Not at all. Calmly, as if he had been waiting to be asked, McMann stepped forward, holding up a Harris tweed jacket which must once have cost at least fifty dollars. While the whole group watched, he went through the pockets with theatrical deliberation, removing pen, pencils, memo-book, hand-kerchief, and so forth. Then he threw it into the centre of the flames, along with his polka-dot bow-tie.

'Oh Spirit of Light,' he intoned solemnly, 'I give you these dead organic materials, that you may consume them.'

'Ahh!'

'Blessed be the Fire of Truth!'

First I wanted to laugh; I felt disoriented. This was succeeded by nervous anxiety, as it finally occurred to me that I was next. Even now McMann was adding his argyle socks to the blaze, separately, with a flourish.

My own socks, tie, and jacket were in plain sight on my chair. I didn't mind about the socks or tie; but I felt intense reluctance to sacrifice the jacket of my only good suit to Ro of Varna. No, I wouldn't do it.

'Roger —'

I refocused. On the other side of the smoky parlour, grouped around the mantel, nine peculiarly dressed people of assorted age and class were standing looking at me. As with one mind, they were willing me to cross the room and throw my clothes into the fire.

'Come on, Roger!' said a plump, motherly looking woman in a green kimono decorated with storks.

'Your guides are watching you now, they're judging you,' a barefoot burlesque comic urged me. 'Don't hesitate now.'

'I – uh.' I believe I muttered something.

'Roger!' an excited woman in a transparent plastic rain-coat exclaimed. 'Don't let the ice congestion form in your brain now, Roger!'

'Zimmern, for God's sake,' a large man in a nylon shirt growled under his breath. 'Participate.'

'Roger.' Verena said nothing else, but fixed her huge dark eyes on me, and held out her white hands, with the long fingers spread apart.

Without any sensation of intending it, I found myself bending to pick up my clothes. Once started, I couldn't seem to stop. I walked across the room towards Verena's eyes, emptied my pockets, and dropped my socks, tie and finally my jacket on to the fire.

'Oh Spirit of Light, I give to you these dead organic materials,' Verena prompted me, 'that you may consume them.'

'Ohspirituvlight, Igiveyouthese organicmaterials, thatyou may consumethem,' I mumbled.

'Blessed be the Fire of Truth!'

It was a cry of triumph this time, topped by Verena's most ringing, ethereal tone. Already hot little flames, like a pack of greedy spirits, were licking at the edges of my jacket. Soon they began to gobble it, growing fatter as they ate. Red, pale orange, gold, they flickered across the smooth J. Press flannel, leaving a black scorched rag, fraying into ash, behind.

And I stood and watched, astonished. The Sophis Project – the social sciences as a whole – did not seem at that moment to provide a sufficient rationale for our actions. No, other factors must be operating here, I thought, as the fire crackled like suppressed laughter. Perhaps someone else, somewhere – possibly Ro of Varna – was conducting a field study on American sociologists. To him, we were the white rats.

12

The first thing McMann and I did next day, the last before the Coming, was go out and try to buy some non-organic clothing. We had been allowed to wear back to our motel those items which had escaped the Fire of Truth, being either more or less non-combustible (like our shoes), or upstairs at the time. It was understood, though, that these things were to be got rid of, if not destroyed, as soon as possible.

We had planned to drive to Atwell, fifteen miles north, to shop. But while we slept the weather had turned bad again, and it was all I could do to drive to the centre of town. Something cold and heavy, between rain and ice, was falling out of the sky; we waded through half-frozen slush between the three places in Sophis that carried men's apparel: J. C. Penney's, Woolworths, and an Army and Navy store.

I had no idea, until I tried, how hard it would be to find non-organic clothes in a place like Sophis, or what they would look like when we found them. Underwear included: McMann thought we had better be thorough. If the Seekers should start undressing again, it would be hard to explain being caught in a cotton T-shirt.

'Hell, who knows?' he said. 'Maybe tonight Ro will tell them to take off all their clothes.'

An imaginary boardwalk movie appeared flickering in front of me, blotting out a rack of pants: Verena standing before the fire, removing all her clothes.

'You think that's what's going to happen next?'

McMann looked at me and grinned. 'I'm afraid not,' he said. 'If they could let themselves put on the kind of show you have in mind, they wouldn't have had to invent Varna.' He moved along a counter. 'Hey, these look okay.'

'They're synthetic, all right. Great if you want pictures of beagles on your undershorts.' I turned the pile over. 'Or fish, or race-horses.'

'Masculine symbolism.'

'Yeah? Here's one with decoy ducks. Pink decoy ducks.'

'It's for the Christmas trade; the wives and sweethearts buy them. Let's get a move on. Here's some shirts.' He began to shuffle through them quickly. 'All right. I'm taking this one.'

'I don't know.' I found my size. 'Three ninety-eight, for that?' I held up a sleazy item with threads hanging from it.

'You're suffering from material clingings, that's your trouble. Christ, did you hate to see that jacket go last night!' McMann laughed. 'I had no idea you were so tight, Zimmern.'

'On my salary, I've got to be tight.' That was true enough; but it wasn't so much the idea of having sacrificed an expensive jacket that bothered me – it was having sacrificed it to Ro of Varna, that vague, self-important, prissy extraterrestrial being. I saw him as a kind of cosmic assistant dean: fond of composing mysterious memos and promulgating needless rules. And it was no use saying he didn't exist. He was very definitely present, like any supernatural being, in the imaginations of his followers. Tall, thin, and fair in his bodily form, according to Verena's description – and probably dressed in non-organic clothing from J. C. Penney's.

Verena fitted into the picture too. She was like some very innocent, very pretty college girl who gets a heavy crush on her adviser (with his connivance), unaware that he is not the dignified intellectual hero of her dreams, but a pompous, vulgar-minded — What was the matter with me, for God's sake? Had my own crush got so heavy that now I was jealous of Ro of Varna, a delusionary creation? 'Jesus Christ,' I exclaimed half aloud, as I went through a stack of shirts without looking at them.

'Come on, Rog,' McMann said. 'You only have to wear the stuff for a couple of days, then you can toss it out if you want.'

'Huh? Oh, yeah.'

'If it's the money that's bothering you, you can charge it to the project. Now let's get going. We've got work to do.'

After loading our purchases into my car, we drove through the falling slush to Ovid's Motel. Ten minutes later I went into the bathroom, where I observed a nondescriptly lower-middle-class young man. He wore a shiny Dacron shirt with a pointed collar, a tan Orlon sweater, and limp brown slacks with an elastic waistband. Another one of Ovid's metamorphoses had taken place. This fellow matched the motel room perfectly: he had the same air of bland bad taste and second-rate anonymity. He was an insurance investigator or small-loans clerk, I decided, or maybe one of those young men who pass out free samples of a new detergent and write down the housewives' reactions. I watched him as he tied Zimmern's striped J. Press tie around his neck, in a pathetic attempt to upgrade his status.

'You aren't going to make it to Atwell today,' McMann said from the other room, looking out the snow-smeared window. 'You should have bought those slippers.' The only non-organic shoes in town in my size had been some fake-Indian moccasins, printed with wigwams.

'I'll manage. I'll wear my galoshes with an extra pair of socks.'

'Your galoshes are made of rubber.'

'So?'

'It's an organic material. Comes from rubber trees. Those Cosmic Love rays'll bounce right off it.'

'Well, Verena didn't say anything about rubber,' I returned. 'And please don't remind her, either.'

'I wasn't planning to. Jesus, you sure are touchy today, aren't you?'

'I'm not touchy,' the man in the bathroom mirror said touchily. I recognized him now. It was Stupid Roger, in his real clothes.

· · · ·

Our job that day was to interview all the Seekers informally to check the present strength of their belief. Did they think our guides would really come tomorrow night? What made them think so? And, in their opinion, did the rest of the group have as much, more, or less faith in the Coming than they did?

I had the car, so I was supposed to go call on Milly, Rufus, Peggy, and the Freeplatzers, while McMann did the household on West Hawthorne Street and Catherine Vanting. In fact, I didn't have to go anywhere. Those Seekers who weren't at Elsie's when we arrived soon showed up, most of them to the neglect of other commitments. Peggy and Rufus, for instance, were cutting classes; as they put it, it was a waste of time to go to some old lecture on history when Ro and Mo and the others had so much more to teach us.

My only problem was getting each of my subjects off by themselves for a few moments of uninterrupted interviewing, and then writing up my notes. So much was going on in the house that the only place I could be sure of privacy was the bathroom. I was in there so often that day and the next that Elsie asked me several times if I were feeling all right, and finally forced me to take some Milk of Magnesia.

Ducking into the bathroom, shutting and locking the door, dropping the lid of the toilet and sitting down on the worn pink chenille cover; taking my notebook out of the sleazy-feeling pocket of those synthetic pants, snapping my ballpoint pen into position – that's what I remember most about the time just before the Coming. On the linoleum between the clothes-hamper and the tub there was a shadow of grime and fluff which gradually darkened. For the first time, Elsie's meticulous housekeeping had slackened. As I sat there, I could hear noises and bustle all around me: steps going up and down stairs, people talking, the phone ringing.

I saw Rufus first. He was sure the Varnians were coming; all their messages to us said so definitely. He thought the other Seekers expected them too; the main thing that worried him was that some of the group – especially the women –

might not be fully prepared. Ro had said that they would come 'in the body', but that didn't necessarily mean in human bodies. What he was afraid of, he said, picking at his skin condition nervously, was that some of the others might be frightened or revolted by the Varnians' appearance, and not realize the true light and power of the spirit behind it.

'You mean you think the Varnians might come with spots, or feelers, or three legs each, something like that?' It was a possibility that had not occurred to me.

'Well, scientifically speaking, we know that other planets are bound to produce different forms of life from what we have here. Their specific gravities are different from ours, their atmosphere, temperature, maybe even their molecular structure might be alien. We have to be prepared for anything.' Rufus ran his hands through his scruffy hair, so that it stood on end like some sort of brownish moss. In the strange collection of non-organic clothes he was wearing, he looked like a different form of life himself.

The telephone was ringing again as I finished writing up my interview with Rufus and left the bathroom. As I started downstairs I saw McMann come into the hall and answer it.

'Hello. Yes, it is. Who's calling? I'm sorry, she can't come to the phone now.' McMann sounded impatient and far from sorry. 'I really don't know. No.' Something in his tone caught my attention. I stopped on the stairs, listening.

'No, b — Uh-huh, but — Well, why don't you try again in a few days? No. No, she's not sick. She doesn't *want* to speak to you now. All right. I'll give her the message.'

I came down the rest of the stairs as he was hanging up. 'What was that?' I asked.

'Oh, nothing: just somebody trying to get hold of Verena. She's not talking to anyone except the group members now. No strange vibrations allowed.' He grinned perfunctorily, and went off towards the dining-room, where Elsie was setting the table for lunch.

'That him again?' I thought I heard her say. I moved nearer.

168

'Uh-huh. I told him he'd have to call back in a few days.'

'That's right.' I could see Elsie as she went round the table folding and placing paper napkins. She was wearing her green kimono and a pair of synthetic bedslippers like mauve dustmops. 'Twice already today,' she complained. 'And three times yesterday.'

McMann said something I didn't catch.

'Well, of course he can't get in here. There's a strong invisible wall of the spirit around this house. No evil emanations can come through it. All the same, it's a nuisance. . . . Three, four, five. I wonder is Catherine coming over for lunch? She might as well, we got enough food for today, anyhow. Could you bring a couple of extra chairs from the front room, please, Tom?'

'I'll get them.' Rather than be caught eavesdropping, I carried in the chairs.

'Oh, Roger. Thanks.' She pushed the door to the kitchen open. 'Better put in another can of the vegetable soup. And cut some more health bread.' She let the door swing closed. 'How many are we going to be now? Six? I can't seem to keep my mind on to material things any more; it's so full of wonderful thoughts of the Coming. I bet it's the same with you.'

'It certainly is,' McMann agreed.

'You know what I think,' Elsie continued. 'I think I'm going to ask Ed to do something about that phone when he gets home, fix it so it don't ring for a while. We can't be bothered any more with that kind of nuisance and interruption, not now. . . . I hope we got enough soda.' She went into the kitchen.

'Listen,' I said, moving nearer to McMann. 'What's going on around here?'

'Shhh.' He gestured with his head towards the kitchen.

'Who was that call from, anyhow?'

'Shut up, for Christ's sake.'

'Now, Roger, if you'll just put these plates around,' Elsie said, coming back in. 'And then maybe you could go

169

upstairs and see if Verena and Rufus are ready to eat. Just knock on the door and tell them lunch is ready. Tom, you can sit here.'

With an air of self-conscious group status, McMann took Ed Novar's place at the head of the table. As I set his plate in front of him, he winked at me.

I found myself sneaking up the steps to Verena's room on tiptoe – easy enough, since I was wearing only synthetic socks. Her door was closed but not quite latched, just as it had been the other day. What were they doing in there? Well, I thought, it's saner to be jealous of a Sophis College freshman than of a being from outer space.

I knocked on the door hard, giving it a little push so that it opened an inch or two. Both Verena and Rufus were fully clothed, and sitting in chairs several feet apart.

Rufus could go down to lunch, Verena said when I had delivered the message. She didn't feel the need of anything: well, all right, maybe I could bring her up some soda; and then wouldn't I like to stay for a private conference myself?

There was a short but intense struggle. Zimmern won, but only just. He had to appeal to Stupid Roger's fear and to his vanity, pointing out that the house was full of people who might easily walk in on him, and that he was wearing blue rayon undershorts decorated with beagles. Well, maybe later, I told Verena. Right now, I was sort of hungry.

About twelve-thirty, while we were eating, Bill and Sissy arrived. Bill had come home for lunch, and then half-way through his vegetable soup he had announced that he wasn't going back to work. Cunningham (his boss) could like it or lump it, that was all. Maybe he'd never go to the office again, who knows? The Varnians might have other instructions for him. Sissy, as usual, backed him up completely. They were both very talkative, full of nervous euphoria. But all the Seekers were pretty high by this time; as Elsie put it, the house was full of particles of positive electricity.

Milly and Catherine Vanting turned up shortly after lunch,

170

and the rest of the afternoon I was busy interviewing. Everyone I spoke to was convinced the Varnians were coming, and all of them, except possibly Catherine Vanting, were enthusiastic about it.

Catherine was in an irritable mood. She had a cold, and complained that she had had to go out that morning in awful weather and buy a Dacron sweater and 'other things' (underwear, presumably) which itched her. She was getting a funny rash; and besides, she was worried about her parents. 'You know, Roger,' she confided, 'I haven't had a real Message from Mother in two weeks. She was just approaching her test for advancement to the fourth plane when she last communicated. I'm sure she's been trying to get in touch with me, but with all this traffic and electricity in the air now, she probably can't make herself heard through the other vibrations. I don't like that at all. Soon as I see my guide, Ko, I'm going to talk to him about it.'

At the meeting that night, before the first hymn, Elsie handed out sheets of aluminium foil to all of us. During Verena's meditation period before supper, she explained, new instructions had come through. To achieve perfect spiritual reception, Ro had told her, we must protect ourselves from contact of any sort with organic materials. Thanks to the ingenuity and devotion of Rufus, who had made a special trip downtown, she was now able to give each Truth Seeker two pieces of heavy-weight foil: a larger one for us to sit on, and a smaller one to place under our feet to prevent the vibrations from leaking out and being absorbed into the carpet. I wondered if they had ever heard of Wilhelm Reich and his orgone box.

The aluminium foil seemed to work: reception was excellent. Not only was there a long Message from Ro but many of the other teachers and guides who were less skilled at interstellar communication got through and sent clear Messages of promise and cheer. They were preparing for take-off, and would be with us soon. The Varnian scientist

Mo congratulated Rufus on his inspiration about the aluminium foil; Peggy was told by her guide not to worry about having cut class. Ko spoke to Catherine personally, assuring her that Mother was now advanced to the fourth level, where she had been welcomed with joyful recognition by Grandfather and Great-Aunt Evie.

Participation scores were running high; I could hardly keep track of all the expressions of satisfaction and agreement – the smiles, vigorous nodding, and cries of 'Oh, wonderful!' 'Yes, that's so!' Bill and Sissy were especially active. Bill retold the story, now more elaborate, of how he had been home eating lunch, and suddenly just as he was finishing his soup he heard a kind of voice humming inside him, telling him not to go back to work.

'That's right,' Sissy said. 'And I know it was a true leading, because this afternoon we lay down for a nap and I had another dream-vision, the clearest I ever had yet. It was like the pastel I made for Catherine of the Zura plane, but much bigger and brighter. The lake of light was sort of vibrating and changing colour in circles, like ripples, and there was a kind of fountain of sparks of vital fire, only bigger than sparks and a different shape, sort of like cornflakes, pouring over the lake right into its centre. I started to paint it, but I didn't get it finished yet.'

'That's a blessed vision, Sissy,' Verena said solemnly.

'Oh, I know that. I was thinking this afternoon, my teacher Solo was right when he said he was going to show me pictures even greater than the ones I'd already seen. But what d'you think it means?'

'It's a sign to all of us.' Verena went into a technical explanation, and then added, 'But you know, Sissy, this vision of yours has a special meaning for you, that's what I feel. It's a sign that a new phase in your and Bill's life is beginning, that your central beings are full of new, vital electronic force, so that if you use it right your deepest wishes will be fulfilled. But let's ask your guides about it.'

Solo and Bo confirmed Verena's interpretation, and sent

172

the Freeplatzers a Message of hope and Cosmic Love. As Verena read it out, Sissy and Bill exchanged a look so full of faith that I wondered if this magic encouragement might not really work. Maybe now Sissy would finally get one of her paintings into the Art Association show, and Bill (in spite of his recent absences from work) would be promoted.

McMann and I had Messages too. He was told to remain calm and of good cheer, for the Coming which his heart desired was at hand, when he would receive even more than he wished for, and would be infused with cosmic vibrations. He was obviously in great favour on Varna. Ro's remarks to me were much briefer, but showed a kind of ambiguous perceptiveness in retrospect:

> LIFTUP YRR IIIEYES ROGERSEEKER BE OF SSTRONG
> SPIRIT   FFOR NOW U SSTAND   AMONG SHADOWSS
> BUT WHEN IN LIGHT

Punctuation and capitalization being missing, it was impossible to say whether the last four words were an incomplete promise, or a question.

McMann was tired when we got back to the motel, but in a state of euphoria equal to that of the Seekers.

'It's going great,' he sighed, dropping heavily on to his bed. 'Am I bushed, though.' He lay back, then sat up again. 'Rog, we've really got it this time. Nothing's going to shake that group now.' He leaned over and clapped his hand on my shoulder enthusiastically. 'Boy, we've got it made. Isn't that right?'

'That's what your guides said.' I agreed with McMann; I just didn't share his metabolism. The tension surrounding the climactic hours of the Sophis Project affected us in antithetical ways. I was wound up tight, while he was all noisy emotiveness.

'We're going to get all the data we need, and then some,' he exulted. 'As long as Verena doesn't call the Coming off at the last minute,' he added.

'You think she might do that?'

McMann shrugged. 'How can you tell what a schiz like her is going to do? She must know, with some part of her mind, that Ro and the rest are nothing but her own mental construct, and mental constructs don't fly around in real spaceships. She could always receive a message that the trip was postponed for some reason. But I think she'll let it go through – the group is so keyed-up now. The explanation will come later, after the let-down. Ro'll say that the Yura waves, or something, prevented them from getting here.'

'And you think they'll swallow that?'

'They'll have to swallow it, to save face. They're too committed now; they may look fools when Ro and his pals don't come, but they'll look bigger fools if they admit Varna doesn't exist, and they've been drinking all that vegetable soup and sitting around on pieces of tin-foil for nothing. No, the group won't break up.' He grinned. 'It's pretty remarkable, you know. This whole thing has been built up for them completely in isolation. They've never had any objective evidence or outside confirmation of their beliefs, no external support at all. Steve Mayonne is really going to look sick. He didn't believe I could find a group like this, you know. He has a theory of how it isn't possible.' McMann laughed.

'I see.' I saw something else, too: a connection between McMann's hypothesis about the Truth Seekers and his position in the Department, even in the world. Opposition would never shake his own convictions, so he wanted and expected the Seekers to hold to theirs. I hoped he was right.

'Let me tell you something, Roger.' McMann leaned forward. 'Those two guys, Mayonne and Ginsman, have been praying for months that this project would be a bust. And I'll tell you something else: they'd do about anything they thought they could get away with to make it a bust.' He nodded his head silently for emphasis. 'You know the trouble

174

I had getting Sally off the Department budget and on to the study? Steve wanted me to hire some incompetent low-classification girl Personnel was going to send over. Just to louse up my project, out of spite.'

'Oh, I don't think Mayonne —' I said. 'I know he suggested that, but —'

'Listen, you don't know anything. You're just a highbrow kid who can't tell his ass from a distribution curve. No offence. But I've been around that department for twenty years; I know what I'm talking about. And that wasn't an isolated occurrence, either. You remember the business with the stationery?'

'Yeah; I remember.' A month or so ago, an order we had sent in for supplies for the project had got lost somewhere, most likely in the departmental office, causing us a lot of inconvenience.

Suppose he was right, I thought. Maybe there had been something funny going on. I remembered Bob Onland's repeated warnings against working for McMann, and the way Mayonne kept asking me almost every week if we'd turned up anything interesting over in Sophis. Why didn't he ask McMann, if he was so interested? There was Barry Ginsman, too, wanting to know the other day if McMann were planning to do any statistical work – 'because I just sent in a big request for computer time, and I'm afraid there'll be trouble if we ask for any more right now'. Was that just a casual remark, or was it a threat?

McMann was right. I had been stupid. A naïve faith in the professional impartiality of one's colleagues isn't the worst error in the world; but it wasn't suited to my ideal Zimmern, the sophisticated, cynical young social scientist from Columbia. Some social scientist: he had been missing obvious interaction clues and failing to report significant data for weeks. Well, at least he could try to make it up now.

'Ginsman said something funny to me at lunch the other day,' I began.

'Oh yeah?'

McMann heard me out intently. It seemed obvious to him that Barry wanted to keep us from coding our data.

'Damn it, you should have told me this right away,' he exclaimed. 'Aw, Christ. By now, it might be too late to stop him.'

'I'm sorry.'

'It was dumb, that's what it was.' He smiled, partially forgiving me. 'Well, forget it. I'll go round to the Computing Centre Monday; maybe I can get some action. I'll talk to Judy Aronson.'

'You don't want me to say anything to Ginsman?'

'Christ, no! Don't even speak to him, if you can help it.'

'All right.'

'You've got a lot to learn, boy.' McMann stared at me. 'You'll make it, though. You're a hard worker, got a good theoretical grasp; all you need is a little experience. You got to loosen up some. You've been a lot of help to me on this study, you know. Hell, I couldn't have done it without you.'

'Thanks. I've learned a lot,' I muttered, grateful and embarrassed. I was surprised by the testimonial; for some time, especially since I had proved so inept a student of Varnian theology, I had assumed McMann regarded me as a drag on the project. 'It's been very exciting.'

'You know something?' He sat forward again. 'We've really got a *study* here. This could be a classic. When these findings are published, a lot of people are going to *sit up*, and *take notice*.' Smiling, he pounded on the bed to emphasize the words.

An important book: not just an article but a book with my name on it that would re-establish McMann's professional status and establish mine . . . Why not? He had done it before.

'Yeah,' he went on with satisfaction. 'I've got plans for us. We've got to take our time, though, Rog, and really follow this thing through. We want to stay with the Seekers long enough after this crisis so there won't be any question of our

176

missing a delayed reaction. We don't want Mayonne and his pals suggesting that the group nexus probably dissolved as soon as we left town, am I right?'

'You're right, of course.' I was so caught up in my present group nexus that I hardly stopped to think what this meant: weeks more of commuting to Sophis, sitting through meetings, avoiding being alone with Verena.

'Now, what I want to do is . . .' McMann pulled a yellow pad towards him on the bedside table and we began to make plans. After the Coming had failed, he thought, there would be a successful effort to justify it theoretically; possibly a new date would be set. Very probably, there would be a campaign to attract new members. That meant that some of his graduate students could come to Sophis and work with us. One of them might be assigned to help me on the political attitudes survey I had originally planned, with a control group matched to the Seekers in age, sex, education, and class.

It was only when I was finally getting into bed that I remembered the question that had been bothering me all day.

'Listen, Tom.' Ordinarily, away from the Seekers, I called him 'McMann'; but that night I must have felt, as they put it, that we were brothers in the spirit. 'I want to ask you something.'

'Shoot.'

'What was all that about the telephone call this morning?'

'Phone call this morning?' He yawned like a good-natured hippopotamus, throwing his head back and showing strong square teeth.

'The one you took, for Verena.'

'Oh, that was Ken,' he said, as if he had never tried to conceal it. Why had I thought he had? 'He's still trying to get hold of her. Persistent, huh?'

'What does he want her for?'

'Wants to screw her, I guess.' McMann shrugged and turned out his light. A shadow fell over half of the room. 'There's no accounting for tastes. Elsie says he's in the possession of a moronic elemental.' He guffawed, yawning again. 'He'll have to wait a while.'

'She doesn't want to speak to him at all, then?'

'Nah. Saving herself for higher things.' McMann lay down. 'Let's get some sleep, pal,' he said. 'We've got a big day ahead of us.'

13

The house on West Hawthorne Street was in disorder when McMann and I arrived Saturday morning. Nothing could be seen from outside, but the door opened on confusion. Chairs stood stacked on top of one another in the front hall, rolled-up rugs leaned heavily against them, and books and magazines lay in piles on the floor. A last-minute Message had come through to Verena in the early morning, and now Elsie and Peggy were ridding the parlour of all dead organic materials in preparation for the Coming.

They were glad to see us. The sofa and the rest of the heavy furniture still had to be carried out, the curtains taken down, and the pictures unhooked from the walls. Elsie was not planning to burn any of these things, which would have been difficult anyhow. The new instructions were to give them away, to 'those that have need'. But that could be taken care of later. The important thing now was to get the stuff out of the room, so it wouldn't block the inflowing spiritual electricity, or harbour malevolent elementals, which were able to lodge in all organic things.

McMann and I were given the hardest job: moving the carpets and the living-room set into the basement. We got the rugs down all right, but Verena's wing chair wouldn't go through the dining-room door. No matter which way we turned it, some part – the ends of its arms, its vestigial upholstered wings, or one of its heavy-clawed wooden feet – caught on the door

Eventually we had to take this chair, and the matching sofa, back through the dining-room and parlour and (after we had moved all the smaller organic things out of the way) through the front door. We carried them down the steps, around the side of the house over the slippery frozen snow, and up on to the back porch, and then it turned out they wouldn't go in through the back door, either. Well, Elsie suggested, hugging herself against the cold as she stood above us on the steps, maybe we could take them down the outside cellar stairs.

As I stood in the backyard, through which a thin, sharp wind was blowing, sucking a smashed thumb and waiting to see if Elsie could get the cellar doors open, I decided Ro was probably right. That chair and sofa were obviously hostile elementals in disguise. Standing there askew in the snow, they looked like a couple of large semi-mythical birds with moulting reddish plumage – dodos, say, or great auks – stuck three-fourths of the way through a metamorphosis into furniture. When we finally got them inside, I shoved them into the corner behind the furnace with as much satisfaction as if they had been Mayonne and Ginsman.

Upstairs, Catherine Vanting and the Freeplatzers had arrived. The parlour was empty now except for two metal lamps and a plastic hassock; everyone was sitting round the dining-room table. Since the piano (dead trees and murdered elephants' teeth) had been moved in there too, it was crowded.

'Hey, Roger,' McMann said to me. 'It's nearly twelve o'clock. Let's go out for some lunch, what do you say?'

'Oh, you don't have to go out, Tom!' Elsie exclaimed. 'I'll fix you lunch. There must be something round.' She stood up. 'You just stay here. Sissy? Bill? You want something to eat?'

'Oh, no thanks, Elsie,' Sissy said. 'We've had lunch.'

'Sure,' Bill said simultaneously, 'that'd be great.'

The Freeplatzers looked at each other. 'We did have a salad plate,' Bill explained, rather embarrassed. 'But I wouldn't mind something more, if you've got enough to go round.'

'Nothing more for me, thanks,' Sissy said virtuously.

'Catherine?'

'Well. Maybe just a little bite.'

180

'I'll see what I've got.' Elsie went into the kitchen.

'Sissy's received another beautiful vision of the Coming.' Catherine gestured at the drawings which were spread out on the table.

'Yes, it came in a dream early this morning. The whole astral universe was spread out in front of me, in symbolic colours. You can take a copy if you like, Roger. I made one for everybody. Here's mine, so you can see the colours. I just jumped out of bed and turned on the light and made it while it was fresh in my mind, with my pastels. See, this here is our solar system . . .'

'We're kind of running out of everything,' Elsie said. 'Roger? I wonder, could you go down to the P and C and pick up a few things? I'll give you a list.'

As I pushed the cart round the supermarket I began to feel hungrier and hungrier, though not for the things I was buying. From Elsie's list, it was clear that lunch (and also presumably supper) with the Seekers was going to be mostly fruit salad, eggs, and vegetable soup. A craving for murdered animal flesh overcame me as I passed the bin of cold cuts, and I snatched up a cellophane envelope of chipped beef.

I paid for the groceries out of my own wallet; Elsie had forgotten to give me any money. It was probably getting to be something of a financial strain for the Novars to feed so many people so often, even if mainly on nuts and Jello.

Outside, a cold wind mixed with snow had begun to blow across the parking lot. I unloaded my cart, got into the car, dug out the chipped beef, and had just taken my first mouthful when I heard my name called.

'Mr Zimmern! That's you, Mr Zimmern, isn't it?'

I started as if caught in a criminal act – which from the Seekers' point of view it was. I swallowed my mouthful of protein and shoved the rest into the space between the front seats. Then I rolled the car window down part way.

'Yes?'

'I'd like to talk to you.' The voice raised against the wind was loud and demanding. A boy about twenty, with bony large features and a crew-cut, leaned in towards me. It was Ken.

'Yes?'

'It's about Verena. I wanted to ask you . . .' He broke off and swallowed for a moment, but still faced me stubbornly, like a student complaining about a bad grade. I met it according to that convention: with silence, eyebrows raised.

'What I want to know is, why can't I see her? I've been calling every day, but she never can come to the phone. And now the phone's out of order, or something. The operator says it's working, but it doesn't ring. I figure maybe her uncle turned it off, he works for the company.'

I said nothing, though I might have congratulated him on this guess.

'I went over there this morning,' Ken continued, 'only her aunt wouldn't let me in. I thought maybe if I hung around, Verena might come by here, or else Mrs Novar might go out shopping herself and I could try again.' He leaned farther towards me. 'I looked in through the window from the porch, I saw they took all the furniture out and the curtains down, like they were moving away.' A flicker of anxiety crossed the clumsy features reddened by cold. 'Listen, are they leaving town or something?'

'I don't think so, no.'

'Then what's the furniture moved out for? Is she just doing over the room? I didn't see any painters' stuff. I mean, what's going on in there?'

Not knowing what to say, I shrugged.

'Last night I went over to Rufus Bell's dorm, but I couldn't find him. His room-mate told me he hasn't been there except to sleep practically the whole week, and he hasn't been to most of his classes.'

'Really.'

I was trying to be neutral and non-committal, but not doing too well: Ken looked at me with hostility. 'Listen, Ken,' I said, trying hard to put more friendliness into my voice. 'Why don't you just wait a few days? It'll all be over soon. Try calling again in a few days.'

'What do you mean, it'll all be over soon? What'll be over?'

Realizing that I had put my foot into it, I said nothing.

'It's some more of that Varna business, isn't it?' Ken clutched the edge of the window glass with his damp, knobby bare hands as if to make sure I wasn't going to get away. 'You and Mr McMann don't really believe any of that stuff,' he said. 'You're just studying them, because they're cranks, isn't that right?'

Suppose I admitted the truth to Ken, would he leave us alone then? Or would he go back to West Hawthorne Street and try to expose us, as soon as he could get a hearing? Would he place the successful completion of the Sophis study above his own ambition, which was presumably (as McMann had suggested) to possess the material body of Verena Roberts at the earliest possible moment? Surely not.

'I have a right to see Verena,' Ken continued loudly, forcing his face into the window, his shoulders hunched against the snow and wind. 'I'm a friend of hers.'

'But she doesn't want to see you, I'm afraid,' I said snappishly; I was feeling the cold.

'She doesn't?' Ken faltered, then recovered. 'How do you know? Did she tell you so?'

I said nothing.

'I bet she didn't!' he shouted into the car. 'I bet she doesn't even know I've been phoning her.' His eyes glittered with suspicion. 'If Verena'd speak to me herself, and say she doesn't want to see me again, I'll go away,' he went on. 'I'll stop calling up, okay. But I'm sure as hell not going to take it from that crazy neurotic aunt of hers.' He wiped snow from his face. 'There was a letter I wrote her too, she never answered it. Her aunt could have just thrown it out. That's what I think. And I'm going to keep going back there until I find out for sure.' Ken shook my window for emphasis in a way that seemed likely to crack it. With a sigh, I reached over and rolled the glass down into the door. His face wobbled forwards, then righted itself. A shower of snow, like dandruff, fell from his hair.

'I can tell you one thing,' I said earnestly. 'Verena isn't coming out today, and neither is Mrs Novar. They sent me to the grocery, to shop for them. You're just wasting your time there. You'd better go home; it's cold.' Taking advantage of the moment, I quickly wound the glass up again, all the way. 'So long.'

I pantomimed a goodbye (brief wave and smile) through the window to Ken's baffled face. Then I started the engine. He fell back a step or two, then stood looking after me through the snow.

I drove towards Elsie's feeling irritable. It was such dirty luck that somebody like Ken should keep turning up to interfere with our study. Of course, there were people like that everywhere, naturally aggressive, self-dramatizing people who were always raising objections and getting themselves thrown out of any group they were in. No wonder Verena didn't want to see him any more. Suspicious too, accusing Elsie of lying to him like that. Well, it was just our luck. We would finish the study in spite of him and in spite of Mayonne and Ginsman.

I was nearly back at West Hawthorne Street before I remembered my packet of chipped beef. Making a quick detour which almost turned into a bad skid, I drove down a side street and parked. While I chewed on the dry, cold animal matter, I wondered whether Ken had a natural paranoid streak. His accusations of us earlier, for instance — Well, of course he was right, then ... I stopped eating. Suppose he was right now? No, not this time. He was just making excuses to justify trying to elbow his way in where nobody wanted him. Maybe I hadn't been really non-directive with Ken, but I had to protect our experimental situation. This was my research project, Verena belonged to me —

To me? Self-exposed, I put the chipped beef down. It wasn't just scientific zeal that made me angry at Ken; it was plain jealousy.

All right. How did I know that Elsie wasn't concealing Ken's phone calls? She was certainly capable of it. How did I know Verena didn't want to see him?

There was one obvious way to find out; by asking her. That meant that I would have to see her alone, though, something I had decided not to do again . . . But this was more important, I told myself. We needed accurate data here; and I could certainly avoid trouble if I really tried.

It wasn't as easy as it sounds to speak to Verena. When I got back, Elsie met me with a cross, impatient expression, and asked what took me so long, everybody was waiting. It might have been better if I had left it until after lunch, but I was in such a hurry that I told her I wanted to see Verena while I was helping unload the groceries; and against all precedent, Elsie refused me permission. Verena was in her room, resting and meditating in preparation for that night, and she couldn't be disturbed any more. It was true, Sissy had been in to show her the vision-painting, but that was different. Elsie had let Rufus go up too. But he had arrived in an awful mental state, with a threatening letter from the College about his work. She wasn't sure she had done right to let him see Verena even so, and anyhow, she had decided that would have to be the end. Verena shouldn't have to have any more contact with heavy earthly minds and their petty problems today. What was my problem, anyhow? Elsie asked. She could probably help me with it herself some time this afternoon when she got a chance. I mumbled that it wasn't really that important, and retreated.

During lunch (very vegetarian and badly prepared) I decided that if Elsie wouldn't give me permission to see Verena, I would have to go without permission. This was contrary to the rules of both the Truth Seekers and the study.

'But I only have to see her for a couple of minutes,' I remember saying to myself, as if that were a complete excuse.

But when lunch was over, Elsie – as if she had some supernatural knowledge of what I was planning – kept getting in my way. Milly Munger had just arrived with a carful of potted plants to decorate the parlour, and Elsie told her I would help.

'Oh, that's wonderful, Roger.' Milly smiled at me. 'Come on in here, then. You see this big bowl of ferns; I want to hang it from the light fixture there. I think it'll make a real pretty effect. If you get up here on to the table, I'll hand them up to you.'

'It won't hold,' Catherine Vanting pronounced.

'Aw, sure it will. It's anchored into the ceiling.'

'I mean this here, it won't hold his weight.' Catherine leaned on the edge of a round folding table, painted green and covered with acne-like rust, which Ed Novar had brought in from the garage. It wobbled noisily.

'Oh, it'll stand it. That metal is strong, like all non-organic substances. Besides, it's just for a minute. Come on, Roger; I'm steadying it for you. Can you hold the other side, Catherine?'

I climbed awkwardly on to the table.

'Careful! That's right. Now the ferns. Sissy, could you hand up the bowl to Roger, so we don't have to let go?'

Sissy came over from the window, where she was arranging plants. A large, round-bottomed metal container, full of fluffy, prickly greenery, was lifted towards me. It was surprisingly heavy.

'There. You got it? Now you've got to get both those chains over the fixture. Oops!' The table tottered, and one of the arms of the chandelier hit me in the face. 'More to the left. No, the other way! Watch it! Aow! . . . Oh, dear! Are you all right?'

I had stepped off-centre on the table, which collapsed sideways with a non-organic crash. I grabbed at the bowl of

186

ferns. It held, but tipped over, so that I came down in a landslide of dirt, roots, and foliage.

'I'm okay, I guess,' I said from the floor.

'Thank heavens.' Milly and Sissy, exclaiming maternally, helped me up. Elsie, who had come running from the kitchen at the noise, was more concerned with the mess on her floor; while Catherine merely stood by remarking thinly that even though this house was supposed to be under a Protection, it looked like some elemental must have got in, and attracted itself to me.

I was like her sister Hallie, she continued, while Elsie went for the broom and Milly tried to brush me off. Hallie just attracted destructive vibrations, not that it was her own fault; but if the eyes of the spirit were opened you could probably see them whirling around thick as flies in her house, getting into the drawers to untidy them, spilling things in the cupboards, and rucking up the rugs to make people trip and hurt themselves. That was one reason why she, Catherine, had refused her sister's invitation to Christmas dinner, the first time in twenty years; she didn't feel it was safe for her there.

Elsie returned with the broom and dustpan, followed by Ed Novar with a step-ladder. As I moved out of their way, I realized I had wrenched, or maybe only bruised, my back.

Anyhow, Catherine went on, she felt she couldn't promise to fulfil any earthly obligations until she knew what Ro's instructions to her would be. As Verena said, we were all putting our lives at the disposal of Varna now. Their plans for us had to come first, she had told her sister, who took it badly. If only Hallie could be brought to see the light! If Ro, or one of the other guides, would just send down a vibration of peace and understanding to Hallie, and to David too, because he certainly needed it as much as she did.

They were all busy now listening to Catherine, cleaning up the floor, and getting the ferns back into their pot. It was probably as good a chance as I would have that afternoon, and I took it, limping unobtrusively out of the room. My back really hurt now, and my heart was operating overtime. Probably shock from the fall, not anticipation, I decided – though as I climbed the stairs I had a quick vision of Verena lying on her bed in a trance, half or less than half dressed in a loose robe.

When I got to her room I didn't even knock; I was afraid she might tell me to go away.

'Hi, it's Roger.' I pushed the door open. Verena wasn't lying on her bed; there was no bed to lie on. Like the parlour downstairs, her room had been stripped of organic materials. The curtains, the braided rugs, and most of the furniture were gone. There was a mattress on the floor against one wall, covered with a couple of blankets, and two folding aluminium chairs; nothing else.

Verena was sitting in one of the chairs, looking out the window. It had stopped snowing, but was still overcast. The pale, hard winter daylight emphasized the pale polish of her skin, the heavy dark-lashed eyes. She looked beautiful but unreal, like a figure in the window of an expensive Fifth Avenue store, frozen in sophisticated fatigue.

'Roger.' She repeated the word like someone memorizing a foreign language, automatically.

'I only wanted to see you for a minute,' I apologized. I shut the door, but came no farther into the room, to show that my intrusion was minimal. 'I know you're tired.'

'Tired?' This, too, was a foreign word.

'I mean, you must want to rest before tonight, and meditate. You should rest. And you ought to eat something.' After lunch, Elsie had brought Verena's tray down untouched.

'I don't feel the need of physical food any more.' Verena answered me as if I were her aunt, with an air of worn reiteration, then smiled faintly. 'My strength is kept up by other means.' She raised her eyes briefly to the ceiling. 'Now that I'm in constant relation with Ro and the others, as they come nearer and nearer to us, I'm nourished continually in

188

the spirit.' She focused on me, and first a frown, then a look of encouragement appeared on her face.

'It's what we all could be, Roger; you too, if you only tried!' she exclaimed. 'If you would only open your mind and heart to the power that's being sent out to you now, every moment; twenty-four hours a day! This is just the beginning for us. I know that now.' Verena rose, and began to walk back and forth in the empty room as she spoke, her eyes dilated, her bush of dark hair lit at the edges from the window behind her.

'Soon, very soon, so many wonderful things are going to be revealed and shown to us,' she went on, fully into her inspirational sing-song. 'And then all of us, even those that sometimes doubt, Roger, and aren't sure of their spiritual strength, are going to be great leaders; we're going to go forth then, spreading truth and healing light all over this planet. That's what Ro has planned for us, what he's been telling us from the beginning, that through us this earth is going to be saved and brought out of its awful pain and darkness. Isn't that right?'

'That's right,' I repeated feebly, leaning against the door to ease my back.

Verena paused. 'You've brought some trouble with you,' she said, and looked hard at me. 'You're in bodily pain, too.'

'Yes, I fell off a table downstairs just now, when I was helping put up some plants. I hurt my back.'

'I'll ask for a healing. But that's not all of it.' She came nearer and concentrated on me even more intently, her head forwards. 'You've got some question in your mind that you want the answer to, but' – she frowned – 'it's not the right one you should be asking. Do you understand me?'

'I don't know. Not exactly.'

'We'll have to get guidance on it. But let's fix up your back first.'

I was still standing against the door; partly to take the strain off my back and partly to demonstrate to both of us

189

that I was hardly there at all, or anyhow, leaving very soon. Verena came over to me.

'Where does it hurt?'

'Here, mostly.'

'There?'

'A little lower. Ow.' Though she was standing so close, Verena had hardly touched me; I winced more from the realization that, in spite of my good intentions, here we were again.

'Yes, I sense it. Pull up your shirt and sweater, Roger, and I'll see what I can feel,' she added, beginning to help me do so. 'That's right.'

Verena put her cool hand on the small of my back, and looked into my eyes with great seriousness. 'Um-hm,' she murmured. 'There's a knotted sensation there. But it's not too bad. Spreads down here a little, too. Way down here, even. You feel it?'

'Um.' I certainly felt it.

'All right. Close your eyes and pray silently, and I'll ask for a healing. There's so much spirit force concentrated on this house now, it ought to be easy.'

Verena was facing me now. She put her arms round me and began to murmur under her breath and rub my lower back gently with both hands. Rationalization set in: suppose I did grab her, that seemed to be what she wanted, so it would be just non-directive; McMann would realize — The hell he would. He would think I was trying to ruin the study. According to his theory, it was Verena's dammed-up sexual energy that had produced Varna; if it were released, Ro and the rest of them would probably scatter like fog before a wind, and there would never be any Coming.

'I feel better, thanks,' I said, pulling away with determination.

Verena opened her thick-lashed eyes, incredibly large at this distance. 'Yes, the waves are beginning to work. Now —'

'I'm all right, really.' I tucked my shirt back in.

'But —'

'I didn't come here about that anyhow, there's something I wanted to tell you.' I hurried on before my resolution could spoil. 'I went out to the grocery store this morning, to get some things Elsie needed for lunch, and I ran into Ken there.'

'Ken?'

'Yes, he's been trying to get in touch with you.' As I spoke, I realized that this was important information. Verena's mouth remained open; her arms fell to her sides.

'Ken! . . . He wants to come back to us?'

'He wants to see you.'

I wasn't sure Verena got the distinction; she sighed with relief and joy, a great gasp of breath.

'Oh, I'm glad.' She began to walk about the room; first to the window, where she stared out as if she might see the grocery and Ken around the corner and about ten blocks away. 'I'm so glad! His spirit is turning towards the truth again, the way Ro said it would.' She looked up at the ceiling. 'I should have had more faith.' She was speaking at, but not really to me now. 'You know, Ken has such a strong impulse to the light. He has a natural gift for learning, and a great intelligence and analytic power. Oh, wouldn't it be wonderful to have him with us tonight! What did he say to you, is he coming here?'

I had distracted her from myself, all right, but instead of being pleased, I was irritated.

'I don't know about that,' I said flatly. 'He just said he wanted to see you, he's been trying —'

'He wants to see me.' Verena gave me her Burne-Jones smile, but almost immediately shifted it upwards. 'Oh Ro,' she cried, 'I thank you for this blessing! I thank you!' She seemed to wobble as if about to faint; then I realized she was kneeling down. 'Oh Ro, my dear guide,' she continued, addressing the light fixture (two bulbs in frosted-glass shades sprouting from an inverted brass saucer). 'You know how I have prayed for this, that you might send waves of truth to Ken's spirit, so that his heart should be touched and he should return to us.'

191

Verena's expression, as she knelt in her bathrobe on the circle of dusty unvarnished boards where a rug had been taken up, should have touched my heart. Instead, it made me jealous and angry. That such a look should be called up by the thought of a clumsy, ordinary, fourth-rate college sophomore like Ken. . . .

'All of us are grateful. Our souls are full of thankfulness for this mercy,' Verena went on, glancing at me. I wondered if she expected me to kneel too. 'We send up our prayers of thanksgiving to you and to the Spirit of Light.' Verena bowed her head and began to repeat one of their prayers. 'Come on, Roger,' she whispered, and though still standing, I joined in half-heartedly.

I left Verena's room no easier in mind than I had entered it. My question was answered: Elsie had been concealing Ken's calls and visits, and she would probably go on doing so. She must have lied to McMann, too, telling him Verena didn't want to see anybody. The problem was, non-directively speaking, what were we supposed to do about it? It was getting too complicated for me: I decided I would have to ask McMann.

I went downstairs, where the women were still cleaning the room and arranging plants, and through the kitchen to the cellar. Rufus, Ed Novar, and McMann were there making non-organic chairs for the meeting that evening. Rufus and McMann were talking cheerfully while they sawed and nailed pieces of plastic; Ed was silently hammering metal rods in a vise. Two of their finished constructions stood near by: a three-legged iron stool which looked as if it had once held charcoal for a barbecue, and a kind of sparkling pink plastic washbasin on feet.

'Hey, Tom,' I said quickly, before I could be invited to demonstrate my low manual dexterity again. 'Like to speak to you.'

'Okay, go ahead.'

I gestured with my head towards the stairs. McMann

frowned. Manifesting our private connection in public was against the rules. I frowned back.

'Well.' He laid his saw down. 'Back in a sec, Ed.'

Since there was no other place to go, I stopped in the kitchen, eased the cellar door shut, and closed the swing-door to the dining-room.

'Yes?' McMann folded his arms and leaned against a cupboard.

'Listen, I saw Ken at the grocery. He said he'd been round to the house earlier today.'

'Oh, yeah? Well, you can tell me about it later. It doesn't look good, us talking together like this.' McMann began to move away; I put out a hand to stop him.

'He said he's been trying to get in touch with Verena, but Elsie said she didn't want to see him.'

'I already told you that,' McMann said impatiently.

'Yes, but I saw Verena, just now, and when I mentioned Ken was looking for her, she was delighted.' McMann said nothing, but his face altered, as if all the muscles had been pulled tight from inside. 'Her idea is that he wants to rejoin the group. I don't think there's much chance of that.'

'No.' We were both speaking in whispers now so as not to be overheard in the parlour.

'He was very aggressive, suspicious. But listen. Verena didn't know he'd ever tried to reach her. Elsie's been keeping it from her.'

'What d'you know? Just as well, though. Let him in now, he'd really mess up the situation.'

'He'd provide another variable.' I said it for the argument mostly.

'One type of variable at a time.'

'Why?'

'Why? For Jesus' sake,' McMann wheezed under his breath. 'This is an experimental situation.' I nodded. 'It's like in a lab, if you're testing your animals on typhus bacteria, you got to exclude tuberculosis. Otherwise you don't know what your results mean. You're supposed to be bright enough to see that.'

'Yeah; I see.' A group of vague, half-formed questions crowded into my mind; I sent them all out again except one.

'It was Elsie told you Verena didn't want to see anyone, then.' I wasn't accusing McMann but supplying his excuse.

'That's right.' He started towards the cellar, then stopped. 'You think Ken's going to try to make contact again?'

'I don't think he'll be back today. I told him it was no use.' It struck me that I had lied to Ken myself, though unwittingly.

'Good work.'

'Tomorrow, maybe.'

'I don't want him here tomorrow. I want the group isolated then. And not next week either, if possible.'

'I got the feeling he'll be back tomorrow, or at least by Monday. I'm not sure, though. He stayed away a couple of weeks last time.'

'A couple of weeks would do. Or make it three. After Christmas he can argue with the group and screw Verena all he likes, I don't give a damn.'

'But when he does come,' I continued, trying to erase the image this called up, and speak in a low, reasonable voice which would not carry. 'If he does come now, I don't see how we can avoid letting him in.'

'That's easy. Don't open the door.'

'I mean, I don't see how we can justify it. Non-directively —'

'Non-directively, we're following Elsie's instructions, that's all.' He smiled, a little restlessly, and moved towards the cellar.

'But that doesn't hold for me. Verena's told me she wants to see him. I don't know if —'

'For Christ's sake, Rog!' McMann interrupted. 'Don't fuss about it like that. Don't quibble. If your Old Testament conscience is bothering you about this petty detail, go talk to Elsie yourself. She'll tell you to keep strangers out of the house. She's already told most of the group members the same.'

I don't know if it was just irritation at McMann's crack; or whether I was so aware of wanting to get rid of Ken myself that I was bending over backwards to be fair – anyhow, I continued:

'Yes, but I don't think —'

'Listen, I haven't got the time to argue about it. I'm running a study.' McMann grinned, but his whisper was like the edge of a saw. 'If you let that little punk in here to ruin it, I'll break every bone in his body. Okay?'

'Well . . . Okay, boss.'

'That's better.' He laughed out loud. Since we had both been speaking under our breath, it sounded like an explosion. 'Now let's get back to work, huh?'

14

The climactic meeting of the Truth Seekers began that evening at sunset: 4.52 p.m. The time was determined by consulting the *Atwell Sun–Advertiser*, not the sky: it had been clouded over all day. Fine gusts of snow still were blowing down through the air, as if someone were shaking an almost empty salt-cellar.

We gathered in the dim parlour, taking our usual places, but on the new non-organic furniture. Mine was a waste-basket which had been turned upside down and topped with a piece of speckled plastic. The only light in the room now came from the three-branched ceiling fixture. Beneath it, the bowl of ferns swayed slightly but continuously in an invisible air current. Its overlapping triple shadow, like that of some feathery octopus, slid back and forth on the floor-boards.

Elsie opened the meeting in second gear, led us through two hymns, and went into a long introductory speech of which I don't remember much; McMann was taking it down while I recorded postures. She had a lot to say about the significance of the occasion, and the necessity of our getting into the right frame of mind for it. If there was even one among us whose soul was still darkened with material greed and doubts, she warned us, it might set obstacles in the way of the Coming. Our guides were near to us now, very near; but passing though the thick layers of spiritual fog next to the earth was the hardest part of their journey. It was only by our all working together, keeping our thoughts pure and concentrating our total mental power, that we could clear them a pathway.

Setting up an alibi ahead of time, I remember thinking. McMann was right; our theory was going to be proved.

Yes, but which one of us was Elsie planning to blame when the Varnians didn't come? Whose doubts would she say had stood between the Seekers and their spiritual guides?

Well, there was one person in the room who participated less than the rest, and knew fewer prayers and lessons by heart; whose expressions of faith were least convincing; who had not so long ago rejected Elsie's offer of advice and counsel.

I looked round the parlour. Over the past weeks I had become habituated to these people, so that though I noted their words and motions in detail, I did not really see them. I saw them now: a group of oddly dressed provincial fanatics sitting in an empty, ill-lit room on an early winter evening. Ed Novar, silent as usual, in his paint-spotted pants and shiny wading boots; Catherine Vanting, tall, pale and bony, her hands knotted into fists on her knees, waiting for a telegram from her dead parents; Bill Freeplatzer, a plump little man in a nylon shirt, leaning forward with a fixed stare; his wife next to him, her head sagging against the wall-paper and a dreamy glaze over her eyes. Peggy; Milly Munger; Rufus. Finally I looked back at Elsie Novar. Her Orlon dress had slid off one freckled shoulder, and she was explaining about positive neutronic waves and the purity of the soul.

They were all waiting for something they had been promised over and over again, which they wanted very much, and for the sake of which they had undergone discomfort, isolation, and social ridicule. When the Varnians didn't arrive, how would they react? According to McMann's projection, they wouldn't give up or disband but would work out some explanation.

Suppose Elsie were to convince them that one member of the group was responsible for their disappointment? Wasn't it possible that they would turn on this person and attack him? I could imagine Bill, Rufus and Ed Novar (in his wading boots) holding me down on the parlour floor, under the swinging shadows of the ferns, while Elsie, half dressed, struck me methodically with some blunt non-organic instrument, and the others joined in a hymn, perhaps 'Nearer My God to Thee'.

I was roused from these fantasies by a real hymn. Elsie had finished her speech, and it was time for Verena to come down to us.

'Light be about you!' Framed in the hall entrance, against a background of stacked chairs, she suddenly materialized, looking less like a real person than one of those larger-than-life cardboard cut-outs you see in movie-theatre lobbies. She could have been set up to advertise some Biblical epic, with that dark mass of hair falling below her shoulders, moist dark eyes and soft open mouth, and lavender technicolour robe, which had just the artificial hue and shimmery texture of costumes in such films.

'In the Eternal Mind.' The Seekers responded in unison.

Verena crossed the room, her robe brushing the floor. She was wearing green plastic beach-sandals. Reaching her chair, she turned and smiled slowly round, from Elsie on her right to Catherine at her left; and then past Catherine, out the window.

'Friends and Seekers of Truth!' Her voice was strong, full of resonance. 'We are met together here for the highest purpose of Light. For now Sol is centred in the Yura field, as we have learned, and tonight is the time of the Whole Lune. Even now our Earth is rotating through the spaces of the universe, towards the darkness oppositing, as we have learned and been told. The time has almost come.' Verena lowered her voice on these last words, but kept the hum in it going, like an electrical current. 'And now we are met here together to welcome our guides and teachers to this Earth. We have been working, we have been praying, we have been meditating, for days, weeks, months, to prepare ourselves for this great time. And now as our guides approach ever nearer to us through our atmosphere, we are gathered here, so that we may work together to assist their Coming in every possible way.'

198

Again Verena looked over to her left, towards the porch window: four rectangles of greyish obscurity, darkening fast, in which the light across the street picked out a curb heaped with snow, a disappearing fence, the scarred side of a tree.

'Oh, the windows,' Elsie exclaimed. 'You want me to put the shades back up? They're out in the pantry cupboard.' She rose, but Verena gestured her down again, as if she were pushing back water.

'No, keep still. We must set no material barriers between ourselves and our guides. Let this room be open and free to the universe tonight, so that all the positive forces of light may flow towards us!' Smiling, Verena flung her arms out as if welcoming a multitude.

Some of the Seekers echoed her with similar smiles; but a few looked apprehensive. Before this, the shades had always been drawn down at meetings.

'We need have no fears tonight,' Verena announced. 'Only good vibrational forces and beings of light can enter here now. Right now, this house, this whole city even, is in the centre of a positive electrical field of tremendous, incredible strength. All dark things and confusion are cast far away, and a great protection of peace and light is over us.' She looked round, checking the expressions of her congregation.

'That's right. We must all relax now and cast any foolish worries we have out of our minds. We've got to put all our individual problems and questions aside now, and clear our brain cells of every material and personal idea, so that nothing remains but the teachings of our guides, and our strong will and desire that they should come ever nearer and nearer to us.'

She seated herself, spreading her robe on either side of the folding metal chair as if it were a throne. 'Oh yes, that's right,' she said. 'Already I can feel the currents of light and power beginning to circulate through this room faster and stronger. Yes! Now, if you'll all concentrate your minds to

199

preserve this flow, I'll try to get a Message for us.' She shut her eyes and laid her hand on the table.

There were to be many messages from Ro that night. Of this first one, I remember only the end:

ALL PEACE HERE MOVING TTOWARD ALL LIGHT AIR FORSES CONCENTRATEDD HERE AROUD   OPPOSITING EARTH WATER FORCE EXPLOSIONZ CYCLONES ON DARKNESS CITIESS

Verena read it out in a voice quivering with awe and surprise. Oh, it was clear what was happening now, she said. We should have been prepared for this. As a result of the approach of the Varnians, all the beneficent forces of the earth had been gathered, by electro-magnetic attraction, on this side of the planet, centering above Sophis. All the good elementals (for there were good elementals as well as bad) had been drawn towards West Hawthorne Street, round which they were rotating in a counter-clockwise, or anti-cyclonic, direction. At the same time, unfortunately but necessarily, there was a corresponding concentration of darkness and confusion on the opposite side of the globe. All the wrong sort of elementals were gathered there, whizzing around clockwise, or cyclonically, creating cyclones. And not only cyclones but hurricanes, tornadoes, and blizzards were to be expected there, and every kind of calamity, great and small: explosions, earthquakes, revolutions, plagues of insects, floods, automobile and aeroplane accidents, typhoid and flu. It was too bad, but nothing much could be done about it; for the protective rays from Varna, which usually shone everywhere equally, were now blocked by the atomic mass of the earth. It was possible, Verena predicted, that many parts of South America would be totally devastated.

Bill Freeplatzer objected that if you dug a hole straight through the earth from Sophis, you would not come out in South America, but somewhere under the Pacific Ocean. That was true, Verena admitted sweetly, but the Pacific Ocean was now lit by our sun, we must remember. That, and the tidal influence of the moon, explained the diversion and central concentration of dark forces somewhere in this hemisphere.

The reception and elucidation of Ro's first Message took over an hour. Rufus related it to his store of popular-science data, Sissy to her spirit picture, and nearly everyone else had some question or comment. The idea that wholesale disaster was about to strike some other part of the world seemed to put them all in a state of happy excitement.

It was after seven o'clock now. No hour had been set for the Coming, though Ro said they were 'very near'. I was starting to feel hungry. I noticed Ed Novar and Milly, too, looking now and then in the direction of the kitchen, where Elsie had prepared an elaborate non-organic supper, mostly coloured Jello moulds decorated with fruit and vegetable slices. Since the guides were known to exist largely or wholly upon spiritual food, it was unclear whether they were expected to eat the Jello or simply admire it as art work.

Verena, on the other hand, kept looking towards the window. I finally realized why: she was waiting for Ken. When the Varnians arrived, she wanted him to be there. Presumably she would hold off the Coming until at least nine or ten o'clock in the hope that he would appear. We were probably in for a long meeting, I thought; I had no idea then how long.

During the next couple of hours we sang all the hymns we knew, we meditated, we recited in unison. There was a long question period, and a short speech by Bill on metaphysics. Verena kept looking out the window. At one point, Elsie and Peggy served glasses of Pepsi-Cola and two small, salty crackers apiece.

At about nine-thirty, Verena went into trance again and received another Message. The Varnians, travelling in their extra-terrestrial space vessel, had reached the outer layer of our atmosphere, and were now circling directly over New York State, like a plane high above a landing field, with their sensitive navigational instruments fixed upon the

201

beam of spiritual desire which we were projecting up towards them.

But our signal wasn't strong enough yet to guide them straight down. It was blocked and diffused by having to pass through the house: through the plaster ceiling and organic floorboards, the upstairs furniture, the attic insulation, and the shingles. What Ro wanted us to do now was go outside and send up our signal direct, through the atmosphere.

'Come!' Verena rose to her feet (looking out the window again). 'Let us go and do the will of our teachers and guides.'

We stood up, some of us a little stiff from sitting so long on metal chairs. Led by Verena, we proceeded through the hall and front door.

It was cold out there, and dark. The ground by the porch was layered with drifts of snow. Verena looked along West Hawthorne Street, and then up at the trees by the sidewalk, which blocked most of the sky.

'Come.' She led us along the path to the driveway, and round by the garage to the backyard, where the sky was less obstructed by organic growths. She walked to the centre of the yard, followed by the rest of the group, and stopped.

'Dear friends and Seekers of Truth!' She raised one arm. 'Let us form a perfect circle. Join your hands, and lift your eyes and your spirits towards the sky! Let your souls reach out and up to our guides above us.'

In the cold obscurity of the backyard, the Seekers moved into a ring. Peggy took one of my hands: her fingers were damp with excitement, her palm hot. Catherine Vanting's hand, on my other side, was cold and dry, but just as tense.

'Let us send up a message of silent welcome with all our hearts, with all the power of our souls!' Verena said.

I was beginning to shiver already, but no one else seemed to notice that we were outside without wraps on a winter night. Verena, for instance, had nothing on but a bathrobe and a pair of plastic sandals. The drifts on the ground swallowed these up completely, so that she might just as well have been standing in the snow barefoot.

202

'Roger.' Verena spoke across the circle suddenly, in an intense whisper. 'You must look up, Roger, you must not cast your eyes and your thoughts down.' I raised my head. 'That's better.'

Bare treetops, the dark bulk of the house on my left, an irregular area of heavy clouded night sky; that was about all I could see with my chin up. The overcast was too thick for the stars or the whole Lune to be visible.

'Let us unite our vibrations now, and recite the Invocation. And as we say these words, let us direct our thoughts wholly to our guides overhead. Oh Spirit of Light —'

'Oh Spirit of Light, within the Mind of God,' the other voices joined in:

> *Let Light stream forth into the minds of men*
> *Let Thy Light descend on Earth.*
>
> *Oh Spirit of Power within the Will of God*
> *Let Power destroy the wrongful works of men*
> *Let Thy Will be done on Earth.*
>
> *Oh Spirit of Love within the Heart of God*
> *Let Love renew within the hearts of men*
> *Let Thy Love descend on Earth.*
>
> *Let Light and Power and Love fulfil the Plan on Earth.*

I mumbled the phrases automatically, swallowing silently whenever I came to the word 'God'. The Invocation had been repeated so often lately that even I knew it by heart. Though dictated by Ro of Varna, it was really an adaptation of one of the prayers used at the Spiritualist church in Atwell, which Milly and Catherine had attended, and to which Elsie had taken Verena.

The blurred echoes of the last word ('Earth') lapsed, and we stood silent in the backyard. I could hear the Seekers breathing and shifting position, the smaller branches of the trees next door creaking as the wind pushed against them, and a car accelerating on the other side of the block.

Somebody coughed; another sneezed. Ed Novar, on my left beyond Peggy, stamped his rubber boots in the dark snow.

Five minutes passed; ten; maybe more. My hands were cramped from holding those of my neighbours, and my feet growing numb, by the time Verena spoke again.

'It is well!' Her voice rang out softly, full of confidence. 'Our signal has been received; our guides are coming down to us. Now let us go in.'

In single file, we tramped back round the house through the snow. McMann and I were last.

'This is it, Rog, this is it,' he whispered, turning to me as we crunched over the frozen gravel of the driveway. 'You can really feel the group will to believe now, can't you?' I nodded. We had stopped by the walk, and a street lamp lit his large, confident features.

'They believe, all right.'

'They're completely isolated. Completely unaffected by reality. Oh boy, we've got it this time.'

'I think we've got it.' I felt encouraged, even excited.

It was true that the group seemed to be united in its belief. As we came into the light of the parlour, shaking snow from our shoes, each face wore an expression of joy and exaltation. The Seekers had waited outside in the cold for half an hour, and nothing had Come. But there was not a word of complaint, even from Catherine, who usually had a morbid fear of cold air and damp.

It was now about ten-thirty. Verena, from the look of her as she took her seat again, would have led the group straight into another session of meditation or singing. But when Elsie suggested that we have an intermission, she agreed, with the sweetness of someone making a concession to impatient children.

I took my turn along with the others going upstairs to 'wash my hands'. As soon as I got the door locked behind me I pulled off my wet, muddy galoshes and then my socks, which had somehow got wet too. Flushing the toilet first to cover the noise, I ran hot water into the tub. Then, balanced uncomfortably on the edge (it was an old-fashioned iron tub with a narrow curved rim and claw feet, probably another elemental), I soaked my numbed feet while recording as much as I could remember of the events of the past few hours.

When I came down, Elsie was passing out more cold, sticky-sweet soda, and some small, brittle health crackers. I had hung my socks to dry on a pipe behind the bathtub, and put my galoshes back on, and I could feel the chill up my legs.

'Let us sing together again,' Verena said. 'We'll start with "Voices Come". Aunt Elsie?'

Elsie went into the dining-room and sat down at the piano, and the meeting began again. Again the Seekers sang hymns, recited prayers, and discussed their imaginary cosmology. There was an artificial air to it now; as of people passing the time politely before the party started. It passed more and more slowly. Verena was still turning to look out of the window, but less often. It seemed obvious now that Ken would not come.

It was Bill, with his bureaucrat's sense of schedule, who first suggested that our teachers and guides would probably reach Earth at midnight, when New York State was exactly 'oppositing' to Sol. This would be the most favourable moment, because of the nature of our sun. As Zo, a Varnian scientist, had told us, Sol was a very young star, and though full of potentially health-giving light and heat emanations, rather erratic. The sun that shone on Varna was mature, full-grown; ours was comparatively adolescent. It still had spots, and sent out irregular, careless bursts of energy which might disrupt an electrically sensitive operation like the Coming.

Once the idea of midnight was proposed, it seemed obvious. The by now slightly wearied spirits of the group revived noticeably. Postures straightened on my diagrams; voices picked up colour. At half past eleven Verena went into a trance for the third time, and received what seemed a quite unambiguous, if slightly scrambled, Message:

REPROACHING NEAR DEARER NEARER TOOTO
LIGHT LOVED SEEKERS AWAITITING IN CLARITY
LIGHT COMINGG WITHOUTSIDE

Again we rose, and followed Verena into the yard. I
wondered as we went out whether it was respect for the
Varnians, or just a class custom, not using the back door
when guests were present. It was about my last sociological
thought of the day. For the next fifteen minutes, I was
occupied with material things. Suddenly all my physical dis-
comforts seemed to have reached the point where they
couldn't be ignored: my head, still aching where the chandelier had struck it; my thumb mashed by the sofa; my
wrenched back; and most of all my feet, numb inside the icy
wetness of my leaky galoshes.

But as midnight approached, and the Seekers sang more
loudly, and recited their prayers in tones of ever-increasing
excitement, joy, and hope, I forgot my bodily condition, and
joined in as if I were really one of them. 'Open my eyes,
illumine me, Spirit divine!' I heard myself chanting in unison
with the rest, as loud as the rest.

Even when we were silent, the effect continued. It was
without effort, now, that I kept my head tilted back, staring
into the obscure air above Sophis, and seeing every shift in
the low cloud cover as the opening through which a 'vessel of
light' might burst. It was a strange state of mind: I still knew
rationally that the Varnians weren't coming, since they didn't
exist; but I felt, if only through empathy, the emotions appropriate to such an event, and the intense pressure of the group
will that it should happen. My heart was beating hard.

It was four minutes to twelve, Bill announced in a radio
newscast voice; three minutes; two minutes; one.

Above the trees to my right the clouds bulged and moved
oddly. What if the Seekers were right, after all? We stood in
a circle in the dark, silently waiting. The pressure of my
neighbours' hands on mine, especially Rufus's on my left,
was painfully intense.

Although no one moved or spoke, it gradually, first by seconds and then by minutes, became apparent that midnight was past. It must have been about a quarter after twelve, though, before Verena broke our silence.

'Let us say the Invocation. Oh Spirit of Light —' Her voice was much louder than before, but thinner. It sounded worn out, as if she were shouting across a long distance, and had been doing it a long while. The other group members joined in, calling up through the clouds in sharp, echoing voices. They would certainly be heard by anyone out walking late on West Hawthorne Street, and very likely in the houses next door and across the yard.

For a moment, I expected a neighbourhood disturbance: opposition from men in pyjamas hurrying out of their homes; calls to the police. But no window was raised; no one, human or divine, appeared.

At twelve-thirty Verena led the Seekers back into the house. They filed into the parlour and took their seats in a stunned, automatic way, speaking to one another in lowered voices.

'I'm afraid something's gone wrong,' Catherine said to Milly. 'I'm concerned there's some dark force keeping our guides back from us.'

'We've got to have faith, Catherine.' Milly didn't sound very sure of it. 'Our guides said they're coming; well, I guess that means they're coming, doesn't it?'

'They could be just delayed,' Bill suggested.

'Friends and Seekers of Truth.' Verena sounded tired, but not discouraged. 'I know our teachers are trying to communicate with us now. They have something important to tell us. I want to ask you all to settle and compose yourselves, and make your minds a pathway for spiritual light, so that their words may reach through to us.'

The Message this time was slow in coming. Verena sat back in the folding chair; her head sagged towards one shoulder, uncomfortably unsupported; the heavy loose hair seemed to drag it down farther. She was very pale in the overlapping low-wattage light, and her sculpturally round shut eyelids, with their heavy lashes, seemed to be set in depressions of bluish flesh; her lips had a strange dark purplish tone. Suddenly her ethereal beauty looked worn thin, half conscious. The complicated ugly shadows of the pot of ferns slid over the skirt of her robe, the thin hand spread on her lap, and the other one clenched on the table, waiting for Ro to take hold of it. The shadows lapped darker at her bare white feet in the plastic sandals. How long had it been since she had slept, or eaten?

Finally, almost invisibly at first, the hand attached to Verena's left arm twitched, and took a better grip on the yellow pencil. Slowly, as if it also were horribly tired, it began to move across the paper, with a peculiar lame, dragging gait; still a white toad, but one with a mortal wound.

It wrote one or two characters at a time, with extensive pauses in between. Once or twice it seemed to pick up speed, but it soon faltered more and more; it gave a nervous jerk, then slumped over sideways and lay on its back, still holding the pencil. It was not dead yet, though. The five legs twitched on spasmodically, still writing their message, but now on the air. Everyone saw it; but none of the Seekers, not even Elsie, dared to speak, or move the hand back into its right position.

Soon the hand vibrated more slowly; it was as if the current first flickered, and then went out. It stopped moving altogether and dropped its pencil, which rolled noisily along the metal table and fell to the floor in the shadows. Verena sat on in the same position, her head fallen over sideways, like the picture of a hanging which used to frighten me in our family encyclopaedia.

'Verena,' her aunt called. 'There's a Message. Verena.' She did not move. 'Verena!'

Verena raised her head, opened her eyes, stared round at us, and finally picked up the paper, reading to herself while we watched.

'Oh, friends and seekers of truth!' she exclaimed at last in a thin, forced voice. 'This is a wonderful Message that has

208

come to us now, a truly wonderful Message. Oh, when you hear this, then you will truly realize what Ro and our other beloved guides are doing for us!' Verena spread her hands, then clasped them together as she spoke, crushing the Message into a ball. It was an unprecedented action, for though she did not always read the Varnians' communications out in full, especially if they were very long, they were always carefully preserved for later study. But the crumpling of the paper was so naturally done, and she maintained her flow of oratory so well, that I doubt if anyone who was not recording posture changes would have noticed.

'Our teachers and guides are near to us now, so near!' Verena's voice was almost firm again, her eyes shining. 'They have received our signal. They have penetrated through all but the lowest layers of our atmosphere, and are hovering in their vessel of light right above us, yes, directly over this house, in the beam of electrical and spiritual energy which we are sending up to them.

'But oh, my friends! What lies ahead of them now is the hardest part of their travel, much harder than crossing all the millions of miles of space between Varna and Sol-III. Oh, so much harder.'

Her voice trembling with emotion, Verena explained that for our guides, those refined and immortal beings, spirits who had transcended the material flesh and were clothed only in pure light vibrations, even moving through the outer layers of our atmosphere was like flying through water. The middle layers, for them, were like syrup; though to their supernal vision, of course, this syrup was transparent. To reach what we thought of as the surface of this planet, the Varnians' spaceship would have to pass through a material substance which to them was as thick and resistant as cereal, or mashed potatoes, to us. If we could imagine driving a car five miles through mashed potatoes, Verena told us, we would have some idea of the task that now lay ahead of our guides as they attempted to draw near to West Hawthorne Street.

'Oh, dear friends,' Verena cried, leaning forward. 'It's so

209

wonderful to think what our guides are doing for us now, that I know all our souls are brimming and overflowing with gratitude to realize it. And I know we're not going to stop now, not for one second are we going to stop sending up our prayers and desires to make a passageway for them to come to us! Isn't that so?'

It was now after 1 a.m. The Seekers of Truth had been waiting for over eight hours for something which had not happened. But as with one voice they answered her: 'Yes, that's so.'

Verena's expression changed from simple intensity to a half smile of hectic triumph. She was not the only one: nearby, Tom McMann grinned at me triumphantly, and I grinned back. Right before our eyes, our theory was being made flesh.

'Then let us go out to them now!' Verena exclaimed. She stood up.

For the third time, the Seekers trailed out in procession to the backyard, and formed a circle. It seemed very much colder now, well below freezing. Either the temperature had fallen rapidly; or, because of fatigue, I felt it more. It was darker as well. The neighbouring houses had all put off their lights, and only the blur of a street lamp was visible through the trees.

'Let us sing together now,' Verena proposed in a tense, ringing alto. 'Let's sing "Coming Nearer".'

> *It's coming, coming nearer,*
> *The lovely land unseen.*

The Seekers all took it up; they knew this one by heart. But outdoors, without the support of Elsie's piano, the voices sounded faint and thin; the cold, slight wind blew them off sideways.

> *Oh, yes! It's coming nearer,*
> *Nearer,*
> *Nearer.*

I was beginning to feel both generally and specifically terrible: hungry, tired, shivering cold, with wet freezing feet and my head and back aching. But that didn't matter, I told myself. What counted was that the Sophis study was working out. McMann and I were going to be proved right: the Seekers would absorb this night's events into their system without a break. At least I hoped so. Because if we turned out to be wrong, what would happen to Verena? What would she do, what would any of them do, if Ro didn't come? If? There was no *if*, there was only *when*.

'The light!' she suddenly cried out. 'Look, the light, over there!'

It was almost too dark to see where her hand was pointing, to one corner of the backyard where, above and behind the trees, there was a reddish glow on the sky.

'They're Coming!' Peggy shouted. 'They're Coming to us!'

'It's growing stronger,' Verena said.

'Yes!' Bill wheezed, breaking into a cough.

'Yes, the light's growing stronger!'

'Brighter!' Sissy screamed, squeezing my hand.

'Stronger and brighter – they're Coming!'

'Shh!' Verena commanded. 'Shhh!'

There was a tense silence. I could see little change in the glow to the south-east, which I realized was probably the reflection of the lights of downtown Sophis on the low-hanging clouds, such as one often sees on such a night. Doubtless it had been there all the time, though only now, when the houses were dark, had it become noticeable. The bulge of light shifted slightly, perhaps, as the clouds shifted over the town, but did not augment.

'Our guides are approaching!' Verena announced shrilly. 'Let us call out to them with all our power. Here we are, here we are! Come to us, come now!'

'Here we are! Us! Are! Come to!'

A confused clamour of voices was raised in the backyard, reaching a crescendo of shouts and then dying off. A minute of silence passed; two; five . . .

211

Finally Verena spoke again. Her voice was lower, but strained with excitement, a kind of subdued scream. 'He is here,' she more or less shrieked under her breath. 'Ro, our beloved teacher and guide, is here, with us now! His light is all around us, he is speaking to us, I hear him! He says —' She paused, as if listening. 'Yes, yes, yes! He says, I Am With You Now. We Are All With And In You Always, For — For Ever. Yes, yes, He says — Yes, he says, I Am Within You! I Am In Man On Earth! Oh Ro, I thank you! Oh, the blessing! Oh, yes, I kneel down and thank you!'

In the half dark, I dimly saw Verena drop to her knees. But the gesture did not stop there; she slid lower, and then still lower, until she was sprawled face down in the churned snow and mud of the backyard. At first we all, I think, assumed she had done it on purpose; we let her lie there for perhaps a full minute, not moving or speaking. Finally Elsie, on her left, bent over.

'Verena? Are you all right?'

There was no reply.

'Verena!'

'What is it? What's happened?' The Seekers broke their circle and gathered closer, around the dark heap on the ground. There was general shouting and confusion.

'Is Ro with us now?'

'What's the matter?'

'What happened? Verena said —'

'Ro came, she said!'

'No, she fainted.'

'Ro spoke to her. I heard it myself, kind of a vibration —'

'Verena —'

'Is she all right?'

'We've got to get her up.' Elsie's voice sounded frightened. 'Tom, help me! Ed, where are you, Ed? Here, you raise her feet up. Come on. This way.'

Together, McMann and Ed Novar lifted the collapsed shape of Verena, and carried her towards the lighted house, with Elsie going on ahead. The rest of us followed after in a crowd, jabbering and exclaiming. I remember that as we reached the front porch, where Elsie was holding the door open, Milly picked up the dragging edge of Verena's robe, now stained with mud and snow, and tucked it over her, covering a white leg bare to the hip.

The Seekers crowded up the steps and into the house behind them, into the parlour among the plastic and metal chairs.

'We'd better take her up to her room,' Elsie decided.

'I'll carry her,' McMann said. 'That's all right, Ed. I can manage.'

'Okay.' Ed Novar let go, and McMann shifted his grip on the mass of inert organic matter and pure fabric, lifting it so that the head and one arm hung over his shoulder. Treading heavily, he carried the load through the group, across the front hall, and up the stairs, followed by Verena's aunt and uncle. Without thinking, I went up after them; so did Milly and Sissy; but as we reached the landing Elsie shut the bedroom door in our faces.

So we came down again, and joined the group members left in the parlour. For the next few minutes, we all behaved like any crowd at a disaster. We milled around, sat down and got up again, went into the hall to look up the stairs at Verena's shut door, and returned. Everyone talked and asked questions; no one answered or listened. Bill insisted over and over again that he knew Verena wasn't 'dead or anything', because he had seen her breathing, while Milly and I kept telling each other or anyone who was standing near by that she had probably collapsed because of starvation and lack of sleep.

Then Ed Novar was heard coming downstairs.

'Verena's okay,' he answered, as the rest of the Seekers hurried to him. 'Yep, doing all right. Just tired out, she was. Elsie told me to say, she'll be down herself in a couple minutes.'

Having delivered his message, Mr Novar went into the parlour and took his usual seat. From the side pocket of his nylon windbreaker he removed a copy of the *Atwell Sun-Advertiser* which had come that afternoon, about ten hours ago. He unfolded it, opened it out, folded it again lengthwise as if he were on a crowded bus, and began to read.

The sense of crisis in the room moderated. I remembered that I was supposed to be a sociologist, and began looking for my notebook. It was getting on for two in the morning now. Some of the Seekers, like Ed Novar, simply sat down and waited for Elsie. Others, as if they had memorized McMann's predictions of their behaviour, started trying to explain and justify the disconfirmation we had received. Sissy began explaining to anyone who would listen that the pink glow in the sky was just the shape of one of her dream pictures, which had shown the symbolic Coming of the Varnians in the spirit. Rufus had some scientific theory which explained everything, while Catherine kept interrupting whenever she could to let us know that her Mother had predicted all these happenings long ago in a message which, if Verena and Elsie had taken it seriously, would have told them exactly what to expect.

But none of these explanations was taken up by anyone else with any enthusiasm, and though Sissy, Rufus, and Catherine continued to offer them round, they did so in a more and more uncertain way, as if they hoped to be convinced themselves. Bill suggested that there must have been a mistake in our lessons somewhere; maybe we had got the date wrong, for instance. Nobody paid him much attention either.

I was listening to all this, and looking vaguely round the room, when I noticed a piece of crumpled yellow paper on the floor of the hall. I went over and picked it up unobtrusively. As I had guessed, it was Verena's last Message, which must have fallen out of the pocket of her robe as she was carried upstairs.

I unfolded the paper and looked at it in the weak overhead hall light. I turned it upside down and tried to read it that way; then I turned it sideways. It was no good, though. The

214

last Message from Ro that I was ever to see, like the first, consisted of meaningless scrawls.

I laid the Message, and my notebook, aside. What I needed was a drink; water at least. I went through the parlour and dining-room to the kitchen. Bill Freeplatzer was there, standing in front of the refrigerator; he started a little as I came in.

'I was just looking at these refreshments Elsie fixed,' he explained. 'Pretty nice, aren't they?'

I agreed.

'It seems a pity our guides could only come to us in the spirit, so they won't be able to partake of them.'

'They wouldn't have, anyhow,' said Milly, who had followed me. 'When you consider our air is like mashed potatoes to them, any kind of food we could prepare on this earth would probably be too heavy. This salad here, it'd most likely be to them like eating rocks or something. I don't know why Elsie made it. Mo told us they don't consume except spiritually after they get their full growth.'

Together, the three of us stared at the nearest moulded salad, a ruby-red scalloped hemisphere like some deep-sea plant or jellyfish. Slices of banana were held in suspension within it; it was decorated with walnuts and whipped cream and rested upon a bed of shredded lettuce. It was just the sort of thing I always pass by with a shudder on the cold table at the faculty club, but at that moment I regarded it with desire. So, obviously, did they.

'It's for those of us here on earth she made these things; isn't that so?'

I agreed, non-directively but with feeling, that it was so, as did Bill. Milly took the plate out of the ice-box and set it on the counter; I found some kitchen spoons in a drawer, and we began to eat. I don't remember any other remark being made until Bill cocked his head at the ceiling, and said, 'Sounds like they're coming down.'

We stopped, listening.

'I guess so.' Milly spooned one more piece of Jello into her

215

mouth, and put her spoon down. I opened the refrigerator, Bill replaced the jellyfish salad, which now looked more like a dividing amoeba, and Milly rinsed our spoons in the sink. Without any further reference to our material greed, we returned to the rest of the group, just in time to see Elsie, followed by McMann, come in.

'Verena is sleeping now,' she announced. 'She was exhausted, that's what it was. She's done so much for all of us, she just wore herself out.' Elsie looked round at the others until they murmured assent and appreciation.

'She said before she dropped off, "Tell them our guides are with us now. They are within us." Isn't that right?' Elsie turned to McMann.

'That's what she said,' he affirmed.

'She wants to be sure we all understand the blessing that has come to us tonight.' Elsie crossed the room and stood in her habitual place, one hand on the back of Verena's empty chair. 'Let us take our seats.'

In a kind of sleep-walking state, I went and sat on my plastic-topped waste-basket. Across the room, McMann grinned at me, still apparently full of energy and interest; Elsie's eyes were bright with determination; but on every other face there was a shell-shocked look – fatigue, discomfort, disappointment.

'Friends and Seekers of Truth,' Elsie began. 'You know this has been an important day in the history of human man on this earth. We've just been present, all of us, we've witnessed the Coming from far across the universe of our blessed teachers from Varna. We've seen how they struggled and exerted to come to us in the material, through the heavy, thick, dirtied air of this world. Well, we tried to help them the best we could, at least most of us did, even up beyond the limit of their strengths.' She raised her eyes towards the ceiling, then looked round the room searchingly. 'But I don't know how it was, the desires of some of us for our guides weren't strong enough, or the thought-waves some of us were sending up were too impure, too full of selfishness and

216

greedy thoughts, we just couldn't make a clear path for them to come all the way this time.' Elsie paused and looked at the Seekers again; none of them met her eyes.

'They got pretty close, though,' she continued. 'Oh yes, thank the Lord, our beloved teachers and guides were down so near to us. Their light shone upon us, yes it did, and their glory was round about us! We saw that with our own eyes.'

There was some response in the Seekers' expressions, but not much.

'Our guides came close to us, and their holy spirit entered into us! It is with us now still. Anyhow, I think each one of us ought to tell what this great Coming has meant to them; how it feels right inside their own beings.' Elsie glanced round the room, but no one volunteered. 'Peggy, why don't you start.'

Peggy, who had been leaning tiredly against the wall, sat up on her kitchen stool. Her long yellow hair was in untidy strings, her non-organic dress crumpled.

'Come on, Peggy,' Elsie half coaxed, half scolded. 'Tell us how the presence of your guides within you feels.'

'Gee, I don't know. I guess I just feel kind of worn out and relaxed. I mean, when we were outside I was all excited and longing for them to Come, but now I'm not.'

'Your spirit is at peace,' Elsie said, 'from the inner presence of your guides. Isn't that right?'

'I guess so,' Peggy agreed without enthusiasm. 'I mostly feel kind of sleepy.' She yawned; Elsie frowned, and looked round the room again. 'Rufus?'

'The inner presence of our guides that have travelled to us across the whole solar system and penetrated into our atmosphere —' Rufus began in a kind of rush, like a student answering a prepared question in class, then faltered. 'Well, I know they must be inside of me, if their electrical waves have made contact inside my brain. I can feel a kind of a humming there, but there aren't any messages coming through yet. I figure the structure of my brain cells has to be

217

altered more before I can really make out what they're saying.'

'You can hear the guides communicating to your individual mind, but you're not developed enough to understand all their language.'

'That's right. Well, right now I don't really hear anything much,' Rufus admitted.

'Not right now, Rufus, but you will.' Though he did not reply, there was doubt on his spotty face. 'Umm. Milly?'

'Huh?' Milly had been dozing; at the sound of her name she half opened her eyes.

'Milly, we want to hear from you what this wonderful new inner light means.' Elsie's spirits were visibly beginning to flag.

'Well, I don't really know.' Milly tried to sit up. 'It's a wonderful thing to have the light within us, but right now it's kind of hard to understand. I feel like I'd lost contact with our guides somehow.'

'That's so,' some of the others murmured; or 'Umhm.'

'You've got to concentrate your forces, Milly. There's a great spiritual power within you, but it can't manifest if you shut it out with doubts.'

'Uh-huh.' Milly yawned. 'It's so late, Elsie.'

'It's past two o'clock.' Catherine said. 'I think we ought to adjourn the meeting.'

'We'll adjourn when it's time,' Elsie said shrilly. 'We've all got to give our testimony first.' She stared at the Seekers. They did not actually oppose her; that is, they did not object or get up to leave, but their expressions were cross and indrawn. They looked, in fact, like a group on the point of breaking up as the result of a severe disconfirmation of their belief system.

Our belief system, too, was being disconfirmed; but I was too tired to care. I looked wearily through my headache across the room at Tom McMann. He was sitting upright, and almost smiling, as if he had not yet realized that everything was going wrong.

'We're going to hear from everyone,' Elsie asserted, in the

218

voice of a tired schoolteacher asking children to recite. 'Hm. Tom? Can you tell us how you feel now that our guides are within your spirit, in all their light and power?'

'I feel that our guides are within my spirit, in all their light and power.' McMann's voice, so much stronger, deeper, and firmer than the fatigued adolescent tones of Rufus and Peggy, Milly's sleepy drawl, or Elsie's shrill whine, practically boomed out across the parlour, making the others look up.

'You felt them entering into it just now, when we were all outside, when we saw the light?'

'That's right,' he agreed. 'We were outside, waiting for the Coming. Then the light appeared above us, and I felt our guides entering into my spirit.'

Written down, that speech might look non-directive, just an echo of Elsie's, but it was nothing of the sort; the group's response proved that. The Seekers were all alert now, watching McMann. I made a warning face at him, but he wasn't looking in my direction.

'You can feel your guides' presence in you now?' Elsie asked eagerly. 'You can hear their words?'

'Yes, I can hear their words,' he asserted. 'I feel their presence, within me.'

'That's wonderful!' Sissy exclaimed.

'Praise be,' Catherine murmured.

Again I tried to signal him to tone it down; by echoing Elsie so affirmatively, he was changing the whole sense of the group. He still paid no attention.

'Blessed be the spirit of Varna!' Elsie said. 'Tom, you are advanced far in the path of learning. I feel the presence of our guides in myself too, but I can't hear their voices clear yet.'

'Tom's intellect is so educated,' Bill put in. 'That's why he hears the guides better, maybe.'

'He's had more practice in using the highest centres of his brain,' Rufus said. 'Isn't that so, Tom?'

'Well, you could say that.' McMann looked down modestly.

'Wait a minute, everybody!' Elsie said. She frowned, considering something, her sharp-fingered small hands working on the back of Verena's metal chair. The Seekers were silent.

'Oh Light of Truth!' Elsie suddenly squeaked. 'Oh pure light of Varna, shine in and around on me, so that I may have a true understanding of the blessing that has come to us this day!' She turned towards McMann, fixing him with her bright mouse eyes, and then back to the whole group.

'Oh, my dear friends!' she cried. 'An illumination of true Light has come to me! I understand now the Message that Ro gave to us through Verena when he was with us outside here. I understand it all. Don't you remember he said to us, "I Am In Man On Earth"? Isn't that so?'

'Yes, that's so,' the Seekers responded. 'That's right!'

'Well, we didn't understand that Message the right way. We thought Ro meant he and our other guides were coming into all our minds, and so when we couldn't hear them any better than before we were discouraged and doubtful. We felt like the Message must've been wrong, or something. Isn't that so?'

'Um, yes.'

'Uh-huh!'

'Yeah, that's true.'

'Well, listen: Ro didn't mean that *at all*. He spoke to us clear, but we didn't understand his words. He meant to say that he was entering into just *one* of us: into the spirit among us most developed to receive him. What he meant to tell us was, I Am In Tom McMann, On Earth!'

15

'I still don't like it,' I said. It was about 3 a.m., and I was walking around the motel room, trying to explain myself to McMann.

'Hm?' McMann grunted and lay back against the padded plastic headboard of his bed. He was drinking beer from a can, and his equilibrium was so good that a vibration of self-doubt went through me. I swallowed and continued.

'It's all wrong, somehow. I think it's been wrong from the beginning. Our being here has made too much difference to the Seekers. Without us, they probably would never have projected anything like the Coming. They didn't really need it. The group was stable; they were perfectly happy meeting once a week to sing hymns and drivel on about astral planes. We were the ones who wanted the Coming, so we could check your theory.'

McMann shook his head, smiling. 'They announced it, not us,' he said. He tilted up the can, swallowed. 'And weren't we right? Not one of them seriously suggested Verena might have made a mistake. Did they?'

'Yes, I mean no, but —' I ran my hands through my hair and turned, facing him. 'But that's what I mean. If we hadn't been there, maybe they would have. You know what Catherine said to me, when we came back into the house that second time? She said, "It means so much to me that an intelligent man like Tom, and you too of course Roger" – that was a second thought though – "still have an unshaken faith. You aren't swayed by the winds of doubt, like Milly."'

'Milly?' McMann blinked a little, and yawned. 'What about Milly? Did she have doubts, then? That's interesting.'

'I don't know,' I said. 'The point I was trying to make —'

'Well, I hope you got it into the record, anyhow.'

'Yes, I made a note —' I dragged my hands up through my hair again. 'Oh, hell!' I began to pace.

'Why don't you sit down, for Christ's sake,' McMann said amicably. 'Have another beer.'

'No thanks. Listen, I mean, if you want to talk about the record. When this study is written up, you know what we'll have to say? "At approximately 2.20 a.m. on December 5, Ro of Varna was accepted by the group as being incarnated in the senior project researcher."'

'You're being naïve again, Roger. You've got to realize this sort of thing is nothing new in the field. Hell, I've got a friend, Burns Walter; maybe you've heard of him. The anthropologist. A whole totem group in Mexico adopted him as their god temporarily. He got his data all the same; better in fact.'

'But this isn't a native tribe,' I argued rather wildly. 'These are American citizens!' McMann burst into guffaws.

'You mean it's against the Constitution? A restriction of their right to life, liberty and the pursuit of happiness? Shit, I've always thought a non-directive investigator would make the ideal deity. A little distant, but so unbiased. Sympathetic to everyone; always ready to listen to you, ready to underline your personal feelings and opinions, and never shoving in demands of his own. Always calm, relaxed, tolerant —' McMann took another swallow of beer. He finished laughing, and smiled calmly and tolerantly at me.

I stared back. It's a sociological truism that you become the role you play, but it's not supposed to happen that fast.

McMann winked. 'Hell,' he added, 'I thought I was doing a pretty good job tonight, along those lines.'

It was true, McMann's behaviour after his metamorphosis into Ro had been a model of non-directive participation. The Seekers, in spite of their fatigue, appeared enthusiastic about this solution to the problem of the Coming, and were obviously looking forward to McMann's guidance in the future.

222

Everyone seemed pleased to be rid of the burden of inner light, and to have their guide visible among them.

'If it wasn't me, it would have been somebody else,' McMann went on easily. 'Once Verena gave out like that, they had to have some source of authority. We knew that months ago.'

'We didn't *know* it; we, I mean you, just theorized it. I mean —' The argument was now back where it had started. 'Don't you see, the whole thing is upside down!'

'Sorry, but I don't. . . . Take it easy, Rog. It's late, and you've had a big day; don't get hysterical. Have some beer.' McMann held a can towards me. 'Come on, you'll feel better.'

'No, thanks.' In the mirror, as I crossed the room, I saw a hysterical lower-middle-class young man with wild hair and a fixed expression. I walked nearer to him and stared into his eyes.

'If you've finished what you wanted to say,' McMann called from behind me, 'let's get some rest. We ought to be back over there early, and it's getting on for four o'clock now.'

I didn't get much rest that night, what was left of it. From 4 a.m. until it began to get light outside I tossed and wriggled, pushed the pillow around looking for a soft place (it was non-organic foam plastic, bouncy and uncomfortable as a beach toy), and listened to McMann's loud, even breathing.

I tried to fall asleep, but my back hurt and there was too much going on in my mind. I kept scanning the whole study mentally, considering all our actions for the past three months, analysing and coding repetitively like some dull, electronically overcharged calculator. I felt feverish too. My head was full of a kind of buzzing ache, in which fragments of thought, words, and phrases, whizzed round, bumping up against each other. At one moment I decided to conclude that what McMann was doing was all right and not to worry about it; the next that he had only convinced me it was all

223

right because of my own inexperience and self-doubt, and by projecting what the Seekers would have called the electric vibrational force of his personality into my mind.

Whatever he said, it seemed awful and peculiar to me that Thomas B. McMann should have agreed to become a divine being; and also that the Truth Seekers should have accepted him as one. That was crazy, wasn't it? If it had been Verena, then I could have understood —

But why did the idea of the group worshipping McMann seem more irrational than the idea of their worshipping Verena? Maybe that only showed how far, without my knowing it, I had been infected by their mental set. If I thought of McMann as a less likely divinity, it must be that I considered Verena a more likely one; that in fact I had begun to believe in her myself.

Of course, McMann had had his turn at being a sort of deity for me once, too. When I read *We and They* back in college; even when I first got to the university and he was an impressive shadow across the hall behind frosted glass – famous, unapproachable, Olympian – the Varnian social scientist who knew all the answers. Ten years ago, when his reputation was at its peak, many more people must have believed in him that way.

When the Sophis study was published, they would believe again. McMann's (and Zimmern's) work on small-group dynamics would explode over the field like light from Varna, if nobody knew how we had biased our results, if we *had* biased our results. If, for instance, the one person who was in a position to know did not speak up and protest and write letters to editors. 'Dear Sir, I think I ought to point out, in connection with . . .'

Was it going to come to that? Was I really planning the betrayal and exposure of someone I had admired, even revered, for years – a great man who had generously taken me into his confidence, into his project, almost fresh out of graduate school? How was I so sure I was right?

If I questioned McMann's procedures, maybe it was from

224

professional timidity, nervous inexperience. Or worse: out of irritation at his heavy-handed kidding of me during the past weeks; or the jealous, small-minded carping of someone who knows he will never have half the reputation, half the originality and personal force of a Thomas McMann.

Or even a still more irrational childish envy. 'Why should it be him?' I had suddenly caught myself thinking at the end of the meeting. 'If Ro's spirit has to go into someone, why shouldn't it go into Ro-ger?' What was the matter with me?

I turned the pillow again, and a disembodied voice within the plastic foam seemed to whisper, 'You become the role you play.'

All right, whoever you are, I said, let's consider that possibility. For months now, Roger Zimmern had been playing the part of a Truth Seeker. And what was a Truth Seeker, typically? It was a nervous, insecure lower-middle-class person who shared with other Truth Seekers false beliefs, irrational wishes, and a distorted perception of reality. Reduced to basic essentials, their Truth was a benign form of paranoia. It was classically paranoid, after all, to believe that unseen forces, evil or good, were plotting the course of your life, and sending electrical currents into your brain.

I remembered reading somewhere that the incidence of mental illness among the staffs of some state hospitals might be attributed to their having to associate over long periods of time with disturbed individuals. That is, paranoia seemed to be catching; even if you weren't pretending to have it already like I had been doing.

Anyhow, whatever the cause, I was now behaving in a very paranoid way: suspecting a senior colleague, one of the top social scientists in the country, of either (*a*) technical incompetence, or (*b*) professionally questionable behaviour. Roger Zimmern imagined that Thomas B. McMann was directing the Seekers' actions for his own higher purposes, as if he were Ro of Var — But he *was* Ro of Varna, Elsie said so. The inside of my head hummed louder. I jerked restlessly around in the bed.

If you suspected you were crazy, that proved you really weren't, didn't it? Only then, if you weren't, you would be crazy to think so. The worst thing about cracking up, if I were cracking up, was that you couldn't trust your own perceptions. On the other hand —

I felt, or thought I felt, really sick by now. Cold and overheated by turns; my back ached, and my head, with the thoughts whirring around in it. I didn't know which ones to listen to, I was getting panicky. All these weeks with the group, I had been so smug, so sure of my own stability. I knew I didn't believe in Varna, so I had thought myself safe from infection. It hadn't occurred to me that if I did catch a psychosis, my delusionary system would take a different form from theirs. Logically, just as the Truth Seekers' beliefs were a distortion of provincial Protestantism, mine would be a warped version of humanism and social science. On the other hand —

A guy I knew in college had a breakdown. His first symptom was inability to make up his mind about anything: depression, insomnia, failure to work, and threats of suicide followed. At length he stopped eating, washing, and speaking; he simply sat in his room until a doctor came from Stillman Infirmary and led him away. He never came back, either.

Lying tossing in the motel bed at dawn, shivering slightly with anxiety, I did not quite conclude that I was going crazy. I told myself that I was over-excited, under a strain, and suffering from fever and exhaustion; that maybe in the morning I would feel better. If not, well, I would just have to break the news to McMann, find a psychiatrist, and turn myself in.

I had drowsed off when the alarm rang. McMann bounded out of bed, and pulled up the blinds with a loud snap. The room filled with cold sunshine.

'All right, out of bed!' he ordered. 'Up and at 'em!'

I pulled the sheet over my face.

'None of that now, Zimmern!' McMann jerked the covers out of my hand and right off the bed. 'Get up!' he shouted. 'Come on, I'm in charge here.'

'I'm tired,' I groaned, struggling to a sitting position.

'You're just out of condition. I'm not tired. All right. Pyjamas off! . . . Pants on!' I was still too dazed to protest. As McMann continued to issue orders, I staggered blearily into my clothes, trying to put the actions and thoughts of yesterday into shape.

'You're a run-down weakling, Zimmern. What you need is some exercise, get yourself into shape, then you wouldn't have this trouble getting up in the morning. Let's do some setting-up exercises.'

'No thanks,' I said, frowning. I had remembered now that I either hated McMann unconsciously or was crazy, probably both.

'Come on. One, two!' McMann started touching his toes.

'I'm 4-F.'

'I don't want any more backtalk from you, Zimmern. Come on.' As I stooped to get some clean socks out of my suitcase, he put a heavy hand on my back and pushed. 'Down you go! And up. One, two. One, two! Touch your toes.' Puzzled, irritated, and just to get it over with, I touched my toes. 'One, two. . . . All right, that'll do. You can go into the bathroom.'

While I shaved, McMann got down on the floor and continued doing exercises, heaving and panting.

'This is the day, Zimmern, old boy, this is the day!' he alternately shouted and grunted, as he executed a series of sit-ups, his arms folded on his broad chest. 'We're going to wind it . . . all up today . . . oh yes we are!'

'Mrh.'

'We're going to show the world.' He stood up and began flailing his arms about like a windmill, touching his spread feet alternately with each hand. 'Come on, come on, come on,

227

snap to it! You can shave faster than that. I want to get over there.'

'I bet they're all still asleep.'

'I bet they're not.' I said nothing. 'You want to bet? Five dollars says Elsie's up when we get there.' I shook my head. 'I'll give you odds. Two to one, okay? Ten against five.'

'I don't want to bet, thanks,' I said, tasting shaving cream.

McMann stopped waving his arms. His face was red from his exertions; I remember thinking casually that he looked crazier this morning than I did. 'Bad sport,' he hissed loudly. 'I hate bad sports. You said bet, Zimmern, the bet is on.'

I made no response; I was shaving.

'It's on,' he insisted, striding towards the bathroom. I backed away involuntarily, but he gripped my shoulder and glared into my face at close range.

'Ow! Hey,' I exclaimed. McMann paid no attention.

'On, you hear? Ro says the bet is on.' He grinned aggressively. 'Okay?'

'Okay.' All right, I thought, suppose I wasn't crazy, and suppose he wasn't just joking —

'That's better.' He let go, still grinning. 'Well, let's get going.'

'Just a second.' Inside my non-organic sweater, I was putting my data into a new order. His behaviour last night, the business about the bet, the exercises – I pulled my sweater down and looked at McMann, who was now running in place by the door, breathing heavily and counting under his breath:

'Thirty-four, thirty-five. . . . Ready?'

'Uh-huh.'

'Then let's get out of here, boy!' He swung the door open. 'On to West Hawthorne Street.'

'What about breakfast?' I was stalling, trying to think what to do.

'Elsie'll fix us something.'

'But, uh. Just a second.' I had noticed the telephone booth by the highway. 'There's a call I've got to make.'

228

'Christ, not now. Who to?'

'It's a – a personal call.'

For a moment I thought McMann was going to hit me, but then he laughed.

'A personal call, huh? Okay, go ahead, but make it short and sweet.'

I hurried across the frozen-slush parking lot, into the phone booth, and shut the door, trying to think fast. What number was I going to dial? I didn't know anybody in town except the Truth Seekers.

But McMann was watching me, walking up and down over there. To gain time, I took a handful of change out of my pocket, lifted the receiver, and put it in. Then I dialled my own number – it was the only one I could remember. The long-distance relays clicked through, and pretty soon I heard the phone ringing back at the university, in Roger Zimmern's safe apartment.

'Listen, Zimmern,' I said to him, moving my mouth exaggeratedly so it could be seen that I was talking to someone. 'I'm in Sophis with McMann, and there's something wrong with him. I think maybe we've both been sort of going mad.'

'Mad.' The word vibrated, echoing inside the black mouthpiece.

What did it mean to be mad? It meant that you had some idea, or wish, so important to you that you were ready to alter your perception of reality, or reality itself, to support it. If the group wouldn't go on believing in Varna, you got in there and pushed it the way your theories had predicted it would go, even if you had to stop being just a theorist and become a prophet or even a god.

McMann was walking back and forth in front of the motel, narrowing the distance each time, and glancing at me on the turn with a snap of his head. 'Listen, hey, Zimmern, tell me what you think I should do,' I mouthed into the cold black plastic. 'But whatever we do, we mustn't say anything to Mayonne and Ginsman, because they're our enemies.'

'Our enemies?' repeated the metallic echo. I heard it like a voice from the heavens, telling me not to be stupid: this was part of McMann's delusion. Barry Ginsman and Steve Mayonne weren't plotting against us – they never had been.

'Are you sure?' I said aloud. I reviewed the evidence rapidly: the supplies delayed, the questions, the remark about computer time – all turned pale and vanished, like flakes of ash in the winter sunlight. I didn't feel relieved, though, but lonely and disappointed. I understand better now about *folie à deux* and the madness of crowds. Paranoia, especially a shared paranoia, can be very attractive. There is a Plan to the universe after all, you say, and I am at the centre of it.

The phone kept ringing. Maybe I really should call somebody at the university. All right, who? It was early Sunday morning, and everyone would be sleeping. Besides, the university was three hours away, and in three hours McMann might be all right again. He was standing by the car now, tapping on the fender with his hand. He looked impatient, but not crazy. Maybe he had just been kidding. If so, he would certainly never forgive me for having called, say, Bob Onland, and announced that McMann was having a manic episode over in Sophis. The trouble is, as a psychologist friend of mine once said, paranoia (or even the suspicion of paranoia) seems to create actions on the part of others which justify it.

McMann saw me looking at him: he smiled and waved his arm. In my glass box, the telephone was still ringing. Roger Zimmern had not answered it, so I hung up and got my money back.

McMann won his bet: Elsie was up when we got there, though not yet dressed: pink nylon ruffles showed below the hem of her kimono, and her dry red hair was loose down her back.

'Blessed be the Spirit of Light!' she exclaimed as she let us in. 'You know, Tom, I was praying that you'd get here early. And I guess you must've heard me calling you silently, isn't that so? Good morning, Roger.'

230

'That's so,' McMann confirmed, in a voice vibrating with confidence. He had been talking steadily all the way to Elsie's in this voice, mostly about the necessity for physical fitness and the impact of the Sophis study on American sociology, once it was published. 'I heard you calling to me silently.'

'Oh, that's wonderful. The true spirit is in you now, I knew it. Let me take your coats. It's what I said. You had any breakfast?'

'No, not yet; we came straight here. Would have been over sooner, only this weakling couldn't get going.' McMann held out his coat to Elsie.

'You heard my prayer, and you came to me direct. Oh, I thank you for that!' Elsie said, taking not his coat but his large reddened hand; she clutched it tight, and bowed her head over it. 'Ro, you are truly with us now,' she announced, raising her face to the hall ceiling. 'I knew it was so. Only Verena doesn't understand. Well, there's not much to eat in the house, but I just sent Ed out to shop. He's got to drive up to the Atwell Supermarket, though, there's nothing open Sunday morning round here. Tom, I have to talk to you.' She had his coat now, and was holding it against herself tenderly. 'You've got to give me your guidance. Just a sec.' She opened the closet door, shoved the other hangers aside, and hung McMann's coat up, smoothing it reverently. 'Can you come upstairs?'

'Surely! That's what I'm here for.'

'I mean, now?'

'Surely, surely!' His voice boomed out much too loud, but Elsie didn't seem to notice. It has always been difficult to tell manic from divine utterance.

'Come on, then.'

'After you.' McMann made a bow of *noblesse oblige*, and followed Elsie upstairs.

I opened the closet door again and hung my coat next to Ro's, thinking. Maybe what I ought to do was get a doctor to see McMann. If he really was mentally disturbed, a doctor could give him something to calm him down; if not,

231

he could calm me down by telling me so. The moment I heard Elsie's bedroom door close, I started for the phone. I had to move a stack of chairs and books out of the way to get at it, and then I had to find the phone book. The drawer of the hall table gave a loud scream as I wrenched it open. There were four G.P.s in Sophis, and I began with the first name. Nothing happened. I tried the next number, with the same result. Finally I realized I wasn't getting any dial tone. The phone wasn't working; Ed Novar had turned it off the day before.

Well, maybe I could turn it on again. I started for the cellar: through the parlour (the non-organic furniture and potted plants looked even odder by daylight), through the dining-room, the kitchen —

'Hello, Roger.'

A pretty young girl in a yellow bathrobe and slippers was standing in the sun by the kitchen table, stirring something in a bowl.

'Oh! Hello, Verena. I didn't know you were up.'

'I've been awake for hours.' She smiled calmly at me.

'How are you feeling?'

'Wonderful, thank you.' She was a little pale, but that was all. Her thick hair was brushed back neatly under a yellow ribbon, and her mouth was red, almost as if with lipstick.

'Would you like some pancakes and sausages? I'm sorry there's no eggs.'

'*Sausages?*'

'I found a can down in the store cupboard.' Verena looked up. 'There's no need to avoid them any more, you know We can eat what we want. Our light is within us now; it's assimilated to us.'

'Uh, yes?' I moved towards the cellar door. What Verena was wearing, I saw, was her original prophetess costume; but the kitchen sunlight, the cord round her waist, or something, had changed it back into a bathrobe.

'That's the wonderful result of the Coming, you see, Roger. The spirit of our teachers and guides is in perpetual contact with our minds now. Oops, the water's boiling.' Verena turned to the stove.

'You too, Roger.' She set the kettle down. 'Your guides' presence is fulfilled within you too. Their light and God's is directing you; all you have to do is listen to it, wherever you are, and you'll know the true way. You don't have to depend on others and follow their commands any more.' She looked at me with her big fringed eyes. 'Why, I can feel you have a purpose in you right now. Isn't that so?'

'Yes, well; I wanted to make a phone call, but your telephone doesn't seem to be working. I think your uncle turned it off yesterday. I thought maybe I could fix it if I went down in the basement.'

'If Uncle Ed turned the phone off, you won't be able to do anything. He's got a key to the box.'

'Oh.'

'How many sausages can you eat?' Verena put a pan on the stove.

'I don't know. . . . There's too much going on here now,' I complained, half to myself.

'I realize it's a little hard to take in all at once,' Verena said serenely, shaking the pan. 'Aunt Elsie doesn't really understand yet, either. If you'd look up on that top shelf, Roger, I think there's some maple syrup there. It'd be in a square can.'

'Sure.' I climbed on to the kitchen stool. 'Elsie doesn't understand?' I wondered what was happening upstairs now, whether I ought to go next door and ask to use their phone.

'No, not yet; she's still clinging to the old lessons. It takes time to comprehend a great change like this, that's all. Oh, good, thank you.'

'She seems to think now that the spirit of Ro is in Tom.' If I went next door, the neighbours would probably listen to whatever I said. Maybe it would be better to drive downtown to the drugstore.

'I know it. That's true in a way, but what Aunt Elsie doesn't see is, it's not just in Tom, it's in all of us equally.

233

She wants for us to go on with the lessons and the messages. She doesn't grasp yet that there's no need for that now.' Verena began taking plates and cups from the cupboard by the sink. 'We can't just gather here with each other any more. That would be selfish. Each of us has got a duty now to go out into the world and spread the individual light of truth that's come into us. Here: take these into the other room, would you, Roger? You can set the table.'

'I've got to make a phone call.'

'Well, Uncle Ed'll be back in a little while; he'll fix it for you. Wait, here's some paper napkins. One, two —'

The doorbell rang.

'Can you answer it? I've got to watch these sausages.'

'Okay.'

I went through the dining-room and parlour and opened the front door. Ken stood there, looking rumpled but determined.

'Is Verena in?'

I hesitated. 'Uh, I think she's in the kitchen, but I don't know if —'

'Thanks.' Not waiting to be asked, Ken pushed past me and started for the back of the house.

'Oh! Ken!'

Now what? I thought, as I listened to the kitchen door swing open and then shut on Verena's cry of surprise and joy. Standing in the parlour, where so many sensational events had been foretold, I had a premonition of my own. I knew that something disastrous was about to happen; but I didn't know what. I started for the front door again, to go and find a phone, but then I stopped. I was afraid to leave them all alone in the house together. Worrying, I circled the room under the bowl of ferns, which swayed slightly to my tread on the bare boards.

'Roger.' Verena sailed into the room, smiling and looking as if she had received a message from outer space. 'Lay another place, will you? Ken's going to stay for breakfast.'

She handed me another plate, cup, and napkin. 'There's

234

been a lot of deception and darkness around here lately,' she added. 'The silverware's in that drawer. Well, I'm going up to get dressed.' She swept out.

'I told you so, Mr Zimmern,' Ken said as I moved the other plates to make room for his. 'That aunt of hers has been giving me a story the whole time. And listen, I guess I owe you an apology. Verena says —'

'Get out of this house.'

We both turned. Tom McMann was standing at the entrance to the parlour, in his shirt-sleeves, with Elsie behind him. He had Mr Novar's hunting rifle, and was pointing it towards us.

'Uh!' Ken said.

'Get out of here, Ken!' Elsie squeaked. 'You should be ashamed! Sneaking in here behind my back, bringing your dark emanations to spread corruption on my family. Get out of here, right now!'

'Put that thing down, McMann,' I heard myself say. It was the first time since I played cowboys in Morningside Park that anyone had pointed a gun at me, and it felt just as much like a game.

'The hell I will. You stay out of this.' He waved me aside with the end of the rifle, as if it were a long, black, pointing arm. 'I know what you came here for,' he continued to Ken. 'You're not fooling me, don't think that. I've known all about you for months. You're working for Ginsman.'

'Ginsman?'

'Yes, Ginsman and Mayonne. All right, get moving, you little fink. And when you see Barry you can tell him I'm on to him.'

'I d-don't know what you're talking about. I c-came to see Verena.' Ken stuttered with fright, but held his ground. 'I don't have to leave unless she asks me to.'

In reply, McMann lifted the rifle and fired. There was an incredibly loud noise. Plaster and paper fell from the ceiling, and shreds of smoke.

'All right!' Ken cried. 'All right!' McMann stood back,

Elsie opened the front door, and Ken ran out of the house, not stopping for his coat.

'And don't come back!' Elsie screamed. She slammed the door.

Smiling gently, McMann set the gun down. 'Well, that's that,' he said. 'Sorry about your ceiling, Elsie.'

'For God's sake.' I ran my hands through my hair. My heart was still thumping. 'What did you do that for? Are you crazy?' I think I said.

'Don't you talk that way, Roger!' Elsie squeaked, scuttling forward. 'Tom did the right thing. The Spirit of Power is in him, and he cast out evil.' She looked up at McMann with admiration. 'Ro is with you now truly.'

Folie à deux again, I thought. I opened my mouth to protest, then shut it. The first thing I had to do was get hold of that rifle, which was now leaning against the flowered wallpaper by the stairs. I moved towards it.

'Eh, Roger, you dumb bastard,' McMann said – not angrily but with the euphoric manner of one who has just scored an important victory and can afford to be tolerant. 'You let him in, didn't you?' I edged nearer to the rifle. 'You know I told him not to do that,' he complained to Elsie.

'That's so, I know you did,' she agreed.

'Well, never mind. We took care of him.' McMann smiled. I put out my hand, but at the memory of his exploit so did he. He picked up the rifle and patted it in a congratulatory way.

'What happened? What was that noise?' Verena appeared at the top of the stairs, barefoot and pulling her dress down hastily over bare white legs.

'It's all right. Nothing serious,' McMann said in reassuring tones.

'It sounded like an explosion, the furnace or something.' Verena came on downstairs, holding the unfastened front of her dress together with one hand. 'Where's Ken?'

'Never you mind,' Elsie said. 'There was an evil force entered into this house, and Tom cleaned it out through the power of Varna; that's all.'

Verena looked round. She saw the plaster and dust on the parlour floor first, then the wound in the parlour ceiling, and finally her huge eyes travelled back to McMann and the rifle.

'You did that,' she said. 'That wasn't right, Tom. Ken came here to seek the truth and light, and you —'

'He came to spread infection, that's what he came here for,' Elsie interrupted.

'He did rot!'

'It wasn't that, he just wanted to see Verena.' I added my voice to the general uproar.

'Yes, to confuse your mind and darken it, just like before, with his physical emanations!' Elsie shrieked. 'And break up our positive concentration of spirit, isn't that so, Tom?'

'That's so,' McMann said.

'Oh, he's so sly,' Elsie continued. 'He knew he had his best chance to get to you now and infect your mind, when you were worn out from last night's efforts and in a weakened condition.'

'I am not in a weakened condition,' Verena cried, pushing back her hair with her free hand.

'Well, if you're not, it's for no good reason,' Elsie squeaked. 'If you're not, then I'm afraid that Ken's already infected you with his elemental earth forces, and it's their strength that's supporting you and holding you up, not your own, isn't that right, Tom?'

'It's so, I'm afraid.'

'It is not so. I feel perfectly well. You don't understand —'

'You're impure now, Verena, and your thoughts are all impure.'

'Ken's purpose isn't what you believe it is,' McMann said insistently. 'He doesn't care about *you*, Verena. He's not your friend. He's an agent of evil forces who want to ruin all of us and destroy our work.'

'McMann, for God's sake,' I exclaimed.

'You shut up.' He waved the rifle at me.

Verena turned full towards McMann and stared at him.

'I didn't know that,' she said, and paused to consider. 'If

237

that's really so,' she said slowly, 'I ought not to see Ken again. . . . You're sure that's so? You're positive?'

'Positive. He's been working with my enemies for a long time.'

'You don't have to question Tom like that,' Elsie scolded. 'The spirit of Ro of Varna is with him now, and through it all things are revealed, the way we were told.'

'I feel so confused,' Verena said, putting her hands to the side of her head. Suddenly, perhaps because the gesture was so conventionally theatrical, I realized that she was acting.

'I guess I need your guidance, Tom.' She moved closer. McMann was still holding Ed Novar's gun, but as she approached he politely pointed it down. 'My mental processes are troubled; I need counsel. Will you help me?' She looked at him wide-eyed, and held out her hands. McMann took one of them, but she still held out the other appealingly.

'Help me, please, Tom,' she asked pathetically.

McMann put the rifle down on the bottom step and took her other hand. 'Sure, of course I will,' he said.

'Oh, thank you.' Verena drew him towards the stairs. As she reached the bottom step she looked at me quickly over his shoulder; from me to the rifle. I hardly needed to be told; I was already edging round the small solid obstacle of Elsie.

'You'll give me your guidance, isn't that so?' They were on the landing now.

'That's so,' Tom boomed manically.

Don't go up there with him alone, I thought at her; you can see he's crazy. Reaching past Elsie, I got one hand on the barrel of the gun, which felt slightly warm, and lifted it. It was unexpectedly heavy, and I almost dropped it again; the butt knocked against the wall.

'Just a sec.' McMann had turned at the sound. 'I'll take that, thanks.' He came down the stairs and pulled the rifle out of my hand before I could react. 'You shouldn't mess around with guns, Roger; somebody's liable to get hurt. Why don't you just go into the parlour now and talk to Elsie; and I'll take Verena upstairs, and set her straight in her thinking.'

238

'That's right,' Elsie urged. 'Come on along, Roger.'

The doorbell rang; two long rings, followed, after a heavy, protracted moment during which we all looked at one another, by a loud flutter of knocks.

'If it's that Ken again —'

'It's probably just Bill and Sissy,' Verena suggested. 'They said they'd be over.'

'Better wait till I have a look out the window.' Elsie started for the parlour.

But I was nearest the front door; I put my hand on the knob.

'Don't open that door! Don't be a damned idiot —' McMann began.

I didn't wait for him to finish but turned the knob and pulled the door open, eager for any interruption. It was Ken again, and with him, this time, were two policemen in overcoats.

'That the guy?' The nearest one indicated McMann; Ken nodded. 'Okay,' he added in the tones of TV drama. 'Hand over that gun.'

16

I still don't like to think much about what happened after that. I realize it's stupid to aggravate myself with guilt because I was one in a long chain of causes. All the same, if I had acted differently, that metaphoric chain, dragging McMann towards Atwell State Hospital, might have been broken. The whole thing might have ended there, if I had supported the story McMann and Elsie first told the police.

With an air of veracity, they claimed that Ken had walked into the house without permission (breaking and entering), that he had refused to leave when asked politely (creating a disturbance), and that he had insulted and threatened them (assault). Elsie described him as a person of low morals and bad reputation, from whom she was trying to protect her niece. The senior cop listened to her respectfully, and told Ken to shut up whenever he started to protest. They weren't interested in what Verena had to say, since she hadn't been there when the scene took place.

Verena herself, possibly, and Elsie certainly, expected me to support this story. After all, for months I had echoed whatever was said in my presence, and done whatever McMann told me to do. Besides, they took for granted, like most people of lower or lower-middle class origin, that you never tell the whole truth to anyone in an official position, especially a cop. They knew that whenever there is any sort of trouble, the authorities will probably blame all the participants – who are in fact all guilty: guilty of causing them annoyance and taking up their valuable time. They will make your lives equally unpleasant, if they can. The more information you give them, the worse it will be for you. The best thing is to say as little as possible.

And possibly this time they were right. If I had backed

McMann and Elsie up, the police might have left after confiscating the rifle and giving us all a lecture. McMann might have calmed down. Later on, if it still seemed urgent, I could have got a local doctor to come and see him; or I could have waited until we were back at the university.

But I didn't consider any of these alternatives for a moment. Instead, my behaviour was a model of empirical sociology: that is, I reported as objectively as I could the observed facts of human interaction, while trying to avoid influencing them in any way; just as if I still thought this was possible.

After that, since at least two of their witnesses were obviously lying, there was nothing for the cops to do but take us all in. In McMann's condition, that was fatal. People with delusions tend to seize on any event as evidence. McMann had begun to think people might be plotting against him; and now, look: Ken had forced his way into the house and had him arrested by the police. Of course, Mayonne and Ginsman were behind it all. They had hired Ken to spy on us weeks ago. Now they had probably bribed the local authorities to have McMann picked up on some false charge and imprisoned during the crucial last phase of the Sophis study. Since Ro of Varna would never have permitted such a thing to happen to his representative on Sol-III, this would effectively destroy the Seeker's faith, break up the group, and disprove McMann's theory.

It was quite logical, therefore, for him to refuse to go to the police station. 'I know what's up, don't try to kid me.' (I can hear his hearty, belligerent voice even now.) 'All I'd like to find out is, how much are you getting for this job? ... Barry Ginsman's a real cheap-skate, so it's probably only peanuts ... Ah, come on. Listen, I'd be happy to double it, whatever it is, and we can all forget the whole thing, okay? Call it a contribution to the Policemen's Welfare Fund, hell, whatever you like. ... Ayeh?' He mimicked their upstate accent. 'Well, get this through your heads. I'm not going

241

anywhere now. . . . Take your hand off of my arm. . . . Listen, if you don't buzz off, I'll make you both wish you never heard of me! I've got a friend or two in Albany. . . . All right, you bastards!'

A large man, in good condition, shouting and striving with all his might against the forces of evil and corruption, McMann was almost too much for the two policemen. Within thirty seconds he had broken a lamp and two of the sergeant's teeth. It wasn't until Ken joined in that he was entirely subdued.

If you've ever been through a crisis – legal, medical, or academic – (let alone all three), you'll know what the next four or five days were like. The confusion, the endless telephoning and explaining, the repetition of the facts until you almost stop believing in them yourself; the series of conflicting plans and decisions, each based upon the opinion of the last authority consulted; the boredom and anxiety of waiting for these opinions in unfamiliar legal, medical, and academic offices; the forms to be filled in; the financial problems — Let's forget it all, as I tried to do after McMann had finally been signed in (technically, signed himself in) to Atwell State Hospital, about fifteen miles from Sophis, and I was back at the university trying to pick up my classes again.

Nearly four months passed. It was early spring, one of those freak warm days in April, when I drove to Sophis again, with my car full of McMann's books and papers. The air was mild, the road clear, the scenery pleasant — I should have been glad to get out, for it had been a dull term at the university so far; but I was feeling uncomfortable.

For one thing, I had never been inside a rural state hospital, and had exaggerated ideas of what that would be like. And I wasn't looking forward to seeing McMann again. His letter asking me to bring the rest of the Sophis data (I had already mailed him all the typescripts, but now he wanted our original notes and tapes too, and a machine to

242

play them on) was completely sane and reasonable. But if McMann were sane, what was he doing in an insane asylum? When was he coming back to the university? That was what the rest of the department wanted to know, what they wanted me to find out.

McMann's letter was not only sane but polite. It had none of the exorbitant jocularity of the one he had sent in January, in which he addressed me as 'Dear Mr Halfassed' and gave directions for wrapping and mailing the material as if to a moron ('... then you get into your little car, put the big package on the front seat, and drive straight to the nearest United States Post Office').

I recognized that tone, all right; it was the one McMann had adopted towards me the morning after the Coming and maintained throughout the days that followed. Whenever I started to speak to him, or later even appeared in the same room, he would grow furious. 'Get that fool out of here,' he would say to whoever was near by, or shout if they were farther off. If I didn't leave at once, he became disturbed and even violent; once in a doctor's office he threw a copy of *U.S. News and World Report* in my face. Finally I gave up trying to converse with him, leaving this side of the negotiations to Elsie, the police, and later on Dr Feinstein from the University Health Centre.

You could say that McMann's attitude towards me was part of his paranoid system; that just as he had the delusion that Ginsman and Mayonne were plotting against him and Ken was their undercover agent, so he believed that I was an incompetent bungler. You could say that, and I certainly tried, but it didn't completely work. If I had been accused of theft, fraud, or murder, I wouldn't have minded; but somehow, even from a madman, the charge that one is stupid and unlucky hits home.

It was partly to put off the moment when I would have to walk down the corridors of a state hospital, and come face to face with McMann again, that I took the Sophis turn-off

243

and drove first to West Hawthorne Street. I hadn't written Elsie that I was coming; indeed, after my long absence I wasn't sure how she would receive me, if she were at home.

It was Ed Novar who opened the door. As tall, dim, and bland as ever; he greeted me formally without expressing any surprise or enthusiasm for my arrival, just as in the past.

Ayeh, he was doing all right, thank you, he replied to my inquiry. No, Elsie wasn't home now, she was up to the store. Well, he thought she would be back in a few minutes. I could sit and wait for her if I wanted. It was quite indifferent to him, his whole manner and bearing demonstrated, whether I came or went.

A perfect neutrality, I thought, after he had left me in the parlour. It was remarkable, really, how little Ed had influenced the group in any direction all the time McMann and I were with them. It wasn't only that he never said or did anything; as we had found, under some circumstances not acting can be a strong, definite act. Rather, he said and did the minimum, or a little less; on the other hand, his being there at every meeting was probably a slight reinforcement. That was how we should have played it ourselves, I realized.

I noticed only a few changes in Elsie's parlour, to which the organic furnishing had all been restored. There were a lot of new straggly looking plants along the top of the radiator, and a large misty pastel over the piano which looked like an oriental version of one of Sissy's vision paintings. On the coffee-table were yesterday's *Atwell Sun-Advertiser*, the *TV Guide, Family Circle*, and *Chimes* ('America's leading Spiritualist monthly'), suggesting that Elsie was keeping up with local events, watching TV again, fixing up the house, and attending the Spiritualist church at least occasionally. Also on the table was a china planter full of what looked like radishes.

I heard the back door slam, and voices raised in the kitchen. Then Elsie came bustling into the parlour, still in her outdoor clothes, followed by Milly Munger.

'Well! Look who's here!' Elsie squeaked, giving me a quick, nervously enthusiastic hug. 'What a surprise!'

'Aren't I glad I decided to come home with Elsie!' Milly exclaimed. 'Real nice to see you again, Roger.' She embraced me in turn, comfortably maternal.

'Nice to be here,' I responded, a little abashed. The quite sincere warmth and interest which some of the Seekers, particularly Milly, felt for me, was something I had chosen to forget; or rather, I had assumed it would end when the study ended. But for Elsie and Milly, of course, there was no study. They had thought, and still thought, of themselves as my friends.

'And what are you doing in Sophis now?' Elsie let a little asperity, and more curiosity, enter her voice. 'You might have let us know you were coming.'

'I'm sorry. I didn't know myself, till about the last minute,' I apologized. Already, as if I were putting on a worn suit every unbecoming fold of which was familiar, I found myself taking up my old persona: inept but basically well-meaning. 'I came to see Tom; I'm bringing him some books and stuff he wants.'

'That's wonderful.' Elsie pressed my arm; she and Milly exchanged a look of approval. 'You can stay over here tonight, you know; there's lots of room.'

'No, I've got to leave tonight.' Stupid Roger shook his head. 'I mean, thanks, but I promised them at school I'd be back.'

'But you'll have lunch, anyhow.'

'Well, I don't want to inconvenience you —'

'Oh, nonsense. Now you just let me hang up my coat, and then you can come into the kitchen and tell us all about what you've been doing with yourself while I get things started.'

Sitting on the familiar corrugated-rubber top of Elsie's kitchen stool, I continued, without consciously intending it, to enact the person that they took for granted. I found myself (or rather Stupid Roger) confessing that though I had looked at the pamphlets on Mental Physics Elsie had sent me a couple of months ago, and tried to read them, I hadn't really understood them too well. Oh yes, I had been trying to listen to my inner voice of the spirit, and doing my best to follow its instructions, when I could make them out. It was true that it was pretty hard going for me alone, but I'd been so loaded down with school work this term I hadn't been able to get to Sophis at all. Elsie, who was arranging cold cuts on a platter, nodded sympathetically, and Milly said she could imagine what it must be like for me working with those unenlightened professors there, that Ginsburg and Mayonnaise or whatever it was.

Yes, it was hard, Elsie said; but I must just go on striving to stay in contact and keeping my mind and body in the best condition for spiritual receptivity and growth. Getting enough sleep and exercise, and eating the right foods, that was very important, much more than most people realized. 'You eat a balanced diet, don't you, Roger, I hope?'

'Oh, yes.'

'You got to do more than count your calories and vitamins though, you know that. You have to be sure you get only real fresh foods, otherwise by the time you come to eat them most of the good is gone out of them. Organically grown is best, if you can find it.' Elsie measured coffee into the pot. 'You remember the lessons we had on food vibrations? Well, of course, all that was directed to a special circumstance; it doesn't really apply in general everyday life. But we've gone into the subject much more lately, and studied up on it.'

'That's right,' Milly put in. 'You see, actually, Roger, the very second a plant is cut from its roots, or pulled out of the ground, it starts to die and lose its nutritive values. That's why I've started growing my own, as much as I've got room for, and so's Elsie.' She gestured at the kitchen window sill, which, like the one in the parlour, was lined with untidy plants, among which I now recognized carrots, onions, and what looked like a potato vine.

'I'll put some of my greens in the salad, and you just see if it doesn't pep you up,' Elsie predicted. 'But what you ought to do really is start growing them for yourself, isn't that right?'

That was right, Milly said; and to get me started, she would give me some pots of stuff she had at home; I could pick them up on my way out to the hospital. 'Aw no, Roger,' she continued over my protests. 'I can always grow some more. Besides, I guess you need them worse than I do. Me and Elsie don't really have to grow our own stuff now, we can get it at the market, since we've been learning to read the auras of food substances.'

And interrupting each other in their eagerness to enlighten me, Elsie and Milly explained that every edible substance has a definite vibration, which is easy to see if you have the gift and practise enough. Good fresh eggs, for instance, have a real bright yellow aura, but the old ones get to be a sort of greenish yellow. The best California oranges give off a pink glow that practically lights up the whole store, once you learn to see it. Of course, there were a lot of things that could influence the vibrations of food besides its freshness. What kind of soil it was grown in, or (say it was a chicken) what it ate, where it came from; even the personality and spiritual development of the people who grew it could be a factor.

The salad was ready now (Elsie said it had a strong golden aura) and we sat down to lunch, along with Ed Novar. Our conversation turned to the other Truth Seekers, I learned that Rufus and the Freeplatzers still came occasionally, say once or twice a month, to West Hawthorne Street for an informal discussion period and an organic supper. Milly came more often, and so did Peggy Vonn ('You wouldn't believe the awful emanations from the kind of meals they give those girls up at the college. Some evenings there's a grey aura on the milk, Peggy says, that practically turns her stomach, pardon the mention.')

Catherine Vanting, on the other hand, seemed definitely to have left the group. Elsie and Milly saw her whenever

247

they went to the Spiritualist church over in Atwell, but she had got pretty hoity-toity. 'You know, I don't like to say it,' Milly added, helping herself to hot wheat-germ rolls, 'but some of us have kind of fallen off in our development since last year. Our thoughts were set more on higher things then, and we were true loving sisters and brothers to each other in our daily life. Why, I remember how Catherine came out to the house Thanksgiving time, and helped me sort out poor Howard's things for the Goodwill and gave me her spiritual comfort. Now she's in touch with her great-uncle that used to own half of Etna, and I don't know who all, she won't hardly speak to me. Well, gone's gone.'

Other former members of the group, I learned, also had new interests. But Elsie and Milly viewed with more tolerance Rufus's study of unidentified flying objects and the possibility of inter-galactic communication; and Peggy's sentimental mysticism, which of late had involved solitary all-night vigils in the dorm and attempts to achieve spiritual union with her patron saint. There were many, many paths to the Truth, after all, and Saint Lucy certainly ought to be a lot better guide to them than some old farmer from Tompkins County that had passed over so full of pride and material greediness he was probably still stuck on the bottom level of advancement.

As for the Freeplatzers, Elsie and Milly hadn't quite made up their minds. Bill and Sissy were both real sincere Seekers, no doubt about that; the only question was if they hadn't got off on the wrong track, taking up so much with Eastern belief.

'Eastern belief?' I asked.

'Uh huh. See, it started when Sissy found out some of her spirit pictures were the same as the designs on those Indian print spreads, the Tree of Life, or something. So that got them started reading up on Eastern art, and then they got on to Hindus, and Tibet, and Yogi, and all that. Well, I don't know.' Milly frowned, and looked to Elsie as if she might explain it better.

248

'It's not that we've got anything against the Eastern Way, Roger,' Elsie said. 'All the great higher world religions are moving towards the same God, we know that of course.' She leaned forward, setting her plump white elbows on the place-mat. 'But what *I* think is, what's right for those orientals isn't necessarily suited to our Western civilization. I mean if you've got all that poverty and real hopeless conditions around you in this life, maybe there's some point in trying to blot out your individual consciousness and think only higher thoughts. It's about all you can do, I guess. But carrying on like that right here in the United States; well, it seems to me it's just negativism. Isn't that so?'

'That's so.'

'It's selfish, is how I look at it.' Elsie sat back in her chair. 'It's not doing anything for others, or yourself either.'

'Well, acourse,' Milly put in, 'that's not how *they* see it. In their minds, they're doing it for the baby, to guide his development.'

'For the *baby*?'

'Yes, see, what they're trying to do is exclude all thought vibrations of pain, or evil, or ordinary material thinking even, that might get into him,' Elsie explained. 'Like, for instance, Sissy won't look at the paper any more, Bill just reads her out the parts he thinks won't do any harm. And if they come over to your home, or you go there, you've got to watch yourself all the time not to mention that anybody passed on, or the sales tax, or anything a person would normally mention.'

'Sissy's expecting a baby?'

'Why, yes,' Milly said. 'Just after Labour Day.'

'I was going to write you about it,' Elsie said. 'Only I guess I was waiting for you to answer my last letter.'

'I'm sorry, I meant to, but ... They must be awfully pleased.' I began counting back from next Labour Day, but Milly gave me the answer before I finished.

'Oh, they are! After all, they been married going on seven years now. And acourse they realize it was due to the high

249

energy concentration of the Coming that made it possible after all that time. It's partly because of that they feel they got to take special care of this child's spiritual growth.'

'I see.' I was impressed in spite of myself. Not that the production of this sort of minor miracle by imaginary forces was so extraordinary – indeed, it was in the oldest tradition. What was extraordinary was that Verena had not only been able to make a barren woman conceive after seven years but had predicted it would happen – when she told Sissy and Bill the day before the Coming that their greatest wish would be granted.

Of course, it was about Verena that I really wanted to hear, but I deliberately put off asking. I waited until lunch was over, Milly had gone, and Elsie was washing up alone in the kitchen. I knew already from Elsie's letter that Verena had left West Hawthorne Street in January, acting according to her own inner light, but against everyone else's; Sissy had had a very definite warning dream about it, and so had Rufus. If I had known in time, I might have driven to Sophis and tried to stop her myself. But by the time I heard, it was too late; she had 'gone off' with Ken.

I took a dish-towel from the familiar sagging white wooden fingers of the holder by the kitchen window, and began drying the dishes. 'And how is Verena?' I asked conversationally, casually.

Elsie stiffened; her sponge stopped on the plate she was wiping, then moved on.

'Like I wrote you.' Her voice was thin and hard. 'Far as *I* know, she's still down in Albuquerque, New Mexico. With that Ken.'

'And, uh.' I didn't know how to put it tactfully. 'Verena and Ken, are they married?'

Elsie dropped the plate into the drying-rack; it struck the sink between the rubber rings. 'Oh yes, they're married, I suppose. If you want to call it that: sneaking over to the city hall in Atwell to some office, and not a soul knowing until it was done, when Reverend Theodore at the Spiritualist

250

Church where Verena used to go with me would have been glad to give her a beautiful service. Or if she wanted, she could have gone to the Methodist church here in town, she was baptized Methodist same as her mother and Ed. But there's some people that walk in darkness, and couldn't stand to have the eye of the Lord shine full on their unions. I guess they're afraid it'd blast them down in their heathen pride and wrong thinking.' Elsie shoved a bristling handful of wet knives and forks into the plastic holder. 'Well, Roger, like I said to Ed, all we can do for Verena now is pray that the light may shine into her spirit again some day and wake it from its miserable blinded condition. Because the pure Truth of God is stronger than lustfulness and lies.' She turned her head and stared at me. 'It's bound to get to her sometime, isn't that so?'

'That's so.' Again, almost automatically, I gave the non-directive response; though, in fact, I was free now to say and do whatever I liked. The study was over; I could call Elsie Novar a narrow-minded, jealous fanatic to her face, as I had so often wanted to. But what would be the good of it? The one thing I had really wanted to say was out of date; the person I had wanted to say it to was in New Mexico, and married.

'I hope it will, anyhow.' Elsie lifted a glass to the light to see if it was clean. 'Because Verena, she's got a great gift of spiritual power, and it's her bounden duty in life to use it.'

'Um,' I agreed. I wondered in reality whether if Verena were to come back to Sophis she would still be able to inspire belief and call up spirits, even if she wanted to. It was more likely that Ken had dissolved her powers for ever. As McMann had once suggested, it was probably prolonged virginity combined with an excess of innate sexual energy that had produced Varna, just as it is said to create polter-geists. Such phenomena are temporary. If I were to meet Verena now that her brief dissociation of personality was over, I told myself, she would be only the ordinary good-looking young wife of a physics major. Nothing to regret.

251

Elsie pushed back a strand of faded red hair with a wet hand, and sighed. Then, resting her forearms in the slack soapy water, she continued, 'I just don't know, though, Roger. Right now, that Ken has got such a hold on her, body and spirit. He's leading her to associate with the worst sort of unchristian people out there, beatniks and Communists and worse.'

'Worse?' I wondered what could be worse, in Elsie's opinion. 'I mean, that's too bad. How do you know?'

'It was in the newspapers, that's how. Some friend of Rufus's, up at the college, he saw it right in the *New York Times*. Here, see for yourself.' Elsie wiped her hands on the flowered apron, and reached into the cupboard by the sink. From behind the sugar bowl, she took a piece of folded newsprint.

It was a two-column photograph, creased sharply vertically and horizontally, as if it had been folded and unfolded often and angrily. Above was the caption 'Campus Protest in Albuquerque Defies Dean's Ban'. Underneath it was explained that 'An outdoor protest meeting, held Saturday in defiance of University authorities, attracted an estimated 1500 University of New Mexico students and faculty. Disciplinary action may be taken against the principal speaker, Mrs Verena Dowd (above) and five others.'

Most of the photo was of a large mob, some with beards and a few carrying picket signs. Because of the distance and blurred focus, it wasn't possible to read any of the signs, so there was no way of knowing whether they were protesting racial discrimination, nuclear bombing, or just some university rule. In the foreground, to one side, was Verena. She was standing on what looked like the top of an automobile, her long hair blowing back; she was holding out both arms, and looking at me with the same wide-eyed incendiary stare I had seen so often here in the parlour on West Hawthorne Street.

A sinking sensation of loss went through me – as if I had just missed a train or a plane. Or, to be accurate, it went through Stupid Roger – awakened today in this house after a sleep three months long. He felt terrible.

I gave the clipping back to Elsie, after shaking my head over it politely, and said I must be going. I thanked her for lunch; I think I even promised to write her, to read those pamphlets on Mental Physics she had sent me and others she was going to mail me soon. I promised to return to West Hawthorne Street as soon as I could manage it.

Elsie walked me to the front door, then stopped, standing in front of it. There was something she had decided she ought to say to me, she announced, before I went.

'Yes?'

'It's about Tom.' Elsie looked aside, frowned, and began gathering up the hem of her apron in one hand.

'Yes.' I tried to put some of Tom's own reassuring resonance into my voice.

'I don't know, maybe it isn't even necessary,' she said. 'When I was up there last week he seemed so well. I was talking to him about Ed's back condition, and he gave me better advice than the doctor, in my opinion.'

'You visit Tom regularly?' I was surprised; none of them had mentioned this.

'Why, sure.' Elsie seemed surprised I should ask. 'I go up there most every week or so, when the weather's good. It's a pretty long drive, specially if it's been snowing. But I know he appreciates the company, stuck out there in the country with all those poor crazy people. It seems to me, considering what Tom did for us, it's all of our duty to visit him as often as we can manage,' she added with slight asperity, giving me a look. I smiled apologetically. 'Milly goes about as often as me, and sometimes one of us takes Peggy or Rufus along; they haven't neither of them got a car. Bill and Sissy used to visit pretty regular too, only now they have to stay away from the hospital, according to their belief, or that baby of theirs might come into this world mentally disturbed.' Elsie smiled sourly and shook her head; I shook mine in imitation.

'Uh-huh.' She paused, then continued in a different tone,

253

bracing herself against the door. 'You know, Tom is such a fine man.' I nodded. 'He has a wonderful spiritual gift, and great intellectual powers too, just about the best I ever met in a human person.... Well, of course, that's why our teachers and guides chose him to be their vessel here on Earth, at the time of the Coming. They singled Tom out among us, among all men, and poured all their great Light and Power into him.' Elsie's face lit with triumph, then faded. 'But you know, Roger, our human brain fibres are terribly weak, compared to the developed minds of other beings. The electric and atomic strain of receiving the full power spectrum of waves from Varna, well, it was just too much even for him. Isn't that right?' She put an anxious white hand on my arm.

'That's right.' I was lying to her, or at least assenting to her lies, wholeheartedly now; more so than I had ever done during the study. But nobody had cared this much about Roger's support, back then.

'It was a wonderful thing he did, taking all that strain and vibration upon himself. He did it for us, Roger, you know. *All* of us.'

'I know.'

Elsie smiled, relieved. 'Acourse, everybody with sense understands that,' she said. 'And they're grateful, too, I'm glad to say, apart from Catherine.'

'Catherine?'

'Ayeh.' Elsie seemed unwilling to go on.

'What does Catherine say?'

'Oh, it's just spite and enviousness.... Well, what she said, it was her opinion the reason some of Tom's brain cells were electrified negatively was they had impurities and sin in them. Just spite.'

'Sin?' I laughed out loud involuntarily. 'I'm sorry. It just seemed ridiculous.'

'That's what I said to Catherine. I told her, I'd like to see you show me a soul on this planet that could stand the impact of that high power charge; just show me one. She couldn't, acourse. . . . Some people, I said to her, have got such dirtied minds they can't tell the difference between true brotherly and sisterly love and ordinary lewdness. But anyhow,' Elsie hurried on, before I could pursue this topic, 'Tom's much better now, practically well. He's made a wonderful recovery. Naturally his guides must've seen right off what happened; and ever since I know they've been working to restore him to his normal condition, or even better.'

'That's fine,' I said sincerely.

'But just in case. I mean, if this should be one of his bad days, not that I expect it, and anyways, I'm sure he won't do anything real disturbing —' Elsie must have seen something of what I felt, for she began patting my arm.

'You don't have to worry, really, Roger. He's nothing like when you saw him last, he talks so quiet and occupies himself with reading and study most of the time. Only if he *should* say something out of the way, you'll know how to take it.'

'Well —'

'Don't contradict him, or try to correct him in his error, is all I mean. Or he might get upset. Just go along with what he says, and everything'll work out *fine.*'

17

Leaving Stupid Roger behind at Elsie's was not so easy. The sound of my feet on her uneven sidewalk, the familiar motor action required to negotiate the slightly uphill turn on to Grand Avenue, every detail of the whole town, recalled him. In a way I was pleased, as if I had recovered part of my past after a period of amnesia. An interesting part, too. At the university (and in New York, I have to admit) nothing worth mentioning had happened for months.

Everyday existence in Sophis was probably boring too, for most people, but not among the Seekers. Crazy things were always happening at West Hawthorne Street, and feelings running high: people were expressing Cosmic Love, singing, crying, denouncing themselves and each other, burning their clothes, quitting their jobs, cutting the telephone wires. In some ways, it was probably more fun being a Truth Seeker than a college professor.

And if I (whom some had called a natural academic type) felt that way, how must it have been for McMann, after twenty years in the same department? I decided I was lucky my role among the Seekers had been one that afforded so little prestige and ego satisfaction. I had less temptation to take it up permanently.

What had happened to McMann was understandable, once you realized he had got stuck in his Sophis role. Just as it was logical for Stupid Roger to fall in love with Verena (and even to run away when she made advances), so it was logical for, let's call him, Clever Tom to become the group leader as soon as a vacancy appeared, and to defend this position with violence.

Of course, there was more to it than that. There must have been some concealed instability in McMann, maybe for years. That combination of professional gregariousness and personal isolation — Why had he never married again, for instance? Why had he published one brilliant book, and then nothing more for nearly twenty years?

All madness, after all (I thought), is just the exaggeration of some norm. Respect becomes reverence; the group leader becomes a prophet or a god. Social science might have left McMann behind, like some outmoded Titan. Among the Seekers, he could be worshipped again as the bringer of Truths of Light, but under another name.

Nothing more was needed but a precipitating cause. What finally drove McMann over the line, I thought, was the realization that his prophecy, like Verena's, had failed. His theory was wrong: after the disconfirmation of the Coming, the group was *not* going to remain united and maintain its belief structure; it was going to fall apart. Rather than stand by and see that happen, McMann altered the data; he changed reality. And, inevitably, he started with himself.

From the road, Atwell State Hospital looked like a small New England college. Red-brick buildings veiled with ivy; curving walks and clipped hedges; wide green lawns and immemorial elms. Even at closer range the illusion continued. The grounds were well kept; I saw an ornamental lake through pine trees. There were no high walls or fences; one of the more modern buildings had bars on the windows, but it might have been the gym.

It was a college during spring vacation, though, empty of students and faculty. In their absence, the campus had been taken over by its maintenance staff: janitors, cleaning women, cooks, buildings-and-grounds men. They were everywhere, grey-faced, badly dressed: sitting on benches in the sun, looking out from windows, promenading the sidewalks in ones and twos. They did not seem pleased to be in possession, but awkward and slightly nervous. When a professor approached, they either pretended not to see him (me) or ran off.

257

Thus, as I drove into the main parking lot, two women in galoshes and scarves scuttled into the bushes as if they thought I meant to run them down. On the path to the administration building, a young coloured janitor with a bandaged head was leaning on an old broom, barring my way. He did not move aside at my 'Excuse me' but stood squinting into space as I detoured round him through the damp bushes.

Already beginning to feel uneasy, I went into the ivy-covered college building and found myself in a small hospital lobby. It was perfectly standard: institutional green walls and floors, glass-topped desk, and brisk white-uniformed receptionist, to whom I stated my business. She spoke into a phone. Dr McMann was at Occupational Therapy; he would be here in twenty minutes.

I walked about. All the seats in the lobby were occupied by shabby, miserable-looking people; I didn't know whether to read their expressions as insanity or just the usual waiting-room fear, depression, and boredom.

'Why don't you go into our coffee-shop, Mr Er – Zimmern?' the receptionist said, consulting the slip she had made out. 'You can sit down there.'

'Coffee-shop?'

'Right down the hall there and turn left.'

I didn't move; I didn't want to go any farther into the building than I already was.

'Here, I'll show you the way.'

'Please, don't bother.'

'No bother.' The woman was determined to get her lobby tidied up. 'I'll tell Dr McMann where to find you when he comes in.' Her voice took on a nurse- or nursemaid-like tone. 'Right this way, now.' She gave me a firm push.

I continued down the hospital corridor, found the sign 'Coffee Shop', and pushed on through swing-doors into a factory or office cafeteria. It looked perfectly ordinary and authentic, and very much resembled the lunch room in the basement of the office building where I had worked the summer I was seventeen. This room was on the ground floor, but it looked like a basement, with heavy square pillars painted cream, high windows with chicken-wire embedded in the glass, and pipes running along the ceiling. There was a counter on one side where you could buy sandwiches, soft drinks, and candy.

The cafeteria, like the hospital lobby outside it and the college campus outside that, was full of maintenance workers; but they looked less incongruous here. It was I who was out of place, as they all seemed to acknowledge by ignoring my presence – gazing past or straight through me as I went up to the counter and waited my turn to be served.

'Coffee, please. Black.' The untidy girl behind the counter did not look at me either. She looked at the coffee as it boiled out of the spigot into the mug, and at the dime I gave her.

'Thank you!' I said cheerfully.

No response; none at all. She must be a patient too. As I turned away from the counter to face the room again, it came over me that I was probably the only normal person there. I was alone in a factory cafeteria with thirty or forty certified madmen.

I took my mug to an empty plastic-topped table and sat down, feeling funny in the legs but ashamed of myself for it. After all, if any of these people were dangerous, they would be in a locked ward, wouldn't they? If they had delusions, they were probably no more dangerous than Elsie's and Milly's belief in the auras of vegetables. What was I afraid of, for God's sake? These people weren't going to attack me; on the contrary, they didn't even seem to know I was there. Here at last, in fact, was a social milieu in which nobody would pay any attention to the presence of a sociologist – a really un-contaminated field.

What I ought to do, I told myself, was take advantage of this opportunity. I should drink my coffee and look around quietly, observing the scene scientifically; that would make me feel better.

The first thing I noticed was that some classification of the data had already been done for me. My chair and table were marked with the name of the room; my mug with the name of the institution. The coat which the girl at the next table had thrown back over her chair had a strip of tape pasted inside the collar, with writing on it. I read it upside down: 'J. Fowler. Ward 9A.' Looking about, I saw pieces of tape on other coats; on scarves, on handbags, on the frames of eyeglasses.

I observed that most of the people present were drinking Cokes; that all were badly dressed; that though some seemed to be sitting together, few were talking. The tone was like that of a plant cafeteria about a month after a strike has failed; nearly everyone seemed sad, preoccupied; nobody was laughing or smiling.

They looked ordinary enough in the mass; but when I began to notice individuals, something happened. I had a book when I was a child called *Saint George and the Witches*, in which it was explained that you could always tell witches, because there was something wrong with them. Not anything obvious: it was only when you looked at them carefully that you would notice their feet were on backwards, their eyes upside down, or their thumbs on the wrong side of their hands.

I observed a teenage boy who was methodically scratching a bad skin condition and making his face bleed; I observed an obese woman eating a sandwich with gloves on. I observed J. Fowler, Ward 9A, who seemed to have cut off most of the hair on one side of her head.

Nobody looked at me still, but I was beginning to feel they were doing it on purpose. I glanced towards the door, and saw a man in yellow-stained work clothes come in; but he came in sideways. He edged slowly around the room towards the lunch counter, sliding his back along the wall and looking from side to side as if anticipating or planning an attack.

I did not feel better. Leaving my coffee, which had grown lukewarm, I got up and went out.

Across the hall from the cafeteria was another set of swing-doors, standing open. Inside was an elementary school library, complete with colourful posters of boys and girls reading ('Books Make Good Friends' one said), low round tables, and even a cheerful children's librarian in rimless glasses and a flowered blouse. I backed away, and around a corner of the hospital corridor, just missing a nurse with a tray of medicine. More double doors faced me now; through the wired glass I saw a high school gymnasium, with bleachers ranged along one side and red basketball lines on the varnished yellow floor.

I began to feel dizzy. It was like being in a dream in which all the public scenery of my childhood had collapsed into one building. I expected at any moment to see my awful fifth-grade teacher, or the doctor who had taken out my tonsils when I was six. Telling myself in a nervous inner voice not to be nervous, I started back down the corridor. Then I heard my name called from the other end, and saw McMann coming towards me.

Even before we were within speaking distance, I knew it was the old McMann; his whole appearance and bearing was as I had first seen it: open, easy, self-assured – above all, normal.

'Roger.' Smiling, he held out his hand, shook mine warmly. 'Good to see you again!'

'Good to see you.'

'How are you?'

I said I was fine; for the first time that day I thought it might be true.

'You brought the tape-recorder and the rest of the stuff?'

'It's out in the car.'

'Great. Let's drive over to my place, and you can help me take it in, okay?'

'Okay.' I smiled; I let out my breath, like a child with a present he has been longing for, but not dared to expect.

As we unloaded the car in front of his building – a small

261

brick and ivy dormitory – and carried his things into a store-room near the entrance, everything confirmed my original impression. McMann was more than just sane again: he was confident, alert, outgoing – in striking contrast to everyone else on the place. He was not blind, or invisible: he seemed to know everyone – patients, nurses, visitors – and they him. Even those who did not respond directly to his friendly greeting smiled to themselves as he pronounced their names – sometimes with a later aside to me: 'Bright old fellow. Tried to kill his wife, but you wouldn't blame him if you saw her.' 'Good-looking girl, isn't she? Used to be a Rockette.'

Catching his tone, forgetting my previous anxiety, I smiled and nodded too, and even shook hands with some of the shabby-looking maintenance men hanging about by the Coke machine in the lobby.

'You got any change, Rog?'

I produced some, and McMann stood everyone to the soft drink of their choice. It was obvious that he was in excellent rapport with these men. They treated him with friendly respect, and called him 'Professor'. Though no one spoke much, and some seemed a little discouraged and preoccupied, there was no sign that any of them might be insane.

McMann had got us coffee out of another machine, and now he led me across the lobby to a sunny bay window where there was a plant stand and two rocking chairs, one occupied by a skinny bald old man with an unlit pipe in his mouth. Instead of greeting him by name as he had the others, or even glancing at him, McMann spoke to me.

'Well, now, Roger!' he said loudly. 'You've come all the way from the university today to see me, so let's sit down, and you can tell me your business.'

The little old man got up, and sidled away down the room.

'What was that about?' I asked.

'Don't look at him,' McMann cautioned me, sitting down. 'He doesn't like it; he thinks he's invisible.'

'Invisible?' I glanced involuntarily at the old man, who was frowning hard; glanced away.

'Yeah. He's convinced he died about five years ago. That's just his ghost you see here, only you're not supposed to see it unless he feels like appearing to you. Well, tell me some news.'

McMann asked me about my own work first: the classes I was teaching this spring, a book review I had written, some of my advisees; he remembered everything. Next he began to inquire, with the same warm interest, after other people in Streib Hall: my office mate Bob Onland, the girls in the Department office, his favourite graduate students. 'And how about my old pals, Ginsman and Mayonne?' He grinned. 'Still plugging along?'

I hesitated. McMann looked all right, he acted all right; but this was my chance to make sure. I threw out a line.

'You're not angry at them any more?' I asked, sounding his mind as if it were a dark lake.

McMann frowned. 'What for?'

'Well.' I wiggled my line nervously, not sure whether a shark might not leap for it, all teeth. 'You used to think they were trying to break up the Sophis Project.'

'Aw, no.' McMann stopped his rocker on the forward swing. 'That was a delusion we had there, Rog, you know that.' He looked at me for a moment seriously (just as I had looked at him), to make sure I was not still crazy.

'Oh, I know.'

'Barry and Steve don't have much use for me' – McMann smiled now, and rocked back – 'but they wouldn't go out of their way to ruin something I was working on. That'd be sabotaging the department. Thinking they had hired Ken to spy on us, bribed the police, that was just plain crazy, you know.' I nodded vigorously. 'Besides, hell, they'd never have the imagination to think up anything like that.' He laughed. 'I would've realized that if I hadn't been so hopped up.'

'That's right.' I was feeling better and better.

'I think it was that damned vegetarian diet that did me in,'

263

he said. 'That, and not really sleeping for forty-eight hours. . . . You too. We were both under a hell of a nervous strain. Only difference was, I tend to boil under pressure, where your type tends to freeze.'

I laughed and agreed. I was beginning to realize how much I, and the whole Department, had missed McMann. Without him, we were a solemn, isolated lot of individuals.

'Yeah, you're lucky,' he added. 'I really lost control for a minute there, when I went after those cops. I saw red, that's all.' He shrugged, smiled.

'You sure did.'

'The trouble was, after that I had to play along with the role.'

'Play along?' I stopped my coffee container in mid-air.

'Yeah. I did one crazy thing, then I had to act nuts for the next couple of weeks to stay out of jail.' He grinned.

'You mean you were *faking*?'

McMann looked at me, then laughed out loud. 'Sure,' he said. 'Didn't you know that? I thought you'd figured it out. That's why I didn't want to talk to you – I was afraid they'd have the room bugged.'

'For Christ's sake.' I shook my head to clear it.

'I guess I gave you a rough time.'

'You certainly did,' I said.

'Sorry. But hell, it was necessary. If they'd known I was sane, that cop whose teeth I knocked out would've got me sent up for six months for assaulting an officer. I had to convince the judge to send me here on a court order, so I couldn't be prosecuted.'

I looked at McMann, my astonishment merging into admiration. So he had done it all on purpose! One brief fit of rage; then, as the walls of social retribution began to grind inwards, to crush him like the man in the Poe story, McMann had leaped upwards, quite deliberately, out through the only possible escape hatch; the booby hatch.

Admiration merged with resentment: 'You could have written me,' I said.

264

'Don't be dumb. They read the mail here.' McMann rocked. 'Anyhow, I thought you knew.'

'That first letter you wrote me — It was a fake, too?'

McMann laughed.

'So you were just playing crazy,' I repeated, lowering my voice, though there was no one within earshot. 'All that time. . . . How did you manage it?'

'It wasn't hard. You've got to remember that when I started, I was still practically a natural.' He grinned. 'I just sort of kept it up. Most laymen have never seen a real psychotic, anyhow. It wasn't so easy fooling the professionals, especially that fellow Howie Feinstein the university sent over. When I got out here, of course, I had a lot of models to choose from.' He glanced down the lobby to where the same men, or others like them, stood by the Coke machine. 'My main problem was the tests they give. I knew some of them well enough to get by; others I've just had to refuse to take.'

'I see.'

'But of course, all along I've had a terrific advantage.' He paused, rhetorically.

'Yes? What?'

'Everybody else here is on the opposite kick from me, you see. They all want to fool the staff into thinking they're normal, so they can get out. The doctors are used to looking for that; but they're not prepared for my sort of game.'

I had to laugh. 'But still — Living here, all this time, pretending to be crazy. It must have been pretty hard.' That was putting it mildly, I thought.

'Nah, not really. The food's lousy, but otherwise I can't complain. It's been kind of fun. Interesting, too. You'd be surprised the things people'll say or do in front of somebody they think is off his nut.'

'But by this time . . . I mean . . . I should think . . .' I stumbled over my question; McMann picked me up kindly.

265

'What you want to know is, what am I still hanging around here for, if I'm not psychotic? After all, I'm probably safe from prosecution by now.' I nodded. 'I'll tell you how it is.' Two white-coated figures were passing through the lobby; McMann lowered his voice. 'Can you hear me?'

'Yes, go ahead.'

'You see, originally I was planning to give myself a month at the most to "recover", and come out in January, so I'd have plenty of time to get ready for the spring semester. But then I began to get interested in things around here. You know, this place is a sociological gold mine. And it's practically unworked. Goffman's about the only guy that's ever done anything important on the asylum, and he hardly scratched the surface. He and his team had to go in as staff members, naturally they missed a lot. There's been some good theoretical stuff in psychology – have you read Szasz?'

I shook my head.

'Well, anyhow, after I'd been here about a week, I said to myself, no point wasting all this time; why not get a little interaction study going? Pretty soon it got so interesting, I didn't want to leave it; and I was getting more ideas every day. So I thought, hell, why don't I stay on till June and do the job properly? I can keep an eye on things in Sophis that way; and besides, I've got a medical excuse from my job, my unemployment pay is piling up back home, no living expenses, all the free time I need, the patients trust me now – it's really the perfect set-up. I'd be crazy' – McMann grinned – '*not* to stay on.'

'But can you really work here?'

'Sure. There were some difficulties at first, but even then my only real problem was where to keep the data so nobody could get at it. I had to hide my first notes under the mattress, and even that didn't work. I came back from breakfast one day and found the guy in the next bed chewing them up and eating them.' He guffawed. 'Of course now I've got a private room, there's no problem. And when I go on to another

266

ward, the nurse or the house doctor will keep my stuff for me.'

'That's convenient.'

'Oh, yes. The staff here has been very helpful generally. There's one doctor here, Dr Hacker – I'd like you to meet him, but he's off today – he knows what I'm really up to, and he does anything he can for me, when I'm under his jurisdiction.'

'They move you around a lot?' I asked.

'I move myself. I can go wherever I like in the hospital, interview any group I want, if I work it right. If I pull the right symptoms, that is. . . . It's incredible how easy it is to manipulate the system here. You collect data on one of the closed wards, say, and then when you're ready to write it up you act more reasonable and get yourself promoted to a convalescent ward like this one, where you can have a room of your own. You want more coffee?'

'No thanks.' It was terrible coffee; bitter, with flakes of wax floating on it. 'Does everyone in this building have a private room?'

'Far from it. It's very interesting how they assign them, actually. There's four or five singles on all the wards. On the bad wards they keep them for the violent cases; here they're reserved for the middle-class patients.' He smiled. 'I pulled a little rank and got one the day I came in. It'll be vacant soon, though. I'm going to mess up now, that's what they call it, so I can go back to the main building and repeat a little time-study of Kahana's. It won't come out the same, I don't think. Those New England loonies were putting him on, in my opinion.'

'Is that what you're working on, time-study projects?'

'No, that's just a sideline. I'm more interested in leadership and interaction. What I'd really like to do is replicate some of the classic small-group studies and see what you get with a so-called insane population, when they think nobody's watching them.'

McMann began to explain his plans to me. I don't recall

267

the details, but I do remember that as he spoke I became more and more enthusiastic and impressed. 'That's a great idea!' I kept saying. 'That's fascinating!'

'I know it is.' McMann smiled, then sighed. 'Only it's a damned big job for one man. If I had a good assistant I could work a lot faster.' He glanced at me. 'There was a smart fellow on this ward who did some good observations for me, but his wife got him discharged.' Another look. 'I could use you around here, Rog. You'd be interested, too.'

'I already am.' I smiled.

'You could get yourself in. If you worked it right.' Though McMann was smiling too, I began to wonder if he were partly serious.

'Yeah; if I threw a fit in front of the main entrance.'

'You wouldn't have to do that. Dr Hacker would help us.'

'What about my classes, though? I couldn't walk out on them in the middle of term.'

'Have you got tenure yet?'

I shook my head. 'They'd fire me.'

'For a genuine mental illness? Not unless they wanted the AAUP to blacklist them.' He laughed.

'They might try it. In June, though —' I suggested, almost serious now myself. 'After exams are over —'

'I'll be out by then.'

'Too bad. Well —'

'If you were here, we could get something nice going on the staff too. The orderlies and nurses. We could split up the wards between us and cover all of them.'

'Um.' The idea of working with McMann attracted me as much as ever; but it was something else that caught my attention: the phrase 'split up'. I realized that if I entered Atwell State Hospital, most of the time I wouldn't be with McMann, but alone in some room full of madmen.

'No,' I said. 'I'm afraid it's impossible.'

'Well, think it over.' He smiled.

It was a final proof of McMann's sanity, I thought, that he

seemed to take my refusal so easily. Getting up, he suggested that I might like to walk around and see some of the hospital grounds. I noticed that as we went out, the little bald old man, who had been loitering at the other end of the lobby all this time, scuttled across the floor behind us and reclaimed his rocking chair.

It was still sunny outside, but colder; a wind was blowing. Lumps of left-over snow, porous and grey-white, lay in the shadows of the brick buildings and under the trees. As we started along the path towards the lake, McMann began to talk about the Seekers.

'Elsie comes up regularly to visit you, she told me,' I said.

'Sure. They all do. Some of them are here practically every week to bring me their problems and get advice. Then next week they're back full of gratitude if it happened to work out, and complaints when it didn't. The ones that don't come, like Sissy and Bill, write me letters. It's a hell of a responsibility, being Ro of Varna.'

'I just heard Sissy's expecting a baby.'

'That's right. Caught it the night of the Coming. I did that, you know, in their opinion.' He laughed again. 'Not personally, I'm sorry to say. It was those big positive magnetic waves.'

'So they're really still keeping all that up?'

'Oh, yeah. They're still committed. The group's holding together fine.' I frowned; Elsie must have been exaggerating things to him, I thought. 'Except for Catherine Vanting. She writes me now and then, but she won't have anything to do with the rest of them. Gone back to the Spiritualists. Elsie comes the most, of course.'

'It must be a nuisance, all that.'

'Oh, it's not so bad. They bring me stuff: food, magazines, cigarettes . . . you know. Elsie does a lot for me. Takes my laundry home, buys me stationery supplies I can't get in the store here, does my mending, hauls my ashes sometimes.'

'Your ashes?' I repeated uneasily.

'Yeah. Didn't you ever hear that term?'

I stopped walking and stared at McMann. 'You mean you've been sleeping with Elsie Novar?'

'Well, we don't get much sleep.'

'But how can you be doing that?' I meant it metaphysically, but he gave me a literal answer.

'Easy. She signs a pass like any other visitor, and takes me out in the car for a drive. There's half a dozen motels between here and Atwell.' McMann waved a hand towards the highway, then lowered it. His relaxed grin began to stiffen as my reaction got through to him. 'If I thought you were going to come the moralist over me, I wouldn't have mentioned it.'

'I'm not. But *Elsie* —'

Again he misunderstood me. 'Hell, why not Elsie? What else do you want me to do? I'm not going to mess around with any of the women here. They're sick. And frigid besides, most of them.'

I looked at the lake, now visible ahead of us through the trees. Incredulity must have remained engraved on my face, for McMann continued:

'I won't insist on it. Every man to his own taste.' He smiled and glanced at me sideways. 'I know you always preferred Verena yourself. I never understood what you saw in her – that overweight, overwrought virgin.' He shook his head. 'But as I remember, you were really stuck on her, weren't you? You were in love with that nutty girl.'

I looked down then at the water glinting through the trees. 'Well, in a way,' I heard myself admit. 'I suppose so.'

'Then why didn't you get off with her?'

'While the study was on?'

'Why not? She was asking for it.'

'But that could have ruined everything!' My voice was rising; I tried hard to lower it.

'Yeah, maybe. But if you wanted her that much, why not take the chance?'

270

'Suppose she'd stopped getting messages? You would've killed me.'

'Sure; I might have tried, at least. So what?' McMann was still smiling, but his voice had gone rough. Was he joking?

'So what?' I repeated stupidly. I felt as if some invisible person had hit me in the stomach. From McMann's point of view, and perhaps in reality, the truth was that not only Stupid Roger but I myself had given up something important, something I wanted very much, for a small-group interaction study.

We had reached the lake. It wasn't much more than a large pond, glittering in the sun and wind like a big piece of crumpled wax paper. A ring of tired winter grass surrounded it, green at the water's edge, and a tall iron fence topped with curved spikes – the only fence I had seen on the grounds. Perhaps because it looked like those fences in the Bronx Zoo, my first thought was that it was meant to keep something, some sort of animal, in. Then I noticed that the spikes curved the wrong way, towards us.

I understood. Everyone at Atwell State Hospital was inside the cage; while there, within that circle, was freedom – release from a lifetime of dirty memories, mistakes, and delusions. It looked like an old fence; it must have stood there for fifty years, at least, barring the way out.

I stopped and put my hand to my head, which was beginning to ache. I tried to order my thoughts; I went back to McMann's first disturbing statement.

'But you and Elsie. I don't understand. She's always been so proper. Adultery —'

'Elsie doesn't think of it that way. For her, it's an honour. A religious event. Hell, not every woman gets a chance to make it with her god.'

'B-but —' I started walking about agitatedly in a circle, waving my arms at McMann, who was leaning with composure against the fence. Anybody seeing us would have thought that I was the patient there, and probably a seriously

271

disturbed one. Indeed, a couple of people on their way back to the main buildings looked at me nervously as they passed.

'Calm down, Roger,' McMann said. 'Get your breath, and tell me what's bothering you.'

With an effort, I stopped circling. Trying to put the case without offending him or sounding priggish, I suggested that it was unprincipled to foster someone's religious delusions so they would do your laundry, let alone for sexual purposes. After all, the Sophis study was finished. What we were supposed to do now was get out of the situation, and let the Truth Seekers go their own individual ways.

As I spoke, McMann's face grew darker. Not just metaphorically: it took on a sullen red tone, as if angry blood were flowing into it.

'What do you mean, the study's finished?' he growled. 'This study's not finished.'

'Well, of course, you still have to write it up.' I emphasized the 'you', as it suddenly occurred to me that McMann might suspect me of having published (or intending to publish) behind his back, like his former collaborators, Sniggs and Murt.

'Write it up? Listen, it isn't even started yet. I told you back in December: this is going to be a long-range project.' His tone was more pleasant, but impatient.

'But you can't go on with it now!'

'Why not?'

'Well, because. Obviously.' My head ached worse. 'I mean, you can't use anything that happened after they decided the spirit of Ro of Varna had gone into you.'

'Why not? We don't have to say it was me the Seekers picked to be Ro. It could have been any of them.'

'Yes, but —'

'We've got to go on with it, Roger. Hell, it's a unique opportunity. A once-in-a-lifetime chance. I know lots of fellows in sociology of religion who would give a year's salary to be in my shoes even now. And when I get out —' He waved his hand at the treetops.

'When you get out?'

'Then we're really going places. The movement's going to expand, just the way we heard at the Coming. You remember. The Seekers are going to go out into the world and spread the Message of Light.' He grinned. 'We've already got a couple of converts here I made in my spare time. They'll be out before I am, and report back to Elsie – they're local people. I figure we'll double the membership in a month once I'm back in circulation, and be up to about fifty in two. By the end of the year, maybe a thousand, or more.'

I realized my mouth was open, and shut it. 'But Verena's left the group. She's out in New Mexico or somewhere, with Ken.'

'We don't need Verena.'

'But you need somebody who can get messages and lead the group . . . You don't think Elsie can do it?'

'Christ, no.'

'You think it'll be Bill and Sissy, then? . . . Milly? . . . Rufus?' My voice rose into greater incredulity with each name. At each, McMann shook his head impatiently. 'Then who's going to lead this movement?'

'I am.'

'You!'

'Why not?' McMann winked.

'It's impossible.'

'Impossible?' He scowled suddenly and frighteningly. I remembered, rather late, that Elsie had warned me not to contradict him.

'But how are you going to do it?' I tried to speak mildly, reasonably. 'You mean, once you get out of here, you're going to go on pretending to be Ro of Varna?'

'Not pretending, Roger.' He gave me a funny, shrewd, sideways look. 'I *am* Ro of Varna.'

'But —' It escaped me involuntarily, like the squeak of a gate.

'You got some better alternative?' McMann's voice had

273

turned threatening again. 'Maybe you think it ought to be you.'

'Oh no.' I smiled rapidly and nervously, as if at a strange, possibly dangerous dog. 'Certainly not.'

'Let's not make any mistakes about it, then.' He smiled back, showing his teeth. 'Let's get it straight now, since we're going to be working together.'

Working together? I opened my mouth, but made no sound.

'All right.' McMann stepped forward, and gripped my shoulders. 'Who is Ro of Varna?' I didn't reply immediately, so he shook me.

'Uh. You are.'

'That's better.' But he did not let go. His smile faded off. 'You know what your trouble is, Roger?' he said.

'Er, no. What?'

'You're a fool. Isn't that so?'

Even in danger, it was somehow harder to agree to this possibly correct statement than to the blatant lie that Thomas B. McMann was Ro of Varna. I didn't answer.

McMann leaned forward, very close. I could see the lake glinting behind him through the bars of the fence, the coarse red skin of his face, and a little state hospital landscape reflected in the pupil of each eye. 'Isn't that right?' He gave me another shake.

I remembered what he had done to the policemen. 'That's right,' I said non-directively.

McMann lowered his arms. 'A fool, and a coward,' he announced. He sighed, and stepped back. 'I'm so tired of fools and cowards. You know that?'

I said nothing, but nodded nervously.

'This God-damned world is full of them.' McMann looked round the landscape, then back at me. 'Why don't you run away now, coward?' he said. 'That's what you want to do.'

I hesitated.

'Go on. Scram.' McMann lowered his head and fixed me with his eyes; then he began to blow through his lips like a

stage madman or a child imitating an aeroplane motor:
'Blrrrrr!'

'Well, okay.' I began to edge off. 'If you want me to.'

'Faster.'

I moved faster.

'See you again some time,' I think I called out, when I was about ten feet away.

McMann took a menacing step towards me; he made a face, and raised his arm. I turned, and began to run.

My first calm sensation, after I had got into my car and was safe away from Atwell State Hospital, was astonishment at myself for having been taken in. Had I really thought McMann could convince a whole hospital full of psychiatrists he was crazy, unless he were actually so? That I had believed in him, even for an hour, showed what an influence he must still have over me; what persuasive force. A remarkable man . . .

But intellectual and personal force – even genius – are no guarantee of sanity. In fact, I thought dismally, it might be easier for someone like McMann, aware of his own superiority, impatient of the opinions and criticisms of the less gifted, to slide over the edge of normality. And because I recognized his superiority, it had taken me that much longer to see, to admit even to myself, what I finally had to recognize: that McMann was mad.

There are several aspects of the matter, though, that keep bothering me. For one thing, when I talk about McMann's breakdown with his colleagues, they and I seem to assume that if he had only stuck to standard procedure, and kept on being just an observer, everything would have been all right. The trouble with that is that we never *were* 'just observers'. We were kidding ourselves from the start, thinking we could go into a group like the Truth Seekers without making waves. Our presence was bound to have an effect, even if we never opened our mouths.

275

I sometimes (though not often) hear social scientists talk about the effects of participant observation on the group studied – but never about the effects on the participant observer himself. Field procedure is based on the premise that you can do something over and over again without really doing it, without its really counting, because you are 'just pretending' to be a member of the group under investigation. Apparently, in spite of all those books and articles on role-playing, we consider ourselves immune from our own laws. We think we're exempt from ordinary moral laws too: when we mess around with peoples' lives, either we aren't really doing it, or it somehow doesn't count.

I have begun to wonder occasionally if sociology itself is absolutely sane. Maybe it's really less crazy, I tell myself, to count yourself in as a significant figure in the group under investigation, even as its leader or prophet, than to pretend you're invisible. . . . Actually, the way I feel now, I would like to quit this profession, if I were trained for any other.

There is another question that troubles me: How many people have to have a common delusion before it stops being a delusion and becomes a religion? Right now McMann is only Ro of Varna to himself and at the most six or seven others. But if things go as he plans, by midsummer fifteen or twenty people may believe he is Ro – by this fall, forty or fifty. And after that, who knows? He has read the literature; he knows how a cult movement is organized, financed, expanded; he knows what mistakes to avoid, how to manipulate large groups —

Besides, with Truth Seeking he has a system, a theology, ideally suited to this moment in history. Everyone now is on the verge of believing in communication with other worlds, 'more advanced' than ours. We keep sending our rockets out, swallowing our disappointment as one planet after another turns out to be made of poisonous hot gas or cold dust . . . A scientifically and morally superior civilization, full of benign interest in us, with a personal 'teacher and guide' for

276

each earthman – what more could anyone want? A year from now there may be a thousand, even several thousand, Seekers of Truth.

Now suppose a couple of thousand people, the great majority of those who know him, believe a certain individual to be a religious leader called 'Ro of Varna'; and that he spends most of his waking life playing that role. Can you still call him 'insane'? Or should we say instead that Ro of Varna is insane to believe he is still Thomas McMann, a professor of sociology? If you are going to determine social identity by time budgets and majority opinion, you will have to take this position.

But the thing that bothers me most is: What if McMann were just role-playing at the end of our last interview? He seemed sane enough up to that point. What if he knows very well he isn't Ro of Varna, and was only trying to scare me: maybe because I didn't want to go into the hospital and work on his new project? Or maybe just for the hell of it. That would be like him. Possibly, if I hadn't already been so nervous, expecting a raving maniac to jump out of the bushes at me any moment, I would have stood my ground and called his bluff. If it was a bluff.

I won't really know until McMann leaves Atwell State Hospital (if he does leave) and comes back to the university (if he comes back). And even if he doesn't, but goes ahead and forms a Truth Seekers movement, I still can't be sure.

Meanwhile, I have no more data – except for one letter he sent a few weeks after my visit. It looks crazy enough; but of course that doesn't prove anything. You see, he might have written it like that on purpose, to confuse the authorities.

Roger-Dodger!
It is the Will of Varna that you instantly acquire the ff. material vibration objects and mail to us parcel post-haste and At Once:

277

Fifty (50) copies MMPI test with key
Ten (10) packets assorted vegetable seeds
One (1) spiral mathematical aura notebook containing
    graph paper And Only graph paper
One and one-half (1½) toothbrushes

Remember! While engaging in this and all material and spiritual activities, STAY AWAKE, Keep Calm, and Beware of Flying Bats.

Your friend and guide
Thomas McMann

A Selected List of Titles Available from Minerva

While every effort is made to keep prices low, it is sometimes necessary to increase prices at short notice. Mandarin Paperbacks reserves the right to show new retail prices on covers which may differ from those previously advertised in the text or elsewhere.

The prices shown below were correct at the time of going to press.

☐	7493 9739 X	**Made in America**	Bill Bryson	£6.99
☐	7493 9767 5	**A Good Scent From A Strange Mountain**	Robert Olen Butler	£5.99
☐	7493 9628 8	**Faith in Fakes: Travels in Hyperreality**	Umberto Eco	£6.99
☐	7493 9797 7	**Nude Men**	Amanda Filipacchi	£5.99
☐	7493 9771 3	**Billy**	Albert French	£5.99
☐	7493 9059 X	**Faggots**	Larry Kramer	£6.99
☐	7493 9896 5	**Nothing But Blue Skies**	Thomas McGuane	£5.99
☐	7493 9611 3	**Folly**	Susan Minot	£5.99
☐	7493 9141 3	**Vineland**	Thomas Pynchon	£6.99
☐	7493 3602 1	**The Joy Luck Club**	Amy Tan	£5.99

All these books are available at your bookshop or newsagent, or can be ordered direct from the address below. Just tick the titles you want and fill in the form below.

Cash Sales Department, PO Box 5, Rushden, Northants NN10 6YX.
Fax: 01933 414047 : Phone: 01933 414000.

Please send cheque, payable to 'Reed Book Services Ltd.', or postal order for purchase price quoted and allow the following for postage and packing:

£1.00 for the first book, 50p for the second; **FREE POSTAGE AND PACKING FOR THREE BOOKS OR MORE PER ORDER.**

NAME (Block letters) ....

ADDRESS ....

....

☐ I enclose my remittance for ....

☐ I wish to pay by Access/Visa Card Number

☐☐☐☐☐☐☐☐☐☐☐☐☐☐☐☐

Expiry Date ☐☐☐☐

Signature ....

Please quote our reference: MAND